I0523114

Hold My Teeth While I

Teach You To Dance

Hold My Teeth While I Teach You To Dance

Mike Johnson

99% Press

Published by 99% Press,
an imprint of Lasavia Publishing Ltd.
Auckland, New Zealand
www.lasaviapublishing.com

ISBN: 978-0-9941015-4-9

Other books by Mike Johnson

Novels
Travesty. Titus Books, Auckland.
Stench. Hazard Press, Christchurch.
Counterpart. Harper Collins, Sydney.
Dumb Show. Longacre Press, Dunedin.
Lethal Dose. Hard Echo Press, Auckland.
Antibody Positive. Hard Echo Press, Auckland.
Lear: The Shakespeare Company Plays Lear at Babylon. Hard Echo Press, Auckland.

Shorter Fiction
Back in the Day: Tales from NZ's Own Paradise Island. 99% Press, Auckland.
Foreigners. Penguin Books, Auckland.

Poetry
To Beatrice: Where We Crossed the Line. Pie Press, Auckland.
Vertical Harp: The Selected Poems of Li He. Titus Books, Auckland.
Treasure Hunt. Auckland University Press, Auckland.
Standing Wave. Hard Echo Press, Auckland.
From a Woman in Mt Eden Prison & Drawing Lessons. Hard Echo Press, Auckland.
The Palanquin Ropes. Voice Press, Wellington.

Non Fiction
Angel of Compassion. TP Press, Auckland.

Children's Fiction
Taniwha. Illustrated by Jennifer Rackham. Beansprout Press. Auckland.

All the monkeys aren't in a zoo
Every day you meet quite a few
So you see, it's all up to you
You can be better than you are
You could be swingin' on a star

Frank Sinatra

PART ONE

1

It was her voice that came first; low, gospel vibrant with a touch of country-and-western melancholy. I could have done without the melancholy, but a touch of salvation is always welcome.

I'll always associate that voice with a small town in New South Wales called Adaminaby, and an Auckland spring that had arrived too early and too warm. It was the morning of another of those El Nino days, fresh to begin with yet sooner or later giving way to a droughty lethargy. I'd opened the side window of my attic office to welcome that early spring in, and was reading about Adaminaby when, through the open window, came the voice of a young woman singing, clear and sweet.

'All my trials, Lord…'

At first I didn't take any notice, I was too deep in the Adaminaby story, which I'd come across while researching Australian droughts. In 1958 a small town in News South Wales called Adaminaby was drowned to create a massive artificial lake, Lake Eucumbene, capable of holding eight times the volume of water in Sydney harbour. Now, as a result of the worst drought 'in a thousand years' Adaminaby is slowly emerging from its watery grave as the lake dries up.

The lake had dropped 36 metres, revealing remnants of the life that Adaminaby residents once had to leave behind, a petrified town in a mud-encrusted time capsule, the Independent reported.

> The receding waters have exposed rusting machinery, broken bedsteads, old bottles, tyres, smashed crockery, and even the odd shoe. Brickwork, stone foundations and doorsteps of dismantled houses can be seen. The Catholic Church's staircase and two gateposts have reappeared. One of the inhabitants, now in his eighties, recalled going to dances in town on a Saturday night, and said that wandering among

the wreckage, dotted with the blackened skeletons
of trees, had been an eerie experience.

A ghostly Saturday night dance; a slow waltz against a backdrop
of blackened trees; a woman's voice, made suddenly louder by a
lull in the wind.
'There grows a little tree in paradise
You know the children call it, the tree of life
All my trials, Lord, soon be over.'
The voice seized me and flung me back through the drought
years to a time and voice I'd clear forgotten. Joan Baez, I said
aloud to an empty room. A voice from my youth, pure and soaring,
recalling nights of white satin, innocence and idealism, love and
faith: a time when the end of the world belonged solely to the
phantasmagoric pages of pulp writers who thought they were just
making it all up.

Some hideous, compelling nostalgia took a hold of me. Not just
for time and place – but a face. Anna's face. After five years, fresh as
the day she died, only younger, much younger. The grief too, fresh
as the day. Whoever said time heals is a fool; time doesn't heal, it
kills. Or at least you hope it does; how could a voice do that to me,
so cruelly?

Later I was to find, in my book of handy quotes, this appropriate
comment from Henry Longfellow, 'How wonderful is the human
voice! It is indeed the organ of the soul. The intellect of man sits
enthroned visibly on his forehead, and the heart of man is written
on his countenance, but the Soul reveals itself in the voice alone.' I
read the lines to my cat, Monckton, who looked suitably wise.

It was the melancholy that got me in all my Anna places.
Similar, perhaps, to the melancholy that possessed the eighty-year-
old Adaminaby resident as he walked through the beached remains
of his youth, the strains of a country dance still in his ears as he
gazed at a marooned yacht, now lying in the middle of the desert-
like landscape. The Tree of Paradise, blighted by the minor chords.
All my trials… I got up out of my chair like a zombie from a Romero

movie and walked to the window. I was all legs and arms. And eyes.

I had to see.

2

I live in a modest two-storey bungalow, with an upstairs corner office I call an attic. It has two windows, one to the front, looking out over Odds Avenue, the other to the side, affording me a cubist slice of the neighbour's one-storied place. What I can see of number 54 Odds Avenue is mostly a big red cube of roof, a green oblong of weedy garden, a wedge of spiny hedge on the other side, and a rust-red corrugated iron fence along the back that looks like it's sneaked in from another suburb where pretences have slipped a bit more. Between the red cube and the green oblong is a small patch of grey concrete that isn't going anywhere. In the foreground, below me, if I put my head out the window and look down, is the wooden fence that separates my place from number 54.

And there, at the edge of the green oblong, was the singer. Crouched, back half-turned towards me, showing a little cheek cleavage – and one of those shrunken white blouses several times too small revealing the midriff and lower back. When she leaned forward, her spine was outlined, a skeletal arc of bone. Her hair touched the earth. She had a loose, rangy kind of figure and she was singing while she pulled things up and dug with a trowel, creating around her a circle of destruction. Dirty blond hair. I'm no fashion buff, wouldn't know a catwalk from a cakewalk, but something about her get-up jarred: the hip-huggers, the hand-me-down blouse, like somebody trying to look like somebody else but not sure how to do it. What it didn't look like was gardening gear.

I wondered why I'd never seen her, before belatedly remembering that the red-roofed house was a rental property and the previous tenants, a professional couple who were never home, had gone. Maybe they didn't need to live anywhere anymore.

'If livin' were a thing that money could buy

As she finished the last long descending note, her head flicked back and her dark blonde hair was blowin' in the wind. Actually, I thought, money does buy livin', and the poor are most certainly dyin'. There's no 'if' about it.

I should have moved away, closed the window, forgotten the girl, shut down on any residual nostalgia and gone back to work. But I didn't.

Blame the music. Blame five years of grief. Blame the empty house or the precipitous spring morning. Blame the cat. Blame age. Make any excuse you like, I kept watching the young woman and she kept singing and dreaming in her weed patch, tossing the weeds to one side and her hair out of her eyes. For that long moment, I stood outside time, like a ghost, watching and waiting, trying to catch a clear look at her face. Eventually I became conscious of myself standing there as fixed as a shop-window mannequin, as if I was doing something sinful or forbidden rather than just taking a sentimental journey.

Next thing, I'll be stalking her down to Donaldson's Dairy and checking through her garbage for mementoes.

Outside, the sounds of a spring morning – the harried rush of cars, the chirp of birds, the distant bark of a dog, the screams and laughter of some children, but I was aware of these things as if from the other side of time and funerals, that other place where the music still lived and hair-tossing blondes were still possible. I remembered the first blonde I fell in love with. Her name was Mary Travis and she sang folk songs with a couple of guys called Peter and Paul (fly away Peter, fly away Paul) and when she sang Blowin' in the Wind her hair did just that. Which was why that ditty became so popular. It was Mary Travis and her blowing hair that did it.

I wallowed around there for a while, a place I hadn't been for a long time. Before Anna. Before Scoop. Before anything. Pretty soon

18

I was rocking back and forward like a baby in a cradle.

'Too late my brothers! Too late, but never mind,
All my trials, Lord, soon be over.'

The spell was broken when a man in a black shirt emerged from beneath the red sloping roof onto the grey strip. He said something and the woman got up slowly. She didn't turn around so I still didn't get a good look at her face. They both stood with their backs to me and stared at the cleared patch of garden as if it were hanging in the Louvre. Her back was sculptured and shapely and probably should have been hanging in the Louvre. I didn't like the shape of his hunched and tense back, though. They didn't do a lot of talking. He turned for the house and she followed him, but side-on to me with her face turned back, as if she didn't want to leave the garden. Her journey to the door was a slowly unfolding tableau. She was loose-limbed, and moved as if she had music in her ears. He moved stiffly, like somebody with hemorrhoids.

In medieval paintings, before perspective came to dominate art, the saints stand around in the air as if on invisible worlds. That's what I was doing, although an ordinary sinner, standing in the middle of the brightly painted air, watching the man and woman disappear beneath the eaves of their house.

3

'What are you working on?' Velvet asked.

'Aussie. Floods, fires and droughts in the age of hot air.'

'You always talk about these things in headings and sub-headings.'

'That's because you're talking to an investigative reporter. Scoop at your service.' I told her about Adaminaby, but it didn't do much to amuse her.

'Fucking sad if you ask me.'

I didn't ask what was sad about it.

'So how's retirement going, Scoop?'

This was an old joke between us, itself in need of retiring. But it kept a bitter edge. Although I was working, I had not travelled since Anna died of dengue fever while trailing after Scoop on one of his mad missions – and Velvet knew that. She'd talked me through the dark days after Anna's death. That's when our friendship started, although we'd met a couple of years before, introduced by the brash Eddie the editor, of Bellweather. He'd commissioned an article on hacking; I said it was too technical for me, so he put me onto Velvet, who came highly recommended, he said. She wrote up the technical stuff and provided some promising leads. Why she stayed on when my grief reached that wrung-out stage boring to others, whose sympathies have been used up, I'll never know. Perhaps she didn't have that much sympathy in the first place, she didn't offer much. I wasn't sure she even liked me a hell of a lot. She just sat with me when there was nobody else. She let me fall to pieces without panicking, and was there when I put the Humpty Dumpty pieces together again. Sort of. Some of the pieces remained missing.

'I'll retire when there's nothing left to write.'

'You mean when the world's turned honest?'

'Something like that.'

She gave a sour smile and stirred her cappuccino with cinnamon sprinkled on top. The dark spice swirled against the whipped-cream top like a gaudy spiral galaxy. It looked fancy beside my humble green tea. We were sitting in our favourite haunt, an unpretentious café near the University of Auckland where she worked in IT, idly watching the equally unpretentious clientele coming and going. A few university staff and office workers.

'What's put your nose out of joint?'

'Work.'

She had two ways of saying that word. The ordinary way, which meant her job at the university, and this way, a quieter, darker tone, with connotations, that signified her other work – her hacking. She hadn't allowed me to quote her in my article, preferring the non-de-plume Xena, after a celebrated warrior princess, and she was careful what she told me – although she said she'd once hacked into the New Zealand Ministry of Defence by accident (of all things!) and had a good old look around before escaping unnoticed. You can always get in, she said, the trick lies in getting in without anybody knowing. I got the feeling she was something of a talented amateur. A hobby with a built-in thrill.

'Firewalls again?' I didn't know much about firewalls except that they were a defensive network protecting soft data. I'd heard of the Great Firewall of China. Hacker troubles meant a firewall somewhere.

'They're getting too good at it. True that.' She spoke mechanically, stirring her coffee, her cinnamon galaxy smeared through the cream. The fragrance of her favourite scent, patchouli, intermingled with the aroma of coffee.

I wanted to know who was getting good at what, but knew better than to ask outright, not in her present state of mind. She did deep-and-introspective with conviction – black hair and dark, expressive eyebrows that knew just how to brood.

To lighten the mood with a touch of whimsy, I told her about the girl next door, the unweeded garden and old sweet songs. Perhaps Velvet was beyond whimsy right then. She didn't seem to get the point of the story, and when she did, she got quite snaky about it. In fact, she seemed to get the wrong idea altogether.

'How old are you, Mr Argonaut?'

'Fifty-five,' I lied. As she would know. I could see where this was heading. Taking the piss out of me was an ongoing conversational delight, originating in those dark days when she would mock me out of my willful grief. I would present a fair target, she would start firing and the fun would begin.

She didn't laugh. 'Fifty-five, that has a good ring to it. But not as good as sixty-five. And how old is this girl next door? I mean, how young is she? Over fifteen?'

I chose to ignore that cheap barb. It's another benevolence of age that you get to stand on your dignity with some hope of getting away with it.

'Maybe mid-thirties,' I said. More like late twenties, I thought.

'And there you were, standing at your window, unseen, watching her. For how long did you say? Five minutes, fifteen minutes, half an hour?'

'Okay, okay!'

'A little rattled, are we?'

She was apparently concentrating on spooning the froth from her coffee into her mouth like a kid eating ice-cream, and flicking me knowing glances from beneath eyelashes that needed no mascara. Since she was in her early forties, and didn't look it, and I was of a more dignified age and looked it, there had never been any question of a relationship between us. Perhaps it's another benevolence of age that one can have a friendship with a younger person without hopes and dreams and hormones getting in the way. Perhaps. But even friendships have to be negotiated, and are one of these eternal mysteries of the heart, more complicated and devious than a climate change summit.

'I'm talking about nostalgia. Like a time slip.' As if, I didn't say, I was actually young again and nothing had happened in those intervening years – just life. 'Music can do that to you.'

'So can a cute backside.'

'You have a dirty mind!'

'True that. But did she have a cute backside or not?'

'She did.' Most certainly.

'And were you not peeping, with avid interest?'

'I don't think *peeping* is very fair.'

'It's called that when you watch someone without them knowing. Noting the details of her clothing, the hip-huggers, the too-small blouse…'

'You've missed the essence of the moment.'

'Did you have your camera? Your long distance recorder? You could re-live this moment digitally, again and again.'

'Missed by a mile.'

Had Velvet actually hit on some hidden sensitivity in me or was I just appreciating, for the first time, a streak of cruelty in her nature? It was loathsome to think that she'd sat with me during the dark days because she was somehow enjoying it. Watching somebody fall to pieces, more fun than pulling the wings off a fly.

'So you're worried you're turning into a Dirty Old Man.'

'Stuff it! You're turning this whole thing on its head, giving it this lurid spin.'

'Am I?

'That's not it,' I said.

'It never is. Or at least it never starts that way.'

I sat there in a huff and drank my green tea. So much for lightening the mood with a touch of whimsy.

'It's the end of the line for you baby-boomers, that's for sure,' she said, after a long consultation with her coffee.

'What do you mean?'

'Don't play dumb.'

I looked around the café, at the careful anonymity it wore. And the people who frequented the place looked quite happy not to have some fancy image to live up to. I searched for signs of other baby boomers, but everybody looked suspiciously young. Baby boomers! How I hate the term. It has the dreadful spangle of tabloid jargon clinging to it. Besides, why should I identify myself with the great surge of sperm released in these shaky isles when the men, horny and ornery, returned from WW Two?

'Baby-bloomers,' I said.

'What was that?'

'Nothing.'

'But you're right. You're a big emotional baby, a baby-bloomer. Did you know that?'

'I thought all men were.'

'True that. Some more than others.'

'You speak from vast experience, of course.'

I knew that would hit home. Velvet had been a loner for longer than I had, and she didn't like to talk about it any more than she liked to talk about her family. She had more no-go zones than a Lebanese playground after an Israeli cluster-bomb attack.

Apropos of nothing, I said, 'Did you know that some Moslems believe that a woman's hair gives off special rays able to bewitch men's minds. Satan's rays. That's why they insist that women cover their heads.'

'When did you last have a woman, Jason?'

'A whaaaa?' Now she was springing this on me.

'Ha ha. 'fess up.'

'Aw, come on, don't push this too far.'

'Too old and past it, eh?'

'No.' That's right, fall into her trap.

'Maybe you're getting too set in your ways, old man.'

'You're not exactly a spring chicken yourself.' It was a weak rejoinder, but reminders of mortality tend to take the edge off wit. Baby boomers are particularly edgy around the subject.

We were silent once more. I busied myself with my green tea while she poked around in the dregs of her cappuccino. Soon she was up for the next round of Strip Jack Naked. Where love might figure in her cosmology, I couldn't guess. Just because you've been wounded in love doesn't mean there's no such thing. Rather, the opposite is true.

'At least show some enterprise! Do some research. Find out who's taken the lease next door, get some names. Track her down. Cultivate your fledgling obsession. Then you could stalk her on Facebook, become her Facebook *friend*.' She dripped with such malicious glee that her spittle sizzled in the bottom of her empty coffee cup. 'Then you can ogle her Facebook pics to your heart's content!'

'Thanks.'

The Facebook business aside, research wasn't such a bad idea. It shouldn't be hard to find who lived next door. Despite Velvet's leering implications, I was curious about the couple next door. If indeed they were a couple. Names. Funny how important names can be. I wanted to know her name. Mary? Angelica? Melanie? Kirsten? Something suitably melodic. A touch exotic. Not a girl-next-door name, like Penny.

Outside, through the plate glass window, Auckland looked pretty buggered in the near 100% humidity. Even the traffic flow looked tired. The palm trees hung their fronds like Jesus on the cross, limp and surrendered. It felt more like the middle of summer than spring. I thought of the things I told Velvet and what she didn't tell me. She'd hit my issues and play her own cards close to her chest.

When we parted she gave me a complicit grin, as if I were up to something. Something a bit naughty. I think she was under the sway of that silly idea that gained some currency in the 90s among panicky baby-boomers that one should grow old disgracefully – or not at all.

4

The next morning, after breakfast and the all-important job of feeding my cat, Monckton, he of the evil eye, I settled down to work. I'm no mouse monkey, like Velvet, but in my role as Scoop the intrepid journalist ferreting out the ills of the world, I'd done my share of link dancing and can find my way around a bit of simple research.

You can find anything you want to find on the net – if you are prepared to pay for it. I fed nine dollars into the wide-open mouth of the Land Information NZ website to do a title search for number 54 Odds Avenue. The owner was listed as a company called Pacific Holdings, and the signature on the title was Molly Rankin, director. I Google-searched Pacific Holdings and got little more than a bright, sparkling home page from which I gathered that it was an investment company with 'wide expertise' in property investment. I had to feed in another nine dollars to get the city council rates evaluation for number 54, which again listed Pacific Holdings as the owner, another nine dollars for the government valuation of the property (with improvements) and yet another nine dollars to do a mortgage search to discover that the property was freehold. Debit-card death by nine dollars a hit. The more I spent, the less I learned.

I contemplated trying to track down the shareholders in Pacific Holdings but decided that would take me in the wrong direction.

Instead, I picked up the phone and rang their listed number. A bright young female answered.

'I'm interested in leasing or buying one of your properties,' I said.

'Direct purchases are handled by the law firm Dogbane & Dogbane,' she said.

'Thank you,' I said.

'You have been talking with Suzie,' she said. I wrote it down. Suzie. Great conversationalist.

The law firm Dogbane & Dogbane just happened to employ my daughter, Marcia, as a lawyer/barrister. It wasn't really that much of a coincidence. Dogbane & Dogbane specialized in property investment; Pacific Holdings were an investment firm. I rang Dogbane & Dogbane and another bright young female answered. In this case I knew who it was, Debbie, the office PA, but wasn't sure if she knew who I was. I decided to keep it simple and not tell her.

'Yes,' she said, '…number 54 Odds Avenue. I'm afraid that's already rented out.'

'Is it listed for sale?'

'No.'

'Who's the renter?'

'I'm sorry, we can't give out that information. Confidential.'

'Is there a phone listing?'

'I'm sorry, we can't…'

'Yes. I know.'

I was tempted to ask for Marcia. My daughter, a modest, practical soul – some thought her colourless – didn't like to be put upon. Fastidious, with a natural streak of caution, she wouldn't appreciate being put on the spot by her father. Confidentiality rules.

As I put the phone down I realized I'd been proceeding the hard way, the long way – a roundabout route to nowhere. With my level of computer skills I see only what Google wants me to see, know what Google wants me to know. If Google is the conscious mind of the net, there is an unconscious mind too, called the darknet, or the dark internet, where no one can follow you and anonymity is assured. Velvet had alluded to it a couple of times, but it was beyond my monkey reach. On the net, you are a creature of your search engines.

But none of that was necessary. All I needed to do was front up to their door, knock and introduce myself. 'Hi, I'm your nosy neighbour. My name's Jason Argonaut, what's yours?'

All I needed was an excuse.

5

In the days that followed a pattern established itself. I would settle at my desk, gather my papers around me like a group of errant children and begin to write. Just as I convinced myself that I was working again, the singing would start and bits of my life would flash by as if I was one of those saints marching through, or had swung too low in the old sweet chariot. I would sneak to the window as if I were the one under observation, and peer into the neighbour's place as at some weird reality TV show, with only a single camera angle, into which the golden girl enters, jeans hugging her hips, hair floating around her face, singing *Corrina Corrina* or *Michael Row the Boat Ashore* or *Tom Dooley* or *One Kind Favour*. Snatches of old songs, folk and gospel stuff from the US of A. Rarely would the man in the black shirt with the unsettling shoulders put in an appearance, and then briefly, purely cameo. I wanted to edit him out of the show, vote him down or whatever they do.

Remembering Velvet's stinging comment, I scrabbled through my storage drawer and found my directional mic. Not exactly CIA grade stuff, and pushing its use-by date, but it did the job. Scoop had used it a few times when there had been problems picking up an audio. I would be ready for her next time she sang!

Sometimes I would hear her voice, but my sole camera angle revealed nothing more than the empty patch of garden, progressively denuded of its weeds. She's probably singing inside, I instructed myself. Still, when I heard her I would lurk at my post, waiting in vain for her to appear. Behind the walls of her house, the sloping red roof, her voice would ring through my middle ear as if through some direct audio feed. Mediated through her voice, my past became a pastiche of song lyrics. Songs popular long before the woman was born. A time when you could swing on a star, carry moonbeams in a jar *or would you rather be a fool...*

When she did not appear at all, either in person or in voice, I still took up my post, believing that my presence at the window, my persistence alone, would conjure her forth like a genie from a bottle. This is seriously fucked, too true, but happened so naturally. When I have to think, the sweat part of writing, I'll walk around my room, so it's natural that I should regularly glide past my side window; it's equally natural that I should glance out and that my eyes should fall to the garden at number 54.

I did see her once, sans voice, back in the overgrown garden, wearing the same low-slung jeans and skimpy white top, only she'd moved to a new patch of weeds and was creating a fresh circle of destruction.

I stood back a little from the window, and to one side, so that in the unlikely event that she should turn and glance up, she would be less likely to spot me. I had a terrible fear that she would see me, and the mic, and that I would have to haul myself off to die in shame. That wasn't about to happen because she always had her

back to me. I longed to get a look at her face. I imagined what it
would be like: sallow and interesting, with high, wide cheekbones
and full red lips. A Californian surfie babe from the seventies. Or
she had a disfigurement, like a livid scar running down one cheek,
or a cauliflower birthmark. As she worked, her shining hair swung
back and forth. Maybe, I thought, those Islamists had a point about
magical rays and female hair.

Naturally, she wouldn't always sing every time she went outside,
and the thought of her down there, without me knowing, saw me
casually passing my window and glancing out until glancing is not
the most fitting word.

Once she dragged out a dilapidated deck chair and sprawled
on it. She had abandoned her jeans for a skirt she had tucked up
around her thighs, exposing a pair of long, thoroughbred legs to
the single bright, all-seeing eye of the sun. My view was cut off
above her waist by the sloping red roof; the detached pair of legs
like a billboard advert for sunscreen or body wax.

I was waiting for the next development, which I hoped would
be to finally see her face, the unencumbered sight of which was
rapidly becoming the holy grail of my vigils.

Instead, I was distracted by the spectacle of a great hawk
balancing in the wind right above her. I remembered hawks from
the rabbit-infested plains of my Canterbury childhood; I didn't
remember seeing one in the city. It looked real yet felt like a
memory. There was something studied and careful and merciless
about the way it hung there, gripping the air, counterbalancing the
wind, eyeing up the girl from the open belly of the sky.

6

'Ever seen a hawk over Auckland city?' I asked Velvet. We were
wandering in Albert Park, enjoying the slap of a sea-breeze. The
turgid heat had eased up. Velvet was moody and broody, with a
breath of sour humour.

'I've seen them in the Gulf islands. Great Barrier and Waiheke, but never here. What would they eat?'

'Road kill.'

'Too slow. That's mynah bird territory.'

Students were lounging on the grass or under trees, some with books open, others holding hands or wrapped in each other's arms as if they were alone. With the sounds of the city reduced to a dull groan, and the shadows of trees playing tag with the light, the scene had a bucolic aspect, as if all were well with the world and the kids might go on that way forever, reading and pashing and dreaming. In the distance, the fluffy waters of the harbour and the crisp, tiny white sails of the yachts bobbing in the Gulf. A perfect picture postcard.

'What's with this hawk thing, then?' We accidently bumped shoulders and a smudge of patchouli lingered on my shirt.

I told her about the hawk, saying it was above my place, not next door. A small lie to hide a much greater one. Velvet would make a meal of me if I told her about the deck-chair and the legs and all. Jeez, I was already a man with a guilty secret. Big lies hide inside little ones.

We had reached the ancient Moreton Bay Fig tree whose uplifted roots had more twists and turns than a Gothic castle. We sat on a park bench under the tree and enjoyed a companionable silence.

'Maybe you dreamed about the hawk.'

'Can you dream when you're awake?'

I got a devious look. 'Maybe some people can.'

'Thanks.'

'According to Wittgenstein,' she said, 'we can't know anything for sure except our own existence. It goes back to Descartes. He said 'Imagine if some malicious devil substituted a false world for the real world. Because we only know the world through our five senses, if this devil had the power to deceive those senses, we would be no wiser. Everything we perceived would be a lie.'

'You'd have to believe in this malicious devil first.'

'He's just a postulate, dummy, but there's no escaping the logic. We wouldn't know if all this,' she gestured to the world, 'was the work of God or Satan.'

Velvet sometimes fancied herself as a bit of a philosopher. The IT philosopher.

'What about this girl next door, Jason, this blonde vision?'

'She's probably the invention of your malicious devil too.'

'Ha! Still spying on her then?'

'Naw. I've given up on that.'

'Sure you have. You lie like a gumboot sucks.'

She looked around as if she didn't like what she saw. Nearby two lovers lay in the grass, gazing fulsomely into each other's face.

'I've got to go back to work,' Velvet said.

'Hey, I ran into a block doing a check on number 54. It's owned by an investment company called Pacific Holdings, but I can't find out who rents, or leases.'

'And you want me to…'

'If you can.' I knew she could. 'You know, hop on your little magic carpet and do a little flying.'

'You're getting lazy, Jason. Can't you bribe someone?'

'I'd ask Marcia, but that would kind of compromise her…'

'But poking around won't compromise me?'

'Well, you're not employed by them.'

'True that. But why should I do your dirty work?'

'It was your idea in the first place. You remember. Do some research! Show some enterprise! And that's what I'm doing. I could only get so far, and now I'm showing some more enterprise by turning to my dear friend, who can do this kind of thing as easy as squeezing toothpaste from a tube.'

I got a crooked grin in return. 'Two parts charm, three parts hustle. That's you.'

We left it there.

As she was leaving, I said, 'About that malicious devil. Would it make any practical difference? I mean, the empirical world is what we've got to deal with, right? Whether it was made by God or the Devil or the Man in the Moon, right? It is what it is. One way or another we are mortal.'

'True that.' But her mind was somewhere else. Already she was walking away, looking, for such an independent woman, oddly vulnerable and alone.

7

The first time I saw her face it was right in my face. Not a fractured glimpse from my window. Her voice might have prepared me for her face – but it didn't.

I was trying to finish my article against a growing sense of hopelessness, a creeping moral torpor and physical enervation. If the world had grown absurd, I had grown absurd along with it. My petty projects had become like the ruins of that deserted Adaminaby. Even seeing my name on the byline was losing its luster.

I was at my computer deep in my crisis of faith, staring at my lethargic sentences, when the doorbell and telephone rang at precisely the same moment.

'Hold on a minute,' I said to Velvet who was trying to tell me something as I paced down the stairs and opened the door.

There was no mistaking her. She was beautiful all right, in a striking way, her fair face darkened with sombre tints. Graceful, strong eyebrows, sky-naked blue eyes, a wide mouth and a heart-shaped jaw. Her blonde hair was done in a fringe at the front just like the real Mary Travis of Peter Paul and Mary fame. When she smiled, those disparate elements made sense and lit up. Everything lit up. The perfect girl next-door.

'Can I use your phone, please?' she said, flashing me the smile. Her voice was faintly foreign. Continental, East European maybe. Not New Zilind, anyway.

'Gotta go,' I said to Velvet.

'What the fuck?' said Velvet. As I shut her off her voice was still cutting the air like a pair of tin snips.

Using her smile an awful lot, the woman edged her way into my front room, but I wasn't complaining. I was blindsided by the wide-mouthed smile and didn't immediately see the nervousness. Actually, I didn't see anything. Just stood there gaping. Here was a person from my own private Reality TV show walking through my door as large as life.

'The phone,' she said louder, as if I might be hard of hearing. She had a soft voice, quite deep; at least I sank quite deep into it. 'Ours is kinda out of order.'

I didn't have wits enough to wonder about this. Everybody has a mobile; the guy in the black shirt with the lumpy shoulders had one. I'd seen with my own eyes.

'The phone,' I said stupidly. 'Of course, of course!' and gestured to the coffee table where the phone lives, waving the phone at the empty holder.

Her amusement was warm and likeable. I banged the phone against my forehead and gave her a helpless look. Just some dumb old guy!

Once she had it in her hand, and I had partially recovered from my idiocy, I saw that she was in a hell of a hurry, her fingers jabbing the numbers like Beethoven at the piano on a thundery night.

'Aunty…' she said, throwing me quick, edgy smiles. 'It's Blue, we've had some connection problems…'

I retreated backwards into the kitchen to give her some privacy, tripping on my own feet and just about falling on my bum. Blue! Jesus! She didn't sound Australian.

She turned her back to me and spoke in a rushed whisper. 'Yes Aunty, I know…I know…yes…I'm sorry, but…what?…yes, she's safe, she's all right, but…yes, I know…but Aunty…no I'm ok…I can't say right now…yes he's…there's a problem…'

The man in the black shirt and lumpy shoulders walked into the room through the still-open front door and approached Blue, but warily, as if she were a dangerous animal.

'We're getting it sorted out,' Blue said into the phone. 'And Reggie's been a great help keeping track of it…'

The man gestured angrily towards the phone as if he had a grudge against it. His face turned nasty. Blue was trying to listen. I didn't like the look of this rooster. East European, Ukrainian maybe. He had a buzz cut on the top and a ratty little tail that hung down his back like a true bogan. His head was the shape of a World War Two German army helmet. His face, distorted by anger, looked, in its pugnaciousness, like an unhappy pig. His mouth was working but no sound emerged. Something was holding him back. Probably he didn't want this Aunty person to know he was there.

Blue was listening hard, ignoring Helmet Head. Apparently not everything was going smoothly with her conversation.

'No… no, I don't think that would be a good idea. At least not yet… what? No! Wrong timing…'

Helmut Head threw down his arms in disgust and made for the door for a dramatic walk-out. But when he got there he turned on his heel. That's when he saw me. He didn't show any surprise, just looked at me standing in the kitchen like a shadow, my cat Monckton by my feet, then dismissed me as irrelevant, strode back into the room and knocked the phone out of her hand. It hit the wall and sprang apart as fast as Blue sprang away from him, as fast as Monckton leapt onto the kitchen bench – a forbidden zone for him.

'I think you've lost the connection,' Helmut Head said to her.

'That was a mistake,' she said.

'Maybe, we'll see.'

He turned to consider me. They both did. He had the face of a thug, but his eyes told a different story. Now the anger was gone he was giving me a cool once-over that didn't miss much.

'After all,' he said to Blue. 'We can't have you reporting to Aunty on the side now can we?'

'I wasn't reporting to anybody, I was doing my job.'

'Yes,' he said, 'and it's time for us to leave this gentleman to do his, and get on with ours.'

'Terrific,' I said.

I got the once-over from Blue this time, but there was some warmth, even a touch of humour in it. A once-over lightly. Suddenly I wanted to show this young woman that I wasn't some fearful old man cowering in the shadows, but a man of character, integrity and courage. A man who would stand up for his home, his phone, and the girl next-door.

'Who the hell are you, barging in here and smashing my phone up?' I said to Helmut Head.

He got that nasty look on his face again and started forward with intent. It didn't seem so important to stand out as a man of character, integrity and courage. It seemed more important to say and do absolutely nothing, which was about all I was capable of doing. After all, I wasn't Jack Reacher. Reacher, the hero of Lee Child's novels, would have taken care of Helmut Head in five seconds flat. Where was Jack when I needed him? I'm here, Jack said, just do nothing, like you're doing now. Maybe pull back into the kitchen a bit. Pick up Monckton. He's less likely to slam you when you're holding a cat.

I didn't have to do those things. Blue touched Helmut's arm in a gesture of gentle restraint. The effect was electric. He froze where he was. One leg out, one arm reaching forward, towards me.

'That's enough,' she said, so quietly I hardly heard it.

He looked down at her hand on his arm as one might look at a fascinating but dangerous snake. The hand was withdrawn, but not hastily. He gave a deep sigh. It might have been relief. It might have been something else.

Blue started in the direction of the door, then turned to me and smiled. It was a real smile, a big friendly one, not afraid of its beauty.

'I'm sorry.' The smile turned apologetic. 'Family matters.'

'They can be trying,' I said.

She subtly nudged Helmut Head, who smiled too – at least I

think that's what he was doing.

'Keep it real, Grandad,' he said.

'Are you always such a hero?' I said.

He gave me a dirty look.

8

Velvet had a well-worn, well lived-in face, as if she'd seen pretty much everything and there wasn't much left of anything. She could be cynical enough; we both enjoyed that. Her manner suggested some hurt in the past, some untouchable scar; we didn't go there. Yet she might've used cynicism, even hurt, as a cover, a sort of camouflage.

Tonight the cynic was uppermost. And something else it took time for me to identify.

'What the hell happened on the phone? You hung up on me?'

'The doorbell rang.'

'Who was it?'

'The milkman. He and Monckton have a deal going.'

'It doesn't work when you try to get smartarse. Did you know that? Has anyone told you?'

'Okay, so it wasn't the milkman. I'll tell you after you tell me why you rang.'

'So I go first.'

'Yeah.'

'Why?'

'Because my story will probably top yours.'

'Okay, I'll play it your way.'

We were in a quiet booth in the Shakespeare Tavern, one of the few surviving old-time bars. In good weather you can sit on the balcony and watch the glass towers of downtown wink at each other. Or sit inside at a booth and stare at pictures of famous rugby teams. The 1905 rugby tour of Great Britain. Why do rugby players always fold their arms for photos? The 1960s fullback Don

Clarke, 'The Boot', sticking another one between the posts. A silver cup, grown too dusty to discern, was framed in glass above the bar. Tokens of an age that was passing. The pub, like many of its baby-boomer regulars, had a demolition order hanging over it. The pokies bleeped away in the corner like neon insects.

A good place for a quiet chat.

'There's something very wrong about your number 54.' She slugged back her wine as if to get rid of it once and for all. 'First, I had a look at Pacific Holdings. It's an umbrella company fronting for a number of investors. Looks normal enough, probably is, except not all the investors are listed. I found money coming in from a bank account that doesn't exist.'

'A handy account. Where does the money come from?'

'Exactly. I suspect some company, or offshoot of a company, using numbers that mimic bank accounts, but I can't trace it. I can't yet determine any physical location for the phony account, but I will.' She paused, looking suddenly grim.

'Does this mean it's dodgy?'

'The party putting money in doesn't want anybody to know.'

'It may have nothing to do with number 54. Pacific Holdings probably has lots of investments.'

'They do, both here in Auckland, and a big Melbourne portfolio.'

'And the investors don't determine what properties are bought and sold.'

'Not normally, that's why they invest in a company like Pacific Holdings. Experts who can invest money for the suckers. But, if an investor wanted to hide the fact that they owned certain properties, they might pay a company like Pacific Holdings to buy it and hide behind a bogus account number.'

'But you don't sound satisfied.'

'Because the usual route would be for the secretive investor to create a bogus company or trust, one that only existed on paper. Then either buy the property outright, or invest in the likes of Pacific Holdings, which itself is probably run out of a couple of closets in Mumbai, and provide a sweetener for that company to buy the target property.'

I thought of my call to the company. The bright and breezy voice of Suzie. Didn't sound like Mumbai, but I knew what Velvet was getting at. The officeless business is increasingly where it's at – it's all on my laptop, sir. Phantom offices for phantom companies. Phantom money in phantom accounts held in zombie banks. There was no end to it.

'But you would have identified a bogus company like a shot, wouldn't you?'

'In all modesty.'

'Then maybe that's the point. This phantom account has you stumped.'

'Not quite. But I get you. The usual route means the usual risks. I had to look harder to see this one.' She drank while she chewed it over.

'Then I had a go at number 54 to find out who's paying the rent. Normally that's easy-peasy. You just hack into the telephone or power companies and look at their billing for that property, and the name that goes with the bill. In this case, all the bills are paid by those lawyers your daughter works for.'

'Dogbane & Dogbane.'

'A hellava name for a law firm. Actually Dogbane is a herb, sometimes called bitterroot, with lovely little white flowers. Toxic to dogs.'

I wondered about cats. 'You must have looked it up.'

'I did, I'm that kind of person. Anyway, the tenancy arrangement is weird. Tenants are always billed for those things – power, gas, telephone – in their names, too. Unless those payments are covered by a tenancy agreement, which is hard to imagine. Must be so, because Dogbane gets the bills and pays them. Wish I had a landlord like that. So I checked for the tenancy agreement, and guess what?'

'I'm 'sposed to say "what".'

'Then say it.'

'Ok, *what?*'

'There is none. No tenancy agreement, no payments made to Dogbane on behalf of number 54. No payments made by said Dogbane to Pacific Holdings for number 54. There are no legal tenants at 54 Odds Avenue; ergo, your wonder-girl and her boyfriend are squatters.'

'Impossible.'

'Exactly, my dear Watson. So, somebody at Dogbane & Dogbane knows who's living there. And that same somebody is probably getting a nice little backhander for keeping it off the books.'

'Why keep it off the books?'

'You're slowing up, Grandfather! Someone is going to great lengths to conceal the identity of your neighbours, your singing gardener, for starters. And how do you know that only those two bozos live there? Because you've only seen them doesn't mean there aren't others.'

'True that,' I said. The idea that there might be unseen people packed in behind the walls of number 54 gave me the creeps all of the sudden. 'What'll you do now?'

'I have a few tricks yet.' She gave me a nod and a wink.

'I could ask Marcia,' I said.

'Don't you dare bring your daughter into this!' She spoke with such vehemence, breaking out of her low conspiratorial tones. A couple of heads turned in our direction. Then I identified what else it was that marked Velvet's mood that night, besides her usual cynicism.

Fear.

'Ok bugalugs, your turn. Time to show me yours.'

I'd lost count of how many wines she'd gone through. Her third glass, or fourth? Calling me bugalugs was a warning. She was hitting it along tonight. As for me, I was still nursing the same brandy as before. Pretty much.

I told her about my visitors. She listened with exaggerated care.

'There's no fool like an old fool,' she commented when I had finished.

I repeated it under my breath. *No fool like an old fool.* I took it that being an old fool was a pretty hopeless fool to be. Young fools have a chance, they can always make new mistakes; old goofies are doomed to go on repeating the same gaffes.

She gave me the look half-drunk people give you when they think they're being very acute. 'I bet she gave you a big smile as she left.'

'Actually, she did.' I felt oddly shamefaced about that.

'Of course she did.' Velvet gave herself, and the room in general, a twisted grin. 'Because she has you wrapped around her battered little finger.' She chucked back the rest of her glass and signalled for another. She suddenly sounded outright drunk. 'This Helmut Head guy is obviously a bully. The girl, Blue – the colour of bruises, you'll note – is trying to get away from him, that's why she needs to use your phone, but he follows her over and barges into your house to continue his abuse …'

Somehow, I couldn't see Blue as the helpless victim; at no stage had she appeared frightened, or even intimidated, just annoyed to have her conversation interrupted.

'He was… wary. Yes, wary but… impotent.' His had been an impotent rage. He couldn't get what he wanted. Couldn't impose his will. 'He was angry because he was helpless.'

'You've said more than you know, Big Ears,' she said. Her fresh wine was rapidly going the way of its predecessors. I wasn't sure that we were having the same conversation.

'Do battered women usually sing when they're gardening?' I asked innocently.

'No, they don't. What does she sing? 'Does your Chewing Gum Lose its Flavour on the Bed Post over Night?''

'Old songs from the fifties and sixties. Like 'Tell Laura I Love Her'. Or, 'The Tender Trap.' Or, 'How much is that Doggy in the Window?'

'She's got quite a repertoire.'

'"Your Cheating Heart' is one of her favourites.'

'She's sucker bait, that's what she is.'

'I thought she was the victim of bullying?'

'Same fucking thing, bugalugs. Same. Fucking. Thing.'

The connecting threads were becoming tenuous. Coherent conversation was a memory.

'Hey, why are you being so aggressive about this?'

She was making me feel guilty. Guilt is one of the loneliest things you can ever experience. I don't recommend it.

With the same twisted grin, she said, 'Just don't forget you're probably old enough to be her grandfather.'

'That's a bit of a stretch,' I said.

Before we parted she grabbed my arm and got sincere. An embarrassing sincerity.

'Don't worry about anything.' A nod and a fluttery wink. 'I'll track the bastards down. Meantime, stay away from them!'

It was a warning that sounded like a curse.

9

My youngest grandson, Felix, known to those in his realm as King Felix, sat in front of a pile of Lego and made his calculations. At five, he still carried a little infant chubbiness, which made him look more lovable than he doubtless was. He had a streak of cunning, that barefaced obvious cunning of a child, at present being employed in scheming which Lego pieces to snaffle before his older brother, the floppy-haired Fintan, turned his attention to them.

Felix looked up at me and laughed, because he knew I saw him and he didn't care. He began snatching all the horses he could see and clutching them to his belly. He'd laughed like that the first time I saw him. He was maybe a month old, and was up on Marcia's shoulder. I went behind her to get a look at his face. When he saw me he laughed as if greeting an old friend from way back; he laughed because he recognised me and I laughed because he was laughing and because I recognised him. We were a couple of old pals, partners in crime, and we were going to have a great time.

Fintan, four years older, floppy-haired and a bit geeky, proceeded to snatch some of the horses from Felix's clenched fists, peeling back his fingers to get at them. Felix squawked and gave me a wounded look as if to say, 'See! See how unfairly I get treated?'

Marcia, sitting on the couch beside me, shushed them both. She had something to tell me and this was making her tense towards the kids. I got onto the floor and started fitting Lego bits together. When I'd fitted a few I'd give them to Felix who would pull them apart while Fintan got on with the serious task of building a castle. When all was quiet on the Western Front, we slipped into the kitchen where we could keep a weather eye on them, sip tea and natter quietly.

'I'm in a bit of trouble at work,' she said.

'Okay,' I said.

Marcia's a neat person. I mean, she liked to keep herself neat and tidy – and her life too. Since the break-up with the boys' father she'd kept a tight rein on things. Because she did her work thoroughly and conscientiously, and was quiet enough not to compete with the alpha egos in the office, it was hard to imagine her getting into trouble.

'I was given a dossier, for safekeeping. Now they want it back. And I'm not giving it back – not yet anyway.'

'Why?'

'The information contained in the dossier could damage… a lot of people.'

'Not good.'

Those who might mistake her modest neatness for lack of colour, might also mistake her reticence for timorousness and miss the moment she will dig her toes in. She's an intensely moral person, is my daughter. As a teenager, she became involved in the animal rights movement and, driven by moral fervour, turned to the law.

She still did a few animal related cases pro bono and could argue forcefully that the world of nature, animals in particular, should have legal representation.

'And the party involved here intends to use the information to wreak maximum damage to all.'

'Even worse.'

Marcia's face wore a stubborn look, reminding me, as she often did, of her mother, Anna. Maybe I idealise her because she looks so much like Anna, with all Anna's mannerisms, except Anna was never quite so prim. Mother or daughter, that stubborn look always meant trouble.

'I suppose you can't tell me more.'

She shook her head decisively, as if she had already said too much.

We watched the kids building. Some elaborate castle was under construction. Marcia sat stiffly beside me, twisting her fingers, nervous but resolute. Somebody was about to find out that prim-and-proper did not mean meek-and-mild, or politeness mean subservience.

'I should hide it,' she said. She was looking at the kids and the unlikely structure emerging, but she was talking to herself, facing up to whatever she hadn't wanted to face up to. Marcia always did the right thing because any other alternative was too messy. She'd done messy once with the boys' father, and once was enough.

'It must contain a real bomb,' I said, trying to imagine what might override Marcia's professional duty, doubtless to a colleague, to return material entrusted for safekeeping.

'That's about right,' she said.

She was using me to think things through, as she'd always done. I'd learned that it wasn't what I said that mattered, but the empathy I showed. In this case, we were hampered by confidentiality agreements.

'What about you? Would you be damaged too, by the release of the information?'

She nodded. 'I'd get smeared.'

'Then common sense, as well as morality, dictates that you hide the dossier.'

'That's what I thought. Which means I get fired. And sued for the return of the dossier.'

'Burn the bloody thing.'

'Don't think I haven't thought about it. Destroying evidence. The vultures would feast on that one.'

In Legoland, King Felix was raiding Fin McCool's section of the unfinished castle, stealing choice pieces to bolster his own construction, and McCool was losing his cool.

'Just one thing,' I said as Marcia stood up. 'Tell me, does this have anything to do with the property next door, number 54?'

'No, nothing.' Her surprise was genuine. 'Why ask?'

'It's just a coincidence. Dogbane administers the property next door.'

'Does it? I didn't know. Probably either Dogbane Junior or his father handle it. How did you know?'

'I googled it. Put money in the slot.'

'Why?'

'To find out who owns it.'

'Why would you want to do that?'

'Maybe I want to buy it.'

'Buy it! Dad, you couldn't afford the front fence. What are you talking about?' I could hear a niggle of worry in her voice: was Dad starting to get funny ideas?

'That doesn't matter. You do what the rich people do. Use other people's money.'

I had my work cut out for me putting her off the scent. Maybe I would have told her, an edited version anyway, but Velvet's words kept ringing in my head. Okay, Velvet, I will not drag my daughter into this.

'Getting nosy in your old age, Dad? Becoming a regular Grandfather Detective.' She rounded up the boys, who made a feeble effort to put away the Lego.

It was lightly said, a throwaway remark, but in that causal moment Grandfather Detective was born. It had a nice ring to it. Scoop had retired. It was GD to the fore!

At the door I said to her, 'You're a smart woman, daughter, you'll figure it out. If I can be of any help, of course...'

She tried a smile on for size and found it didn't fit.

'Actually, Dad, it's not smart women, or men, that we need; it's good ones.'

So we took our leave. And the kids gave Grandad a shy hug. Shy hugs are okay. As we shared those brief moments a weird feeling came over me, that I was hugging them for the very last time and would never see them again. Maybe all farewells should be like that.

10

...then the telephone rang.

Velvet seldom rang, the call the day Blue and Helmut Head paid their visit was the exception rather than the rule; she was a texting and Facebook person, so at first I didn't recognise her voice. She was speaking low, as if there were someone else in the room.

'Listen carefully,' Velvet said. 'You've got to get out of there.'

'Do you know the time?'

'5.30 a.m. You say you're an early riser.'

'What's the panic?'

'No panic, I just want to get you out of there.'

'You mean into an old person's home where they strap you to the bed when you become obstreperous, and God help you if you live to be a hundred? You could spend twenty obstreperous years strapped to a bed. Imagine that.' I stumbled out of bed, into my dressing gown and into the kitchen to put the jug on.

'You're not listening. Get out of your house, spend a few days away, go skiing on Ruapehu. Hit the nightclubs in Eketahuna. Go visit your long-lost aunt in Christchurch.'

'What are you talking about. I don't have a long lost aunt, in Christchurch. And I've never heard of nightclubs in Eketahuna.'

'Then go stay with a friend.'

'Is that an invitation?'

'Not for a moment.'

'Jesus, what's going on? You can't just…'

'It's number 54. It doesn't exist.'

'Whaaat?' The jug boiled and I poured a restorative cup of green tea. The only way to start the day. I pulled the living-room blinds and looked out at the street, glimmering in the last of the night's darkness. I felt very obstreperous.

'First I checked the police files to see if they had any record of calls out or complaints or anything. Nothing, but that's not unusual. If you never cross the cops you fly under their radar, but it's rarer than you'd think to have a totally clean record. An overdue library book, parking fine, outstanding bill, anything that can be traced to a particular address will put something on the record. For number 54 there's not just a clean record, there's no record at all. As far as the police database is concerned, number 54 Odds Avenue doesn't exist.'

'And that means I have to do a runner?'

'Listen, learn and be wise. Next I checked out the SIS. Curiouser and Curiouser. You know in the movies when people are trying to get into files a big ACCESS DENIED notice appears. That's stupid because any file that's tagged like that will be lit up in neon for someone like me, like a big invitation really. A red rag to a bull. But number 54 is sitting there, unobtrusively, and when you access the file guess what you get?'

'Nothing.'

'Right! No documents, no security clearances to hurdle, no firewalls, just a blank screen. Nothing to hack into. Nothing to find. Nowhere to go.'

I imagined walking along a street, going up to a door, going inside to find not a house but a blank space God had forgotten to colour in.

'I checked two other security-related databases with the same result. Number 54 Odds Avenue is a black hole.'

'And that's bad?'

I looked out the window, half expecting to see men in dark coats with dark hats pulled down over their shadowy faces sitting in dark cars. Keeping an eye on number 54. And my place.

'Someone with some grunt has gone to great lengths to camouflage number 54 and will doubtless go to great lengths to keep it that way.'

'Ooooo – am I supposed to be scared?'

'Better off scared than smartarse.'

'So what are they doing next door? Manufacturing anthrax? Making a dirty bomb for Tama Iti? Hiding Osama bin Laden, who never died and has been living in New Zealand all along running a friendly local suburban dairy?'

'Whatever it is, they don't want anybody prying.'

'Fine. They can stick to their business, and I'll stick to mine.'

'Famous last words. If you end up as somebody else's collateral damage I'll blame myself forever.'

'Velvet, I appreciate this, but…'

'Get the fuck out of your house.'

'This doesn't quite add up. You're not telling me something. I mean, why should I be hounded from my own, mortgage-free home like a beaten dog just because the law doesn't have a file on the house next door?'

A dark car with the two men in dark coats that I'd been half-expecting to see drove slowly by. They must've left their hats at home. As they passed number 54, the driver gave the place a good once over. He was Asian – Korean or Chinese. I only got a brief look in the streetlight and the raw dawn.

'Okay, hardhead, have it your way. It's your funeral. But lock your windows and bolt your doors. That Californian surfie girl of yours is certain to be bad news. Put a curtain up over that fucking window. Ring me the moment anything happens and I'll bring my SWAT team in to pull you out.'

'I have enough teeth left to eat my toast.'

'Yeah, but I bet you cut off the crusts.'

'What are you going to do?'

'Back to the other end of the piece of string. Pacific Holdings.'

'You've let this thing get a hold on you, Velvet.'

'What do you mean?'

'I mean, I don't care any more. I asked you to look into it on an idle whim…'

'No, that's not true. I suggested you check it out because you were nosy and you came back to me when you got stuck.'

'Whoever, whenever. The point is, we can forget it. I've met the neighbours now, they dropped by, remember? If I want to know them better I can just pop over and say hello and have a nice cup of tea.'

There was a lengthy silence as I enjoyed my tea.

'Don't do that,' she finally said. 'You don't know who or what these people are. Stay clear. Don't play the clown. Pull your head in and keep your nose clean.'

'Okay.'

Dawn came walking in on stilts.

11

Pulling my head in lasted only until the next time I heard Blue singing. Velvet had over-reacted, I decided, and pushed the panic button too soon. Or there was something serious she wasn't telling me. Sooner or later she'd cough it up. So, I'd got back to work on the Aussie article. It felt good to shape up to the deadline. I was back in control of my life, on top of things again.

An old standard recalling amateur nights at the jazz club. It was all about rising up and singing and spreading wings and flying and all the wonderful things awaiting the little sleeping child. I'd sung it myself to Marcia to get her to go off to sleep when she was toddler.

I shimmied to the window and there she was. But not alone. There was a young girl with her, about eleven years old. A neat sheen of dark hair and very pale arms. A skirt that looked like a school uniform. They were both in the garden looking at the general devastation of weeds.

I'd just arrived when Blue swung around and looked directly up at the window, as if expecting me to be there, and a smile flew through the air.

Busted! Or summoned?

The catch was sticky, so I bashed it with my elbow. The ancient brass catch snapped, sending its screw-top spinning across the room, and the window flapped wide.

I rustled up my top falsies and flashed a smile back.

I leaned out into the world. 'Are you okay?' I called. Stupid, since any one of a number of neighbours might be listening. And her answer? Ask me to throw a rope?

'Fine!' She gestured to the girl, 'This is Sparta.'

Sparta? The ancient Greek city dedicated to the arts of warfare? Why did these people have weird names like Blue and Sparta? Why not ordinary names, like Max and Jack and Madeline?

'Hello Sparta!' I waved to her and she waved back. An oval face and a wide forehead. Black eyebrows.

'Hello Mr Grandad,' she called gaily.

Blue laughed and it was mellow, like those little bronze bells the Buddhist monks ring to get enlightened. The monks I mean, not the bells.

I laughed too.

'What shall I call you?' Sparta said.

'Mr Grandad will do fine.' Grandfather Detective at your

service.

This time they both laughed. Two bronze bells; one, lighter, airier.

I wasn't so much busted as becoming part of the family!

I didn't give Velvet's warning a second thought.

12

After all the excitement I couldn't work, couldn't rest, couldn't do anything. On one hand Velvet was urging me to flee the house, and on the other I had friendly folk next door who didn't seem like a code-red alert. Unless every smile and wave contained some implicit threat. Funny, when I thought of Velvet it was as if a shadow had fallen over her, some Mordor-type darkness. Out my window, the bright sunny world of a spring morning was all too real, all too ordinary.

A couple of days passed and no word from Velvet. With every passing hour her silence became less reassuring. Maybe hacking was more dangerous than she let on. Maybe her paranoia, if that's what it was, was justified.

'Why do you do all this hacking? For love or money? Or just for a thrill?' I'd once asked her.

'To steal things,' she'd said.

'What kind of things?'

'Things to construct a platform.'

'To do what?'

'More hacking, of course!'

Ha ha. Circular logic. Very funny until it isn't.

'You're just saying that because it's the sort of thing I'd say.' I was used to her being more direct.

'Then maybe what I'm saying is, back off Big Ears.'

And I did. But now I was getting frightened, not so much for myself as for her. Surely she would tell me if she were in out of her depth.

I put a curtain up over the offending window, a nice thick red one that Anna once bought for our bedroom, until she decided she didn't like it and took it down. It was in a box of old linen stuffed with memories. It glowed like a red sun in my office, creating a perpetual sunset.

I found my Aussie article exactly where I'd left it when Gershwin's 'Summertime' had wafted me to the window, finished it with a willful lethargy, loaded it into an email and banged send before I could think twice. That's the wonderful thing about email – there's no *quick-take-it-back* command key.

I was going stir crazy. Time to act. Get out of the house. Get away from Monckton. He gave me a lazy-eyed look that could have meant anything. One day I'll buy that book about discovering the inner life of your cat by studying its paws, and I'll know all of Monckton's lazy-eyed secrets.

13

I arranged to meet Eddie at the Swanson, a little café around the corner from the Bellweather offices. I'd planned for the two of us, nice and cosy, but he brought along Jerzy and Margery. Margery, the prude-faced redhead, officially Eddie's PA, effectively ran the magazine. Her cold-bitch approach, a foil to Eddie's bluster, belied the usual redhead stereotype. Jerzy was from Poland, and was once a great photographer. Then he'd become more interested in cameras than the photos they took. Then it was computers and the dizzy world of digital, and that was the last of a great photographer – although he was a whizz at faking images in photoshop. Jerzy lacked the normal social graces, and knew more conspiracy theories than Nexus magazine, but we'd hung out a few times when he'd processed photos for my articles. Like me, he wasn't on Bellweather's payroll, but a freelancer.

Eddie made a big show of paying for the coffees. He approved of my article on Aussie. Good solid stuff – Bellweather never did puff pieces – and he'd just loved 'that Adaminaby stuff'. Good ol' Scoop could still do the business. Letters and blogs about the hatchet job I'd done on evidence manipulation by so-called Global Warming sceptics were still flowing in. I'd called them lots of names like 'deniers', 'contrarians', 'rejectionists', 'flat-earthers', 'lobbyists', 'astroturfers', 'sock-puppets' and 'trolls', who sowed only doubt, confusion and fear. It was an angry piece, and Eddie, on the advice of Margery, had almost rejected it as 'too emotional'. He published it when I got emotional about him rejecting it – and was glad he did. Lots of controversy, lots of hits on Bellweather Online. His online advertising jumped with the increased hits. Maybe they didn't know about sock-puppets.

'We've got a weird one,' Eddie said when they'd settled to their coffees, me to my green tea. This café peddled the worst green tea in town, a single stale tea-bag in a teapot of half-hot water.

'It's a tip-off.'

Eddie hated tip-off stories. Genuine whistle-blower stories were like manna from heaven, and as rare, whereas tip-off stories tended to get murky. Depending on the source. Eddie had contacts all over the place, from Greenpeace to the police, but Bellweather was into serious commentary on contemporary affairs, not some scandal rag. Nevertheless…

'Spit it out.' I pretended to sip my tea.

'In this case, Eddie, said, 'it's not so much the story as the source.'

'The build up's killing me.'

'Some vessel, with secret cargo, will shortly leave Melbourne for China. I suspect something highly toxic. Too toxic for the normal traffic.'

We both knew that there was a huge, largely unacknowledged, export of toxic waste from Australia to China. One of free trade's dirty little secrets.

'And what would China do with it?'

'Feed it to their kids.'

'You're a sick man, Eddie.'

'The world, Scoop, not me. The world! I'm just trying to run a magazine.'

'Who's the source?'

Silence around the table. Lots of discordant clattering and clacking of cutlery. Lots of looking the other way.

'Ministry of Defence,' Jerzy finally said. He dragged his lower left eyelid down so a vodka-reddened orb showed grotesquely.

Silence dug a foxhole. Eddie seemed to have lost his bonhomie.

'There's nothing we can do with the tip, not from here. We can check ship departure schedules for the next month but what's the point? We don't know what we're looking for. And the paperwork, it'll be all kosher, whatever. No bill of lading would say, 'one dirty bomb', would it? It'll say the ship's carrying nuns to Lourdes or whatever. Pipelines to Pipelinestan.'

I began to see the light. 'And you want me to go to Melbourne to check it out on the ground…'

'No, he doesn't.' Margery said. Margery Razorblade. She dunked her gingernut in and out of her coffee faster than a pickpocket at work. 'The magazine can't afford it.'

'That's right,' Eddie said weakly, 'I just thought you might happen to be going…' He tailed off because he couldn't finish the sentence. Couldn't tell me he wanted me to fly on my own wallet.

I didn't want to disillusion him. 'It's alright Eddie, I don't do fieldwork any more. I'm retired, remember, on my porch in my rocker with my pipe.'

'But you don't have a porch, or a rocker, or a pipe.'

'I can improvise. And I have a cat.'

'That's a start,' Jerzy agreed.

Eddie held up both hands in a gesture of defeat. 'It annoys the hell out of me. It might be a story. It might be a big one.' That was a torment. For Eddie, every story, every prospect, could be a big one. 'It's too vague. Even if you were to go Melbourne…'

'… I probably couldn't find anything.'

He nodded, reluctant to drop it.

'And what's your interest in this?' I asked Jerzy.

'MOD contact's mine,' he said. 'Smart Johnny. Can spot a doctored photo at a hundred metres blindfolded. A real pro. There's a whisper going around. It's so hush-hush I don't think *anybody* knows.'

'Just a fucking whisper,' Eddie said. 'I can't get any confirmation from, ah, the usual sources.' Greenpeace often knew about stuff like this and Eddie had a couple of friends there.

'Too bad.'

'What about your source, Jason?'

Ah, out comes my name. I read once that everybody has an animal they take after. At first I thought dear Eddie was a weasel, but that was too cheap a shot. He was actually a snuffling burrowing, snuffling creature, like an anteater or an aardvark.

'Who do you mean, Eddie?' Although I knew perfectly well. 'Meilin?'

Eddie nodded.

Meilin. The name threw me back to my glory days when Scoop scooped his biggie, a full exposé of China's Three Gorges Dam project. It had won me several awards and, as they modestly say, catapulted me to fame, if not fortune. The Three Gorgeous Damn, as the child Marcia liked to call it. I couldn't have done it without Meilin. He was my guide, chief researcher, translator, and rode shotgun for me at every turn during the writing of the story. We went to China and interviewed people and photographed stuff, focusing on the lives of displaced people and the huge environmental risk of the project. How Meilin swung it I'll never know, but impermeable bureaucratic barriers seemed to dissolve at a quiet word in the right ear. Favours owed. Protection from high places. I played the innocent, well-intentioned writer, which fooled nobody, which was the intention. But we didn't get arrested and we got out with the story. Somebody inside China wanted the world to know, I figured.

They were all looking at me.

'Don't hold your breath,' I said.

'Would he want money?' Margery said in a thin voice.

'You can't bribe Meilin.' The thought amused me. The added thought, that I never quite knew who Meilin was working for, did not.

As we were leaving, I told Eddie off the cuff that I was going to do my next article on China's energy policy. He didn't fight me. He had a look on his face you could almost call thoughtful. 'Global warming, again,' he said.

'It's *the* issue,' I said.

14

Home, and Monckton let me know I'd forgotten to feed him. When I rattled some little star-shaped biscuits into his bowl, he looked at me askance. So I read him the label which assured him that his star-shaped biscuits contained all the goodies a cat would ever need. They even had different colours. He was not impressed.

Then I noticed.

My place had been frisked!

I'd love to say, in the tradition of the genre, that I knew this by some super intuition, a pricking of my thumbs, a subconscious awareness of a subtle misalignment of elements. But no, the frisker jerk had left my computer on.

I always powered it down when I left. Switched it off at the wall, don't ask me why. Call it fear of power surges. Now, powered up with nowhere to go, my desktop grinned at me like a happy hound. I hadn't bothered with a password protect for my desktop; I was a journalist not a secret agent. Spooks are welcome to hack into my files anytime they've got nothing better to do. I publish everything anyway, or try to. Coming into my house, sitting at my desk and bumming around with my files didn't make a hell of a lot of sense. It wasn't until I was sitting at that same desk staring at the screen that I realized the frisker mightn't have turned my computer off because I disturbed him.

So he, or she, might still be here.

So I did that routine you've seen a thousand times on thriller and horror movies, where the slasher-bait goes from room to room saying, 'Hello is anybody here?' or 'Come out I know you're there,' or 'Come and slash me, I'm ready' and other such inanities, until they get what they're asking for. Those scriptwriters have no shame. But that's exactly what I did, just as on the big screen. Turned on all the lights, did a boards-creaking-tension-rising scene creeping up the stairs; opened the cupboards, looked under the bed, checked the window locks, peeked behind the arras, paid my taxes and cleaned my chimney.

Nobody. Nada.

And no signs of a general search. Nothing broken, nothing missing, nothing out of place.

So why didn't the jerk just hack into my computer from the safety of his own bunker like any decent spook?

Looked like the work of a rank amateur to me.

Still, I prowled from room to room looking for those subtle indications of a serious frisking. Too subtle for Grandfather Detective. I could smell something, however, a faint sweat in the air, a sense of psychological if not physical disturbance. Somebody had passed this way.

So I went back to my computer, my only real clue.

Then I found the files and everything changed.

There were three of them, sitting innocuously on my desktop where I was sure to find them, ordinary looking Word docs.

I didn't want to open them, suspecting some sneaky virus that would gobble up my desktop and all within – but that did not compute. If whoever-they-were wanted to wipe my computer, why not infect it directly? Or get out an ax; a very effective method for rooting hard drives.

The first document was three pages of Chinese writing and meant nothing to me at all. The second was a map, but with no latitude or longitude marked, just a grid; I had no idea whether it was up, down or sideways, and, since there was no ocean, there was no coastline to indicate location. The third looked like a photograph of circuitry, which meant about as much to me as the Chinese. This was accompanied by more Chinese arranged in columns, could have been anything from a poem to a shopping list.

Then the shoe dropped. Someone had broken into my home, and my computer, not to steal anything but to give me something. To put files on my desktop. And leave my computer on to make sure I noticed. Did that make sense? Why not just email me the stuff? But then, emails can always be traced. *Track 'n' trace*. I'd heard that expression. And, I wouldn't have opened attachments from an unknown source. I never do. Not even the spams promising pictures of pretty Russian girls looking for husbands. I confess I opened one of those once and the girl had looked so sad I didn't have the heart to open any more. Yes, I'd have deleted it, along with Viagra pills, penis enlargements, and our Prime Minister's weekly 'Key Notes'.

But why bother in the first place? The documents meant nothing to me. What was I supposed to do with them? And why Chinese? Tell me why.

It couldn't be Eddie. Breaking and entering wasn't his style. Eddie was too important in his own mind, striding the hallways of publishing in a double-breasted suit to sneak around playing cheap tricks on his feature writer.

Family matters intervened. Marcia and the boys were at the door, but it occurred to me, as I went to let them in, that up till now it had all been a lot of fun because Grandfather Detective had no case. No crime had been committed. No dame had sashayed into my office, crossed her legs, inspected her bright red nails, creased my palm with some green and a phony story and looked dangerous. All my dame had done is try to use my telephone and sing 'Just Walk on By' to a bunch of weeds.

Now a crime *had* been committed, albeit a minor one. Breaking and entering. I thought, somewhat superstitiously, that my amused embrace of the grandfather detective persona somehow *necessitated* a crime. A disturbing idea, particularly as I was the victim. I'm an empiricist at heart; I like my cause and effect to stay firmly in line.

Causality is a jealous god.

15

I put it to the kids. I told them, in my Grandad story-telling voice, of the mad king who wanted to reach heaven, so set to work to build the highest tower he could. Then I flashed a few pictures from Brueghel of the Tower of Babel. They loved it.

I proposed that we marshal and commandeer every available Lego piece, from many sets bought over the years, for one grand tower, one definitive high castle, using every last piece, after which we'd retire for some naughty flavoured yogurt.

Weighty considerations for little brains. The broader the base the higher the tower, but the more pieces used on the base the fewer for the tower. We settled on a star-shaped base to support a vertical tower, the rule being that the tower couldn't fall over. If it did, we had to go back and strengthen the base. This task was doubtless as impossible as the original, but it caught the imagination of Fin McCool and King Felix. With considerable concentration, Felix stuck bits together for the very top, which made him King, while Fin and I toiled on the buttresses.

We were doing it. We were building the Tower of Babel, right in the living room.

When the doorbell rang.

I thought it was Marcia, who'd left the boys with me rather hurriedly while she dashed off to do something. But I was wrong.

'Hi,' Blue said.

'Hi.'

'Hi,' Sparta said.

'Hi-de-hi,' I said.

I hadn't noticed that Sparta was Asian. Chinese, I guessed. A clear, intelligent face, classic almond-shaped eyes.

'I'm sorry,' Blue said, looking over my shoulder at Fin McCool and King Felix busy building the Tower of Babel.

'I'm sorry too,' I said.

I didn't know why I said that and neither did she, but we carried on regardless as people do, as if we'd said something that made sense.

'I'm interrupting you.' She had an accent, very faint. Possibly Australian.

'My grandchildren.'

'Wow!' Sparta said. 'That's lots of Lego.'

Fin looked up and noticed Sparta. She can have been no older than twelve and as exquisite as a Ming vase; Fin was nine and a floppy-haired geek. He blushed hard enough to add an appreciable point-something percentage to global warming. While he was in disarray Felix swiped a few of his pieces.

I introduced everybody to everybody. The boys affected a great indifference, but Sparta was apparently charmed.

'Your grandchildren are very lucky to have such a grandfather,' she said in a light, formal voice. 'You have several generations of Lego here.' She wore her hair quite short, simply parted in the middle, and a short black dress with long white socks up to her knees. Looked like she was in training for a Starbucks' adolescence.

'Thank you,' I said. 'Lego wasn't invented when I was a kid.'

She was making her own private assessment of me, letting me know, maybe, she wasn't fooled by the doddery old man act. I had a feeling that sooner or later I'd find out the results of that assessment. In the meantime, I let her know that I was returning the favour.

'But you had Meccano sets,' she said.

'How did you know that?' It was, in fact, a Meccano set my parents gave me when I was eight that spawned my lifelong interest in science. I started out as an aspiring engineer. Meccano was a big thing in the 1950s, when I was knee high to a duck, but how did Sparta know?

Her answer was lost to the sweep of social interaction.

'Such wonderful boys,' Blue said. 'You must be very proud.'

Sparta slipped easily onto her knees and joined the boys. From above, I could see that her hair had been neatly parted and combed to a shiny dark luster. Fin graciously offered her a pile of Lego pieces, which she graciously accepted – all done without much eye contact – and, after some serious thought, King Felix gave her a few pieces too, begrudging and magnanimous at the same time. Maybe it was the purity of those amazingly clean white socks that got him.

Quietly, Blue said, 'I came to apologize for the other day.'

'Aw, shucks.' *Shucks?* I don't think I'd ever used the word in my life. Why should I? I'm not Huckleberry Finn.

'We had a bad day.'

'Got out on the wrong side of the bed?'

Something passed across her face, a hesitation, a carefully hidden double-take. Maybe she misconstrued what I said. Maybe she thought I was coming on to her, Christ! Maybe she hadn't heard the expression before; a whole swathe of popular expressions is disappearing from the language faster than you can say Jack Robinson; nowadays, you can't trust anybody under sixty to understand good idiomatic English.

She smiled anyway; the kind of smile that banishes doubt to Siberia and wipes rational thought cleaner than a virus ravaged hard-drive. 'Does it make any difference which side of the bed?'

'It might. Depending on the kind of night you had.' Another double-entendre! What was wrong with me?

She gave a sophisticated flourish of her left arm and wrist suggesting a passionate and theatrical character who had seen more of *those* kind-of-nights than you could shake a stick at; neatly balanced by a gauche curtsey of the hips, a knock-kneed, ankle-tapping, adolescent shyness. It was a prize performance, and there're no lollipops for guessing who fell for it, hook line and sinker.

'You don't have to apologize,' I said. 'Your friend only smashed up my phone.'

'We had a high stress day. Reggie got agitated.'

Reggie? I thought 'Reggies' existed only in PG Wodehouse novels or Archie and Jughead comics where he plays rival to Archie for the favours of Betty the curly blond and Veronica the straight haired brunette. Or Biggles. Wasn't there a Reggie in Biggles somewhere? If not, why not? I bet not many dear readers remember Biggles, the intrepid World War One pilot immortalized by Capt WE Johns.

So Helmut Head of telephone-smashing fame became *Reggie*?

'Are you and, ah, Reggie… together?'

'When we're not apart.'

We both laughed. Not only did she look like a Californian surfie girl, she had the casual, easy-going, outward manner of one. Easy on the eye, easy to talk to − what was there not to like?

'Are you staying long, next door?'

She shrugged, but with her whole body rather than just her shoulders.

'Probably not.'

'And Sparta, is she staying with you?'

'She's on holiday. From Singapore.'

I was dying to ask who she was but it didn't seem polite to be so obviously nosy.

'Sparta. That's an unusual name. How did she get it?'

'She chose it herself. Suits her, doesn't it?'

In some respects it did. There was not just a neatness but a precision about the girl, an economy in the way she handled the Lego pieces, a naturalness in her erect spine.

When she rose, Sparta left a legacy in the form of a stronger base for the grand tower, having used all her pieces to buttress both boys' projects rather than rival them with her own, and they thoroughly approved. Fin smiled shyly at her. She smiled back and his eyes glazed over.

'Check your mailbox,' Blue said as they were leaving. 'You'll be getting an invitation.'

As the door shut behind them King Felix commenced, with

grim fury, to destroy the Tower of Babel.

16

I thought a lot about that visit, went over it in my mind to locate what it was that made me uneasy about it, besides my own clumsy behaviour – I hadn't even offered them a cup of tea – but there was nothing to indicate that the visit was anything other than what it appeared to be.

Unless it was a scoping exercise. A reconnaissance.

I picked up the phone with Velvet's warning in my ears. All I got was her answer phone, so cute – *I think, therefore I leave a message.* Another cheap joke at Descartes' expense! I can't think, therefore I don't exist.

I didn't leave a message.

No choice remained but to break out my secret weapon: Mazzie 323. The never-ending car. The little sedan that could. Mazzie was the nearest thing I had to a reliable companion since my wife died – if you don't count Monckton. I kept her in a lean-to; off-road at least, but merely a roof, a single wall to the north-west, where the worst of the storm rain comes, but she never complained. She was proudly rustproof, almost. I kept her waxed and airbrushed where she needed it.

There she was, just as I have described, in all her humble glory. Like a magician I flourished the key and slid in behind the wheel. No sinister computers for Mazzie, controlling your windows and locating you on somebody's GPS. Just a good old honest-to-god car with manual locks and window winders. Not like some modern cars I've heard of that, when you slide in behind the wheel, ask you to prove that you are sober. Mazzie wouldn't dare.

Mazzie was a vintage Mazda 323; archetypal enough to be anonymous, just like its owner, yet distinctive enough to the connoisseur's eye to be noticeable. Perhaps the most unaggressive little car ever built except for the Fiat 500 and the Morris Minor, but we don't want to go there. It was a golden oldie, two-door; I'd looked after it, gone into boot for it, replaced doors and rubber seals from deals I found on Trade Me. I'd put the word in here and there. I knew when to grab a radiator going cheap, and a spare pair of headlights or those expensive plastic casings that wrap around the tail-lights. I gave her a soak up once a week at the self-serve car chalet service, which consisted of a water gun, a soapy brush and a parsimonious slot machine. I'd served Mazzie well and Mazzie had reciprocated. She loved those lube and oil change jobs I gave her every six months.

As I nosed out onto the street, a large black sedan cruised past. I'd seen it before, and the Asian guys in it. They probably lived around here.

The old social institution of just dropping in on someone is on the wane; given this age of texting, tweeting, blackberrying, and facebook-fucking, it's so easy to text ahead and say 'c u in 10' it now seems rude not to. I have a mobile I seldom use; you'd be amazed how easily I get by. It's supposed to be a smart phone but a phone can only be as smart as its operator. So, unheralded, I turned up at Velvet's place when she should've been home to try my luck. It was 6 pm.

Mazzie knew how to get there, which was a good thing because I'd half forgotten. In the greying afternoon of a grey day all the streets in Mt Eden looked the same, full of offices pretending to be old houses. There were some old houses, at least the facades, the inside having been reinvented, that were respectable family homes for the well-off. Then there was Velvet's place. An old house nobody had got around to reinventing because the sagging exterior put the punters off: a nice bit of camouflage, I thought, noticing the datura and wisteria that had colonized the unused end of the deck where a couple of old armchairs were succumbing to time in a mossy doze. It looked like a student hang-out.

Using my accumulated knowledge from wasted years reading

crime fiction, I cunningly parked around the corner.

I loitered outside her house under the shadow of my fedora, scoping the place, keeping out of the orbit of the yellow, UFO glow of the streetlights. It wasn't any place special, but looking at it gave me a funny pang. This is where Velvet lived. I didn't come here often; I mean I'd hardly ever been here; I'd always met her in the city. The question of visiting each other's homes had never arisen. It was as if I'd forgotten that she was a real person with a real home to go back to, a room to get lonely in. Wipe the dead flies from the windowsill, sneak a quick drink from the vodka bottle. Face up to the night. She didn't even have a cat.

I couldn't bugger around forever, so I fronted up and rang the doorbell. Some hairy looking dude met me at the door. Grandad Detective had a senior moment. Velvet rented, she didn't have the whole place, did she? Maybe she had a room or lived around the back. I couldn't remember. Whatever, it wasn't worth a panic attack, but it hit me in that same funny pang place. Velvet: I hardly knew her.

The guy who answered the door wasn't dusting off the welcome mat. He was a hairy dude in jeans. That blonde, curly hair that grows everywhere, even on his face.

'I'm looking for Velvet,' I said.

'Velvet?' he said in an American accent.

'She does live here, doesn't she?'

He considered me. We had a moment. What I learned from it was that Hairy Dude was protective of Velvet, a self-appointed threshold guardian, and I liked him for that. He didn't return the favour.

'I'm an old friend,' I said, with a subtle emphasis on the 'old', and my best imitation of a friendly great-uncle smile. He wasn't impressed. He just stood there looking at me.

Velvet solved Hairy Dude's problems by appearing at his side.

'Jason. What are you doing here?'

'Field work.'

Hairy Dude gave me a last unconvinced look and quit the scene.

17

Velvet led me to her quarters, a bedroom-lounge with a bit of a kitchenette. The kitchenette was great if you had to cook for only point-five of a person. She put on a record, I mean real vinyl not your digital stuff, and it was one of my favourites, 'Let it Bleed'. I was happy to do that, and appreciate how Mick Jagger had sounded when he was a little red rooster, but I was puzzled by why she put it on. Was it a bit of a dig, baby-boomer music? It was not as if we were about to have a party. Indeed, although the Rolling Stones scratched away with a promising beat, Velvet stood by her kitchenette facing me with a stony face, making no effort to be nice. A more sensitive soul would have realized he was not welcome and got out fast. As it was, I pretended everything was normal and talked about this and that until she got sick of it.

'What was it you wanted?' she said at last.

A little speech ran through my mind. How about an explanation, Velvet? You push the panic button, want to hustle me out of house and home because some unnamed force has laser weapons rotating in outer space zeroed in on number 54 Odds Avenue. Or maybe there's a drone up there ridden by some gum-chewing kid in Oklahoma with an itchy trigger finger and a hard-on. Then I discarded the speech.

'It's got to be a joke, right? You were pulling my tit.'

'Joke?'

'Yeah. Ha ha. I've got to get out of my house. Big giggle.'

'No joke. No joke at all. I'm surprised you're still there.' There was a flatness in her voice, a coldness in the room. 'You just can't take a hint, can you Jason? And do what I say on *trust*. Which means without asking questions.'

'That's true,' I said. 'Because it didn't feel right. I mean, you didn't explain. Just this bolt out of the blue.' Blue! Jesus. 'I thought it was a big joke. Let's spook Scoop.'

'No you didn't.'

'Where's the threat? I met the girl next door again. She might be a bit ditsy but she seemed nice enough.'

Like a hungry dog on a piece of meat, Velvet was onto that. 'You met them? How?'

'Why so aggressive, Velvet? What the hell's wrong?'

'Just tell me.'

'The nice girl next door, came over to pay her respects, and apologize for the incident the other day. It seems she's not that happy with her partner, a punk called Reggie. And she had a sidekick, a cute twelve-year-old Asian girl called Sparta.'

'Ah ha. I see the way the land lies.'

'I don't think you do.' The heat was rising in my face. Must've been the stuffy room. There was something of a nasty edge to this banter tonight.

'I think I do. You really shouldn't be wandering around loose, Grandad.'

'Hey, why do you say that?'

She ignored the question. 'So you let them in?'

'Of course. What was I going to do, slam the door in their faces?'

'Yes. Better, you shouldn't have been there to answer the door.'

'It was all very harmless. They didn't grow fangs or anything. I had the boys with me and Sparta played Lego with them, very diplomatically too.'

'You mean they came in when Fin and Felix were there?'

'You say that like it's a terrible thing.'

'True that. You don't know what you're playing with.'

'Tell me then.'

'You should have just got out.'

We bartered on back and forth without getting anywhere and I got tired. Younger people can always wear you down. Best to play up the exhaustion and make a pitch for pity. I don't know if that worked, but eventually she turned up the music. Jagger was singing about being screwed by some bar-room queen in Texas.

I thought she was trying to drown the conversation, but she came and sat close to me and spoke in a voice low against the music. 'I found out more about Pacific Holdings, and about the non-existent bank account which, it turned out, can be traced to another company which, in turn, seems to have an interest in number 54 Odds Avenue.'

'What company?'

'For your own sake, I'm not telling you.'

'That's a good one. Not new, but always good.'

'Tell me, were some renovations made next door before your Blue & co moved in?'

'As a matter of fact, yes. How did you know?'

'There was a little trail of payments from Company X to Pacific Holdings to Dogbane & Dogbane to a builder who put in the original bill. We can be pretty sure that most of the 'investment' money put into Pacific Holdings by Company X goes into the maintenance of number 54, which suggests that nobody at number 54 is working or earning any money. A scan of Inland Revenue files confirms it. No one with an IRD number lives at 54. So I had a wee look at the Department of Internal Affairs. No one with a passport lives at number 54. Or a driver's licence. I checked the accounts of all the major banks. There're no accounts registered to that address. Your girl next door is a ghost. She can pass through bureaucratic walls like a ghost through real walls. I don't like that; I can't do that. Everybody leaves a trail.'

There was a pause as the band played on. 'It's mysterious, but is it necessarily scary? Maybe a witness protection deal. A safe house way off the radar in little ol' New Zealand.'

'Maybe. But whatever it is, you are best off right away from it.'

'Why are you playing the music so loud?' *You can't always get what you want*; true enough, but the London Bach Choir was pumping loud enough to lift the lid off the back of my head and fill it full of angel's wings.

'Because I don't feel safe.'

'That's the bit you need to explain.'

'Imagine you're a burglar. You steal into somebody's house at night. You know the occupiers are away because you saw them leave. You find a safe hidden in a laundry cupboard. As you proceed to crack the safe you become aware that *somebody is watching you* from the shadows. You can't see them, but you know they are there. So you drop everything and run. The watcher runs after you. No matter what you do, what clever twists and turns you make the watcher stays with you. You cannot shake him. Your art cannot protect you. You are followed all the way to your home. Now the watcher knows who you are and where you live.'

She bit her lower lip, already red and sore.

'I see,' I said. I wasn't sure that I did, but it seemed like the right thing to say. Sounded as if she was in a lot more danger than me.

'Whoever it was, followed me through the darknet, and that's supposed to be impossible. Everything is encrypted in such a way that your movements can't be followed.'

'And the house you're talking about breaking into is Company X?'

'Right.'

'And the safe is in the laundry?'

'They had some interesting looking code hiding behind some special protection.'

'And you're into stealing code.'

We didn't say anything for a while. Jagger went on expostulating on the agonies of a 1960s adolescence.

'This watcher, how did you know?'

'That was spooky. Whoever it was didn't try to do anything. Didn't try to stop me. Just lurked in the shadow. I had this powerful sense of presence, you get it if somebody is riding with you, tracking you. I didn't panic then. Maybe they were testing their security systems or something, Seeing how far I'd get. What freaked me was not being able to shake the tail. There's a software that enables pursuit like that, called Bloodhound, but you need a skilled operator to do what that trace did. And big money behind you. I hit something big, Jason. Like, Pentagon sized big.'

She let that sink in.

'And now somebody has planted a bloody great flag on my hard drive.'

I gestured to her laptop.

'No. I did it at work. They traced it to my work computer at the University of Auckland,' she said.

'That's a relief,' I said.

'Not necessarily,' she said.

Velvet sat stiffly, her hands in her lap. She was urging me to leave in a big way, but wasn't ready to ask.

'You're holding out on me too, aren't you,' she said.

I didn't say anything. That's a trick I learned from the Jack Reacher novels: stay silent; manifest latent power. In my case it didn't work that way; Velvet just took it as the sign of weakness.

'Go on, spit it out,' she said, like encouraging a cat to cough up a fur-ball.

I decided on the direct approach.

'Did you break into my house and put some files on my computer?'

She looked offended. 'What the fuck are you on about?'

'Somebody walked into my house and loaded some files onto my computer.'

'What kind of files?'

'Some Chinese stuff. And a map.'

She rubbed her hands together in her lap. She was one big Gordian knot of tension. Whatever she was thinking she wasn't sharing. 'Somebody could be setting you up.'

'How?'

'By putting incriminating material on your computer. You wouldn't have to understand it – just the fact of it being there would be enough.'

'Why would anybody do that?'

'To get some leverage over you. Or take you out if you get too bothersome.'

This was very plausible, but there might be another explanation. Velvet herself might have done it for reasons as yet unclear. Something she hacked and wanted to hide. And couldn't email.

'You think this is connected to number 54?'

'I assume nothing. Number 54 may have nothing to do with it. At least directly. I mean the people there, these women that have infatuated you, may know nothing, but say it was a witness protection program, those doing the protecting might have an interest in putting you over a barrel, especially if they know you've been poking your nose in. If next door is being watched, how do you know that your little vigils at the window were not observed?'

'I didn't think of that.' What I did think of was the noir car with the noir Asian guys with shades sliding past.

'What are you up to anyway? Playing detective?'

'Grandfather Detective at your service.'

'You're more full of shit than old kitty-sand. Just a nosy old man, that's all.'

'Yeah, that too.'

But she wasn't going to laugh. 'And the first thing anybody checking you out would find is that you're an investigative journalist. That wouldn't be reassuring to a witness protection team.'

'You really think that's what's up?'

'I have no idea. It just fits the data. It's the most benign explanation.'

The record ended, but the silence went on scratching as the needle sought closure in a repeating loop.

She walked me to the door. At least she did that much, or she was just making sure I didn't get lost on the way out.

'Where's your car?' she said, looking up and down the street.

'Caught a taxi,' I said. 'I'd had a bit too much green tea.'

'Don't be silly, where's the car?'

'I parked it around the corner.'

She gave me a quizzical look; I swear she was about to break into a grin. But she didn't. She just shook her head and went inside.

18

I woke next morning to the news that the University of Auckland's computer system had crashed. An unknown virus was blamed.

I hadn't slept well. I'd kept thinking about Velvet's watcher in the shadows, and the darknet like some murky underworld, and ghostly bloodhounds. Like a swimmer underwater, this was the world that Velvet moved in, a virtual world of real threats. Give me the clear light of empirical research any day!

The story was on page three of the morning paper. The head of the University's IT section, a Dr Wayne Morse, said that it might take several days to restore services. He had no idea where the attack came from. 'Some people do this sort of thing for fun,' he said. Dr Wayne Morse, the story went on, was in NZ on a scholarship from the University of Maryland, the top IT facility in the U.S.

The story gave no exact time for the attack. Maybe at that very moment Velvet and I were talking about tracers and bloodhounds.

My first instinct was to ring Velvet, so I did. The thought that clawed at me, of course, was that her activities and the computer crash were related. I remembered the bleak look on her face when I'd said it was a good thing she'd used the university computers and she'd said 'not necessarily.' Maybe she had been imagining something like this.

'I think, therefore I leave a message.'

I didn't leave a message, but while the morning still had legs, I rang Jerzy, the mad Polish digital man.

I said, 'Jerzy, what would it take to bring down a university computer network?'

'A good education?'

'What else?'

'The newspaper article is crapula. That Morse guy's lying through his teeth.'

'How do you know?' You had to be careful with Jerzy; whatever you talked about you were never far from some idée fixe, never far from an instant harangue on, say, the Russian Anarchist Bakunin, or the glory of the Ghibli anime studios in Tokyo.

'No such thing as an unknown virus. Viruses are quickly identified. Worms are sneakier but too slow. No, no, no. No virus.'

'Then what?'

'Fucked if I know, and fucked if I don't. It's more likely to be a monumental screw up. Sheer stupidity serves. Entropy rules. He must cover his arse.'

'We'll watch that space. Maybe his head will roll.'

'More likely they'll make him Vice Chancellor.'

Sitting in my mailbox, in an unstamped mauve envelope, was a silver-edged, scalloped invitation card. It was inscribed by hand, in neat yet curly script.

Dear Mr Jason

Here's hoping you are available this coming Friday,

at 11 a.m. for tea and biscuits at number 54 Odds Avenue.

The humble 'Mr Jason' was an affecting ingénue touch, but tea and biscuits? I could see Sparta standing in a card shop looking for invitations appropriate for old pooh-bahs like me and Jane Austen, not quite aware of its quaintness. Or it could be singin'-the-blues Blue, pulling the old man's tit.

I stood the invitation card up on the table and stared at it. Friday was a couple of days away. Then I picked up the phone.

'I think, therefore I leave a message.'

So I set out to satisfy my growing curiosity the only way I knew how. Keeping number 54 under observation day and night. I was now convinced, without a shred of evidence, that the occupiers of number 54 had something to do with the university computer crash.

I set up my camp stretcher under the window and catnapped with one ear twitching. Kept the curtain if only for camouflage. Dusted off my digital camera and set it to take a shot every ten seconds, subtly poking out under the curtain. Watched Odds Avenue too, googled any cars regularly parked in the vicinity. Got my exercise walking vigorously around the block a couple of times checking out the house that backs on to 54. Tahatai Street, number 73. I could look down the driveway of 73 Tahatai to the red iron fence, beyond which lay the weed garden and the silent number 54.

My obsession became my Modus Operandi, my MO as they say in police procedural novels. Unlike many older people, I don't have a problem with a bit of insomnia. I could stay up at night and watch the moon pass over number 54, feet up, mind in neutral.

My camp bed was nothing like the cruisy air-mattresses people take camping with them these days, rather a veteran of World War Two, a narrow strip of thick military green canvas stretched between poles that locked in place with steel brackets, bequeathed to me by my dad. Quick and easy to erect and sheer luxury I'm sure compared to hard ground. Lying in it, on my back, I thought of my dad, lying in this same bed just as I was, staring up at some foreign sky.

It was all oddly satisfying in a fortress-mentality way. I had my laptop, my mobile, my fortitude, my old gas camp cooker and billy to make tea without having to go downstairs. And, last but not least, I had my cat, a comfortable presence. Felt like a real Kiwi bachelor, I did. Even thought of ordering in a case of baked beans. I kept the window open for interesting sounds. Luckily the weather was still unnaturally clement. I put on a nice wooly New Zealand-made jumper and felt quite snug. Like a bug in a rug.

Doubtless, I was playing myself for a fool. Number 54 surely would be clamped down tighter than a drum of radioactive waste; somebody would be making sure that absolutely nothing happened, that nobody came or went or so much as farted in the wind. So your beloved GD, and his faithful purring sidekick, were harbouring their forces for a massive waste of time.

Everything was quiet at number 54. Too quiet. In an important respect, something had changed. Blue no longer came out to weed the garden to the tune of 'Red Sails in the Sunset'. Or lay on the deck chair with her long legs in the sun. There were no cheery hellos to a friendly old grandad at the window. This indicated some kind of circling of the wagons at 54.

A blanket of silence descended. To wile away the time I read the latest Lee Child novel. It has always struck me that although Reacher owns nothing, just the shirt on his back, he always seems to have a bewildering array of modern weaponry at his command, and I have to tip my cap to Child for his precise research into all these goddamn killing machines, always assuming that Child is not, like his hero, a mass murderer.

But I had a weapon too. Lying on that WW2 camp stretcher, soaking up the memories of my father, it floated into my mind. I found it lying like a piece of dark jewellery on a snug satin pillow in an innocuous old shoebox in the wardrobe. An ancestral weapon, a World War Two Luger automatic, a precision made lethal-weapon with the classic, angled grip. Plus twelve rounds of reserve ammunition. My dad had solemnly shown it to a wide-eyed young Jason when he was about ten. I couldn't have told Jack if it was a .38 a .45 or a bad night on the town, but I could tell him that, for a museum piece, it worked just fine.

'It's not legal,' his dad confessed, letting young Jason hold it, feel the weight of it in his child hands. 'Lots of soldiers smuggled back German weapons. This one was taken from an SS Officer, who formally surrendered it.' His dad's voice took on the special tone he used to talking about the war. The same tone people use when talking in a church. 'Classic German engineering. Does the job.'

The ten year old held it in his hands, aware of a sudden solemnity.

74

This thing killed people. Did the job. Like the camp stretcher.

'It'll be yours when I'm gone,' his dad said.

And it was, there in my closet, well-oiled and preserved, and had hardly been fired for sixty years except for testing.

I took it to my observation post, shoe box and all, trying to hold it casually, and put it under my desk. Chekov said that if there was a gun on the wall in Act 1 it would have to be in somebody's hands by Act 3, and I had a bad feeling about the damn thing. It might be a family heirloom, but it held out some implicit promise. I'm here, I can always be used, it said; used twelve times in fact, if the need arises.

Ha! Reggie better not come here now, throwing his weight around. He might find himself staring down a Gestapo barrel.

19

My vigils at the window unexpectedly paid off. The following evening, as twilight faded to night, Blue and Sparta walked into the garden, deep in conversation. They didn't glance up at the window. I broke out my directional mike. I couldn't play it loud enough to hear, or they might have heard it, so recorded it for later. Blue, in jeans, talking earnestly away, hunkered down like a cowgirl, maybe so she wasn't towering over Sparta.

And Sparta speaking her share, straight-backed, composed, in a schoolgirl's blouse and skirt with black shoes and white socks pulled up to her knees, but speaking deliberately over Blue's right shoulder, as if to someone standing behind and to the right of Blue.

They didn't pay the weeds the slightest attention.

I didn't catch a word; their voices, while urgent, were low.

Blue put her arm over the young girl's shoulders. Protectively, I thought.

Then they went inside.

As they passed under the shadow of the eaves, I fancied that it was Sparta who had the power, however it may appear. Something about the way she walked. Like royalty. And Blue as her shadow, nurse, faithful retainer.

As soon as they had vanished, I closed the window, secured the curtain for good measure, and hit playback on recorder.

It came through loud and clear. Every word of it.

In Mandarin.

Chinese is an inflected language. You have to be able to sing it. I can sing along but I can't understand it.

There was Sparta's voice, sharp and fast; I didn't have to know the language to know she was using it well, and to great effect. There was a certain imperiousness in it, the hint of command, but there was also an appeal in it, a passionate appeal strapped in a formal delivery. Blue answered with equal fluency, in more measured tones, too careful to be reassuring, subtler in their implications. And was there not a threat? An evocation of some nasty power. Sparta bit back, but the weakness was in the hurt. The hurt was the biting back. Blue put her arm over Sparta's shoulder at that point, I guessed. Her voice dropped into full contralto, a thrilling and emotional response to Sparta's hurt. I didn't understand a word, but it made my scalp prickle.

Their voices blurred as they went beneath the accursed eaves.

Those spooky voices wouldn't go away, mainly because I kept playing them back all the time.

It was time to go see Meilin.

Which I did. Later, I was to wonder why I didn't print out the strange Chinese files on my computer and take them to Meilin too, and what the consequences would have been if I had.

Meilin did not particularly want to see me, especially unannounced at dinner time, reluctantly inviting me into his main room, which was clean and sparse but for a capacious settee and matching chairs, outrageously comfortable. He was about to start on a plate of prawns, sprouts and salad with hot buns. He placed the plate in the middle of the table, meaning for me to eat with him

Chinese style, so I pretended, to satisfy protocol. For him I was one of those crosses in life one has to bear. We'd had our glory days of the Three Gorges Dam. My Scoop days. Since then we'd worked on a couple of projects with some success.

You don't stuff around with Meilin at the best of times, so I played him the tape.

His face didn't change as Blue and Sparta chirped away. I knew that the less he revealed the more he was feeling. He did the Asian poker-face thing really well, and liked to use it on westerners. Even me. When the tape finished four minutes 25 seconds later he didn't say anything. I didn't say anything. He chomped away on bean sprouts. Silence has a different value and purpose in Chinese conversation I'd never figured out.

'The young girl is from mainland China,' he said at length, 'probably from the northern provinces. There's a touch of Korean. There are also traces of upper echelon Beijing. The elite. Old Party or new oligarchs. She's very well educated. Very. But she's spent enough time in Hong Kong to give her an inflection. A street inflection, which is strange given her high status. She's amazingly articulate.'

He was talking to himself, trying to figure it out. I thought about how good Sparta's English was, how exact her pronunciation, not the trace of a 't' turned into a glottal stop. Better than Meilin's, and he'd worked as an official translator for the New Zealand government.

'You say she's eleven or twelve, but Asian girls are deceptive to the western eye, and can have very light voices. She sounds like sixteen or seventeen.'

'No older than twelve,' I said.

He let that pass.

'The western woman is also remarkable.' He looked at me, openly curious. 'What does she look like?'

'Like a Californian surfie babe from the 1970s. You know, long blonde hair, extended torso, legs all over the place, a cute butt…'

but maybe Meilin didn't know. Not his cultural territory.

'This is no bimbo, whatever her persona,' Meilin said quietly, taking a prawn delicately in his fingers. 'She speaks Mandarin better than I speak English. She has to be a native speaker, learned it in China, maybe Shanghai. A hint of Singaporean, which would explain being bilingual. Maybe born in Singapore and moved to Shanghai at an early age.' He briefly considered the prawn before popping the tail into his mouth and gently sucking out the meat.

I remembered thinking she had some trace of an East European accent in her English. That had been a hasty judgment. I knew Aussie accents, and South Africans, the Brits and Irish and the Yanks, but I didn't know what a European Singaporean sounded like. A native speaker of Mandarin and English. All those fifties hit parade shibboleths had led me astray. Caught me out in nostalgia-land. And yet, she did sometimes have an Aussie twang. Meilin was struggling with similar contradictions in her Mandarin.

'Fascinating,' I said. 'I'll write a paper on it. But what did they say?'

'It was an on-going conversation.'

As he explained it, Sparta said that, for the thousandth time, it was not going to work. 'It' wasn't explained. She said that 'he', whoever he was, was not going to like it, and further, 'it' might precipitate a crisis. Therefore Blue was going to have to rethink her position. And Blue had replied that all was under control. That somebody called Aunty would not dare intervene, and that yet another somebody called Reggie was not a problem. That 'it' was after all a fait accompli. Sparta replied that Reggie *was* a problem, and if he got any worse, she would have to move against him, which would spoil everything and leave Blue with a mess to clean up. Blue replied, consolingly – which is when I think she put her arm over Sparta's shoulder – that the holy ones wouldn't allow any fuck-ups and that everything was on course.

And that was it.

'Holy ones?'

Meilin shifted in his seat, but comfortably. He was making short work of the buns.

'It's a classical reference. Literally, it means The Immortals – probably code for something they can't talk about.'

We both thought about that.

Meilin said, 'but the word is inaccurate in English. The 'Immortals' lived in the Tang dynasty. There were eight of them, including one woman. The dates of their deaths are recorded. They are half-folklore, humans of extraordinary powers. Each had their…area of…expertise.' Meilin's English was being pushed, something I didn't often see.

What, or who, I wondered, would merit a code name like that? The highest of the high in the Chinese power structure?

Meilin might have been wondering the same, but all he was doing was chomping on a bun as if nothing else in the world existed.

I gestured to the tape. 'How do you read it?'

He didn't want to answer or he was too busy eating.

In the end he did. 'I don't get the relationship between these two. It is very intense and open on one hand, very intimate, but on the other hand, they are like strangers, negotiating, closed off from each other. The power shifts are harder to read. It appears that something has happened, or is happening, that has caused a rift between the two. The girl has considerable leverage, I don't know what it is; her threat to move against this Reggie sounded real, and your surfie girl has some kind of ultimate power she doesn't want to use.'

'Who are these people?'

His hand paused over the dish. Another prawn had its head stuck up invitingly. He didn't take it.

After a long pause, he said, 'They are not the kind of people a wise man cultivates.'

I pondered that one.

He couldn't tell me much more. Or wouldn't.

At the door he said, 'How are your grandchildren?'

I nodded politely and said the right things.

'And your daughter?'

I did the same as before. I didn't quite get it. Someone was pulling a chain at the back of my neck.

'I'm glad,' he said. 'I have family. In Szechuan.'

He'd never talked about his family before. I didn't know what to say or why he was telling me this right now, so I kept nodding and saying the right things, trying to decode the hexagram of his face.

'Filial duty,' he said.

'Very important,' I said.

We both nodded.

He made sure the tape was in my pocket before I left.

20

I was looking forward to a little holiday from the Godzilla of the plot. A little Mozart, Mozzarella and Malbeck. Followed by one of those rare, satisfying sleeps lasting from ten at night to six in the morning without a prostate pee call.

I'd no sooner put Mazzie to rest and was about to do the same, than two ominous figures materialized out of the dusk. It was a perfect film-noir. They had everything: the walk, the coats, the angle of the neck. Only the fedoras were missing.

They were either hoods or cops.

They were cops.

There were two of them, a taller one and a squatter one. Tweedle-dum and Tweedle-dee.

The taller one, who looked like he needed massive injections of Vitamin C to save his face, loomed over me, flashing his wallet. I was coherent enough to give it a look. He was a Detective Inspector with a Maori name I was too rattled to take in. As far as I could tell it was bone-fide. His hair was combed up at the sides with a suggestion of a duck's arse at the back, like Elvis Presley. In fact, Mr Detective Inspector had something of the brooding presence of the early Elvis.

The other was a short, bumptious-looking man with ginger tendencies and of notable ugliness.

'Are you Jason Argonaut?' the tall one said.

'You got me.'

'Is that your real name?'

'My professional name. Ever heard of a famous writer called Mike Smith?'

'That's your real name.' It wasn't a question. He knew that I knew that he knew.

'The word 'real' is debatable.'

He gestured to the short one. 'This is Detective Sergeant McDonald.'

'Charmed, I'm sure.'

Sergeant Haggis gave me a dirty look.

'Shall we talk inside,' the tall Maori guy with the ravaged face said. I decided to call him Elvis.

'I don't know,' I said. 'It's late. Way past my bedtime.'

Elvis nodded as if he were agreeing with me. 'Of course we can always talk at the station. We have some nice cozy interview rooms.'

I could imagine.

I thought of pulling an old man act, you know, I've had a big day chasing my tail, come back tomorrow after I've had a snooze and a freshen up and hid my illegal Luger. Then I thought of those cozy interview rooms.

'Ok, come in, but on one condition.'

He and McDonald raised an eyebrow at each other like Thomson and Thompson of Tintin fame.

'You don't poke around in my papers or anywhere else. I'm an investigative journalist. I've got sources you'd need a million lawyers to get hold of.'

'You're pretty defensive, Mr Argonaut.'

'I'm a public figure.'

Elvis looked around the kitchen. 'Looks like you haven't cooked in here for a while,' he said.

'I like to eat out,' I said. I didn't know what he meant; my kitchen looked perfectly normal. Maybe he just wanted to put me off balance.

'I don't think so,' he said.

Don't fool with these guys, I could hear Jack Reacher say. Jack is wise in the ways of cops and their world. Best to heed him.

I sat them down at my all-purpose lounge. The settee and easy chairs were arranged in a semi-circle around an old fashioned fireplace, which made it hard for them to adopt a dominant position. They rose to the challenge, however. Wherever Elvis sat he was the head of the table. Some people are like that. And some people, like McHaggis, prefer to stand.

'You're a friend of a woman known as Velvet Reed,' Elvis said.

My heart sank, as novelists were once allowed to say. I went cold all over, which is another. Some heartless force was trying to insert a sharp chisel between my scalp and my skull. It was fear.

'What's happened to her?'

'Why should anything have happened to her?'

'Why are you here?'

'She's been reported missing.' He watched me for a while. 'Not at home. Didn't turn up for work today, or yesterday.'

This couldn't be a simple missing person case. Not enough time had elapsed for the cops to be pushing panic buttons and keeping a senior detective like Elvis up past his bedtime. A day off the radar was neither here nor there. This had to be about the computer crash. Her sudden disappearance would naturally bring suspicion upon her. She should be busy assisting them with their enquiries.

'I beg your pardon?'

Elvis had said something.

'I asked you if you visited her the night before last.'

'Yes.'

'What time?'

'Early evening. Around six.'

'What did you talk about?'

'Old times, personal stuff. I was feeling maudlin. We played The Rolling Stones.'

He and McDonald did another Thomson and Thompson act, although this time it wasn't up to scratch. I don't think Thompson, aka McDonald, understood the meaning of maudlin.

'When did you leave?'

'About an hour later.' How long does it take to play *Let it Bleed*?

'What was your relationship with Velvet?' Haggis Face demanded. He remained standing. I think sitting would have made him look too short.

'We were just good friends,' I said. It might have sounded a bit flippant, but I didn't feel that way; it was simply the truth. The more questions they asked, the more I began to wonder if Velvet had had something to do with the computer crash, and had in fact done a runner. In which case my good friend was in deep shit.

Elvis did most of the play. He was polite and professional, and seemed happy with my answers. McDonald, on the other hand, looked less and less happy. Some rat was nibbling at his acorn. He left it till we got to the door.

'Was Velvet involved in illegal hacking?' He contrived to make his gingery eyebrows look formidable. Probably scared the hell out of shoplifting kids.

'She never told me.'

McDonald looked dissatisfied. Elvis looked bored; he was tired and wanted to get home. He gave me a card with his number on it.

'We'll meet again,' McDonald promised me.

21

Alone at last, I broke out the brandy, sat in my favourite chair and did some serious thinking. It didn't do much good. I couldn't believe anything bad had happened to Velvet, but I feared it. She freaked out because someone hacked back at her when she did a little probing into number 54. The Eye of Sauron noticed her. The university computer crashed. She thought it best to get out of Dodge. She gets a bit jumpy sometimes. It sounded all right, but it didn't convince me. Why hadn't she rung in sick at work or something? And why hadn't she told me she was going? A hue and cry was the last thing she'd want.

I thought back to our last meeting. Mick Jagger poncing away. The walls have ears. What if she'd lied, or not told the whole truth? What if she'd cracked that safe and found something? A saucer full of secrets. And just maybe something really bad *had* happened to her?

A second glass of brandy did nothing to clear things up.

Nor the third.

Mazzie complained about being stirred up so early in the morning, a chill in the cylinders and all that, more choke please, where the hell are we going and it better not be up too many hills. Cough cough.

Mazzie and I commiserated together as I steered her towards Marcia's place. You can make the harbour bridge old girl. We can make it together.

While I drove I rang the number Detective Elvis had given me.

Instead, I got through to McDonald. Smart move of Elvis's.

'I want to know if Velvet has been found?'

'Where are you, Mr Smith?'

Ah, so it's Mr Smith now.

'I'm going to see my grandchildren, if it's any business of yours. Now tell me about Velvet.'

'Did you know that it is an offence to drive and talk on a mobile, even with earphones.'

'Don't worry,' I said, 'I don't have any earphones. Has Velvet turned up?'

'No.'

I hung up. He was right. It is dangerous to drive and talk on a mobile.

Marcia didn't understand why I turned up early. She wasn't the only one. The kids were getting ready for school. For King Felix, being only five, this was his first year. He liked school, having greatly extended his kingdom there.

He came running out at me and threw his arms around my knees, which was a bit of a risk. 'Grandad! Are you coming to school with me?'

'I wish,' I said. 'I could probably learn something.'

'I bet you could do good drawings.'

'I'm not so sure,' I said, remembering the pots of colour we had at primary school. The colour would be mixed from a powder. If the teacher was feeling mean, you got a thin mix that ran down the page. A thick mix that stuck to the page in globs meant a happy teacher. Huge rolls of coarse paper. Slap-dash-bash. We were all Jackson Pollocks at heart.

Marcia stood to one side, watching me like a stoat watching a chicken.

'I'll walk them to the bus stop,' she said tersely. 'Back in a mo.'

Christ, when I was five I was running wild in the backcountry blackberry land of Hanmer Springs, filling my lungs with alpine air, free as the breeze, as open as the sky, as lively as a hare. In our class photo for that year, 1952, I had bare feet. Didn't need any other. If my mum had taken me to the bus stop I'd never have lived it down. Besides, there wasn't a bus stop because there wasn't a bus, just a few streets and fields and trees and mountains and sawmills and a school house that was built like they built rural railway stations in those days, peak-roofed in red iron, clad in overlapping timber and painted off-yellow. Standing there in Marcia's kitchen, I thought I caught that mountain smell, the edge of it. Maybe it was the pine fragrance in the dishwashing liquid.

Fintan gave me a high-five as he left.

I paced the kitchen trying to figure out why I was there.

I started at the blunt end. 'Velvet's gone missing,' I said.

Carefully, like a lawyer probing a witness, Marcia asked all the right questions. I told her about the cops, my last visit to Velvet, Velvet's hacking story, the university computer crash. Certain details I omitted. I didn't let on that I knew who lived next door, or about Blue and the rest of it. I was doling out the truth to Marcia as if she were still a child and I couldn't seem to do anything about it. Treating truth as a lolly-scramble. Some of the lollies roll out of sight and never get found.

'You think her disappearance has something to do with the computer crash?'

'I can't rule it out.'

'Which in turn has something to do with her investigation into number 54?'

'Something's frightened her.'

Marcia thought for a long while. Amazingly clear-headed is Marcia. An orderly mind. I'd hate to face her in a court of law.

'So you see a causal connection. As with a crime. Her investigation of number 54 led to the computer crash which *led* to her disappearance.'

Put like that, the way a lawyer would put it, it didn't sound so plausible. She exposed the assumptions I was working on. Possibly there was no causality at work at all. Velvet's investigation, the computer crash, her disappearance, all just happened – nothing more than a cluster of events in time.

Carefully, I said, 'Velvet would never of her own will disappear like this unless… unless, she was involved. Or.'

'Or,' Marcia prompted.

'Or she's dead.'

'Is that what you think? That she's dead?'

'I think that's why I came to see you.'

I was quivering, on the edge of something. Tears, I don't know what.

86

'Steady up there, Pops.'

'I'm steady,' I lied. 'I can't think of any other reason she would fail to turn up at work, or ring in, or something. She was fanatical about things like that. As bad as you.'

'That's really saying something.'

I pulled out my rarely used mobile and used it. When it started to ring I handed it over to Marcia. I heard Velvet's tinny voice saying, *I think, therefore I leave a message.* That joke had passed its use-by date.

Marcia and I stared at each other.

'And she didn't call. She'd know I'd be freaking.'

'This is wild talk.'

I did my best to shrug. I think it means *whatever* in shoulder language.

'Dad, do you kind of… love Velvet?'

I wasn't ready for that conversation. Another time.

'Have you heard of a company called Pacific Holdings?' I asked her.

I thought I saw it, that shock of recognition, but I could have just read it into the fever of the moment.

'No, why?'

'Pacific Holdings owns 54 Odds Ave.'

'The senior partner, Arthur Dogbane, probably administers that contract.'

Marcia's unease was growing, making me curious.

'Pacific Holdings are an umbrella company. Velvet was investigating one of its investors when all this blew up in her face.'

'Dad, you didn't need to know all this stuff just to buy the house, for God's sake.'

'I know! Velvet just got carried away. By the challenge.'

'But Dad, you were never serious about buying! You've got no money. I don't understand all this.'

Which was because I hadn't told her about the singing, or Blue, or Blue and Reggie's visit, or Sparta – and I didn't want to tell her.

The less Marcia knew the better, which, on reflection, could have been the way Velvet had been treating me. And might be the way Marcia was treating me right now.

'Velvet's a hacker, a raider. She got on the trail of something.'

I told Marcia of Velvet's breaking and entering metaphor. The safe and the watcher in the shadows. As the story unfolded, Marcia became more agitated. Pale.

'You know something about this?' I asked.

Being an upright person, Marcia had trouble lying. Especially to me.

'I can't tell you,' she said. 'But I can tell you that what worries me has nothing to do with your number 54. And nothing that would lead to an attack on the university computer system.'

'Ok.' I didn't know whether to feel reassured or not.

'The best scenario is that Velvet's gone to ground.'

'And what's your best scenario? With that dossier I mean.'

'I've brought myself a few days grace on that one,' she said tightly.

We said nothing while Marcia briskly put away the boys' morning mess.

When I left I had tears in my eyes and no idea why.

22

I rang Elvis' number again at midday. I was chewing my fingers to bits by this time.

I got through to McDonald again. We were having far too much to do with each other.

'You're very anxious, Mr Smith,' he said. 'Have you reason to be?'

Why did poor McDonald try to be so clever?

'She's missing,' I said, as if talking to someone somewhat slow on the uptake, like a desk sergeant, 'and I want to know if you have any information?'

'Were you two having a relationship?'

Here we go again.

'We were just good friends, I've told you already. That's what happens at my age.'

Don't ask me why I liked to jerk his chain. He just did that to me.

'Nothing new to report, sir,' he said, as if someone might be listening in to the conversation for instructional purposes.

We both hung up.

I sat around waiting for the sky to fall in.

That didn't happen so I rang Jerzy.

'Jerzy, do you know what a bloodhound is?'

'Didn't think high-tech was your field. Thought you were a global warming man.' He made it sound like a circus act: the strong man, the funny man, the human cannonball, the global warming man.

'I'm full of surprises.'

He said, 'Listen carefully, I'm only going to say this once and then I'm going to hang up. And you are not going to quote me. I don't exist.'

'Jesus.'

'Say it!'

'I'm not going to quote you. You don't exist.'

'Bloodhounds are the killer drones of the virtual world. Once aroused, they can shadow every key you touch, your every mousey move, and can wipe your hard drive cleaner than a baby's bum at bathtime, no messy viruses needed. They hunt hackers. They may activate a real human to monitor and control the counter-hack, like, if the bloodhound runs into too much tricky stuff. And these humans are the best in the game, born with Nintendo thumbs.

'Who are their bosses?'

'Anybody with hard cash and the need. There has to be a hell of a lot of money involved at the very least, these cyberbrats eat lots of junk food. You're talking governments, big corporations, black ops, that kind of stuff. It's only legal if you know which side of your nose you're tapping.'

Jerzy hung up.

Jesus, I never saw the computer world as so scary, you know, the Creature from the Black Lagoon; but in this case the Black Lagoon was the virtual world of data systems, and that world had bred its own Terminators. Maybe, as in that Japanese horror movie, one of them had crawled out of Velvet's computer screen and sucked her in.

It was with a new respect that I awoke the computer. This fucking thing could bite. Strange virtual creatures called Bloodhounds are out there, all too eager to sniff me out. Astro-drones that could laser my hard drive in nanoseconds.

I noticed, as I opened the map, that the doc had not been saved. It was just sitting on the desktop. I realized that if I hadn't opened the documents, they would have just hung there with provisional virtual status only, like an immigrant without a work permit. Now I'd opened them, I either had to keep them open as unsaved docs, save them, or delete them. Opening them had already committed me.

I went for the map first. Full coloured, it was quite detailed and clear, but there were no longitude and latitude coordinates and I had no way of knowing up or down, let alone where I was. The topography was there, mountains, flat areas, as were certain symbols, but there was no decoder for reading them. I isolated a couple of wandering blue lines I designated as rivers. There were brown lines I designated as roads, not many of them, no obvious urban areas; I had the feeling I was in remote territory. Staring at it didn't get me very far; I might as well have been looking at a map of my own brain. I once read an essay by a teacher with the wonderful name of Stanley Fish. He showed his class a list of names and told them it was a poem; the suckers went right on ahead and began interpreting the list as if it were a poem. So, says Fish, we form interpretive communities: perhaps there is no thing-in-itself.

Deep waters for an old journo, but looking at the map made me feel like an interpretive community of one – I didn't know what I was looking at. And there were no suckers around to tell me.

Then I noticed an oddity. There was a faint colour division up or down, or sideways, that divided the map. I used the division to create an up and down. I designated up as north and down as south. That was fun. So with the right side as east, the left as west (I got all dyslexic around that), I had a colour disjunction that ran from north to south. The east side colours were subtly enhanced, with some areas highlighted. I was momentarily interrupted when Monckton jumped up beside me, which he didn't often care to do. He looked from me to the screen. Looked like he knew something I didn't. Trying to see it the way a cat might see it, I looked back at the screen and saw faint arrows, thicker than roads, rivers and topography, arching from west to east. I'd seen arrows like that in graphic representations of military movements; Hitler's pincer movement into France, that kind of thing. But here they were hidden, like palimpsests, only visible when you looked at them through Monckton's eyes, and had a solid grounding in Stanley Fish. They were in pale violet.

I went to print it out so I could look at it in hard copy, but Jack Reacher forestalled me. Not a good idea, I had to agree with him. Any print job would be noted somewhere – time for a little practical paranoia.

That left me with more questions than McDonald's has burgers.

23

The morning of *tea and biscuits.*

The phone woke me. I reached out from under the sheets and grabbed it.

It was my pal Joe. Aka Elvis.

'What did Velvet tell you about her hacking activities, Mr Argonaut?'

'Nothing too specific. I knew she did it.'

'And you knew it was illegal?'

'I didn't ask. I mean, it's a murky area.'

'Do you know why she was doing it? Was she working for somebody? With anybody?'

'Not Velvet. She's a loner.'

'How do you know?'

I didn't. Not really. He let it pass.

'I know one thing though. Velvet wouldn't have done it for money. It was the thrill of the thing she enjoyed.'

'How do you know?'

Again, I didn't. It was my understanding of her character, my reading of her as a person, and I told Elvis that. He wasn't terribly impressed. 'If it was a secret she wouldn't have told you, would she?' Cop logic for you.

I saw an opportunity. I didn't want the cops to know about my interest in the house next door. None of their business was how I thought of it. But if Velvet was in trouble because of her investigation into number 54, in other words, because of me, the game had changed.

'She said something about a company called Pacific Holdings. A passing remark.'

I could hear Elvis writing it down. Let's see what crawled out from under that rock.

'Has she been normal lately? Her usual self? Or has she seemed worried?'

I didn't like the drift of these questions. 'There's been no sign of her, has there?'

'Just answer the question.'

'What about her driver's licence, passport, bank cards, clothes…?'

'Please answer my question, Mr Argonaut.' I could hear it in his voice. We were a mere step away from one of those nice, cosy interview rooms.

'She's been a bit moody, but then, she's like that.'

I remembered her face the last time we'd met, with Jagger pounding behind.

'And maybe something else.'

'What else?' He had all the patience of a dentist extracting teeth.

'Fear. She was afraid.' Saying it out loud like that to Inspector Joe made it real to me. Brought the fear right into the room.

'Of what?'

'I don't know. She didn't tell me.'

'Okay.' He heard the break in my voice and eased up a bit. 'And by the way, she didn't take anything with her.'

'I see,' I said. 'She's dead.'

'What makes you say that, Mr Argonaut?'

'If she'd done a runner, she would taken stuff. Wallet, clothes.'

'Unless she has cash.' His voice was cool and silvery. 'In fact, if someone is serious about disappearing the only way to do it is to leave *everything* behind. All ID. Velvet would know that.'

He wasn't trying to reassure me. Just working through his cop logic with no particular feelings in any direction. I had my own logic. Like tearing the petals off a daisy, but instead of *she loves me, she loves me not* it's *she's dead, she's alive, dead alive, dead alive*, the daisy petals withering in the air.

The Godzilla clock ticked on.

I decided to dress in black. At least in the trouser department. My formal looking Mountain Trail pants, loose, flexible for kick-boxing Van Damme style, and a long, creamy white shirt Indian kurta style, informally open at the neck. Like a photograph, I look more effective in black and white. I boast a spray of patrician hair, if fluffed up, above eyebrows not formidable perhaps but nominally intelligent. Definitely a patrician nose, late Roman Imperial, a little worse for two thousand years of wear and tear but still serviceable.

So the big moment had finally come. In that respect the virtual world of fiction is as much subject to the arrow of time as those of us who toil through the real world, such as it is. Sooner or later that appointment rolls around, be it with the dentist or death. It's our daily *dues ex machina*. The inconvenient unavoidable. Entropy.

Tea and biscuits.

Sparta opened the door before I could knock. I took that as a mark of respect. She bowed her head gracefully. She was stunningly dressed in a formal, full length, pale-blue-sky-sublime embroidered frock, high-waisted in the traditional Chinese manner. Wild swans and all that. Her shoulder-length hair had been lifted and turned a couple of times into what my old aunt Aggie would have called buns, revealing the delicate freshness of her neck and throat.

'Hi Grandad.' Like an American teenager.

'Why do you call me that?'

'Because you are Grandad to your boys, the Lego boys.'

I had to smile. The Lego boys! Whadda team! A brief picture of Fin and King Felix fighting over some Lego prize. Like a horse. Or a guy who slots into a horse to make a horse-and-guy.

'You are looking very royal today, Sparta,' I said. Regal, that was the word, but I wasn't sure she would know it. 'Just like a princess.'

'Thank you,' she said, accepting the compliment like a real lady.

She led me into a hall, with rooms off to each side. There was a closed doorway on the left, which I guessed to be a bedroom, and one on the right partially open. I tried to take a sneaky sideways glance inside, didn't see much but what looked, crazily, like the back end of a coffin. More likely some kind of polished wooden cabinet.

Blue met us halfway down the hall. In contrast to Sparta she was looking super casual in sloppy blue jeans and a sloppy white top and a just-got-out-of-bed hair-do money could never buy, shining blonde strands playing helter-skelter with her face. She gave me a huge Californication smile. Yeah, yeah, I thought, and you speak Mandarin like a native. Who the hell are you, Blue? What's your real name? And I'll bet my mother's milk you haven't really just tumbled out of bed.

'God knows what you think of us,' she said, pretending to hide her mouth with her hand, as if she were too embarrassed for words.

'I love your singing,' I said. 'Whenever you sing 'Georgia On My Mind' I can hear the orchestra. À la Ray Charles. It's a pity Ray never heard you sing.'

'Is that when you started watching at the window?' she asked casually.

'Around then.' I could be casual too. 'I heard your voice first. 'Ol' Man River'. That's me. Not many people around here sing while they pull up weeds. In fact, not many sing at all, or pull up weeds for that matter.'

'I can play the guitar too. I'll play a song for you. Some day.'

'I'll hold you to that.'

We entered a spacious living room, built around a red brick fireplace, kitchen at the back. There were chairs around the fireplace, but loosely, with plenty of walking space. An eight-seater table of polished kauri was positioned beside a large window affording a generous view of the tall paling fence separating number 54 from my place. It looked more like a sculpture than a table. Great if you do lots of entertaining of people you want to impress. Against the other wall, by along from the fire, was an upright piano, very modern and expensive.

The effect was of a rather luxurious dining room, rather than the more prosaic 'living room'. Some gentle eastern music was playing in the background. Everything perfectly pleasant.

Blue led me away from the table to the lounge area where Reggie was standing, his pugnacious face looking almost thoughtful. I didn't get then that his type only become thoughtful when they feel threatened. Then they think just fine.

'Thanks for the phone,' I said in a friendly voice, you know, let bygones be bygones.

'What?'

'The phone you smashed. My phone.'

'What about it?'

'Thanks for the new one. I got it in the mail. It took a bit for me to figure it out. Bit technically challenged. Works fine.'

Reggie looked at Blue, who shrugged.

I could see the question forming on his lips, *You got a phone in the mail?* And I could see the awareness dawning that I was taking the piss out of him, when Blue pulled him back to his social duties as co-hosts in their Punch and Judy show.

I wasn't the only guest.

A tall, grave-faced Asian guy on the other side of forty stood quietly by the fireplace. Reggie introduced him as Mr Wang. Reggie was making a real effort. Mr Wang and I exchanged courtesies.

Blue retreated to the kitchen where she and Sparta fussed as girls are supposed to. Reggie joined them for a moment and returned with a pot of green tea, already steeped, pouring it into small, handleless cups etched with stylised willow branches. For your good health, and perhaps to line the stomach for the harder stuff to come.

'So you are an investigative journalist, Mr Argonaut?' Mr Wang said as the thimbles were recharged. The tea had a smoky edge.

How the hell did he know that? One of my fan club, perhaps.

'I write for a living. Shameful but true.'

He smiled. 'I've heard that all journalists desire to write a book.'

'Probably. It's the great delusion of the age that everybody has a book inside them. It's like saying everybody has a tree inside them. Or a turtle.'

Mr Wang was not to be deflected. 'You did an article on the Three Gorges Dam, with Meilin Xiang.'

'You are very well informed, Mr Wang. But I'm not here in my professional capacity. I'm here for tea and biscuits.'

Mr Wang smiled.

'Ah, just like the British,' he said. 'But we're closer to lunchtime than morning tea. I think our hosts have something more in mind.'

24

Reggie, who was now playing master of ceremonies, called us to the main table where he, Blue and Sparta had already gathered. At its centre was a stainless steel pot, the size of a large wok, but steeper, with a fluted funnel in the middle. A small charcoal brazier beneath emitted a blue flame and its contents, veiled by the broth's smoky sheen, bubbled away. But you could see a small armada of chilies floating on the surface. There were five sets of small bowls, side plates and chopsticks arrayed around it, and wedge-shaped platters with rolls of meats, stacks of tiger prawns and other fruits of the sea, long-tendrilled mushrooms, bok choy, spinach, sprouts, assorted greens, condiments, and a wooden board with red and white glutinous cubes, laid out in a grid like a checkerboard. Reggie scooped the cubes into the broiling liquid, then the vegetables, meat and seafood.

I wasn't too gob-smacked. I'd spent enough time in China to know how they like to party, and to what lengths they will go for an honoured guest, for I supposed that's what I was, or what I was being invited to feel.

Reggie guided Wang and I to our seats, sitting us together. Blue and Sparta sat opposite us while Reggie did the honours at the head of the table. Reggie allotted each of us a clear liquor with an oily consistency in small crystal glasses, full to the brim.

'*Baijiu,*' said Reggie. 'Chinese sorghum wine. High octane fuel. Perhaps Mr Wang would propose a toast.'

Mr Wang inclined his head in acknowledgement of the honour. He studied the glass. 'To 5,000 years of history!' He raised the glass – 'Gumbai!' – threw his head back and drained it in a single gulp.

Everybody followed suit. I knew the drink. But still gasped to suppress a cough. Not much shy of 60%, I guessed. Probably illegal under the local liquor act. Strong enough to stir the dead. But this was top shelf, not the sickly kerosene workers in blue overalls siphon from gaudy tins, purchased from street sellers for a few yuan.

At Reggie's direction I lifted my bowl to a carefully ladled assortment of the hotpot's contents. The pungently hot, chillied broth was almost a relief after the baijiu. A tingling numbness set in under my tongue, like a mild anesthetic. Wang, however, was already gesturing Reggie for a refill, though he did not immediately propose another toast.

A sense of expectancy nagged at me – Chinese are great believers in reciprocity, so I proposed a toast of my own and made sure to empty my glass in Wang's emphatic fashion. A little etiquette goes along way in the East.

'This one's for Blue,' I said, 'who has the voice of a jazz singer. Here's to old sweet songs! Gumbai!'

I'll drink to that! Gumbai!

Reggie topped our glasses again.

'Are you Sparta's father?' I asked Mr Wang ingenuously, playing the vague-old-man.

He demurred. 'I'm a friend of the family.'

'Which family?' I picked up a tiger prawn in my chopsticks and inspected it.

He gave me a quick look, enough to tell me that he was not fooled by my geriatric trip.

Reggie prodded at the cubes bobbing in the pot and, satisfied, scooped two into my bowl.

I split the darker of the pair using my chopsticks like a knife and gingerly maneuvered one half into my mouth. It had the consistency of jellyfish, with a sharp tang on the finish.

'Do you like our *xuedoufu*?' Wang asked, eyebrows slightly arched.

'Very good,' I said, 'but what is *shoe doh fu?*'

'Doufu, you say it 'tofu',' said Wang. 'And *xue* means blood. Xuedoufu – blood-tofu.'

'What kind of blood?'

'Ah, can be duck-blood, chicken-blood, pig-blood – almost any kind of blood.'

Couldn't imagine Kiwi tofu eaters going for it.

'This one is pig-blood, Reggie said. 'Like black pudding, right? An English delicacy.'

'Yummy,' Sparta said.

'Reggie made it,' Blue said, 'he's just too modest to say so.'

Reggie did his best to blush, and didn't quite get there.

Conversation wasn't that easy. But the *baijiu* wet the palate and loosened tongues – at least my tongue.

I burbled on about the joys of scientific research, and passed a couple of comments about global warming, but I wasn't making all that much sense, even to myself. I just wanted to know who these people were. Blue watched me all the while, hardly looked anywhere else, and said nothing much, just made encouraging noises to keep me going; she seemed to rest content with the creaminess of her skin and the blondeness of her hair. Reggie didn't have a lot to say for himself. But he did say one thing.

We were talking about music, Blue having offered to put on some western music that might be more to my taste, maybe some Leonard Cohen. I declined, suspecting a little mischievousness on Blue's part; it was too early in the day for Cohen's crepuscular melancholy. Maybe some classical? No, I was content with the discordant chimes of the Chinese music.

'I can't stand Leonard Cohen,' Reggie announced abruptly. 'Or Neil Young. Or Bob Dylan…' He sure knew in detail what he didn't like. 'A bunch of whining, moaning minnies.'

'What do you like?' I asked politely, trying to more accurately place his accent, spearing a piece of *xuedoufu* on my plate. East European was too tempting, too easy.

'Stravinsky,' he said, 'You won't find anything to match The Rites of Spring. Or Stockhausen. His was electronic music before electronics.' He picked up some *xuedoufu* in his fingers and wiped it into his mouth like a baby with mush.

I had to do a rapid re-evaluation of Reggie. I didn't know that thugs like him were into modern classical music, but then again,

I didn't know any thugs. Maybe Reggie, chef and classical music aficionado, wasn't a thug after all and I had been deceived by appearances.

'And I like Berg, too,' Reggie said, when he had finished, or rather half finished swallowing his mush, 'when I'm feeling mellow.' He picked up a roll of ham and sucked on it, perhaps to demonstrate.

'He never feels mellow,' Blue assured me. 'Believe me, he's a boy-racer at heart.'

'So was Stockhausen,' I said, and Reggie gave me a bleak smile.

We all drank. I didn't know about Berg but I was feeling pretty mellow.

'And who do you like?' I said, turning to Sparta, who was being the model of decorum.

'Aaah: Neil Diamond?'

'Wrong answer,' I said.

We both laughed, and I threw back another tumbler. I didn't know kids came this smart. I didn't know she even was a kid. Maybe these guys ran a vampire franchise, had been around for countless centuries, and were pulling my tit before the gory stuff. A coffin in the back room and all that. That was why the spooks were onto them. Here I was laughing and drinking and sounding off like a donkey in a nest of slavering vipers.

But try and talk sense into a donkey.

'Hey Sparta,' I said, after my next tumbler of the elixir. 'Do you go to school?'

'No. I'm tutored at home. I have a very wise teacher.' She patted Blue on the leg. There was something almost proprietorial in that action, like a master patting the head of favourite pet.

'Are you some kind of princess?'

Everybody went on doing what they were doing, assiduously eating, but I sensed that something new had entered the atmosphere, like a ghost stealing unseen into the room.

'Yes,' she answered primly.

'So where are your parents?'

'They are away busy being king and queen.'

Blue laughed. 'Don't be fooled Jason. She may be a smart kid, I'll give her five gold stars for that, but she can fantasize like any other kid. She's got one hell of an imagination, don't forget that.'

'I won't,' I said.

'She sure the hell thinks highly of herself,' Reggie said. He bit the head of a tiger prawn and munched away.

'Of course she's a princess,' Mr Wang said indulgently, like a doting uncle.

'Thank you,' Sparta said, inclining her head in his direction, every inch the princess.

Reggie looked ready to spit on the floor. Maybe the prawn didn't appeal.

'I'd like to propose a toast,' Sparta said, lifting her glass of lemonade.

We readied our thimbles.

'To Chang O, Goddess of the Moon,' Sparta declared.

We drank.

'Didn't she commit some crime?' I said, struggling to remember the popular myth.

'That's right,' Sparta said. It was her turn with a king prawn. She started with the tail, nipping off a piece in a fairly ladylike manner. 'She stole the elixir of immortality from her husband, who'd received it in payment for shooting some excess suns out of heaven. When she took the elixir she found herself floating up to the moon, where she remains in exile, with only a jade rabbit and a woodcutter for company.'

'The poet Li Po liked to compose verses to her,' Blue said.

'I lift my cup to
the moon, my shadow and me -
together, we make company.'

'The poet was a solitary drinker,' Mr Wang observed with some gravity. 'One should not drink with only his shadow for company.'

'Ah!' Sparta said, 'but he was not alone, he had Chang O for company.'

'He was trying to fool himself,' Mr Wang said. 'Make the best of a bad situation.'

Blue got up and went to the piano. At first I thought it was a classical piece she was playing, even Berg perhaps, but then I recognized the melody, and after a moment it came to me. She was playing Neil Young's song 'Helpless' in a classical style, with trills and frills and variations. She came in singing the last verse, also in classical style. The lines about windows behind stars and birds throwing shadows were full of nostalgia, haunted by childhood.

The big birds of the song reminded me of the hawk I'd seen hovering above her, and I quietly finished off the verse. *Helpless.* In the face of all that. *Helpless helpless helpless.*

25

'You know something,' I said to Blue when she had finished the final trills, 'nobody sings any more, you know, as they go about their daily business. People used to sing as they worked, sing in the shower, sing their way through life, can you credit that? The Maori sang their way across the Pacific Ocean, thousands of miles. They did it on the power of song.'

Reggie looked fatigued but Mr Wang was enthusiastic. 'It is true. The ancient poets affirm that it is only through song that some of the gods and goddesses may be approached. Have you read *Songs of the South*? There was a belief in Tang Dynasty times that music could melt ice. I'm not sure about heavy metal though.' Had Mr Wang just made a joke? It was hard to tell.

'You mean we can sing our way to nirvana, Mr Wang?'

'In nirvana there is no singing because there is no song.'

This sounded very wise and Zen to me.

'How do you know?' Blue said to him. 'Have you been there?'

Mr Wang turned to me. 'Don't get your knickers in a twister,' he said clumsily. 'That is the right expression, Mr Argonaut?'

'Not my knickers,' I said, trying to concentrate on the subtext here.

'I don't like Nirvana,' Sparta said. 'Their sound drags. Kurt Cobain sounds like a voice in a well, drowning.'

'Well, yes,' I said, 'that's a fair description,' wondering why the hell we were talking about music.

In the end I decided they were just humouring me. All this shadow-play just to make me feel good? Reggie looked like he was asking himself the same question.

'Are you in business, Mr Wang?'

'Import/export.'

'That's what they all say.'

'What?'

'The term covers a multitude of sins.'

Mr Wang turned helplessly to Blue who shot back a quick line of Chinese. Didn't even look at me. Didn't so much as blush. Like she knew I already knew.

He nodded. 'Multitudes.' And he didn't look too unhappy about it.

'What about China importing toxic waste?'

'We have plenty of our own.'

'But there's money to be made in it.'

'There's money to be made in anything, if you squeeze it hard enough,' Reggie said, hacking at his mouth with a toothpick and trying to smile at the same time; he thought he'd made a joke. He was still picking away at the rolled meats, sucking at them as if they were giant spliffs.

Blue looked away. Suddenly I wanted to talk to her, alone. To ask her....

'Mr Wang, I'm very intrigued that China banned James Cameron's Avatar.'

'I can't speak for the Government, Mr Argonaut; I'm just a trader.'

'This is not an interview,' I laughed and sat back in a relaxed fashion. I'd learned that if you do this sort of physical action people will mirror you, like monkeys, and do the same thing; by apparently being disarming you disarm your opponent. Very Zen. But Mr Wang did not follow the rules, and continued to regard me intently.

Nonchalantly, I tossed back my next tumbler. 'When you catch me doing film reviews you'll know I'm on the scrap heap.' He begrudged a smile. 'I'm just curious. I thought you might have an opinion. Isn't the film just a harmless, schmaltzy fantasy?'

He did some Zen meditation over his bok choy, chewing in careful circular motions. I was glad I was not the bok choy being pounded to pulp so methodically.

'The film is *not* a harmless fantasy, Mr Argonaut. It merely pretends to be. Actually, it is a clever piece of propaganda, directed against the development of the Earth's resources. In China we have,' he spread his fingers as if tabling a show of cards, 'minorities and dissonant groups that might identify with the blue people of Pandora. But you know this, from your work with Meilin Xiang on the Three Gorges Dam.'

Twice now, he'd mentioned Meilin's name. What if he knew that I'd seen Meilin recently. Was he trying to tell me something? Dropping a hint.

'A lot of people were displaced,' I said.

He nodded grimly, 'More than you know.'

'I liked Avatar,' Sparta said. 'Better than David Bowie.'

Blue and I shared an amused moment. Mr Wang was left right out of that one. 'Major Tom to Pandora,' Blue said.

Sparta took a second, delicate bite at the prawn. 'It was magic, but only in 3D. It felt like you could put your hand out and capture the blessings of the trees. On Pandora there were no machines, no prisons. People could jack into nature through their hair.'

'Green propaganda,' Mr Wang said without malice.

'A load of shite if you ask me,' Reggie said, sounding peeved that nobody had. 'Pretentious shite too, the worst kind. Sentimental to the eyeballs.' Here was another side of Reggie – the literary critic. 'Go to Pandora and fuck a blue alien, who needs it?' He snapped a toothpick in half and threw down the bits.

Argument over as far as he was concerned.

'No blue aliens for you, eh Reggie?' Sparta said with a discernible emphasis on the word blue, throwing in a bit of Aussie twang in case he missed the point. He didn't, and lifted his upper lip at her in acknowledgment. 'Still,' she went on brightly, 'you have to admit that a fuck's a fuck.'

There was a sudden choked silence around the table. This was not the way a princess talked. Yet somehow it didn't sound like an obscenity coming from her, with her precise intonation, but Reggie didn't see it that way. I could see all kinds of retorts running through his head and out the other side.

'Bad language makes your mouth foul,' he said. 'My grandmother had the answer for brats like you. Sand-soap and water mouthwash. And lots of Hail Marys.'

'I was only quoting,' Sparta said mildly.

'Quoting who?'

'It's a saying, or truism, popular in certain uncouth quarters, origin unknown.' Uncouth? Where did this girl learn her English?

'You are a scholar?' I said to Sparta. There was enough tension in the air to rack up my blood pressure by 20 points. There were so many elephants in the room I'd lost count.

'I get to hear things,' she said, without a trace of humour. 'That particular little nugget I heard from Mr Reginald himself.'

They're all covering up, I thought. Like actors in a play. A play put on for my benefit, but tensions will show. In a position of weakness, the smart man doesn't force any issues, Jack Reacher advised. First, figure out where the hardware is – who's packing? In this case, Reggie was packing, easy to tell. Wang was harder to read. Blue could be packing. Even Sparta. Everybody and their dog could be packing.

That's when the party turned pear-shaped.

26

Abruptly, three people entered the room from the hall. I guess that's the disadvantage of living at the back of the house – you can't see who might be coming through the front door.

The first was a regal looking Asian woman I guessed to be Chinese. The hint of the traditional in her sleek, modern dress, the cut of it, the pattern, there was no time for speculation. She was about 70, with a face hard enough to be kiln-fired. The way she carried herself, and looked contemptuously around the room, made her look tall. A couple of smart-looking Asian heavies flanked her; dapper and light on their feet, polite heavies. One looked older, even smarter. These two are killers, Jack Reacher advised me. The woman too. They are certainly packing. Not triads. These guys are something else.

I was about to stand up, as you do when people enter the room, especially a well-dressed, matriarchal-looking woman, but nobody else moved and I was momentarily disoriented. Do the Chinese stand up when people enter the room? Or was this a case when normal etiquette did not apply?

'Looks like I missed the banquet,' the woman said in firm, clipped English.

'Aunty Wu,' Blue said. 'If we'd known you were coming we'd have saved some bounty of the sea for you.'

Reggie picked up a rather sad-looking prawn and offered it to the woman.

'We're putting an end to all this silly fantasy right now,' she said. To Blue, she said, 'This was a stupid idea from the start. It was never going to fly. I told everybody, but nobody listen. Everybody too smart. Aunty Wu, they say, she's losing her nerve, jumping at shadows – and now you see what happens. Aunty Wu was right all along.'

Reggie leaned back, his hand subtly, or so he thought, reaching inside his jacket.

'Don't even think about it, Hive,' Aunty Wu said.

Hive? Was Reggie about to turn into Hive? What kind of name was that?

'You've made the wrong move, Wu Lin Yang,' Blue said. 'It's bad luck to interrupt high tea with an honoured guest.'

'Ah, Fang Runru finds her tongue at last. Bet you don't use that name here. What do they call you, Tarzan Jane perhaps?' She tittered as if from behind a fan. Her heavies smirked.

I shifted my chair, to get a better view of the action. I could see, beyond the smirking heavies, to the partially open doorway in the hall. I had a clear view of what was obviously a coffin, no mistaking it. Some expensive, dark polished wood with fittings that had the dull gleam of real gold. It was one fancy coffin.

Regal Woman turned to Mr Wang. 'Ah, Mr Wang, you do have a habit of turning up. Here and there.'

Mr Wang inclined his head in a formal gesture of respect but said nothing. His attitude suggested that none of this had anything to do with him.

The woman called Wu Lin Yang turned her eyes on me. There was no warmth in them. 'Who are you?'

I didn't care for her tone.

'I'm the honoured guest.'

'What gives you the honour?'

'I'm an elderly neighbour. A wise ancestor. These good people asked me over for tea and biscuits. Perhaps you'd like some of this wonderful spread. Or a little *baijiu* perhaps.'

'Elderly? You're probably younger than I am.'

'I doubt that.'

If she got the compliment it didn't show. She placed her hand on Reggie's shoulder. 'You can unfreeze now, Hive. Just drop the Napoleon act, you know, guns on the table, please.'

Reggie threw a squat looking handgun on the table.

The younger heavy walked smartly forward and snapped it up.

Behind them, the coffin lid opened. A frail, skeletal arm held it up. A moment later a cadaverous face appeared.

Madam Wu turned back to Mr Wang, 'What about you, Mr Wang, are you packing, as the Americans say.'

Mr Wang nodded and reached into his side pocket. He drew forth a pack of cards, opened them up, shuffled them, cut them, and turned up the Queen of Spades which he offered to Madam Wu.

It was the coolest thing I'd seen for a long time, but I had other things to look at.

Spider-like, a pair of legs appeared on the edge of the coffin beside the cadaverous face. A human body emerged like an insect from a chrysalis. An old Chinese man, even older than me. Much older.

Great-Grandaddy Vampire. Nosferatu.

Finally, having dealt to the lesser players, Madam Wu addressed Sparta. 'Ok Jiao Ming, on your feet. We're leaving.'

Sparta didn't move. The atmosphere ratcheted up a few knots. My blood pressure did the same.

Softly, Blue said, 'Think again, Wu Lin Yang.'

'Aunty Wu,' Sparta said. 'Why assume I want to go with you?'

Why talk in English? For my sake? For Reggie's? Or did they prefer to do their confrontations in a neutral language.

'Daddy wouldn't approve of this, Aunty Wu.'

'Such a correct young lady, aren't you, Jiao Ming. Such a prissy prig. And you're so smart you're nearly always right. Daddy would *not* approve. But there are things that Daddy doesn't know. He doesn't get the big picture. And neither do you. Face it, Runru has made a mistake, put this place in jeopardy. She blows the whole silly plan. So you're either coming to Aunty Wu like a good girl… or my friends here will offer their assistance.'

'I don't think so,' Blue said, pulling her hair from her face and fixing it in a swift ponytail. She sat straight in her chair, arms loosely by her side. Despite appearances, she didn't seem like a Californian surfie girl any longer.

'Seems this is a family affair,' I said. I stood and lifted a final tumbler into the air, 'but it's really time for me to be going... I can find my way to the door. Thank you, lovely time. I know just one ancient Chinese salute: *Among friends, there is never enough wine.*' I tossed the hard stuff to the back of my throat.

Nobody said anything. Nobody moved. It was like they were all watching TV.

As I put the thimble back on the table, Madam Wu said, 'You didn't say your name.'

'Mike Smith. And I'm about to leave.'

'Mike Smith?'

'I've got a birth certificate to prove it.' How many people can use their real name as an alias?

As she considered my answer I realized that she was wondering if she'd have to kill me.

Surely, there's no need to kill a befuddled old man. One too many thimbles, not too nimbles. Out the door before you can sneeze. On the run. Away with the breeze. Lucky old sun. But the looks on all the faces told me that my act had cut little ice, and I wasn't going anywhere. Meanwhile I could still see the back room, and that old Great-Grandaddy vampire had extricated himself from his coffin and was creeping, and creep is the word, towards the door. He had bat ears that stuck out each side of his shaved head, like Lon Chaney in The 0Son of Dracula.

The older, more suave heavy leaned forward and dropped some Mandarin into Madam Wu's ear. Squeaks and bubbles.

'Ah! So you're the famous Jason Argonaut!'

She turned resentfully to Wang, 'Why didn't you tell me?'

Mr Wang said something to her in Chinese which sounded like get it over with, or get over it, or how's your father. He could have been asking for directions to the men's rooms. Which, come to think of it, I was starting to need myself.

'That's not why I'm here,' I said. I didn't sit down. I don't subscribe to the notion that people shrink as they get older, and could still use my height. I was no Jack Reacher, but even with five and a half inches knocked off his height, I could still stand tall. If Aunty Wu could play regal, I could too. I still had a bit of Einstein hair to go with it, remember. 'I live next door. Said hello to Blue and Sparta one day. She invited me today. It's nothing more complicated than that.'

'I should shoot you,' she said. 'It would be instructive to others, who don't seem to be taking me seriously, it would get rid of somebody who's pretending to be a garrulous old fool, but who could turn into a major pest, and best of all, it would serve as a warning to any other scooper-snoopers to stay well clear. To your editor, particularly.'

'It sure would,' I said. 'But I'm the one who would take it personally. He'd still have to get the next edition out.'

I thought of pointing out that the cops might show an interest too, but Jack Reacher observed that it might not be a good idea to threaten Aunty Wu at this stage. Or any stage.

The old vampire entered the room naked but for a Samurai-style loincloth.

'This is not Detroit, or Hong Kong.' he said in raspy voice. 'Start shooting, very soon police arrive. Untoward attention will accrue.'

Everybody turned to meet him. There was a hush in the room, as if a god had just entered. Shock and awe. But Aunty Wu and her packing sidekicks looked more surprised than anybody else.

Aunty Wu did a stiff and formal bow. 'Grandfather,' she said. 'I didn't expect you.'

'Obviously. Now, let's get rid of silly guns.' He faced the younger heavy, who had taken Reggie's pistol. There was no menace in it, yet I had the feeling that this old skull 'n' bones could have taken them out quicker than look at them.

'You know,' the old man said to the room in general, 'it is called common sense but it is most uncommon. Rare in fact. And never found around guns.'

The younger heavy carefully placed Reggie's gun at the old naked guy's feet. Then, after a moment, pulled a pistol from his waist and added it to Reggie's. He wouldn't look at Aunty Wu. The older heavy added his pistol to the growing pile.

Old Nosferatu turned to Aunty Wu. Feigning indifference, she loosed a small handgun from somewhere on her person, it was too quick to see, and put it on the floor with the other hardware. Then the grand old man looked at Mr Wang, who stoically drew from his sock, movie-style, a thin curved knife. He held it out, tenderly holding the blade, so the old guy, old Nosferatu, could grasp it by the handle and add it to the pile.

I was starting to like this old guy. He had charisma. He had style. I gave him the nod, one grandfather to another. Grandfather power! He could kill everybody in this room in five seconds, Jack Reacher said. Even me.

I shouldn't have given Nosferatu the nod. It just drew his attention to me. There was no particular camaraderie in his smile. Surely, I thought, he couldn't be Aunty Wu's grandfather, even he wasn't that old. Maybe grandfather was some sort of title of honour. Like Godfather.

'No weapons,' I declared. 'But I do have a reserve pack of MallowPuffs in the kitchen. They'd make a mess out of somebody's face.'

Nobody laughed. Apparently they didn't appreciate slapstick. Didn't understand the wonderful weapon farce can be in the face of terror.

To Aunty Wu, the old man said, 'This nosy fool has already attracted the interest of the constabulary, who paid him a visit the other day. And you come busting in here like some kind of cheap triad madam, interrupting my meditations.' He netted us all in his gaze as the most experienced fisherman can net a myriad of whitebait no matter how swift the river or lean the season. To me he said, 'The older you get, the less you want to contemplate mortality. The more you have to.' Except for a dry, archaic quality, he spoke English almost perfectly. Some of his vocabulary choices, however, seemed odd to me, oddly old fashioned. When were the police last called the *constabulary*?

At the same time, his words gave me a lightbulb moment. Something from my random strange-but-true collection. A sort of Asian cult, corporate type high-stress guys (don't know about the women) who buy their coffins in advance and lie in them with the lid down for a set time every day, just to get used to the idea of being dead. To contemplate their mortality from the inside, as it were. To stare into the satiny darkness. Watch their balance sheets dissolve in the corrosion of time. Face their terror, then their nothingness. Bully for them! I don't want to get used to the idea. I'll have plenty of time when I'm really dead to do that.

Then Aunty Wu did something truly amazing. She dropped to her knees and prostrated herself at the Vampire's feet. 'I was afraid for Jiao Ming,' she said into the floor. 'I had bad dreams about Fang Runru.'

With the fluidity that would have made a twenty-year-old blush, the Vampire flowed into a squat and bent over so his face was close to hers. He rocked back on his heels easily, like a little girl having a pee. 'There's no shame in fear,' he said gently. Then he switched to Mandarin, chanting in a sing-song voice. I guessed it was poetry because it sent a chill up my spine.

Both of them rose. Aunty Wu looked shaky. Her face was a mess, but there was hardness in her stance.

I should have shut up, but couldn't help myself.

'Why are you talking mostly in English?' I said to the old vampire. Once a nosy old fool, always a nosy old fool.

'Because English is my language of choice in this country. English is the language of guns, best language for talking about pieces and pigs and packing and death and bottom lines and nine millimetre headaches. I reserve my Mandarin for the ancient poets, who must be read aloud, and discussions of those poets. The right language frames discussion. Right thought, right action.'

I really did like this guy, despite insulting the English language (I mean English is as blunt as you need it to be; subtleties will accrue, however), and insulting me. He rocked. (How would you say that in Mandarin. In two syllables?) He was my role model, my hero.

The old man rested enquiring eyes on Blue, who faced him calmly, with a half smile. 'You know I dislike guns. They're so heavy to carry around.'

The old man did not return her smile. 'Things have not proceeded the way you intended, Fang Runru.'

'I know,' she said, looking dead serious now. She let forth a stream of Mandarin, as if she felt more comfortable in that language for what she wanted to say.

'Unintended consequences plague the rational mind,' he said when she'd finished.

Very quietly, she said, 'You are very generous, Grandfather.'

'A great mess is what I'd call it,' Aunty Wu said.

They all fell silent, on the brink of saying things they couldn't say. Why not? Because I was there? Because Mr Wang was there?

'We have to take Jiao Ming,' Aunty Wu said to Nosferatu in a shaky voice, moving in behind Sparta, her fingers clawing the back of the chair as if they had intentions of their own. 'This place is no longer secure.'

Nosferatu looked skeptical. 'So this is a rescue mission, with lots of guns.' He was speaking to Madam Wu but was regarding me thoughtfully.

Aunty Wu was reluctant to agree with him.

The Vampire turned to Sparta, who was watching him quite dispassionately. 'Jiao Ming, do you wish to be rescued by Aunty Wu?' he asked respectfully.

'I may need to be rescued, Grandfather, but probably not by Aunty Wu.' The way he spoke to her and the way she said 'grandfather' convinced me that he was her grandfather, and that Aunty Wu had used the term as a way of ingratiating herself with Sparta in this present crisis. 'That would be… there is an expression in English.' She pretended she had forgotten, pretended she was just a schoolgirl a mere three years older than the floppy-haired Fin McCool.

'Jumping from the frying pan into the fire,' Blue said, suddenly sounding very Australian. Funny the way her accent veered around.

Aunty Wu tried to look patient. Her spider fingers returned to their nest.

Reggie was on his feet. "Fuck this! This is just a fucking charade! Now watch this, arseholes…' and the arseholes watched as he did a forward roll, hands over the back of his head, hitting the floor with the left shoulder, coming up right side on top of the guns and produced from the pile of weaponry his original hardware, business end first, in his right hand, grinning, pointing that same business end at ol' Nosferatu's head – all in a single fluid movement.

Which side was Reggie on? I wondered. Surely he should be pointing the piece at Aunty Wu.

The old vampire smiled down benignly at him. 'You've been practicing,' he said.

'The old cunt dies if anybody moves,' Reggie shouted. Suddenly he sounded Australian too. He and Blue were some kind of matched pair. The Jack and Queen of Spades. Except she spoke native Mandarin.

Nobody moved.

Reggie covered everybody one by one, me included, as he got to his feet. As the tiny black hole of the barrel passed by me, I heard death whistle in the wind.

Still nobody moved.

Nosferatu's benign smile did not waver. The smile intimated that far greater sins had been forgiven than Reggie could conceive.

Reggie eased himself backwards. Still covering everybody by turns. It was a busy pistol.

Still nobody moved.

He got to his feet.

He started to look puzzled. How come no one was trying to take him out? What would he do now? Now that nobody else was doing anything.

He didn't know. Nobody knew. Nobody spoke.

Get ready to go under the table, Jack Reacher said. Gotcha, I said.

Reggie found his voice. After all, a gun can't say very much, just bark one sharp syllable. I bet he found his voice a bit too high-pitched for his liking. 'Everybody pisses off, except me and Fang Runru and Jiao Ming, just the way it was. Grandfather can go back to his coffin. It's been a nice morning.'

I was more than ready to accept his invitation. But still nobody else moved. We were all frozen in tableau, like a house of wax. We needed some fairy dust to whisk us back into action.

Then Reggie began to wonder what he would do if nobody did anything. Start shooting? That didn't sound very sensible, even to Reggie.

'Jiao Ming stays here,' he said. 'Otherwise nobody gets paid.'

It occurred to me, probably belatedly, that maybe the precocious Sparta had been kidnapped. By Reggie and Blue, perhaps. Then Aunty Wu arrives with heavies to save her niece, not knowing that the girl's awesomely powerful grandfather is in residence in his coffin. His presence here meant there was a bigger game in town than rescuing kidnapped nieces.

'Why don't you stop him?' Aunty Wu said to Nosferatu.

'I don't have to,' the awesome old guy replied. I wondered if I could become his disciple, and be as awesome as he was. Except the word awesome has been debased to a point where just about anything can be awesome, even a fucking ice-cream, and I should cross it out and find another word – except it's the right word.

The old guy's right, Jack Reacher said. Reggie's all dressed up with nowhere to go.

'Ok,' Reggie said, 'we'll play it that way.' To Mr Wang and me he said, 'The suit and the peeping tom can leave now.' The black hole of the barrel did a he-loves-you-he-loves-you-not dance between the two of us. I guessed it would end up loving neither of us.

Mr Wang and I looked at each other. We both wanted to walk. Badly. So why didn't we? Because we both looked to the awesome old guy, aka Grandfather, aka Vampire. He was as silent as a stone Buddha. His eyes were cast compassionately down at the pile of weapons at his feet. So we were stone Buddhas too, our eyes cast down. Apparently the suit and the peeping tom were not leaving. Not because leaving was more dangerous than staying, though it might have been, but because nobody was doing anything. Nobody could break the spell.

Reggie knew how to restart the clock. He pulled the trigger. A real spell breaker. His shot took out the plate of half-eaten bok choy in front of Mr Wang and ploughed into the fine kauri colonial table. Food flew everywhere, accompanied by kauri chips. A bit of Wedgwood china wedged in Mr Wang's hand. Pristine blue ran with human-grubby red.

I went under the table.

A quick chaos ensued above, but no more shots were fired. Muffled scuffles and suppressed cries. It was surprisingly silent, like lovers fucking under a blanket. I assumed Reggie was being dealt to with the minimum of fuss. One gunshot is one too many; two is many too many.

When Blue finally looked under the table, she found herself staring down the barrel of a German made World War Two Luger automatic. Good to go.

'You cunning old bastard,' she said.

'I didn't come down in the last shower,' I said.

I didn't shoot her.

Or anybody else.

PART TWO

27

I slept but I didn't feel rested; I dreamt but didn't feel purged. I wondered if I was awake at all, and what woke me.

The answer to that last question was easy enough: a none-too-subtle rapping on the door. Nevermore! Some rapping at the door you can't mistake. The Law! Old Bill himself. I threw my silly, old-maid's dressing gown around me.

I got out of bed and battered my way through the silence to the door, thinking about yesterday's tea and biscuits.

I didn't have to shoot anybody. When I came up from under the table, Luger in hand, Nosferatu greeted me with a joyful smile. He was hugely amused, and so was I. Grandfather to Great-grandfather. Life was such a fucking joke!

But, out of the chaos of impressions, I'd taken one thought with me to bed that night: *something had precipitated Aunty Wu's intervention.* Something had happened to upset the apple cart. And Blue was getting the blame.

I'm sure there are better sights to see half awake and hung-over than the Law, in the form of the tall, ravaged-faced Elvis, aka Detective Inspector Joe Potiki, and his sidekick, McHaggis himself, the persistent Detective Sergeant Donald MacDuck.

'Do we talk to you inside or at the station?' McHaggis said. In one of those nice, cozy interview rooms, no doubt. At this tender hour.

I made myself and them a cup of tea. They certainly weren't eager to arrest me, but were as watchful as a couple of caged tigers.

I settled them with their teas.

I waited and said nothing. I wasn't here to entertain these guys.

Elvis said, 'When did you last see Velvet Reed?'

'I've already told you,' but my heart had already begun its long descent into hell. 'Have you forgotten? Lost your paperwork?'

'Tell us again,' McHaggis said.

So I did. How I arrived at her place, how some unimpressed

guy with a hairy face met me at the door. How we sat around and talked about old times and other boring stuff. I didn't tell them about Mick Jagger, or the sinister bloodhounds that hack back at the hackers. The last thing I was ever going to talk about to Old Bill was number 54.

Elvis didn't look bored at all. He was apparently weighing my every sin of omission. Where would I fit in Dante's levels of hell? Surely, among liars the withholders of truth would suffer the greater evil, since their sin is more subtle and beguiling. The outright liar is at least naïve enough to wear his sins upon his sleeve.

McHaggis was more openly skeptical. He wasn't fooled by a tosser like me.

'Dr Wayne Morse, who leases the property and lives there, said he cannot remember ever seeing you, except that one time.' That had to be Hairy Dude, getting the knife in. But where had I heard that name before? It rang a loud bell.

My voice broke open like the shell of an egg. There was a blind, blighted creature trying to emerge. 'What's happened? You're not here at this ungodly hour with your tea growing old to ask me how often Velvet and I met at her place.'

Elvis was the one to say it, quietly and without fuss. 'Velvet Reed is dead.'

He kept talking, talking, but I heard nothing. The long nightmare had begun. I was adrift in my own toxic ocean to beach myself again and again on the sandspits of grief. Steady up, Jack Reacher said; people die, it keeps them busy. It had been a game to me, playing at being Grandfather Detective. Packing an antique Luger. Impressing the grandkids. Impressing the blonde next door. Impressing Sparta. Making an old vampire laugh.

No one was supposed to die.

No one ever is, Jack said.

At that moment I died. Or something inside of me did. I had to face the days knowing that my inquisitive folly had led to Velvet's death. Velvet! Who was worth a million Blues no matter how many languages they spoke. Dying inside, I caught up with the fact that I loved Velvet. Had loved Velvet. You don't know what you've got until it's gone. I'd killed Anna by dragging her into fever country, and now Velvet had fallen victim to my stupidity. Nothing more to be said, 'game over' as they used to say when there was some kind of game worth playing.

'When did this happen?' I was amazed that I still had a voice, could still talk.

I thought for a moment he was going to say something standard like, 'We're the ones asking the questions here,' but he didn't. He just didn't answer.

'You haven't left town in the last couple of days, have you?' McHaggis asked.

'You know I haven't,' I said. I didn't quite see where he was going with this.

'You rang me from your car, where were you going?'

'Home. I'd been to see my daughter.'

Jesus! I was a suspect.

Elvis said, 'If you have any information… anything we can use…'

'Ms Reed didn't have that many friends,' the gingery Scotsman said.

'I didn't know.' That was true. I'd always known she was a bit of a loner but she seemed to know lots of people.

Elvis said, 'Mr Argonaut, was Velvet in trouble?'

This question hit uncomfortably hard this time around. I didn't think I could lie. I sensed that if I did, Elvis would know and it would be hello cosy interview room.

'Yes, maybe. But only in hindsight. I thought she was just gloomy or depressed, I told you before.'

'Did she give any clue at all. Something to do with her family, her job, her hacking?'

'I think you're leading the witness,' I said.

If he thought I'd made a joke to relieve the tension, Elvis gave no sign of it. 'Did she say anything, anything at all, something you can see now? With hindsight?'

I tried to ignore the sarcastic edge. Monckton ran up and rubbed against my leg, providing me with some blessed respite. 'Please excuse me while I feed the cat,' I said to them. 'Otherwise, we'll get no peace.' While giving Monckton his allotment of multicoloured biscuits, it occurred to me that I had a golden opportunity to put the cops on the same path Velvet had been on – and see what happened. Would cops start getting murdered, the police computer go down?

'Did you check out Pacific Holdings?' I asked.

Elvis shrugged. 'It's a property investment and development company. Nothing irregular.'

'Velvet said that one of the investors in the company had a non-existent bank account.'

'Which investor?'

'She wouldn't tell me.'

'Was she going to look into it further?'

'I guess she was.' *Or maybe she already had.*

'Why?'

'Beats me.' A truth that flew pretty close to a lie.

Sergeant McDonald chipped in. 'I had a wee look at Pacific Holdings' portfolio. They own a bit of property in Auckland, rentals and the like, and the funny thing is that they own the house next door to you, number 54.'

I shrugged. 'Funny coincidence alright.'

'That's what I thought,' McDonald said.

'Why was she investigating this company in the first place?'

'She didn't tell me. She was reluctant to talk about her hacking.'

'I'm not surprised,' Elvis said. 'Last time we spoke,' he consulted his notepad, 'you said that she was afraid of something. What did you mean?'

'She didn't say anything. It was just a feeling I picked up.'

'And you said that she was dead. How did you know?'

'I didn't. But I felt it in my bones. There was no other explanation for her disappearance that made sense.'

'What about the university computer crash. Could she have had anything to do with that?'

'If you mean, would she have been technically able, I guess so, I don't know, you'd need to ask an expert. But if you're asking if she might've been involved, I don't see why she would. I mean, it was her job to maintain the system. IT, she kind of loved it and hated it. I don't see any motive.' More likely, the forces she had aroused destroyed both her and the evidence of what she'd done.

'Did she talk a lot about her job?' He was writing in the notepad now.

'Just the usual stuff. Staff politics.'

'Did she mention any glitch, recently, any problems with the system.'

'There are always glitches. That's what her job is, to sort them out. Was. Her job was. Jesus.' I was numb all over, as if my body didn't belong to me. At least my mouth was still moving; I was still able to talk. I could hear my voice saying things.

'Did she ever talk about virus attacks?'

'From time to time. Again, that *was* her job. At least as I understood it.'

'Did she ever make reference to commercial espionage, or sabotage?'

'No.'

'Did she always work alone, hacking I mean? Did she work with others?'

'I doubt it. Velvet was a loner. By nature.'

Elvis sat back and Haggis leaned forward, rubbing his hands on his trousers as if to clear the palms of sweat. Maybe in anticipation, he was so eager to play bad cop.

'Did you and Velvet have an argument that evening?'

'I told you, we just chatted about this and that. Gossiped.'

'Why did you visit her in the first place? Just an idle chit-chat?'

He made it sound unlikely.

'Basically, yes. It was a social call. Bit of a catch up.'

'Even though you'd never been there before?'

'Ah…'

'You just went for no particular reason, out of the blue, just like that.'

'Yeah.' Go ahead and prove otherwise, Scotty.

'Bit of a coincidence that she was murdered later that night, don't you think?'

They both observed me keenly to get my reaction. They must've got an eyeful.

'So you didn't have an argument?'

'Sorry to disappoint you.'

I fussed around with Monckton again to give me time to think. I was too numb to think. These clever bastards were tearing me to pieces. McHaggis clearly had his own narrative for what happened that night, one in which I played starring role as murderer, and now he was digging for a motive.

'What time did you arrive?'

'Sometime after five.'

'What time did you leave?'

'After six. I don't know exactly. When did she die?'

'A bit after seven.'

I said nothing. Sadness grew in the silence like a black flower.

'Where did you find her?'

Haggis ignored the question. 'You did go straight home after visiting Velvet? You didn't stop off anywhere?'

'I've told you, I came straight home.'

'Any indication that she was going out again?'

'No. How did she die?'

Elvis and Haggis exchanged a quick look.

Elvis said, 'She was strangled. Something thin, like a bootlace.'

I tried to imagine it, then didn't.

'Was she… assaulted?'

A stupid choice of words, but Elvis understood me. 'No bruising, except for the throat, no indication of sexual assault. She was fully clothed.'

McHaggis took up the story, 'It looks like a stealth attack. Someone crept up on her from behind. Or someone she knew well who didn't have to creep.' He was watching me closely, doubtless for signs of guilt. Thought he was very clever, he did.

'Death would have been swift,' Elvis said.

The mercy of a swift death. Praise the Lord!

'She was found in Albert Park among the roots of a Moreton Bay Fig. Covered up with leaves,' Elvis said.

Velvet and I had sat under that tree only a few days ago, and had walked past it many times, those gothic roots, the half hollow trunk.

'Unbelievable,' I said. In more ways than one. 'Why should Velvet have gone back to the university after I left, and why walk across Albert Park?'

'Good questions,' McHaggis said. 'It looks like she was followed to the park and killed – or her killer was waiting for her.' He rubbed his meaty, freckled hands on his trousers again.

Oh Jesus, light of the world.

I picked up Monckton and held him close. 'I think I want to be alone now,' I said. I sounded like a child.

'Of course,' Elvis stood up. 'We realize this is difficult for you,' he said.

McHaggis didn't look like he realized any such thing.

'By the way,' Elvis said. 'What state was Velvet's apartment in when you left?'

'State? It was okay.'

'Was it tidy?'

'Tidy enough. Velvet's no slob.' *Was* no slob. 'Why?'

'Because Velvet's room had been thoroughly turned over.'

'You mean searched?'

'It looks like that.'

'When?'

'We don't know. Any time after her death.'

I didn't say anything. They were watching me so hard I should have turned to stone.

I had my Humpty Dumpty moment then, and fell off the wall. My mysterious documents! It was Velvet who had broken into my house and manually put those docs on my hard drive! Velvet, my phantom intruder, took out her insurance policy as best she could as the deal went down. She knew she'd tripped a landmine somewhere out there in the pitiless reaches of virtual space. She must have wanted me to do something with those documents.

I walked them to the door, shuffling along in my slippers like an old man.

'Just one more thing,' Haggis said as they reached the door. They always do that, you know – leave a final question as a parting shot from the door. 'Did Velvet have any boyfriends? Lovers?'

'From time to time, I think.'

'Did she have a current one, then?'

I thought about it. If she had, would she have told me about it? No reason to, unless it was bothering her; no reason not to, unless it was bothering her.

'Not that I know of,' I said. 'Why?'

'Would you have been jealous?'

He was priceless, was Haggis. He had me taped as the jealous murderer. A crime of passion, no less! It's either love or money, so if it's not money, it must be love, however improbable that might seem.

I lay down and slept and dreamed that a great hawk hovered over the city, its wings casting blinding shadows on anybody who looked up.

28

I'd read somewhere, maybe some Ed McBain police novel years

ago, that if you can find out *why* a murder was committed you would know *who* the perp was. That sounded wise. The only lead I had for a motive was a murky 'big player' Velvet had found out too much about, an identity hidden behind security firewalls so thick a neutron couldn't get through.

After the cops left, I took to my old post at the window and looked down at number 54, perhaps for the last time. It felt that way; my voyeur days were over – if they had ever been. I looked at the patch of cleared garden where it had all started. I remembered Velvet casually, teasingly perhaps, telling me to find out about number 54. The wall I ran into. How I then asked Velvet to crack the wall for me. Which I was convinced she did. Now she was dead while I was still alive and undeserving.

Next door looked unchanged, and why should it look otherwise? Everything was frozen in time, as in an amber fossil. Nothing moving. The roof jutted out at the same annoying angle, a corrugated iron fig-leaf without the fun. The patch of garden was the same crop circle of song. But Blue was not about to emerge to do any gardening.

I abandoned that window for the other window, the glowing screen, and went into Facebook. Facebook welcomed me back (after a very long absence). Velvet was aware of my feelings about Facebook, and regarded them with tolerant amusement, as a civilized, rational mind regards the terminally superstitious. It's true that I'm a hopeless Luddite when it comes to Facebook; it has a sly intelligence to it; it's half aware, like a synthetic being, and it watches every move you make and it never forgets. I do my best to avoid it, but in this case duty called and there it was, Velvet's Facebook page. A sunny picture of her smiling at somebody on her right, unaffected and natural. There were grieving notices, tributes, mostly from her IT friends at Auckland Uni. People seem to have lots of friends when they die. I found the funeral notice, the day after tomorrow, time and place. The notice was signed simply 'Queenie, on behalf of all the *whanau*'.

Queenie. Velvet had spoken to me about Queenie. When she was nine or so she ventured alone around a headland at Bethells Beach to see what life she could find in the rock pools. She was squatting by a pool when Queenie found her and, as if Queenie had mysteriously known it was there, she showed Velvet an octopus lair with a real octopus inside, undulating darkly with lots of sliding legs, and told Velvet the secret of the octopus.

'What is the secret of the octopus?' I'd asked.

'It grows in the octopus's garden,' she'd said.

'What is it?'

'Queenie said if I told anybody it wouldn't be a secret anymore and the octopus would die.'

'Then how did she find out?'

'I didn't think to ask her that. I was only nine, remember, and I was very impressed. I didn't have the benefit of your logical brain.'

I got out of Facebook as fast as I could.

29

The next morning, waking unrefreshed, I asked myself, standing under a long shower, what should I do? Front up to number 54, confront them with Velvet's death and see what happens. Read the signs.

It's very unlikely, that the inhabitants of number 54 had anything to do with Velvet's death despite the drama of tea and biscuits. It was only when she went into the ownership structure of Pacific Holdings that Velvet hit pay dirt. Number 54 had been merely the doorway through which she had passed to get to the more dangerous stuff. I picked a professional assassin for Velvet's murderer. Someone completely anonymous. Flies in one day, does the deed and flies out the next. In and out. And the cops find nothing. Stashing the body in the fig tree roots was not a serious attempt to conceal it, just enough to give the killer time to get out of Dodge.

On the other hand, I thought, as I showered and towelled, chugged some muesli – I preferred light summer crunchy, even in winter – sculled some dandelion coffee to massage the liver, and saddled up. Number 54 was the only clue I had the cops didn't have. Time to throw a spanner in the works. Turn over a stone, see what crawls out.

Sparta answered the door, dressed in dark matching t-shirt and tights, like a school kid off to the gym. Her hair was damp and curled.

'I'm sorry to just drop in.'

She invited me in.

'Did you bring your gun? That relic one?'

'Yes.'

'Can I see it?' Such innocent enthusiasm.

'Okay.' I extracted the Luger from its secret hiding place somewhere around my waistline.

She held out her hand.

I gave it to her.

'It's marvellous,' she said, turning it over. 'So simple in mechanism, so brutal. The finest steel. Highly effective at short distances. If looked after, this antique will live to outshoot most of the Kalashnikovs around nowadays.'

'You seem to know a lot about guns.'

'I know more about art. Bauhaus is my favourite retro style.' She flourished the weapon for my admiration. 'This weapon is pure Bauhaus. The ultimate fusion of form and function.'

'Is that right?' This kid never ceased to amaze me.

Blue arrived. She was wearing a skivvy top and track pants, her hair pulled back in a simple ponytail, like the gym leader. The pretty, wholesome girl next door, off to a workout.

'What are you doing?'

'We're looking at Grandad's antique pistol,' Sparta said primly. She held it forth for Blue's inspection. Blue took it, turned it over in her hands, and gave it back to Sparta.

'I'm sorry to drop in on you like this,' I said, suddenly wondering how I was going to pull this off. 'I have to ask for your understanding, your indulgence even…' They looked at each other. Only grandads spoke like this. Not even grandads. 'My best friend in the whole world has been murdered.'

There it was in all its abrupt truth.

They took me down the hall – all doors closed this time – through the lounge dining room, with the long table, replete with bullet gouge, to the kitchen behind, sat me at the kitchen serving bench and provided me with a restorative herbal tea. From there I could look through a ranch-slider back door to the garden and the swathe of dead weeds. I thought I could see new weeds springing up.

'Who murdered your friend?' Sparta asked. The Luger was dangling negligently by her side; she seemed to have forgotten about it.

'I don't know, the police don't know. If God knows, he's not saying.'

'Do you believe in God, Grandad?'

'I think I do. But this God would be of the beyond-anything-you-can-conceive variety. I'm allergic to dogma.'

Sparta nodded and smiled, as if someone had offered her an ice-cream. I think she liked my answer.

Blue was keeping me under careful observation; I was being hung up to dry under Californian skies. 'You have a particular reason for telling us about it?' she said.

To Blue, Sparta said, 'You don't understand him. In his own time, he would have revealed his purpose. Our job was to allow him that courtesy, since he is in mourning, but you come blundering in and pre-empt it all.'

She handed the Luger back to me. I'd hate to play you at Poker, Grandpaw, Jack said.

'Thanks,' I said to Sparta. 'Of course Blue is right, so I'll give her the courtesy of a direct answer. When Velvet was murdered, she was investigating the ownership of this house, number 54.'

Blue didn't miss a beat, 'And why was she doing that?'

'Because I asked her to. I was thinking of buying the place. Have been for some years. An investment.' Having told the lie once, it rolled off the tongue the second time. Telling it twice almost made it the truth.

Blue and Sparta didn't react. Perhaps that's what happens when people hear you tell a lie.

'We don't own this property,' Blue said. 'We know nothing about it.'

'Is that why you spied on us?' Sparta asked.

'No. Blame Blue's singing for that.' And I've already told you that. Sparta was testing to see if I'd change my story. I began to sweat.

'You are a researcher,' Blue said. 'You have quite a reputation, Mr Jason Argonaut, investigative reporter. You know how to access information. You could easily have discovered the name of the law firm, or company, Pacific Finance or something.'

'Pacific Holdings. Discovering who they represented was much harder.'

'Why would you want to do that?'

'Because I like to know who I'm doing business with. I'm old fashioned that way.'

I sipped my fragrant tea. It was exquisite.

'You think we had something to do with your friend's murder?' Those pie-in-the-sky eyes were so artless.

'Let's put it this way. When I came for tea and biscuits the other day, I witnessed some very strange events. Weapons were presented. A shot was fired into your table. An ancient got out of a coffin. It's not surprising that I start wondering. I'm a wondering sort of person.'

'So you come here, alone with your Luger, which you promptly hand over to Sparta, to confront your prime suspects?'

'Don't worry about my health. If I don't report every half

hour to my lawyer, I turn into a police bulletin and number 54 has choppers hanging overhead. Guys in black suits and automatics with red laser sights come sliding down on cables. By the way, where's Reggie?'

'You've got a wonderful imagination - and Reggie's... not around.'

That 'not around' sounded a bit sinister. Velvet 'wasn't around' either. What if they'd got Reggie to take out Velvet, then sent him back to Siberia to chill? Oh well, you should be able to take out a couple of girls, Jack said. Laconically.

'You mean for a drink?' I said.

'You're undertaking your own investigation of your friend's death?' Blue asked.

'I'm just angry and confused.'

'We've already had a visit from the police.'

'You have?'

'Yeah, a tall Maori guy with a face, and a little square ginger guy with an attitude.'

'What did they ask you?' I hadn't expected this.

A smile played around her Mary Travis lips. 'If we'd seen anything unusual, you know, out of the ordinary, happening next door, at your place, at number 52.'

'Looks like *you're* the prime suspect, Grandad,' Sparta said, making it sound super exciting, like winning a prize.

'And what did you say?'

'That you were a wonderful, polite neighbour and we couldn't wish for better.'

'She did, she did!' Sparta did a momentary cheerleader act. 'You should have seen her! She had the tall one eating out of her hand.'

I could imagine it.

'What about the other one?'

Sparta wrinkled her nose prettily. 'Not the short one. He was a sourpuss.'

Blue went on. 'And I didn't say a thing about your vigils at the window, keeping us under observation, peeping at me in the garden.'

'It's true!' Sparta said, taking me impulsively by the arm. 'She kept quiet about everything. She's a fabulous liar.'

'I don't doubt it.'

What was this I sensed? A trade off?

I said, 'I told the police nothing about certain events at tea and biscuits…'

'That shows great wisdom, Grandad,' Sparta said solemnly.

But we did not have a deal. I had no common cause with them in withholding information from the police. They had more to hide than I did. I sat there feeling helpless. I didn't know what to say. There was nothing to say. I was on a fool's errand, just as I thought.

Sparta leaned forward and put her delicate hand over my gnarly one. 'Grandfather, we don't know who killed your friend.' She spoke with that straightforward honesty of a schoolgirl.

'Sparta,' I said, 'have you been kidnapped? Is that what that Aunty Wu episode was all about?'

'You are correct, I am a hostage. In a technical sense.'

A technical hostage.

'In such a situation, it is the hostage who holds the power,' Sparta said.

'Too smart for her own good,' Blue said to me.

I took a punt. 'Of course, the holy ones wouldn't allow any fuck-ups, right?'

Sparta clapped her hands in joy. 'What sharp ears you have, Grandfather. And you can understand Mandarin too! How clever.'

Blue brought out some biscuits. I drank exquisite tea, ate the biscuits and kept quiet. The Luger was heavy in my pocket, but what power did it afford in this situation? The power to go berserk and shoot them both so fast not even the old vampire could scamper out of his coffin fast enough to stop me.

'But that's all you're going to learn,' Blue said. 'It's enough for

you to make sense of tea and biscuits, but that's all. Call it the need
to know principle: the sharpest way to cut a wave is with a wave.'

That sounded to me like a Chinese saying translated into
English.

'But I haven't made sense of tea and biscuits.'

'I don't think you have a story, Scoop,' Blue said.

I didn't ask how she knew my nickname; nothing surprised me
anymore. If she'd asked about the health of Monckton, I probably
wouldn't have turned a hair.

'I'm not looking for a story. I'm well over Scoop now. I just want,
very badly, to understand why Velvet was killed. What if she found
out something about what is going on here – whatever that is, the
hostage situation.'

'There's nothing going on here,' Blue said, 'but a close family
matter that really isn't anybody else's business.'

'Sometimes the left hand never knows what the right hand is
doing,' I said.

'You are quite awesome, Grandad,' Sparta said. 'You have the
makings of a Chinese sage.'

'Jason,' Blue said. Her voice alerted me. And her posture.
She was sitting tall, like a queen, and there was nothing cutsie or
Californian about her at all. 'We have a complicated situation here,
it's true. And we can't tell you about it because it's private. I drew
you into this when I tried to use your phone, which is my fault, but
there's nothing happening here of any interest to anybody else.
Nothing your friend could have discovered about us would put her
life in danger. Sparta's stay here is because of a disagreement in
the family. A very Chinese matter. It looked scary with all those
guns, but I want you to understand that we are not engaged in any
criminal activity.'

It was a pretty speech. I said as much.

'So who are you, then?' I said.

'I'm Sparta's nanny,' Blue said. 'She may be precocious but
she's still just a kid.'

'She's a fabulous liar,' I said to Sparta.

'Not this time,' Sparta said, looking sombre.

'Does that mean she's your jailer?'

Pie-faced, she said, 'Oh no, that's Reggie's job.' And she grinned like a naughty monkey.

We all grinned. Bit of a clown, was our friend Reggie.

The silence that followed was not comfortable. I didn't sip my tea and pretend that it was.

'Why didn't you go with Aunty Wu when she came to rescue you?' I said to Sparta.

'Aunty Wu was not rescuing me,' she said, quite pedantically, but didn't elaborate.

Roundabout and roundabout and roundabout we go. Just like Pooh and Piglet. The more they tell me, the less I learn.

Blue was regarding me with concern, like a niece or a daughter who has noticed errant tendencies in an aged one. I thought she was going to lean forward and pat my hand.

Blue said, 'Do you know the tale of the six blind men and the elephant? Each took a hold of a different part of the elephant. It is a snake, declared the one who had its trunk. It is a vine, said the one who had its tail. It is a palm tree said the one who had its ears. It is a wall, said the one who encountered its side… None imagined an elephant, not in their craziest dreams.'

'It's a pretty fable,' I said. The moral being, I thought, is that I should not go on asking questions since I will never understand the shape of the beast. This is a fancy babe, alright, Jack said. There was a touch of admiration in his voice.

'I don't care about the elephant,' I said. 'I just want to know why Velvet had to die.' I wanted to blurt something about Marcia and the grandkids too, and how I was afraid for them because I couldn't help but think that Marcia was somehow involved, but didn't.

Blue considered me gravely. Then she left the room, returning a moment later with an instrument which looked like a zither but with fewer strings. Carefully, she placed it flat on the table, which was gleaming with late morning light creeping in under the eaves. She leaned over the instrument, all concentration, gold hair dangling all over the place.

She began plucking at the strings with a bone pick. I didn't recognise the tune until she started singing, gutsy and slow, an old song called 'The Last Dance' all about that special person saving the last dance of the evening for the love stricken singer. More melancholy versions of the song suggest that it might be a forlorn hope. The zither thing sounded the chords, but in an offbeat, Chinese manner; plangent, poignant, too slow to give an affirmative upbeat to the chorus, about how she would be in his arms for the rest of the night. The way Blue sang it, it sounded like a lament. A funeral dirge. The girl would forget who was taking her home and in whose arms she was supposed to lie.

Instead of crying, I got up and courteously offered to dance with Sparta. She courteously accepted. We danced, quite sedately since the tempo was bluesy and slow, yet not without some art. We did a waltz shuffle, the girl matching my rusty timing exactly. Her head only came up as far as my chest, one slim arm raised to my shoulder, the other around my waist. Her perfect solemnity was perfect.

All that was lacking was the pale moonlight of the song.

One-two-three, one-two-three, Sparta and me.

And Blue's voice.

Dancing a last dance with death.

For a moment there, I thought Velvet came into the room.

Sparta alone led me to the door. The house was quiet. I didn't hear any coffin lids creaking or the clickety-snap of weapons being readied. I decided I wouldn't invite them to dinner. We were nearing the front door when the hall door, which had been closed when I'd come for tea and biscuits, opened and Reggie came out. Incongruously, he was wearing an apron with an embroidered pattern on it. He was carrying some used coffee mugs and plates.

Behind him I could see a couple of computer screens and, on the wall behind them, a poster, a lovingly angled shot of some hypermodern racing car. A nice bit of petrolhead pornography. His eyes passed through me, across me, as if I wasn't there. It wasn't anything personal; our Reggie was deep in thought.

'Are you in danger?' I asked Sparta quietly as we reached the door.

'Not immediately.'

'I enjoyed our dance,' I said formally.

'You're very brave, Grandad.'

I smiled bravely.

'Perhaps,' she said, 'I might play with your grandchildren again.'

I thought it was a veiled threat until I heard the thread of loneliness running though her voice. Just a kid without any friends.

'I'll see what I can arrange,' I said. A lump in my throat. Maybe that lump was the lie I was telling. Or something else.

'Anytime,' she said.

30

That night I dreamed of Anna for the first time in many years. I was back at the crappy crematorium, scene of Anna's departure from this world. The large crematorium is empty but for me and one other mourner, a woman who keeps her back to me.

Hidden engines beneath the floor hum and vibrate. The platform supporting the coffin jerks forward. Like a piece of luggage on an airport conveyer belt, it does a stilted shuffle through the hairpin bend of mortality, waiting to be claimed by a helpful hand on the Other Side. The coffin lurches behind an august purple curtain that reminds me of the corrugated drapes that hung across the screen in our local picture theatre before they turned it into a cut-price clothing market. The coffin suddenly tilts, balances for a moment of ontological uncertainty before, to the crank of well-oiled wheels, plunging into the flames which greet it with a victorious roar. The crematorium shudders – sounds of the organ swelling to cover the noise – and spurts forth an ashy blessing, kissing the roofs and gardens of the surrounding suburbs with the lightest, most delicate and dissolving touch. Homeopathic doses of Anna spread across half the city.

Then time runs backwards. The tears on my cheeks trickle up into my eyes. The flames of the kiln become the fires of creation, giving birth to the coffin, which runs backwards, uphill, into the crematorium.

The other mourner finally turns to me. It is Velvet.

There won't be anybody burning my body, I hear her voice say, so clear and sharp in my head it woke me up to a gun-metal grey dawn.

The day of Velvet's funeral.

Perhaps a person isn't dead until they have been 'laid to rest' by the living. Up to that point they might be quite restless, presumably. Funerals are for the living, however; the dead are well over it. 'Laid to rest' happens in the minds and the hearts of funeral goers, if at all. If they can leave the ceremony with easier hearts, a little lighter in the face of mortality, it has done its job.

Nobody should spend too much time in the company of graveyards, I said to Jack Reacher. But he wasn't around, which was his privilege being merely a fictional character and all. I still hadn't sorted that out. After all, wasn't I a fictional character too, mostly? Grandfather Detective, Jason Argonaut, Scoop the Intrepid Reporter, and finally the most fictional of all, Mike Smith, the name on my birth certificate. A wholly hypothetical person massaged by years of bureaucratic invention – a birth certificate, marriage, death. And Jack is not just a fictional character, but an archetype famous world-wide, the lucky bastard; a very tall, polite, seriously handsome, cold-blooded killer; and he gets the girls, let's not forget – a stranger, lone ranger. If you wanted to be cruel you could say he is more real than me.

Nobody should spend too much time in the company of

graveyards; it is not the dead that are buried there, it is their fictions. As soon as I walked into that South Auckland hall I was blitzed by the understanding that Velvet had significant Maori *whakapapa*. Olive skin and dark hair yes, but with the sweet racial mixes we're getting in Auckland anything was possible. A harpoon struck my old whale heart. Why hadn't she talked about it? The mourners were talking about someone called Whiro Tatua. If it weren't for the reassuring sight of Elvis and Haggis – who perhaps subscribed to the theory that murderers appear at the funerals of their victims – I could have been at the wrong funeral. Velvet – another fiction put to rest.

The coffin was real enough, in pride of place at the front of the hall. Unopened.

Lots of people I hardly knew, who just as well might have been fictions, milled about. I recognized Hairy Dude, centre of the university IT crowd. A couple of bros, one with a thick dreadlocked pony-tail, checked me out in case I was one of those old pensioner ghouls that haunt funerals for a cup of tea and a club sandwich.

Overhearing introductions, a penny dropped. Hairy Dude was Dr Wayne Morse, head of the IT division at Auckland University. Velvet's flatmate and boss were one and the same. This had to be significant. Velvet had often told me about her flatmates and their fucked-up lives. That this detail had never emerged seemed significant too.

I phased in and out of the ceremony, the songs, and eulogies, losing all sense of time and often of place. A man who had introduced himself to everybody as Velvet's brother, Hiko Maui Tatua, said how so far beyond anybody's comprehension her murder was, and how everybody was praying for a swift arrest. I liked the look of Hiko. He looked tough, and there was a dignity and seriousness about him that was attractive. The other men, I noticed, especially the guy with the pony-tail, treated him with deference.

A distraught looking Maori woman with wild faux-blonde hair – mid-to-late fifties, I figured – kept looking at me and giving me the evil eye. She was standing beside an older Maori woman, at one point pulling on her arm and indicating to me with her head. The old woman, bless her, didn't demean herself by looking at me. I was grateful nobody else took any notice of me. I didn't want to start explaining who I was. I was somebody's forgotten uncle and I was happy to stay that way.

And it did stay that way, at least until after the ceremonies.

Then, Hiko himself, and the pony-tail guy, approached me, accompanying the old woman I'd seen earlier. She looked like Velvet would have looked in a hundred years time. Hiko offered me his hand.

'You're Whiro's writer friend, aren't you? The journalist.'

'Yes. Jason Argonaut.' I took his hand.

Detective Joe was loitering off to one side, balancing a cup of tea and club sandwiches. I checked the exits.

'I'm Whiro's elder brother. Hiko.' He gestured courteously to the old woman. 'This is Mavis Tatua, our *kuia*. Whiro's mother.'

'Named after Mavis Rivers, the jazz singer.' The old *kuia* gave me a sudden gap-toothed grin. 'Except she could never sing as good as me.'

I laughed. A light chuckle was called for, but I have a loud, braying laugh, totally unsuitable for funerals. Everybody looked my way for a moment. It's okay, just that silly old bugger – who is he anyway?

The old woman looked pissed off. 'You think I can't sing as good as Mavis Rivers?'

Hiko gestured to Ponytail, 'And this is Johnny Watch Tatua, Whiro's younger brother.' A likeness to Velvet made the tall man's face familiar; the same wide apart eyes and longish jaw. But whereas with Velvet, those features made her face look interesting and ruggedly beautiful, on Johnny Watch they made for one mean, ugly-looking customer. No smile. And no handshake.

'I could always carry a tune,' Velvet's mother said. 'But Whiro couldn't.' She said it as if that meant something.

'You and Whiro were good friends, eh?' Hiko said.

'Not really,' I said. 'I thought Reed was her real name. We'd make jokes about Velvet Underground and Lou Reed.'

'Reed was her father's name,' the old woman said. She gave me a look, like she knew me, or at least knew my type. The unreliable type. Maybe the same type as Velvet's father. Take a walk on the wild side.

'Whiro liked her secrets,' Hiko said. He probably meant it to make me feel better, but his tone veered towards an inner darkness, a secret resentment of his own.

Just then I felt Velvet go past as if she'd just walked by. The smell of her, her perfume, was strong. Patchouli, I'd never forget it. I sat down heavily, spilling tea over my club sandwich. Old man loses his balance. Nothing to panic about.

'What's wrong?' It was the distraught woman I'd noticed earlier who spoke. Maybe fifty-five, a bottle blonde with a small, tough face, pretty enough as it goes after a life of hard knocks. She pushed in beside Mavis, not rudely but intently. 'What's wrong,' she repeated, staring at me as if I'd suddenly turned into a scaly alien.

'It's *her*, isn't it?' she said when I didn't answer. 'She's not at rest, is she. Like a bloody blowfly in a bottle, she is.' She gave me a quick, hard look to see if I was going to be offended. Encouraged by what she saw, she continued, 'A flipperty-gibberty if ever there was one.' She waved her tea-cup at me and I figured it contained more than Earl Grey.

'I thought I could smell patchouli,' I said. Going crazy should be done at home, decently alone, with maybe Monckton to comfort me.

Mavis regarded the other woman sternly. 'The murdered spirit can't rest until justice is done.'

'Amen to that,' the blonde woman said, lifting up a cup as if to toast. 'And the devil take the hindermost.' She winked luridly at me. Guess I was of the hindermost. 'I know who you are,' she said. She didn't sound happy about it. 'Whiro used to call you Mr

Nowhere Man.'

'It's nice to be recognized,' I said.

'I don't know why she'd want to fool around with an old bastard like you.'

'We didn't *fool around*,' I said. And you don't exactly look like a spring chicken yourself, but I didn't say that.

'Keeping you in tow, was what she was doing. Where she could keep an eye on you.'

'Why would she do that?'

'Let me tell you one thing, Mr Nowhere Man, Whiro never did nothing out of sentiment. *Nothing.*'

'Did she talk to you?' I asked the woman. I meant about me.

'It's all very well for you.'

'I'm sorry…?'

'So am I. But you're a sorry bastard if ever I saw one.'

'I'm grieving like everybody else, if that's what you mean.' Out of the corner of my eye I saw Inspector Joe edging closer.

'That's not the fuck what I mean.' Her voice on the rise, faux-blonde hair over her face. She had another pull at her cup.

Two large, very friendly guys appeared each side of her. 'Come on Queenie,' one of them said in the softest of voices.

'And the sorry bastard's going to be a hell of a lot sorrier,' she said. Crazily enough, I liked her.

The two guys looked at me with no apology.

'Maybe he's got a bad conscience,' Johnny Watch said, talking to me but looking at everybody else.

Elvis was quietly keeping a weather eye on our little party. I was suddenly convinced that everything I did betrayed me; like a guilty murderer, I was jumping at shadows.

'She was just passing by,' I said. 'A whisper in the wind.'

Velvet's mother said, 'When Whiro was little, I used to sing to her when she couldn't sleep. She used to say that my voice had arms, soft arms to carry her. I sing to her now, maybe her spirit can sleep.'

She threw her head back and broke off into 'Now is the Hour' in a voice quavery and soulful. Others joined in, perhaps happy to be relieved of their conversational duties. Pretty soon everybody was singing 'Now is the Hour', swinging gently back and forward, some linking arms. Sergeant McHaggis stood stiffly at attention.

An old war song, but it fitted fine when you listened to Velvet's mother sing it.

31

'All hands on deck,' I announced coming through the front door. Monckton leapt to do my bidding, which somehow landed him in front of the fridge. 'You're getting too fat,' I said. He gave me his starved look. I gave him a handful of cat biscuits. He looked at me askance, a look he'd been practicing for a long time. 'They're as good as the real thing,' I told him, but he didn't seem convinced.

I headed straight for the cupboard where I suspected I'd find some brandy – a bottle one third full. That would be enough. More than enough for my brutal purposes.

I paused at the cupboard door and took a careful survey of my comfortable downstairs quarters. It all looked depressingly normal. Everything sat where it should. The afternoon light struck familiar poses. Monckton crackled away at the biscuits. Since Anna's death, the place had slowly assumed the appearance of a widower's pad. A Nowhere House for a Nowhere Man. Did Velvet really say that? Jeez.

I got the bottle out of the cupboard, unscrewed the cap and poured.

'Here's mud in your eye,' I said to the walls and tossed back the drink. It was suitably vile.

Then the phone rang.

I gave it the evil eye but it didn't stop ringing. Monckton did the same but it went on its merry way. I downed the first drink and poured a second, wondering if I was just imagining the scent of patchouli in the air.

'Jason?'

'The better part of him.'

'It's Jerzy here.'

'What a pleasant surprise.'

'Are you drunk?'

'Getting there.' I tossed back half the glass.

'Remember the conversation we had a day or two ago?'

'Yes.'

'You might be interested in this. I told you it couldn't be a virus, but it's worse than even I thought. I thought they just fucked up. Ha!'

'Spell it out.'

'We have the mother of all systems' crashes. Total blitzoid. Everything: hard drives, back-ups emergency systems for saving data in case of a crash, every damn thing one-and-all, wiped as clean as a baby's bum at bath-time. Turned to slag. There'll be no retrieving of data, you can bet your hoary beard on that.'

'You sound excited about it.' Last time we'd spoken he didn't want to so much as fart sideways on the phone, now he was as garrulous as a bar fly on speed.

'I am! It would be like an astronomer witnessing a supernova, or… or…'

'I get the picture.'

'But you don't. What did Velvet say?'

I didn't remember mentioning Velvet to Jerzy. In fact, I remember deliberately not saying who my source was, even not revealing the gender.

'Why are you telling me this, Jerzy?'

'Hey, chill! There's gotta be a reason for a cyber attack like this. I knew Velvet had to be your source when you mentioned that bloodhound thing. And she was in thick with Morse, so I thought…'

'What do you mean, she was in thick with Morse?'

'They lived together, for Christ's sake. Bonky-bonk and worky-work together. They're the prime suspects. I thought she might have said something…'

Hang up, Jack Reacher said.

So I hung up.

They lived together, for Christ sake. Bonky-bonk and worky-work.

Not an easy thought to hang up on.

Don't have the third drink, Jack said as I was pouring it. *There's somebody in the house.* Look at Monckton. Monckton was not acting normally. His ears were down flat, his tail was twitching and his eyes had narrowed. He looked up at me and gave a silent meow.

'I'm going to check out the house,' I said.

Best stay where you are, Jack said, or, better, leave immediately.

Fuck that, I thought. This is my house, my castle; I'm not going to be driven out of it by fear and voices in my head. That's two drinks talking, Jack said. It's your funeral.

Monckton jumped up on the table, which is forbidden.

I checked out the house. Downstairs was clean. I crept up the stairs to my office wondering why I was tiptoeing.

At the top of the stairs, a figure materialized out of the shadows as if from nothing. A man, but slight, wearing a black body suit like a ninja. He seemed relaxed, not like an intruder in somebody's home. He was Chinese with a small round face and cropped hair.

'You come with me, no?' he said, his accent strong.

'No,' I said.

'You come please,' he said.

'No please,' I said. Get away from him, Jack commanded.

Too late, I leapt to obey. The ninja's hand was on my neck, squeezing something – and the rest is history.

32

I woke up all at once, immediately, as if I'd never been out and was still standing at the top of the stairs. My eyes flew open like the eyes of the dead in zombie movies. No cozy transition. I was lying on a bed, on my side, facing a blank wall with a door in it. I sat up and took stock. I was okay, in one piece; not bound or handcuffed or anything exciting. I got up and did some exercises just to make sure everything was working. I couldn't remember anything since the stairs. Maybe I had concussion. Concussion is a funny thing; you can have it and not know it. Of course I had not received a blow, just a funny little squeeze on the neck. The room was windowless and featureless except for the cot and door. Like a cell except a cell has more amenities. What would happen when my bladder caught up with me?

I checked out the door. Not much to check out, just a depressible handle that didn't depress.

I sat back down on the bed and felt around in my memory. Found a hole into which the last hours had disappeared. The edges of the hole were sore. How long would it take before claustrophobia set in? Imagine a lift, a lift that isn't moving. With me inside.

The door opened and an Asian man in a suit walked in, a man I knew.

'Mr Wang,' I said cheerfully.

Behind him came another man wheeling a tray with coffee, a poached egg on toast and a couple of cakes. He was in loose, baggy pants and a t-shirt, and looked like a ninja. I recognized him and gave him a sour look.

'I thought you might like some refreshments,' Mr Wang said.

'I don't drink coffee,' I said. 'Do you have any green tea?'

Mr Wang nodded at the ninja who took the coffee and exited.

'You're going to tell me how sorry you are that we have to meet again under such unfortunate circumstances,' I said.

He nodded. 'I *am* sorry.'

I tucked into my egg on toast and waited.

'We mean you no harm, Mr Argonaut, we just have to keep you here for a few days.'

'Until it all blows over?'

He didn't confirm or deny.

'Or for my own safety?'

He didn't confirm or deny. A fountain of information, was Mr Wang.

'You could have invited me in the normal manner.'

'We ran out of time.'

'I can walk faster than the ninja can carry me, I bet.'

'I can't tell you why you're here, Mr Argonaut. But you will be well treated. We'll find you a better room than this.'

'Now you're getting me excited. But I want to know something, just to put my mind at rest. Did you guys kill Velvet Reed?'

'We did not.'

There was something in his intonation – maybe just his Chinglish.

'But you know who did?'

Wang shrugged.

'Are you protecting me from her killers? I mean, I must be high on their list. Or are you protecting the killers?'

Wang said nothing. He appeared to be thinking about something else.

The ninja returned with the green tea. It was delicious. Wang and I sipped our tea like a couple of old friends.

'People are going to know I've disappeared,' I said, as if engaging in light conversation. 'My editor, for example. He has this thing about deadlines, ringing me up all the time, keeping track.'

Mr Wang gestured negligently. Eddie was taken care of. Easy-peasy.

And, I wanted to add, my daughter, Marcia, will be worried. She'd probably ring the police. Inspector Joe and dear Sergeant McDonald would be very interested also.

'Someone will have to feed Monckton, my cat,' I said. 'He's too lazy to catch mice.'

'Your cat will be fed,' he said. Friendly neighbours, perhaps. Did Blue and Sparta know about my abduction? Or were they behind it? I'd gone to them with my questions about Velvet – and now this.

I didn't have any more cards to play so I waited.

'There are documents on your computer. A map, a photograph of a circuit, and some Chinese writing. Where did you get them?'

'I didn't. Someone broke into my house and put them there.'

Mr Wang considered this. Wang wouldn't need a computer whizz to tell him I had not received them by email, or sent them on. He might even know that I was not at home when the documents were put there. But who had given him the idea that there were documents on my desktop in the first place? Somebody who knew Velvet?

'What have they got to do with anything?' I said. 'They don't mean much to me, of course.'

Wang didn't answer. He had no problem taking his time, letting the moments slip away as he did his thinking. I had time to polish off the eggs on toast, sample a little sweet cake, and drink the last of the tea – which must have been of the finest quality since it did not grow bitter and retained its lightness to the end.

'Who do you think put the documents there?'

'I have no idea. How'd you know they were there?'

He smiled. Perhaps at my silliness in expecting an answer.

A completely new idea occurred. Since the documents meant nothing to me, maybe they weren't intended for me at all, but for the person led to find them, Mr Wang himself. If that were the case, Wang was being set up. And, since Wang would himself suspect this, all this questioning of me could be an elimination exercise. He wanted to cross me off his list.

'Perhaps some work-related matter? I believe you are intending to write a new article on China.'

He could only know that by talking to Eddie, surely. And why would Eddie talk to Wang?

'Yes, China's energy policy. Are these documents related to that?'

He didn't answer my question. The ninja came and took all the breakfast stuff away. Our pleasant chat over breakfast was slowly morphing into an interrogation.

'You see, Mr Argonaut, I can't discount the possibility that nobody broke into your house, and that you got a disk or memory stick from, what do you journalists say? – a *source* – and put it on your computer yourself.'

'*I* can discount that possibility – sorry about you.'

'What were you planning to do with them?'

'Nothing. What would I do with them?'

'You might have found some way to put them to use. Maybe try to get them translated.'

I had nothing to say because he was perfectly correct. It would only have been a matter of time before I got around to them.

'Don't you find it odd, Mr Wang, that soon after those documents appear on my computer, my friend Velvet Reed is murdered?'

'Are you suggesting Ms Reed might have put them there?'

'If she knew she was likely to die, she might.' Perhaps in the hope that they might, eventually, lead me to the killer. Once I'd figured out what to do with them.

Wang inclined his head in something less than a nod of agreement.

'Shortly after the documents appear on your desktop, you visited Meilin Xiang. What did you talk about?'

I was getting tired of the fact that my life was an open book to these people. Where I went, what I did, what was on my computer. Walk into my house and out of it at will, like ghosts through walls, they could. 'We talked about how China might meet the challenges of global warming, particularly the waning of the great rivers.'

'Ah! So you are planning another collaboration with Meilin.'

'Not exactly.'

'You played him a conversation you recorded between Fang Runru and Jiao Ming. Why didn't you show him the documents at the same time?' So Wang had been talking to Meilin, and Meilin had told him about the conversation. Why would Meilin do that?

'I've asked myself the same question. I think I just forgot.

Getting forgetful, you know.'

'I don't think so. Why did you record the conversation?'

'I thought maybe Blue was going to sing.'

'You were spying.'

'No. I mean, yes, but innocently. I got distracted, hung-up on Blue, the new girl next door. With a voice like a fallen angel.'

Mr Wang went silent again. I didn't know what he might make of fallen angels.

Shortly after that he got up and walked out.

33

My new quarters were clean and correct, like a motel or a well-kept guest room. A light, fluffy duvet, towels folded at the end of the bed and a small ensuite bathroom with ceramic ducks flying up one wall. A TV, even a small bookcase filled mostly with old Robert Ludlum and Jeffrey Archer novels. A kitchenette complete with electric jug, an unopened box of green tea bags and some cubes of sugar. And two fresh, dry dishcloths. No fridge.

A sliding glass door led to a small balcony with a view over some glasshouses and well-tended gardens. Quite a spread. But the glasshouses blocked out most the view except for the sky, which wasn't offering any clues. Instinct told me I was out west somewhere, close to the Waitakere Ranges but facing the other way, east. If we were on flat land, buildings would show behind the glass houses, suggesting that the land was sloping eastwards. The illusion of freedom was severely compromised by steel bars embedded in the concrete balcony walls and fixed to the lintel above. Goodbye sky.

I had a shower and used one of the folded towels. It was yellow. I waited for something to happen. Then I waited some more. Big action hero. I turned on the TV and found the 5pm news. I wasn't on it. But America was. Congress was hung up on extending America's debt beyond the 14 trillion ceiling. Tropical storms were pushing wet, windy weather onto the North Island. Auckland was in for a blow. Some politician was playing the race card. A little girl got washed down an open drain. I turned off the TV. Played the silence card.

When the ninja came in with my evening meal – poached fish and lightly fried veg, very nice – I tried to engage him in conversation, but all I got was a sweet, modest smile. He moved with grace and fluidity, as if he had no bones. Not much taller than Fintan and as light as a girl. When he left, and the silence moved back in, I began to feel the reality of incarceration, even as pleasant as this. The silence had a decidedly permanent feel to it. The thin edge of a greater and profounder silence. The silence of dungeons and tombs.

I lay back and took the opportunity to do some thinking. Was Wang in with the crowd at number 54, as it appeared, or was he part of another faction, like Aunty Wu? How many factions were operating, and who was the old vampire? Plenty questions, plenty no answers. One explanation did make sense. Wang, or more likely an agent of his, had killed Velvet – he was lying about that – and was trying to make sure that the information she'd discovered had spread no further. If she'd placed some of it on my computer, where else might she have placed it?

Wang denied killing Velvet, but didn't deny he knew who did it. That, if he was telling the truth, made him a smaller fish than the one really jerking the line.

Soon I had nothing left to think about but Marcia and the boys. I was guilty because I hadn't spoken to Marcia since Velvet's death, and there was Marcia in trouble herself at work. I thought back to my last meeting with my daughter, standing in her kitchen, the boys just gone to school, her face pale at the mention of Pacific Holdings. She'd known something. Always so stubborn and independent! Too proud in her quiet way to ask for help. And I hadn't rung her, had no update on her hot dossier.

That big stew kept me going till dawn.

By the time the ninja arrived with my breakfast – scrambled eggs done with parsley and oregano, quite beyond compare – I felt all used up. Besides turning me into a foodie, incarceration did nothing for me. The novelty had worn off. The glasshouse which dominated the view did nothing but reflect back at me. It wasn't healthy. My options were limited. I could make a nuisance of myself, overflow the bath or something, but that seemed pretty childish.

'I want to speak to Mr Wang,' I said.

The ninja smiled, did a little bow and gestured to the food.

'Mr Wang,' I said.

He nodded and smiled. Maybe he didn't talk much. Had taken religious vows or something.

As I neared the end of my breakfast – deliciously cooked but somehow ashes in my mouth – two men entered the room. One was Wang and other my old colleague Meilin Xiang.

Meilin pulled up a vinyl kitchen chair and sat opposite me at the table. Mr Wang stood, just behind him and a little to one side.

'Why didn't you show me those documents when you brought me the tape?' Meilin said. He gave no sign that we'd ever been colleagues, or friends.

'I've been through this with Mr Stonewall over here,' I gestured to Wang, 'I don't know, except that I didn't think it was a good idea to print them out. Why? Was it a mistake?'

'The best mistake you ever made.'

'How come?'

'Because Mr Wang doesn't think it was a mistake. He sees it as an adroit and careful move.'

'Is that good?'

'In one sense it is. It proves your discretion. He's confident you didn't show the material to anybody else.'

'And in the other sense, the bad news side?'

'Being clever makes you a less predictable factor. Being a writer doesn't help.'

'Are you in with him, Meilin?'

Meilin looked pained. 'I'm here to vouch for you. In fact, I'm here to get you out.'

'Okay, let's go. I've already packed.'

'Not so fast. Mr Wang will release you only on certain conditions.'

These turned out to be that I wasn't to write anything about anything except how keen China was to go green, that I wasn't to talk to anybody about anything, especially my editor, except about how keen China was to go green, that I wasn't to have any kind of communication with the residents at number 54 – and of course I wasn't to talk to the police.

I listened carefully to the list. Like a kind of house arrest of the mind. I couldn't think anything about anything except...

Before leaving I asked Mr Wang a question. 'What is the secret of your green tea?'

He smiled. 'Add lightly roasted brown rice husks,' he said. 'In the Japanese fashion.'

I walked out of there on my own two feet.

It's all too easy, Jack Reacher said.

34

'Can I open my eyes now?'

We'd been driving for five minutes.

'Who are you?' I said to Meilin once I could see, noting with satisfaction that my instinct had been correct and that we were out in the tatty land of the Westies.

'I was attached to the supreme Central Committee of the Chinese Communist Party. I stood on a few toes. Got myself semi-banished to New Zealand. Worked as a translator for your Prime Minister.' Was that a hint of condescension in his voice or just his minimal, measured delivery?

Attached to the Chinese version of the Politburo. As high as you could get. Again I remembered the way obstacles seemed to vanish before him during the Four Gorges Dam investigation. A word here, a word there; no bribes required.

'Were you assigned to me, for the Four Gorges project?'

'I volunteered. A crap job but someone had to do it. It was a way for me to get back to China, reestablish a few connections, assist in my rehabilitation.'

'But you let me get my hands on some pretty hot stuff. Was that another indiscretion, get you sent back for another stretch in these shaky isles?'

'No. I let you get your hands on some pretty hot stuff. But not the hottest stuff.'

And Scoop thought he had the lowdown.

'But, you know, your record on Four Gorges complicates matters for Mr Wang.'

'How did you get me out?'

He shrugged. 'We had a chat.'

'Did you pull rank on him?'

'It's not that simple. You don't pull rank on Mr Wang.'

'I see.' But I didn't.

Outside the car window, Auckland's urban landscape reassembled itself. Wasn't much improvement on the Wild West, just fewer trees and old cars in driveways. More tasteless apartment buildings trying to look tasteful or giving up on the job.

'I badly need you to tell me what's going on,' I said. 'Can't see what harm it can do since my lips are zipped, but I've got a feeling you're going to tell me that what I don't know can't hurt me or some such brush-off.'

He lifted his hands from the wheel and raised them palms up. 'No brush-off. Just that some things are beyond your limited comprehension.'

'I may look like a barbarian, but I can think like Lao-Tze.'

'Once barbarian always barbarian. Never think like Lao-Tze.'

So I quoted him a line and verse, something Scoop had once committed to memory to impress his Chinese connections:

'When the great Way is forgotten
kindness and morality arise.
When wisdom and intelligence emerge
the great pretence begins.
When there is no peace within the family
there are filial children.
When the country is confused and in chaos
loyal ministers appear.'

Meilin grinned. 'Barbarian can mouth the words, but never penetrate their inner meaning.'

'Try me.'

Apparently driving suddenly occupied Meilin's attention.

'The more I know, the better prepared I am, the better decisions I make, the less likely I am to make a stupid mistake. I'm like a bull in a china shop, forgive the pun, but I'm a blindfolded bull.'

Not sure if he knew the expression, but he got the drift.

'Big international events are unfolding. China's response has to be carefully coordinated… across many powerful factions, not just within the Party, but… other factions. The girl you know as Sparta, Jiao Ming, is the daughter of the Boss Man of one of these factions, the most powerful of all. She is being held as…. a token of… good faith. A pledge perhaps, my English is uncertain here. But this pledge holds the whole alliance together. She could not be held in China, since there is no neutral ground there. New Zealand is conveniently out of sight. Very small scale operation, perfect camouflage.'

'So Mr Wang reports directly back to the Boss Man.'

'That is a natural deduction, but in this case false.'

'So who does?'

'Fang Runru.'

Blue! In my amazement I forgot to ask who Wang did report to.

'Runru is very important. She puts a pleasant non-Asian face to the house. Good for camouflage. Also she is responsible for Jiao Ming's personal wellbeing. But more, she answers to the Boss Man.

She was born and raised in China. Australian mother, American father. Rare in China but not unknown. Both parents had high trade links. Blue shows early aptitude for languages. Speaks several dialects of both Mandarin and Cantonese. Takes Chinese name. Studies Chinese classics in their original forms. Becomes martial arts adept. Goes to university aged fourteen to study maths. Makes friends easily. Sings with informal, expat nostalgia band in Bejing called The Blue Moons. Recruited by the Boss Man aged eighteen. Quickly becomes his most trusted agent, especially in matters to do with the West. Very useful. Looks good. Can move at any level of International and Chinese society. Almost.'

He was reeling this stuff off as if reading it from a dossier, her file, which he might have been doing – he had that kind of mind.

'What about Reggie?'

'Reggie is something of a mistake. He was placed there by another faction, as part of the deal, but his role is confused. Or rather, he may have some role I am unaware of. He is part bodyguard, but his real job is to keep an eye on Blue, keep everybody honest. His problem is he fell in love with Blue, which is never a good idea.'

'He has a funny way of showing it.' I thought of Reggie freezing when Blue put her hand on his arm.

'Blue needles him all the time. You know, he can speak Mandarin okay, but Blue and Sparta switch to Cantonese to share secrets. Makes him paranoid. Thinks she's plotting behind his back.'

'Maybe she is.' I told him about Blue's first visit, Blue's conversation with somebody called Aunty. Reggie's grand entrance and attempted bullying of Blue.

'Reggie is loose-cannon, prob'bly won't be staying too long at number 54.'

Prob'bly. He seemed about to say more, but thought the better of it. Finally he said, 'There may be more to him than meets the eye.'

'Could Blue have been… ah… negotiating with Aunty Wu, perhaps behind Reggie's back?'

'Poss'bly. Aunty Wu was a mentor for Blue before Blue went to work for the Boss Man. '

'Who is this Wu? She really an Aunty?'

'She is a family member, related to the Boss Man, but she represents other factions. She never liked the set up at number 54. Big argument with Boss Man. She was going to take Sparta and execute some plan of her own. But...' he gave a short laugh, '...she didn't know the old man was there.'

'What difference did that make?'

'All the difference.'

He said nothing for longer than was comfortable.

'So who is the old guy? You know, he just stood there, unarmed, stark naked, and everybody threw their hardware at his feet.'

Meilin grinned again. He seemed entertained by the story. 'This is rare sight for barbarian to witness. It was the ancient's *chi*. Of everybody in the room, he had the most *chi*, so everybody throw down their guns. Guns useless against that kind of *chi*.'

Of course I knew the Chinese term *chi* but had never penetrated its inner meaning. In my barbarian way, I saw it as a kind of ultimate coolness. Maybe that wasn't too far off. 'So who is this *chi* man?'

'That I cannot tell you. The wise man refrains from further inquiry.'

What about a persistent idiot? 'Is he some kind of martial arts wizard?'

Meilin drove. The traffic was thickening. We were in the middle lane. All around us there were impatient automobiles. Meilin was not impatient.

'That may be the best way to think of it,' he said.

Beyond my limited comprehension, obviously.

We were getting closer to home, but I was reluctant to let go of the conversation. I had yet to ask about Velvet's death and the uni computer wipe-out, but there was something I wanted to know first. 'Did you know all this, about number 54, before I came to you with the tape?'

'No. In general terms, maybe; I was informed that something was happening here. But I was not in the loop. Unless something came to my attention. As it did. Me not knowing was like a control test. If I hear nothing, given my contacts, then the operation is going well, the camouflage is holding. If I get to hear of it, there must be leaks. Then I am briefed. Then I have to take care of things.'

'Like me.'

'That's right, like you.'

'Are there others like me? To take care of.'

A ghost of a smile. 'Gratefully, no. You're a one-off.' I thought then that maybe he admired me, a nice little boost to my much bruised ego.

'What about Velvet, she a one-off too?' A one-offed. Taken care of.

Further silence inside and road rage stuff outside. Squally rain came down and stirred up some dust. Didn't make Auckland look any more romantic. The silence, however, was not comfortable. Meilin was weighing his options. He would tell me some pretty hot stuff, but not the really hot stuff.

'I don't know everything. It's just as important for me not to know everything as it is for you not to know much at all.'

'The Dao of secrecy,' I said. And quoted:
'The way that can be told is not the eternal way.
The name that can be named is not the eternal name.'

'Perhaps the barbarian has penetrated a little closer to the inner meaning.'

'So what can you tell me?'

'Wang came to the same conclusion as the police. You are a suspect. Velvet was having a sexual relationship with one of her flatmates. You visited her the night she died.' Dr Wayne Morse again! Little wonder he was so lacking in manners. I vowed that the next time I ran into him I would punch out his lights.

'But Wang didn't ask me much about Velvet, everything but

that. He was more interested in the stuff on my computer.'

'That's his way. Mr Wang… he is in class of his own. He works through… misdirection. Keep you looking somewhere else. Clever interrogation. No need for Chinese finger-traps or water torture. He finds out what he wants to know and doesn't even have to kill you afterwards because you don't know what you've told him.'

'That's nice. So what did he find out?'

'You did not kill Velvet.'

'He figured that out all on his own? What about Mr Loose-cannon Reggie?'

'Possibility has been checked. Almost impossible.' Again the ghost of a grin, 'he has, the police would say, an… alibi.' Meilin had a little problem with the pronunciation. 'But agents could come from overseas. Hong Kong. Hit men. Easy.'

'If Wang suspected me then he had nothing to do with it.'

'That's right.'

Yes, that was right, unless Wang, and maybe Meilin, wanted me to think that way. Debriefing by misdirection.

The squall passed over and the sun came out. A ragged sky did a parabola over downtown Auckland. The sky-tower urged upwards. Pot of gold at the end of something dirty in the sky struggling to be a rainbow.

We pulled up outside my place.

'So you don't know who took out the Uni computer?'

I didn't expect a straight answer, so knock me over like a feather:

'Chinese Government. Central Committee. Serious faction.'

'You won't come in for coffee?'

He declined with the briefest of gestures.

'The map,' I said. 'Troop movements.'

'What makes you think that?'

Ah, had his attention. 'Faint broad arrow strokes on the map. I've seen something like that before. I'd guess Korea. Chinese troops moving into Korea?' I was flying on half a wing and a prayer, anything to keep him talking.

You know,' he said, after a long time with his hands still on the wheel, 'for a barbarian, you almost think like a Chinese.'

35

I re-acquainted myself with my house while Monckton re-acquainted himself with his food bowl. Everything looked the same, smelt the same, felt the same, but I couldn't shake the sense that something had changed. Maybe it was me who'd changed.

I gave Monckton a cuddle – he looked like he might forgive me – and came to a decision. Time to draw a line under this whole thing, wash my hands of it. Keep my nose clean and do what Wang suggested, write my article on how keen China was to go green and forget the big bad world. Forget the weird and wonderful inhabitants of number 54. Not my business. This grandfather detective stuff was just make believe. As for Velvet's death, that was police business, Elvis and McHaggis were up to the task. The killer would probably turn out to be Hairy Dude, Dr Morse, who killed her when she tried to dump him. Something obvious like that. Like those contrived thrillers that steer your attention elsewhere while the killer stalks you in the shadows of the plot. Misdirection, the Wang trick.

Hide, keep my head down. Maybe the bad guys won't see me.

On the strength of these resolutions I made a humble meal and sat down with the cat to watch TV and be a normal person watching TV with his cat eating his humble pie. Yet, as I watched the news with its daily jumble of the trivial and the momentous, I couldn't help keeping an eye out for a something big, something so secret the Chinese would take out a New Zealand university computer system to protect it. The university computer crash was on the news. A solemn faced guy said that a virus had wiped all memory from the hard drive and back-up systems. Nerds were working around the clock to retrieve whatever, a new enrolment program was up and running, blah blah… I stopped listening because I recognized the solemn-faced guy with the American accent. It was my old pal Dr Wayne Morse, sans beard. From bushy to gaunt. Dr Wayne Morse, head of the University of Auckland's IT division. Worried blues for a worried mind.

Then I had my big thought of the night. Elvis and McHaggis would only get so far. They would be misdirected, sidelined; squashed, if need be. Reassigned, most likely. Polite guys in suits would appear, and nothing more would happen. That plot line killed off, officially.

I looked around at my place. Suddenly it wasn't my place. I was still in the motel replica with a view over glasshouses and bars over the balcony. Not to mention the ninja waiter. Meilin's rescue and the return to my house and cat was a fantasy. I was still in prison. I'd turned my house into a prison by making my solemn promises *not* to do this and *not* to say fucking that: to say nothing about nothing, and, as King Lear says in the great play, *nothing shall come of nothing*. Oddly trivial but profoundly true, Mr Wang.

I snapped off the TV and went upstairs to do some work. The mysterious documents were gone from my desktop, no surprises there, but nothing else had changed.

I pulled up the notes I'd made for my China article. There was plenty of potential. I was sure that with Meilin's help I could do another Scoop, stage a grand comeback in the same arena as my former triumph – China. To hell with the going green thing, I'd look at China's response to global warming. Something of the same as I'd done for the Aussie piece, only grander and more ambitious. Look at the effect of glacial retreat on the rivers. Get some inside stuff, courtesy of Meilin who, to keep me sweet, would supply me enough information, not too much and not too little – to put me on the map again. *We will give you every support.* Yes, Mr Wang, I'm sure you will. I will have a second fifteen minutes of fame. A few old journos will pause over their abused keyboards and shake their heads; good old Scoop, they'll say, he's not past it yet. He can still turn up the goods. Eddie will pat me on the back and explain yet again why he can't give me a bonus. Life is sweet if you don't eat too much chocolate, they say.

As if idly playing around, I fed 'cyber warfare' into Google. I skipped Wikipedia, and an invitation to 'keep up to date with trends in the defence industry,' by attending a conference entitled 'Cyber warfare: Europe 2012', and went straight into 'China admits existence of cyber warfare team'.

> China has admitted for the first time that it had poured tens of millions into the formation of a 30-strong commando unit of cyberwarriors called The Blue Army. The team is reportedly trained to improve the security of the country's military forces and to protect the People's Liberation Army from outside assault on its networks.
>
> The Blue Army, believed to have already been in existence for two years, is currently under the Guangdong Military Command. Although supposedly established for defensive purposes, most governments across the globe fear that revelation is likely to confirm suspicions that cyber attacks on their systems do indeed originate from China.
>
> Xu Guangyu, a senior researcher of the government-backed China Arms Control and Disarmament Association, said:
>
> "The internet has no boundaries, so we can't say which country or organization will be our enemy and who will attack us. The Blue Army's main target is self-defense. We won't initiate an attack on anyone."
>
> The PLA daily reports that the cyber-warfare team emerged victorious in a simulated cyberbattle to defend China's military networks against a

series of virus attacks, junk mail barrages and stealth cyber intrusions from an attacking force four times its size.

I wonder how many other countries are this prepared.

Searching for more on the mysterious Blue Army didn't get me very far, predictably. Nor did it get me anywhere trying to work out why the Chinese Politburo felt obliged to wipe the computer network of an insignificant New Zealand university. All I had was the instinct that it was somehow connected to those accursed documents.

I was at home, I was working – it seemed that way. But all I was doing was waiting for the next Plot Development. That's the difference between Jack Reacher and me. By this stage in a story Jack is out there killing a whole lot of scumbags, creating the next Plot Developments for himself, driving the agenda, the quintessential active protagonist; me, I'm sitting around home watching TV waiting for the sports news to finish, or skipping around websites. No wonder modern fiction is in such dire straits; so much cutting to the chase no one knows what they're chasing. How many guys can Jack kill in one book? As many as you put up against him. How many dead scumbags does it take to hold the reader? As many as he can eliminate in seventy thousand words. The flasher these books get, with their seductive, glittering, embossed covers, the less substantial they become. They become almost ghost-like, the Twilight of fiction. It is as if the great literary heritage of the world is being sucked out from the inside by one of JK Rowling's Dementors.

Good luck, said Jack. I'll stick to my scumbags. You stick to yours.

36

It was afternoon before I rang Marcia. Morbidity of mind had prevented me from ringing her already, I decided. The phone would doubtless be tapped. Mr Wang had accepted my assurances of good faith with good faith, but he would know the moment I lapsed. I didn't want to think about what might happen then.

Marcia didn't sound happy. Didn't sound aware that I'd been taken out of circulation for a couple of days. Or like she wanted to talk to me at all.

'You okay?'

'I'm okay. The boys okay?'

'Yes, they're okay. *Dad I've lost my job.*'

I had that cold all over feeling again, just like they say in novels. I'm sure all the colour drained from my face, and my blood, wherever it had retreated to, turned to ice as well. All of those things.

'The dossier.' I said.

'That's it.'

'I thought you'd bought yourself some time with that one.'

'I ran out of time.'

'So what did you do?'

'I refused to return the dossier. Said I was taking legal advice. So I get fired. All my effects have to be returned to the company, so my man will get his dossier anyway, unless I now steal it.'

'Where is it?'

'That's better left unsaid.'

Monckton scratched the back of my chair, which he knew I hated. It was a signal to put him outside.

'I keep thinking I've done the wrong thing.' She sounded like a little girl talking to her Dad, because her Dad knew everything.

'No. No you didn't.' But I wasn't sure. How would she and the boys fare with no job? With morality, there's always a price to pay, the price we least want to pay.

'I can get another job,' she said, apparently reading my mind. 'That's not the point.'

No. The point was the principle at stake. It always is with morality: that point beyond which you cannot be pushed whatever the price. Morality is never truly a choice.

'Why can't you leave the dossier with a disinterested third party?'

'No such thing.'

'Why did this person give it to you in the first place?' My guess was that her unnamed tormenter was a senior partner in the firm. Mr Dogbane. Or Mr Dogbane, perhaps. I knew they came in senior and junior versions.

'Because this person was afraid. Now this person is angry. With me.' So scrupulous, she wouldn't give away the gender of her oppressor.

'And now I think I'm being followed.'

'Is that possible?'

'Well, it's unlikely, but I think something's happened behind the scenes to up the ante, to make the information in the dossier more destructive than it already was.'

'I wish you could tell me what you're talking about.'

'So do I, Dad. But because I'm doing this, and getting fired for it, it's even more important that I keep confidentiality.'

There wasn't a lot more to say. She was as wary of the phone as me. We fenced around a bit. We agreed to meet again soon.

'Give my love to the boys,' I said.

And put the cat out. He sat on the step and stared at me, mildly resentful. That questioning look that cats are good at. 'Go into the world,' I commanded him, 'and do catty things. Be a real cat. An active protagonist cat.'

Distracted by something, Monckton looked away. He'd lost interest.

The afternoon sky looked innocent enough, if a little glazed. Humidity was up again. Time to play my role as harmless old geezer keeping his nose clean and his head down, and wander to the local Indian dairy for this and that and some Monckton food, thinking about Marcia. I walked past number 54 with barely a glance. None of my business. I had my ritual conversation with the dairy owner, who was from Calcutta, and who called me Professor. He had been a public servant before coming to NZ, and boasted a certain education. He asked me what I thought of the latest stock market crash. I told him we were witnessing the demise of capitalism and that small businesses like his own would be unlikely to survive. He treated my analysis with great satisfaction. 'It's all the government's fault,' he said.

I was returning home, still playing the geezer, still thinking about Marcia, when everything turned pear-shaped. The plot sprang its next development. A big, older American car low down in its springs pulled over about twenty metres ahead of me, nose into the footpath. Go up the next driveway and don't look back, Jack Reacher said. I obeyed. I walked up a stranger's driveway as if I lived there. There was no car or anybody around. Curtains pulled. Silence within. Behind me car doors slammed, preternaturally loud in the dull suburban air. I continued to the back of the house. Nothing much there. An old fashioned circular washing line with some washing on it that creaked in its socket with the wind, an awning, a locked door, a window that hadn't been opened since Adam was a cowboy. Over the back fence, Jack said. I'm too old for these action hero scenes, I said, struggling over the fence. In fact moving with surprising alacrity. I could see my place up the street, a couple of houses over. Behind me the pitter-patter of eager little feet.

I was in somebody else's back yard. I stumbled over a garden. A little girl on a tricycle watched me without expression. I smiled happily at her as I dashed past. Fun and games! A woman's startled face stared at me from a kitchen window. Down the driveway, onto Taraire St, a woman's scream from behind. Never a dull moment. I guessed the woman at the window had rushed to her back door, and the sight of whoever was coming over the fence after me was not reassuring. The child set up a wail. Maybe my pursuers forgot to smile properly. I've always had a way with kids.

All around me endless Auckland suburbia, undulating volcanic waves of it. Turn right and go back up the next driveway, Jack said. I did it. Footfalls hit the street behind me. This house was silent, but the woman next door was still shouting and yelling. The back fence to this place was just a few strands of stretched wire. I went through it like a kid chasing a ball, grazing my leg on the wire. This place had no garden. It was a wild mass of uncut grass, a disgrace to the neighbourhood really.

I was too disoriented to know where I was, but a thickish hedge appeared to my left. Go through it, Jack said. I flung myself at the hedge, no looking back; I could hear the clumping of heavy feet well enough. I tore my way through the hedge, leaving bits of clothes and flesh, but I didn't care; no way was I going to be abducted a second time. Behind me male voices were shouting instructions.

The new backyard I found myself in was familiar, but I'd never seen it from this angle. The red corrugated iron back-fence on a lean, the bit of garden with a patch of weeds cleared, but now growing back.

Like a rat in a maze, I was in the backyard of number 54, Odds Avenue.

One more fence and I was home. I could lock the door and stick Monckton onto them.

'He's pretty quick for an old cunt,' a voice from the other side of the hedge said. I knew that voice.

Although hesitation can be fatal, I hesitated. Bang on the back door for help? No way. So I headed across the garden for my fence, angling for the house, thinking I could cross over about half way to Odds Avenue, cut off from view as much as possible from the garden.

A swearing and cursing came from behind as the bros made jihad work of the fence. I got around the side of the house before they made it through. All I had to do was nifty over that fence and I was home and hosed. But I didn't feel that nifty. Age was catching up on me, and the fence presented an even face of boards with all the cracks running vertically; it had been braced on my side. A pole-vaulter wouldn't have had much trouble. Behind me, out of sight, there came hoarse consultations. Then the back door opened with a bang and a light, clear voice, asked the gentlemen if she could help them, like a somewhat over solicitous shop assistant keen to up her sales for the week.

Sparta.

If she could distract them, I might have a chance with the bloody fence. At the same time, as I eased my way further along the side of the house, I thought maybe I could make a run for the low, front fence, hop back onto Odds Avenue and home the longer but easier way. Behind me voices rose in anger. Losing an old bugger over a few fences was a serious hit to their pride. Sparta spoke again, quieter this time, so I didn't pick up what she said. There was more shouting. Somebody yelled 'fuck this!' Then there was the sound of thumping and bodies hitting the earth. I had an image of Sparta, in her twelve-year-old school-girl outfit, spinning and kicking and taking out the bad guys like Summer Glau on speed.

I'd reached a side window, which looked in on the room with the coffin and the old vampire. I resisted the urge to look, but it didn't make any difference. Apparently undeterred by the sunlight, the old vampire was looking out, right at me, a few inches from my face, separated only by a pane of dirty glass. He looked at me and I looked at him. I cracked first and gave him a sickly grin. He raised one eyebrow in mock surprise. I could never do that. Raise one eyebrow while keeping the other flat. It must take a lot of practice.

Probably you don't have much else to do lying in a coffin all day.

Then I heard an angel singing. It was Blue. Singing an old Frank Sinatra standard.

'Have you heard it's in the stars, next week we collide with Mars…'

Blue was making her way to the back of the house.

The vampire's eyes never left my face as Blue's voice faded as she reached the back door. I heard her voice rising in clear command. The commotion, the thumping and banging stopped. 'Who are yous jackasses?' I heard her say in a broad Aussie accent. Further thumps and curses followed.

The ancient lowered his lone raised eyebrow. If I could penetrate to the inner meaning of this enigmatic muscle movement I would say he was telling me to fuck off. Get going while the going was good.

It was over the fence for me. And so it was, fear forcing a certain youthful agility to age, I did my own chi thing over the wall without losing what used to be the family jewels.

38

Monckton, who was sitting on the back doorstep, gave me a scared look as I arrived, and decided that the best policy was to run inside for the fridge. I locked the hell out of everything, knowing it wouldn't matter when push came to shove. I might as well get into bed and pull the blankets over my head.

Instead, I wondered who to ring. Elvis and Haggis? All that would result is that they would hassle me. Cops are like that, you hassle them and they'll return the favour. Still, I was a grown man wasn't I? I could stand on my own two feet, face my demons without running to papa every time.

A ring on the doorbell heralded the next plot development, polite but insistent. Before opening the door, I rang the police. I was getting through to Elvis, when the big Maori guy with tatts, Hiko and Johnny Ponytail came through the door. Then the surprise of the day. The frazzled blonde from the funeral, the one Hiko and Johnny Watch had to hustle away: Queenie. She gave me a lavish smile. It was all right except for the teeth.

Johnny Watch is packing, Jack said, but he's an amateur. The guy had a bruise on his forehead like a thyroid third eye. Rage was pushing out the other two eyes.

'I'm sorry,' Hiko said, 'for the misunderstanding.'

Johnny Watch looked pained.

'What misunderstanding?' I said

He hesitated.

'Looks like you've been thrown into a gorse bush, Mr Hiko,' I said. He was too big and broad to have suffered the hedge lightly. Pity about his leather gear.

I invited them in.

'We just have some visitors,' I said loudly to Elvis, who had stayed on the line. 'I'll ring you back in twenty minutes.'

We sat around in my living room, Hiko and Johnny Watch sat on the couch. Queenie and I sat on easy chairs at angles to the couch. We were ready for a round of spin-the-bottle.

'That was our mutual friend, Inspector Elvis.'

'You rang the cops?' Hiko looked puzzled. Johnny Watch looked pissed off. Seemed like he and I had got off on the wrong foot. Queenie stared at me.

'No rush, I'll ring him back soon. He'll be expecting a call.'

Hiko considered it. 'Very clever,' he said.

'Us oldies need to keep our wits about us, since we're not as agile as we used to be. Scrambling over fences is a boy's game. Of course, sometimes girls get to play too.'

Johnny Watch hit the side of his head as if he had some insect lodged in his ear. 'You know,' he said to Hiko, 'I don't like this piss-taking old cunt. Why are we so nice to him? Let's just beat the shit out of him – then he can make all the calls he wants.'

Queenie cackled like a witch in a Roald Dahl story. 'I'll tell you one thing, boys, he's sure got you steamed up. Couldn't nail his skinny arse over a couple of fences. Then get taken out by some freak manga chick with a high kick – and a fucking Miss Bondi with a forearm like a footballer. Never seen anything like it. You boys, Gary and them others that fucked off, all on your backs waving your paws in the air like helpless puppies.' She turned to me. 'You have a real talent for trouble, Grandpops.'

'You can choose your friends, but you can't choose your neighbours,' I said, wafting into the kitchen. 'Tea anyone? I was about to have one. Had a strenuous day.'

Hiko nodded, but his eyes stayed level. Johnny Watch looked at Hiko as if to say, what are you going to do with this old cunt?

'I've got some nice green tea here. Organic. Very strong flavour.'

'You got anything stronger?' Queenie said. 'I've had a strenuous day too, Grandpops, chasing around after these niggers through other people's property, scaring little kiddies and happy housewives. You know,' she said to Hiko, 'the reason why you couldn't catch an old man is that your arse has got too fat. I never realized that until today, when I had to trail around after it.'

I put a teapot, cups, sugar, milk and chocolate thins on the coffee table, and gave Queenie a hefty slug of brandy.

'And it waggles back and forward like this,' Queenie sea-sawed her palms in imitation of moving buttocks. 'Like a bloody Poly.'

'Remind me why we brought you along?' Hiko said to her.

Queenie glugged some brandy and beamed at me. 'I'm here because Grandpops and I kind of established a rapport, you know at Whiro's funeral. These guys didn't mean to chase you. It was your fault for running away. Looked suspicious. Like a man with something to hide, y' know?' She gave a conspirator's wink.

I didn't quite remember the funeral that way, but I nodded. 'If it's old and runs away then chase it, is that what you're saying?'

'It doesn't have to be old,' Johnny Watch sneered. I didn't realize he had a sense of humour.

Queenie cackled again and tried to slap my knee. Unfortunately, her chair was a little too far from mine and her hand fell through the air, almost unbalancing her. 'Fuck,' she said, and sculled the rest of the glass, maybe before she spilled it. Then she waved the empty glass at Hiko. 'And don't tell me I've already had enough, because I haven't and I'm going to have more! So fuck you!' She turned to me, the glass swinging through the air to line up on me as if it were a firearm. 'Fill her up Grandpops, and,' she added generously, 'have one yourself.'

'You're sure better at the rapport thing than Johnny here,' I said, pouring myself a short one for appearances sake. 'He looks like his watch has stopped.'

Queenie squirted some brandy on the table. Hiko sank his teeth into a chocolate thin as if it were made of bone. Johnny Watch snarled at me, lips drawn back over nicotine-stained teeth.

Calmly, Hiko said, 'We didn't mean to frighten you. We just wanted to talk. About Whiro's death.'

'I thought the pansy with the beard did it.'

'No you didn't,' Queenie said. 'That arse couldn't squash a fucking bug if he was sitting on it.'

'Well, what about you guys? You're pretty good suspects. You know, some family thing. Families are funny that way. Velvet never talked about you guys so maybe there's some skeleton in the closet rattling its bones. For starters, look at young Johnny Watch here, looks to me like he's got a violence problem. He's just itching to beat up an old man!'

Johnny Watch was on his feet in a flash, more than eager to prove to my point. The knob on his forehead was pulsing like a cop light.

Wearily, Hiko waved Johnny Watch down.

'And I ran,' I said, just for the books, 'because I thought you were going to abduct me. I'm over being abducted.'

'We was going to invite you over to our place, for a little smoke and drink, you know, bit of a chat,' Queenie said, voice cracking with insincerity, or maybe parody.

'So why's hair-trigger boy here carrying a gun?' I said, gesturing to the fuming Johnny Watch. Good move, Jack Reacher said.

'You silly fucking sausage,' Queenie said to Johnny Watch, and tossed back the rest of her glass. 'You'll get us all fucking arrested.'

'That's not a bad idea,' I said. 'Armed men, home invasion.'

Wordlessly, Hiko held out his hand. With a poisonous look at me, Johnny Watch handed over the gun. A skanky little pistol. .32, Jack said, No accuracy over about 10 metres. Some Asian clone of a Russian clone. Clearly, a weapon beneath Jack's dignity. Hiko emptied the magazine and laid it on the table. He put the empty gun in his pocket.

'I'm very reassured,' I said. 'I'll tell you what, let's cut a deal. You give me the gun and I'll come to your place and have a smoke and drink and a decent cry.'

'A man after my own heart!' Queenie croaked triumphantly, slamming down her empty glass.

Johnny Watch's jaw went loose. It didn't improve his looks.

Hiko was not sure. 'You'd come with us?'

'Have to make a quick call first,' I said, pocketing the brandy and picking up the phone.

I knew just what to say to Elvis.

39

We piled into the old Holden with the squishy suspender belts and farted off towards South Auckland. Hiko drove, Johnny Watch beside him; I sat in the back with Queenie and a big guy who suddenly turned up and jumped in the back, squeezing Queenie between us. 'We're good to go,' the new guy said.

'Meet Gary,' Queenie said. 'He had a run in with that Bondi blonde of yours. Very quick it was. A flick of her lily-white wrist.'

'Shut the fuck up,' Gary said.

'Pleased to meet you too,' I said.

Queenie dug her elbow into me as she clawed something out of her pocket. A spliff, ready rolled. 'I think we need to chill out,' she said. 'Everybody around here has got a rat up their arse.' Her elbows went again as she fished out a lighter. I could add rib bruising to my aches and pains.

'Christ,' Hiko said. 'Can't you hold till we get home?'

'I'm at home right fucking here,' Queenie said, full of outraged innocence. 'I've spent more time in the back of this fucking car than you could shake a stick at. Fuck it! I own this fucking car, remember? Who pays for the fucking rego? And what about your last speeding ticket? I had to pay the fucking bastard, didn't I?'

Hiko slid the window down as Queenie, full of righteous indignation, lit up. She took a couple of heavy hits, then handed it forward to Johnny Watch. Johnny hesitated, then, shrugging, took the joint, took a few quick hesitant tokes, like a boy behind the toilets, and handed it back to Gary. Gary looked at it. Blew the end of it so it glowed red. 'Naw,' he said, and handed it to Queenie who, after a quick couple of tokes, handed it to me. I took a toke. It was strong. No pig without a wig. Bad move, Jack said. Trust me, I said. I took another toke. Winked at Queenie, and took another quick one. 'Jesus, Grandpops,' she said, 'You sure had me fooled.'

'How hard can that be?'

'Don't push it, Jimmy. I can see you're a bad boy.' She waggled a reproving finger at me.

'Being good would defeat the purpose of life,' I said with airy abandon. I was suddenly a debonair character out of an Oscar Wilde play.

Again, the witchy cackle. I could get to like it.

I blew on the end of the joint, just like Gary had, watched the innards glow, then handed it over to Hiko. 'If you can't beat 'em, join 'em,' I said to Hiko. 'Yeah right,' he said, and took it.

Cars in other lanes whirled around us like grey sharks.

'Hello,' Johnny said as we were coming onto the motorway. 'We've got a tail.' He was staring into the passenger mirror.

I resisted the urge to turn around. Felt a bit vertiginous up there on the flash and whizz of the motorway, the city shifting below.

'I see them,' Hiko said, handing the spliff back to Queenie, who went broody over it.

Gary was squinting out the back. The grey sharks surged around. 'I see them,' he said. 'We got the Asian invasion on our trail.'

'Don't fuck with me,' Hiko said.

'It's Mr Panfried and Chicken kung fu. They cruised by when you was inside the geezer's house.'

'Why didn't you tell us, for fuck sake,' Hiko said, banging his hand on the wheel.

'How's I t' know? There's fucken Asians everywhere. So they drive past, so fucking what?'

But I knew what. Mr Wang was not about to let me out of this sight. For all he knew I was being abducted.

The traffic sped up in the right lane and the car following us, a modern BMW, which had switched lanes, was forced to come up alongside. I didn't know the guy driving, but I knew the passenger. It was the ninja. Maybe he was bringing me a cup of green tea. 'Nice car,' Johnny Watch said. The flow of traffic altered again and the pursuers had to surge on ahead. Johnny Watch slid down his window and gave the BMW the fingers.

'Good one,' Hiko said as he slewed the car to the left, heading for the first exit ramp, overstressed suspension providing the obligatory squeal.

'Great to have guys like you on my side when the chips are down,' I said.

'They're real crackers all right,' Queenie said.

'I wouldn't go back to Queenie's place, if that was where you were going.' I said.

'What do you mean?' Hiko said.

'I mean they'll just be waiting for us there. They'll have the address from the car registration.'

'Just like fucking cops,' Johnny watch said.

'That's right, just like fucking cops. Only much worse.'

'Know about these guys, do you, Grandpops? Why're they

following you?'

More to the point, why were they letting the bros see them?

'Just drive somewhere random, before they pick up our trail again. Park somewhere and we'll sort it out, here in the car, Queenie's home.'

'Fucking right! And where's the brandy, big-boy? I saw you slip the bottle into your pocket.' I forked it over. 'And how come I can feel Whiro around you. At the funeral, you just about fell over.'

'I just felt faint,' I said to Queenie.

'Felt faint did we?' she said, mimicking my South Island accent. She glugged at the bottle. It didn't seem to placate her. She took a vicious toke on the spliff. Her face was a totem wreathed in bitter fumes.

Hiko found a discreet place on a side street with view overlooking the motorway. Neat, inconspicuous parking spot. Hiko turned around to face me. Johnny Watch just kept looking ahead as if we were still driving.

'I can only talk under the threat of torture,' I said. 'Your Mr Panfried and Chicken kung fu have a boss man, and the boss man lets me out on the condition that I say nothing about anything. But I can't do much if you threaten to torture me, can I? I'm an old man with a low pain threshold.'

Johnny Watch got it first. He swung around, bringing a lighted cigarette with him. He jabbed the cigarette at my face. 'I've got a whole packet of them,' he said. His grin couldn't have been wider.

Queenie did her demented hen laugh. 'I'll tell you what, I'll give you a fucking kiss. Will that qualify?'

'Cut the crap,' Hiko said. 'Okay, I'll kill you if you don't tell me what you know.' He sounded deadly serious. The car went quiet for a moment. 'Now, why are those gooks following you?'

I opted for the simple answer. 'Because they think I have something to do with Velvet's death. Just like you guys.'

'Why should they care?'

'I thought you might be able to tell me,' I said.

'Whiro's involved in triads?' Hiko said. Nobody commented on the present tense.

'These aren't triads. They're big players in some larger game, which I've been trying to see.'

'Was Whiro involved with them?'

His question gave me pause. Velvet was a loner, I'd always seen her that way. Was it possible she was acting as a part of a larger group?

That would change the picture.

'If so she never told me.' I faced that possibility with a stab of bitterness. She told me so little. Maybe that's what she liked about me.

'Where the fuck do you come into it?' Hiko took the brandy out of Queenie's lap before she knew what was happening and took a grim slug.

'Except for Morse, I was the last to see her alive. We talked about some stuff, but she was holding back. She was afraid. But these big players think she might have told me something, so they're keeping me nailed down.' As good an explanation as any. Make up enough lies and one might turn out to be true.

'Yeah, and maybe you're holding back something now,' Johnny Watch correctly diagnosed. He passed his cigarette dangerously close to my wrist. 'The man who lies is the man who cries.'

'Help,' I said, 'I'm being assaulted.'

'Was she hacking?' Queenie said. 'I always told her that hacking would fuck her one day.'

'There's some connection to the university,' I said. 'Their computers went down. Maybe Velvet knew too much about something. That IT guy, Dr Morse, he's involved somehow.'

'No shit,' Gary said.

'She was sleeping with him,' I said. The words left an unpleasant taste in my mouth. I took the dormant spliff from Queenie's claw-like fingers and sucked it back to wakefulness.

'Why didn't she talk about you guys?'

'Maybe she thought we'd eat you alive,' Queenie said

'Maybe cook you first,' Johnny Watch said. Hiko laughed. I laughed too, too late and too loud. It wasn't that funny.

'Fucking stuck-up bitch, miss fucking IT. I could fucking kill her, if she weren't already dead.' Queenie spat at the front seat, missing Johnny Watch's collar but close enough to call. 'None of us was good enough for her. She never told you about us because she was ashamed of us.'

'That makes sense.'

'Fuck you.'

'When did you last see her?'

'I told you, she was ashamed of us.'

'You didn't see her on the day she died?'

'I'd've spat in her face if I had.'

'What did she do to piss you off?'

'No, Queenie,' Hiko said.

'One thing you can say about me,' Queenie said, 'is that I never hold a grudge. *Utu* doesn't wash with me. *Utu* is crap. Not like other people. Like Hiko here, her elder brother, he's a dark one. And like herself. Once she got the knife into you the devil himself couldn't pull it out.' She took the brandy back from Hiko and gave it to me. Peace offering. I swapped the spliff for the brandy. Peace offering. I took a grateful slug or two and handed it to Johnny Watch. Peace offering. 'All this torturing is thirsty work,' I said to Johnny. 'You can say that again,' he said, and took the bottle.

'Wait a minute,' Hiko said. 'We didn't kill Whiro, we know that. This isn't about us.'

'Finally,' Gary said, 'somebody talking some fucking sense.'

'When did these Asian guys turn up?' Hiko said.

'A few days ago. They kidnapped me and took me somewhere. That's where I met your Mr Chicken kung fu. He brought me tea on a little trolley. Very polite.'

'Do we have to put up with this?' Johnny Watch said to Hiko. He blew on the end of the cigarette, which glowed malevolently.

'Let's make his dreams come true.'

'One thing I'm sure of,' Queenie said. 'He may be a cunning old shit, but he never killed Whiro. He was soft on her. And he's got a cat.'

To Hiko I said, 'The boss man came and interrogated me. And none of this waving smelly cigarettes around. He was a professional. Even met me socially beforehand, to check me out.'

Hiko pulled a crumpled piece of paper from his pocket and gave it to me. A sentence was scrawled in ballpoint: *Jason holds the clue to operation Golden Fleece.* It wasn't signed.

'It's her writing,' Hiko said. 'She wrote to me when I was inside. I'd never mistake it.'

'So you are holding out on us,' Gary said, making it all clear, like he was used to dealing with stoners, cretins, the elderly, and those generally slow on the uptake.

'What's operation Golden Fleece?' Gary asked.

'I don't know.' A joke, maybe. Jason and the Golden Fleece. Ha ha.

'Don't know's not good enough,' Johnny said. His cigarette skimmed my wrist, singeing hair. I felt the scorch of it on my skin. To think I'd given him this crazy idea.

'Jesus!' Queenie hit Johnny's hand hard enough to shower bits of burning tobacco everywhere. Gary, Queenie and I scrambled to brush them out before we all got burnt. A moment of cursing and high farce.

'You can't torture the bastard in my car,' Queenie said, as if the car would take offence.

'It was his idea,' Johnny Watch said.

I said, 'Before she died some documents mysteriously appeared on my computer. Velvet must have put them there. Maybe that's the clue…'

'Did you bonk her?' Queenie said.

I said, 'Sweetheart, I haven't bonked anybody for so long even *you* are looking like a prospect.'

The men all snorted, as if they had prize coke in their snozzes.

Queenie gave me a look, as if about to kiss me or kill me. Then she gave her best witchy cackle and slapped me on the leg hard enough to revive old bruises.

'But now of course the documents have gone.'

'None of this is adding up to anything,' Gary said in disgust.

'Join the crowd,' I said

'Fuckin' clueless.'

There was a lull in the conversation as everybody except Gary nodded solemnly.

As if making a casual comment on nothing much at all, Queenie said, 'I'll tell you what though, those girlfriends of yours next door sure did a good job of knocking us out while you scrambled over the fuckin' fence, you old goat. They covered your ass.'

I didn't like that. If there was one thing I couldn't talk about it was number 54. Wang would know, somehow he would know.

'What makes you think they were covering my ass? They didn't see me.'

'Sure they did. Going over the fence. That little Hentai chink could hardly stop laughing. She musta seen you before, to laugh like that.'

'They see me going to the shop. More likely they were just repelling invaders.'

'Horse shit. The boys had hardly got through the hedge when that crazy chink came up and kicked them all so hard in the cods they couldn't get up, couldn't hardly breathe. She didn't stop to say hello how's your fucking father, or can I help you, like a polite little chink would.'

'You know more about it than I do,' I said.

'I think Queenie's got a point,' Gary said, 'I think the old cunt's still holding out on us.'

Hiko looked at me hard. 'Queenie does have a point.'

Headlights drew up behind us.

'How the fuck did they do that?' Johnny Watch said. 'I couldn't do that.'

'They'll always find you,' I said. 'And I'd take it real easy with these guys. The girls were just the entree, these guys will give you the mains.'

'Sure,' Johnny Watch said, but I could see his paranoia eating away at him.

'I wish I knew who these guys are,' Hiko said as two figures got out of the car. Like any good fighter, he hated fronting an unknown quantity.

'I've already told you,' I said. 'They are guys you don't want to know. Just believe me. Let me out and then drive away.'

Nobody said anything. The guys stood by their car, one on either side, without moving.

'You'd better let me out,' I said. 'It would be easier for everybody.'

Again nobody spoke. The men didn't move. Finally, Hiko said, 'Too easy. If these smart boys know something about Whiro's death, I want to know.'

'Yesss,' Johnny Watch said through his teeth.

'I dunno,' Gary said.

'It's my fucking car,' Queenie said. 'They better not lay a finger on this car.'

'It's all right,' I said, snapping the door handle, 'I'll let myself out.'

'Not so fast, Grandpops. The brandy's not finished.' Queenie clutched my arm like a wallflower at a country dance.

The men began to walk towards our car, slowly, carefully, professionally.

'Stay in the car,' Hiko said.

'Naw, fuck that,' Johnny Watch said. 'Gives them all the advantage.'

He opened the door, got out and stood beside it.

Hiko fretted. 'Fuck it.' He had the cheap pistol in his hand and was slotting the cartridge into it. It was my turn to curse. In the excitement I'd forgotten to confiscate the gun.

'You'll have to get out too,' Queenie said to Hiko. 'You can't let Johnny play lead on this one.'

'Fuckin' right,' Hiko said and got out of the car.

'Leave me with the gun,' Gary said, but the voice of sweet reason came too late.

When Hiko got out of the car the men paused.

'What do you want?' Hiko called. 'Why are you following us?'

It wasn't the ninja, but the other guy who spoke. 'We want to talk to Mr Argonaut.'

'What about?'

The guy didn't answer. The two of them began to walk forward again, very leisurely. Hiko let them get close enough and pulled out the gun. He aimed it at the guy who spoke. Both men froze. Hiko had chosen his distance carefully, the men close enough to shoot but too far away for them to do any high kicking.

'Tell me why you're tracking Mr Argonaut,' Hiko said.

'Please. We need to talk to him. He's in the back of your car.'

'Damn right I am!' I shouted, pulling loose from Queenie and stepping out of the car. Queenie scrambled after me, cursing. Only Gary was left and he didn't look like he was going anywhere.

'Okay,' Hiko said. 'Do your talking.'

'Mr Argonaut,' the guy said, 'would you like a lift home?' You couldn't ask for a more polite Asian.

I hesitated, calling on the Wisdom of Solomon. 'These people are family of Velvet, the woman who died. I'm sorry about the gun. They're grieving and a bit touchy. They were about to take me home, actually. Maybe you could follow us, just to make sure we get there safely.' I flashed a big hearty smile around. 'We were talking over personal matters.'

Apparently Hiko didn't like the initiative drifting from him. He made a big show of affirming his stance and steadying the gun, which was steady enough as it was.

'You're after the geezer because of my sister. Why? What was my sister to you lot?'

The polite man spread his hands. 'We know nothing,' he said. 'We just here to take Mr Argonaut home.'

'Why? Is he under house arrest or something?'

Again the man spread his hands. 'We just drive,' he said.

'They might be right,' I said quietly to Hiko. 'You know how it works. These guys are just grunts.'

Hiko thought it over. Johnny Watch didn't. That was the difference between them. Johnny was tired of being out of the action. He started forward. 'Maybe *someone* needs a bit of encouragement,' he said, like a tough guy from a noir thriller.

'No,' Hiko said. 'I got a better idea.' He shouted. 'Take us to your boss. Somebody who can answer my questions.'

The man's open-palmed gesture turned into a shrug of helplessness. 'I can't do that,' he said.

'Fuck you can't,' Johnny Watch said, and kept moving forward.

Then the man moved. Fast. Too fast for Hiko to shoot. Next thing he had Johnny Watch in a face-to-face bear hug, arms locked around his lower spine, and, swinging Johnny around to place him in Hiko's line of fire, squeezed tight. Johnny let out an agonized roar, like an animal.

Hiko didn't waste any time. He swung around to line up the ninja but the ninja wasn't there. In fact, he was right on top of Hiko, lowering him gently to the ground and taking the gun from his slack fingers. Hiko never knew what hit him.

'Nifty eh?' Queenie said. 'I could do with a couple of them around my place, clean out all my deadshit whanau.'

'Shall we go, Mr Argonaut?' the ninja said.

'Do I have a choice?'

The other guy lowered Johnny to his feet. Johnny stood there looking like he didn't know what planet he was on. I didn't look at him as I went past. I didn't look back, but I heard Gary open the front door of the car and heave himself into the driver's seat.

So I got into the back of the BMW, with the ninja. The other guy drove.

For two guys who wanted to talk to me, they had surprisingly little to say. Nothing, in fact.

No brandy or spliffs either.

40

Monckton gave me the evil eye when I left the house the next day. He was probably spying for Mr Wang, as if Wang needed help in that department. Not that I cared anymore. Let Wang follow me around till doomsday, which surely isn't that far off. No sitting at home and growing my toenails while Velvet's murder hung over me like the hangman's noose, Wang be damned. In fact, having Wang's angels looking out for me might play my way if I got too deep in the shit.

I parked Mazzie at an inconvenient distance from the University and set out to track down Dr Wayne Morse. There were PA's and other gatekeepers but I got through by flashing my press card around.

Dr Morse's office was small and cluttered, dominated by a large flatscreen. He looked small and cluttered too, sitting behind it. He wasn't pleased to see me, and had no reason to be.

'You! The investigative journalist?' He drawled the words out, American style.

I nodded modestly. 'Didn't Velvet tell you? During some nice pillow talk.'

He looked even less pleased.

'But I'm not here to do a story.'

I remembered what Meilin said about Wang's questioning – interrogation by misdirection. I wanted to know the events on the day of Velvet's murder, so I asked him about the computer crash.

'I can't talk about that,' he said, 'it's under police investigation.' He sat stiffly, as if somebody was poking him in the back with something sharp.

'I doubt they'll find anything.'

He bit his lip. He looked harried, like a man on the run. Hair dishevelled, fungus returning to the face. He didn't want to look at me. I didn't want to look at him either, but every day throws up some necessary evil.

'Was Velvet involved with the crash? We have a series of events that need precise timing. I saw her around six, after work. The computer crashed at some unspecified time that evening, the same evening that Velvet goes missing, presumably murdered. Have I forgotten anything?'

Something in the question resonated. He closed his eyes for a moment and swayed in his chair.

'I've told the police all I know.' Yeah. Name, rank and serial number.

'Me too. Look,' I pretended to drop all pretences, 'I know you don't want to talk to me, but I was Velvet's friend. I want to know what happened to her.'

'I don't know what happened to her.'

I could always try the thumb-screws, or a bit of water-boarding.

'Did you sleep together that night?'

He jumped as if I'd pricked him with a pin. 'No.'

'Why not?'

Morse stared at me morosely.

'Did you lie to the police about that, like you're lying to me?'

'You'd better get out. You can't just barge in here...'

'But I can.' I loomed over him in my best Jack Reacher style, looking as dangerous as I could, a man ready to crush any worm that stood in his path. It wouldn't have fooled any self-respecting worm.

'I can't tell you anything.' His voice took on an unpleasant whine.

'Ah.' Morse was terrified, but not of me.

'Had any new people come into her life lately – any Asians, for example?'

Again, like the needle on a lie detector machine, the pin-pricked jump. 'I didn't notice anything, really.'

All I had to do was ask the right questions and the guy was an open book.

'Did she have any visitors in that last week, besides me?'

'That I know. A woman came around. An aunty or some such. Velvet had already left for work.'

'When?'

'The last day.'

'What time?'

'Around 8 a.m.'

'Fifties, skinny, frazzled blonde hair?'

'I've told you to get out. Want me to call security?' The worm, still uncrushed, was trying to turn.

Queenie? Queenie had denied seeing Velvet – or had she?

'Please understand – I can't talk to you. There's nothing to say.' He was threatening to turn into a wheedling worm.

I did my best looming act. 'Why can't you talk? Somebody got to you, told you to say nothing about anything. A big built Asian guy, Chinese actually, goes by the name of Wang.'

This time he looked like he'd sat on a hedgehog.

'You lived with her. Worked with her. Was she having any personal issues?'

'I don't know,' he said miserably. 'She never told me much.'

'I know the feeling.' I quit looming. He wasn't worth crushing.

'By the way,' I said when I got to the door, 'why were you so hostile to me when I came around on that last night?'

'I don't remember that.'

'Sure you do.'

I closed the door when I went out.

41

I had to go to the Bellweather office downtown to find Jerzy.

'Ah, our occasional visitor,' Eddie greeted me. 'So nice of you to drop by. Look everybody, it's Scoop! Remember him?' Everybody said 'Hi Jason' and I said 'Hi everybody.'

Eddie took my arm and drew me aside, a bad sign. The nearest quiet place was Margery's office, where she did her accounting voodoo. She was sitting at her desk looking at her face in a compact mirror, maybe admiring her burnished copper hair. When she turned her cold eyes in my direction, I saw the flash of something that was not her normal contempt – wariness perhaps.

Eddie sat me down. 'I've got, like, shitty news,' he said. He always put 'like' into any sentence when he was nervous, an old bad habit that surfaced from time to time. He took a quick look at Margery, as if there might be some comfort in her cold face.

'Did you ever try and follow up that story?'

'What story?'

'The ship. From Melbourne to China. Remember?'

'Ah… Now I do.'

Eddie looked relieved at my memory loss. 'Then you didn't speak to your Chinese friend about it?'

'Meilin?' I remembered now, the conversation at the Swanson. Jerzy's involvement. 'It slipped my mind. I've had a hectic week.'

'Well that's okay then, because, you know, you wouldn't credit it, but that lead, Jerzy's lead… turned out to be a bum steer.'

'A bum steer?'

'Yeah, a fucking ghost ship.'

'I thought Jerzy's contact was high up. Ministry of Defence no less.'

'That's right,' he said. 'But in this case the MOD screwed up. Jerzy's contact was misled. A bunch of documents turned out to be phonies. So up the garden path we all went. Dum-de-dum!'

'Wouldn't you know it.'

'I thought, like, I smelled a rat when I couldn't get any independent confirmation of the story.'

'Good thing we didn't put any money down,' Margery said.

'This is the great age of crackpots,' Eddie said.

Perhaps it was because I had been with experts that these two seemed like such hopeless liars. Eddie was as jumpy as Dr Wayne Morse had been. Even Margery Razerblade looked rattled.

'You seem nervous,' I observed.

'Pissed off more like it,' Eddie said. 'Just as long as you're not wasting your time on a wild goose chase.'

'I haven't been, up till now, but you've made me curious, Eddie.'

'How so?'

'Cos you may be full of shit most of the time, but you're not a natural liar. I mean, you don't have a flair for it.'

To Margery Eddie said, 'I'm going to take that as a compliment, because I'm a glass half-full type of person.'

To which Margery replied, 'I'd take it as an insult, but then I'm a glass half-empty type of person.' And she gave me her cold fish-eye look, enough to freeze a cub reporter to the floor, but I was made of sterner stuff and I'd been in training.

'I've always thought that depended on what was in the glass. So why don't you just tell me who got to you and we'll take it from there.'

They both stared at the floor. Nothing much there but our feet.

'Was it a Chinese guy, about so tall, goes by the name of Wang? Gets around, from what I hear.' Everywhere I turned Wang was standing in front of me.

Eddie shook his head. Margery put a warning hand on his arm.

'Come on, you can tell ol' Scoop, he won't say anything. He can put it in his bag of secrets. He's got all sorts in that bag.'

Eddie found his bluster. 'Let's just forget the story, right? It was, like, a dead duck before it quacked. Let's move on, talk about your China article. How's it going?'

'If you're trying to frighten me off this story, it's not working. I'm not frightened enough. Who got to you?'

'We're not trying to frighten you, for God's sake. Why should we?'

'Because someone has frightened you. You and Miss Razorblade here.'

Margery gave me a filthy look. If she weren't such a cold fish I might have thought she loathed me.

'So the story isn't a bum steer, is it?'

Eddie held up his hands in a gesture of surrender. 'All right, all right. Once you latch onto something, you never give up – like a fucking limpet.'

To Margery I said, 'I'm going to take that as a compliment, because, in Eddie's case, I'm a glass half-full type of person. He's never let me down yet.'

She said, 'He doesn't listen to me. I've been telling him for years to dump you.'

'He can be stubborn that way,' I said, turning back to Eddie. 'Come on Eddie, 'fess up, who leaned on you?' I thought of looming over him, as I'd done with Morse, but figured it wouldn't work in Eddie's case; Eddie was a small guy so people loomed over him all the time.

'The Ministry of Defence,' he said.

That took the wind out of my sails. 'You mean Jerzy's contact retracted?' I looked around for the culprit.

It was Margery who answered. 'His superiors retracted for him. We got a visit from some fairly top brass.'

'So there really is a story. A hot one.'

Eddie nodded. 'We've been officially notified that it's a hoax.'

'What did Jerzy's contact say?'

'That he'd been leaned on.'

'What are you going to do?'

He waved a weary arm, the arm of a man with too many burdens to bear. 'Get a real job.' He touched the top of Margery's coppery hair, very lightly. 'Maybe I'll have a raging affair with my super hot PA.'

Margery offered him a face like a chisel.

I got out while I was still intact and hunted down Jerzy.

I found him sitting in front of a large flatscreen doing some

Photoshop work on an advertisement.

'I could do with some photoshopping of my mugshot,' I said. 'That one you have is old, I'm younger now.'

He swung around. 'Jason, you old has-been, what are you doing here?'

'I work here, remember? The brains of Bellweather.'

'If you've come to pick mine, you're too late.'

'What do you mean?'

'One of any number of things.'

'You know Jerzy, strange things are happening to me.'

'Is this a shaggy-dog story?'

'Everybody I meet is either lying to me or talking in riddles.'

'Some days are like that.'

'I've got a simple technical question for you, buddy boy, so there's no need to run and hide.'

'Okay. I'm a bit out of kilter. I didn't like the MOD turning up. Where I come from, when the men in black turn up, people disappear.'

'Must be one hell of a cargo on that ship.'

He nodded. 'Or they don't know. Spooks get upset when something new crops up. First off, put a lid on it. Screw it down tight.' He tapped his head. 'The military mind, you have to understand it.'

'I can hardly credit that they came here, in person, to the office. Talk about overkill. Eddie must've just about crapped his pants. A phone call would have done the job.'

'Actually, I don't feel comfortable talking about it. If this country keeps going the way it is, it will be just like America. That what you want?'

'A systems crash, like the university one, could it have been done from the inside? You know, somebody slipping a big nasty into the computer. An inside job rather than a hacker attack.'

He chewed on his tongue. 'In theory yes, but I don't see the point.'

'To cover your tracks?'

'With software that powerful you don't leave any tracks. And you probably don't want copies of it floating around on disks or memory sticks. I mean, to do it manually would be… would have no finesse. No elegance. Too messy. No cyber-warrior would ever think that way.'

'But is it possible?'

'Oh yes.'

It had been a crazy idea, that Velvet might have been involved in the computer crash, acting under pressure from someone like Wang. Would Wang murder Velvet afterwards to further cover his tracks? Hardly. No finesse. Too messy. Besides, Meilin had already told me that the Chinese government was behind the computer crash, and the Central Committee was unlikely to work through someone like Velvet. Unless it was the other way round: Velvet had stumbled on the plot to crash the university computer and was trying to stop it. And got murdered for her pains.

'However, *mein freund*, an insider might have helped another way. I mean, by opening an imported file that shouldn't be opened. By springing Pandora's box. Slip it through email in camouflage as an ordinary attachment. Have your insider cued to spring it. The released software, call it Pandora, immediately obliterates the evidence of the crime along with everything else. That's quite elegant. No firewalls to deal with. The Trojan Horse principle.'

'Wouldn't a copy of the email be held by the server?'

He grinned deliciously, 'Either your insider deletes the message from the server first or Pandora takes care of that too. Child's play.'

'Would Pandora have to activate immediately, or could it wait, wait for the insider to catch a plane to South America?'

'All Pandora would need to do is wipe the email from the network and the server and lie cloaked until the appointed moment. Child's play.'

'Would that be the most elegant option, in fact?'

'Hardly. A bloodhound would pass through the kind of firewalls a small scale network like a university would have like a neutrino through custard, and along with it of course comes Pandora. The box opens. Instant obliteration. Besides…'

'Yes?'

'Insiders are messy because they're people. And planes to South America can get delayed.'

42

Elvis and Haggis-face met me at the entrance to the Bellweather offices as if they had just arrived.

'Gentlemen, long time no see. What's up? Discovered Velvet's murderer yet?'

'Mr Argonaut,' Elvis said, 'we'd appreciate it if you'd come down to the station with us and answer a few questions.'

Ah, we'd gotten to that point, finally.

'One of those nice cozy interview rooms you've told me about.'

'That's the one,' Haggis said.

Police stations remind me of hospitals, only worse. There are horrors hidden away behind their scungy walls.

'Can we talk in your car? Police stations give me a dry throat. Make my tongue stick to the top of my mouth.'

Haggis face gave me a filthy look. He had ways of unsticking tongues.

'Okay,' Elvis said

Once in their car, one of those glaringly anonymous grey sedans, Elvis in the back with me, Haggis in the front behind the wheel, Elvis pulled out a tape recorder and quickly fed in the time, location and those present. I had to state my name and address. As I did so, Haggis pulled the car out into the traffic.

Elvis bowled first. 'Mr Argonaut, when you rang me last night, some people had just arrived at your place – who were they?'

'Velvet's family. Where are we going?'

'Why did you want to ring me back in twenty minutes?'

'It was an insurance policy. I doubted their intentions.'

'Explain.'

'According to Dr Elisabeth Kübler-Ross there are four main stages to grief. Denial, anger, negotiation, acceptance. They're stuck at the anger stage. Looking for someone to blame.'

'You?'

'The thoughts crossed their minds, just like it did yours.'

'So who were they?'

'What's going on? Where are you taking me?'

'Just tell us.'

So I told them, the model cooperative citizen, that's me. Did my best to describe each one.

'What mood were they in?'

'Jumpy.'

'Who was jumpy?'

'Johnny Watch for a start. He was carrying a gun. He offered to beat me up.'

'What happened to the gun?'

'Hiko confiscated it. He played the leader.'

'You went for a drive. Why did you do that?'

'They weren't comfortable talking at my place. I think my cat put them off. He's got an evil eye.'

Haggis was driving slowly, turning lots of corners.

'What did you talk about?'

'Velvet. Now look you guys, I've been cooperating right down the line. But if you want answers to further questions without holding me, which is not a good idea, you'll have to give a little and tell me what's going on. And where we're going.'

'Why is holding you not a good idea?' Haggis said. It was clear what he thought.

'I'm sure you'd prefer a willing, cooperative witness to a reluctant, lawyer driven one. I want to know who killed Velvet as badly as you do.'

Elvis flicked a quick look at Haggis. 'The man you know as

Johnny Watch was murdered last night.'

I said nothing. This didn't feel like Wang's work. Too inelegant. There was a third force at work. One far less elegant.

'How was it done?'

Elvis looked at Haggis, who proceeded to deliver his coup-de-grâce with relish. 'It's a hard one. You see, Mr Cooperative Witness, Johnny Watch's corpse was delivered to his family's door at 7.30 this morning. Cooked, roasted in fact, garnished with vegetables and herbs.'

He waited a decent time for me to absorb that indecency.

'Now… Mr Argonaut, you went for a ride with four members of the family and you talked about Velvet. How did you get home?'

I didn't want to have to talk about Wang's outfit, not so much because of Wang but because of the can of worms it would open with the police. I thought that the police would have been reined in by now, if not by Wang then Defence – where were the guys in grey suits? How come this dog-and-pony show was still on the road?

'How did you get home?'

'Some guys picked me up.'

'What guys?'

Haggis had turned into Taraire Street. I knew now where they were going.

'Inspector, do you remember that second call I made last night, before I went for a ride?'

'You said you thought you were being followed.'

'Well it turns out I was. By these two Asian guys. They followed us and broke up our little party, which wasn't such a bad thing. We'd been drinking brandy.' I talked Elvis and Haggis through it, pretty much exactly as it happened, Hiko pulling a gun, Johnny Watch playing the hero, the turning of the tables, the disarming of Hiko, Johnny Watch's humiliation – I had nothing to lose telling the exact truth.

'What did these guys say to you?'

'Nothing. Not a word. They took me home and drove away.'

'What do you know about them?'

Finally, we cruised to a halt outside my place. I wanted to jump out of the car, run inside and bolt the door.

'They've been around a couple of days. Keeping an eye on me.'

'Any ideas who they are?'

'Until last night I thought they might be you guys.'

Elvis snapped off the tape recorder. 'Sergeant McDonald, with Mr Argonaut's kind permission, please have a look around his house for any items of interest.'

Haggis didn't wait for my kind permission. As he shut the door behind him, I called out, 'Watch out for the cat. He's wary of strange-looking visitors.'

Elvis placed the tape recorder in my hands. I looked at it. It was off.

'Now give it to me straight. Who are these Asian guys.'

I didn't hesitate. 'They work for a big-shot called Wang. Ever heard of him? For a while I thought he'd somehow stymied your investigation of Velvet's death, that you might be in his pocket. I can see you're not.'

Elvis was looking grimmer with every sentence. 'Carry on,' he said.

So I told him about getting kidnapped, Wang's interrogation, my eventual release – I didn't mention Meilin. I also told him about Wang's instruction to me not to say anything about anything.

'What interest could Wang have in Velvet's death?'

'That's the big question.'

'Who is Wang anyway?'

'All I know is that this business frightens the hell out of me – when I'm not pretending to be brave. There are forces at work here bigger than an aging science journalist, or even the Auckland Police.'

'Do you think Wang is behind the murders?'

'No.' I spoke slowly, thinking it out as I went. 'The manner of Johnny Watch's death is carefully calculated to give offence, and to enrage Velvet's family. Big cultural insult. Wang wouldn't want that. I got the impression that he was trying to calm troubled waters. Somebody else is stirring the pot.'

'Brother and sister both murdered. We looked to the family first.'

'Nice red herring. I think Velvet stumbled onto something big, which doomed her. Johnny Watch probably tried to track down the two Asian guys who humiliated him and ran into the wrong people.'

'All we know is that he went off on his own after the incident with you and was never seen again.'

'And that's probably all you'll ever know.'

He nodded heavily.

Haggis appeared at my doorway bearing a package triumphantly in his hands.

'Just tell me one thing,' I said. 'You must've retraced Velvet's movements in the few days before her death. Is there any indication of anything like this? That she'd gotten in over her head?

'No.'

'Any gaps? Times you can't account for?'

He hesitated a fraction too long.

'When?'

'The last day, she arrived on campus at eight-thirty a.m. Someone saw her. But she didn't check in until ten.'

'What time did the computer system go down?'

'Sometime in the evening, we think.'

'You think?'

Reluctantly, he said, 'We don't have access to that information.'

'Ah!' I said. 'And did you discover why Velvet was in Albert Park after hours?'

Again he hesitated. He glanced at Haggis, who was having a discussion with Monckton at the front door. 'She was heading downtown to the bus stop on Queen Street.'

'Didn't she take her car?' I was becoming more confused by the moment.

'She did, and parked it right outside the university clock tower. Somebody sabotaged it.'

'How?'

'Removing the distributor cap.'

'That would do it.' No attempt to hide the sabotage, I noticed. Distributor caps don't remove themselves.

'Did you find it?'

'In a plot of begonias.'

Haggis had crossed the road, opened the car door and, with a dour flourish, held up a large evidence bag.

There, as if floating in its own amniotic fluid, was my WW2, precision-made German Luger automatic.

43

I had a nerve trying to see Queenie on the very day young Johnny Watch turned up on their front lawn, roasted and ready to eat, but I couldn't help myself. A quick search through the phone book soon revealed the address. I parked down the road, and walked past on the other side of the street. There were people everywhere at Queenie's place, spilling out onto the front lawn and the street in a hubbub of loud conversation. Big women with scarves over their heads and men with black looks. Lotsa heavy dudes. Lotsa weapons. There was a continuous, loud, quavering wail from several women's throats that unanchored the street from its mooring in the earth and set it on an ocean of sorrow.

By a stroke of luck I saw Queenie straight off. She was standing apart from the crowd, a glass of something in one hand and something burning in the other. She was staring my way. Then she wobbled over the road towards me. I didn't know if she were zonked or stunned by Johnny's death, or both.

'You're a fucking bad omen, Grandpops, did you know that? Everywhere you go… death follows.' It was Queenie all right, but all the fire had gone. She spoke slowly, in a wan, slurred voice. Like sludge. Definitely both.

I saw no way of beating about the bush, not with Queenie in the state she was in. 'Why did you go and see Velvet the day before she died, and why did you pretend you'd had no contact with her?'

'You know,' she said mechanically, 'you could get killed hanging around here.' I got a death's head smile. I suspected something a little bit harder than the booze and dope. Heroin perhaps.

'If you hated Velvet, why did you visit her?'

She took a long time to focus her pinball pupils on me, fix me in her field of vision.

'I never hated Velvet. *She* turned her back on *us.*'

'So why visit her?'

Queenie looked vacantly around the street. Maybe she was thinking up some lie to tell me. Maybe she'd forgotten the question. Behind her, on the other side of the street, someone had separated themselves from the milling crowd and was watching us. It was Hiko.

'To show her up. By being nice to her. Nice cuzzy-bro.' I got a crooked grin. A little of the old combustion returned to her eyes. 'Better than spitting in her face, eh?' There was no witchy cackle, but there might have been on a better day.

'How were you nice to her?'

'By delivering a little package sent to her here.' Her death's head grin turned into one of triumph. 'That was the beauty of it, you see. *I* was doing *her* a favour. How's that for a right Christian gesture?'

'You'll get to heaven before they close the door, Queenie. What was in the package?'

'How would I know?'

'Because you'd look.'

'Um… s'pose I would.' She drifted off again. 'Nothing but a stupid little memory stick thingy.' She took a slug with one hand and a drag with the other. Every time her elbow bent her mouth opened.

'Just like Velvet. Never do anything straight.'

Hiko started across the road.

'Did you put the stick into your computer?'

'I don't have a fucking computer. Velvet should never have got involved with them. I only have a car, and Johnny managed to trash that before he got trashed.'

I touched her cheek to mine. 'I'm sorry about Johnny,' I said.

'Get the fuck out of here,' she said.

I did, but maybe I left it a second too late. Hiko altered his course to intercept me. I quickened my pace. Unfortunately, because of the angle he was taking across the road, I couldn't retreat to my car and was walking in the wrong direction. Hiko quickened his pace too. No jumping back fences this time. I'd have to circle the block to get back to my car. No way I was going to get that far. I kept going as fast as I could without breaking into a run. Maybe there'd be a shop at the corner I could slip into, ask the owner to ring the cops. Footsteps pounded behind me. There was a ragged roar from the crowd.

I'd just passed a parked car when the passenger's door opened, Haggis got out and stood in front of Hiko. I have to admit that I was pleased to see his ugly mug.

'We're taking Mr Argonaut into custody,' he announced. 'For his own protection.'

Hiko stopped. Several other men gathered. Among them I spotted Gary. Elvis was already out of the driver's door and was heading around the bonnet to collect me. The men bridled. Haggis's imperial tone of voice got them as much as anything, and for a moment it was in them, it was there, to rush the cops and overpower them. There were enough on hand, and more arriving. The whole street seemed to be there.

Haggis didn't show any fear, I'll give him that. In fact, he puffed himself up like a little frog, ready for action.

'Hiko,' Elvis said loudly, grasping my arm, but he was speaking to them all. 'No point in facing an assault on police charge. The old man had nothing to do with Johnny's death, you know that.'

'If he turns up here again we'll beat the shit out of him.'

A hundred eyes turned on me. A hundred voices murmured agreement. It was my moment.

'Duly noted,' Elvis said, all calm, while Haggis bristled. It must be an offence to make threats to citizens, even pathetic ones like me, via the police. Elvis guided me swiftly around the street side of the car, opened the back door and pushed me inside, hand on head in the time-honoured fashion of arrest. I hoped he was just putting on a show.

As Elvis stepped up to his door, he said, loudly, 'And you won't need to visit him either, will you?'

'Fuck you,' Hiko said, 'fucking useless pigs. What are you hanging around here for anyway? Why aren't you out nailing Johnny's killers, nailing those Asian arseholes?' There was an ugly snarl of agreement among the bros, and one or two younger ones, eager to follow in Johnny Watch's footsteps, started forward towards the car.

'Get in,' Elvis said to Haggis.

Haggis stood on his dignity for a moment. But no more than that.

Fists thumped on the boot as Elvis hit the gas.

'Time to take you down to the station,' Elvis said.

Haggis beamed and wiped his whiskers with the back of his hand like a cat in front of the traditional bowl full of cream.

That's how I finally got to see the inside of a cozy little interview room.

44

Marcia and the boys were waiting for me when I got home. After five hours of helping the police with their enquiries I was in need of a stiff drink and a soft bed, but I didn't have to be an anxious father and grandfather to see that something was wrong. The two boys, dressed in their best, were sitting upright on the couch like two stooges in a school play. Marcia was sitting in my easy chair, but there was nothing easy about her posture. I felt a stab of familiar guilt. With all the drama of Velvet's death, I had forgotten about Marcia.

'I'm leaving the country,' she said. 'Taking the boys.'

I poured myself the stiff drink. I was half way to that soft bed. 'When?'

'Later tonight. To Melbourne.'

'Why Melbourne?'

'I've got an interview for a job – and I thought I'd stay over for a couple of weeks or so.'

'Good. Good. I'm glad.'

I drank and waited for her to say what she had to say. I half-heartedly dragged out the Lego but the boys ignored it. Fintan was listening intently to the conversation. Felix, for once still, was staring slackly off into the distance. Even Monckton's attentions didn't interest him.

'Dad, a couple of years ago our firm facilitated a deal between a Chinese firm and a company of receivers in New Zealand to buy some NZ farms going cheap. The deal seemed to be all above board – but it wasn't. About six months ago a fellow lawyer at Dogbane & Dogbane gave me a hard copy of a dossier of documents, originals not copies, proving that our boss, Mr Dogbane Senior, engaged in corrupt practices to facilitate that deal, and got a hefty kickback for his services. Politicians are involved. My colleague gave me the dossier, afraid that Mr Senior was onto him. A week later, my colleague's office was searched and trashed. A couple of other offices were rifled. Not mine. I'm too insignificant.' She took a long, deep breath. 'So now my colleague wants the dossier back because he's locked in a death struggle with Mr Dogbane Senior and doesn't care if he brings down a bunch of innocent people, and the firm, with him.'

'But don't you have a moral obligation to let this information out, whatever your colleague's motives?' *The truth must out*: the journalists' old faith. 'And why should you care about your corrupt boss? Your corrupt ex-boss.'

'Dad! Get subtle here. Dogbane Senior is on the skids anyway. Give him another six months. My colleague is being vindictive, and because it would be easy for Dogbane to implicate the whole firm in this, and take others down with him, it'll be a train wreck for a number of people who I've worked with for six years, honest people unwittingly dragged into this. My reputation will go down the drain too. I'd have to turn snitch and dob in both my colleague and Dogbane. I'd never get another job in Australasia. So where is your moral obligation now?'

'The devil's always in the detail,' I said, 'in law and morality. Where's the dossier?'

She patted the bag jammed into the seat beside her. 'It's staying with me at all times.'

'Does your colleague know you're leaving?'

'Hell no! He'd have the cops onto me.'

'Did you look at the dossier?'

'Sure. In for a penny, in for a pound, isn't that what you used to say, Dad?'

'It's what Scoop used to say.' I wanted to sit beside her and give her a big hug, yet even as a child Marcia wasn't a huggy person. She valued self-possession above the comfort of warm fuzzies. Pluck, we used to call it, a highly prized quality. In Marcia's case, however, there was something of the stiff upper lip in it.

'I did a quick investigation of a Chinese investor company involved in Pacific Holdings. A secretive company called Golden Fleece, registered in Hong Kong. It seems Golden Fleece has its golden fingers in a number of pies, very big pies, including military research and weapons production. They keep out of sight.'

'What? Did you say Golden Fleece?'

'You're not going deaf are you Dad?'

'Not in a million years,' and I cupped my hands behind my ears.

She laughed briefly.

'Our Mr Dogbane was having direct secret negotiations with Golden Fleece, which is operating under the cover of Pacific Holdings. Golden Fleece has quite a little property portfolio, including your house next door, just as you said. There's something odd about that too.'

'What?'

'Golden Fleece pays Pacific Holdings for all expenses relating to number 54. The tenants apparently pay nothing.'

'That is odd,' I said, trying to pretend I didn't know. Marcia was now on the same trail that Velvet had followed. Lacking Velvet's skills, she wouldn't hit what Velvet had, I hoped.

Marcia flourished the dossier. 'There's enough dirt in here, Dad, to bring down Dogbane and the rest of us, a couple of cabinet ministers, maybe even the government – selling off New Zealand for personal profit.'

'There's nothing new in that.'

'True, but you don't often see it spelled out like this.'

'Then don't sit on it! Let it come out and things fall where they may.'

Very quietly she said, 'I wasn't going to sit on it forever.'

'Ah.' Always the good lawyer, she'd know when the time was right to strike.

'But Dad, Golden Fleece is dodgy. There might be something going on next door that you'd want to keep clear of.'

'I'm good at staying out of trouble.' *Jason knows the secret of the Golden Fleece.*

'I'm sure. I can't help thinking…'

'Spit it out.'

'Dogbane's computer system has been hacked into. Somebody had a good old look around. I know your friend Velvet was a hacker… just all a horrible coincidence. Unless… Dad, did you ever suspect that Velvet was engaged in espionage?'

'I didn't suspect it. No.'

'I think it's dangerous for you here, Dad. Come with me to Melbourne. We'll all go to ground for a while.'

The boys' eyes riveted on me and I knew this was the upshot of the visit. Would Grandad come with them? They wanted Grandad to come with them. I could see it in their eyes, and they were curiously still, the way kids are when adults are deciding their fate.

'Dad, somebody is following me and it's not Dogbane, or my colleague. So who is it? That's the question that scares me. What if it's Golden Fleece? And they want the dossier.'

'Can you be sure? Maybe Dogbane Senior knows about it.'

'He doesn't, or I'd know fast enough. As for my colleague, I told him that I've put the dossier in a safe deposit which I'll access tomorrow. He approves of my carefulness. He thinks I hate Dogbane as much as he does, and that we are in cahoots. And besides…'

'Besides what?'

'These guys following me are Asian. There's no reason why Asians can't be private detectives, but why would my colleague hire them to follow me? Not his style.'

Wang. Everywhere I looked. Even Marcia. I felt sick.

'Golden Fleece is in the firing line too. They've engaged in corrupt practices, bribery mostly. They'll want to keep the lid on this as much as Dogbane. So they might come here, Dad, looking for me. You wouldn't be safe.'

'We could have a party.' I could invite some of my ninja pals.

'Come with us, throw some things into a bag, grab your passport and let's get out of here. I want you to come.'

The kids stared at me with big eyes.

'What about Monckton?'

'Don't be silly. We can make arrangements for a bloody cat.'

Monckton didn't like that comment and stalked off.

I could feel it inside my chest, like a stone. A core of stubbornness perhaps. A core of selfishness. I looked at the boys.

'I need you now, Pops,' she said, voice husky with strain.

'I can't,' I said. 'I mean, I can go with you for a couple of days and help settle you in, but I can't stay, I can't hide away.'

Her moment of vulnerability quickly passed; she was probably ashamed of it. Needing her Dad at her age!

'So you're going to stay here and play hero, is that it?' Her voice was harder than I think she wanted.

'You won't be able to escape them, Marcia. They'll follow you to the airport. They'll follow you to Melbourne. They'll follow you to the gates of hell. Doing a runner on the red-eye is only going to tip off Golden Fleece that you have the dossier, if they don't already know.'

'I've thought about all that. But I can't stay to face the music in the morning. I *can't* hand over that dossier. I won't! Let them come looking for it.'

For the first time in this whole roundabout saga I caught the scent of the murderer.

I went to the boys, knelt down in front of them and looked at their solemn faces. Well, Felix was solemn because he was in tune with the moment, but Fin was more than solemn – he was scared. He knew what was going on.

Without getting up I turned to Marcia. 'And I can't in all conscience let you go with that dossier. Think of the boys! Leave it here. Then go to Melbourne, do your interview, go to ground for a while, fall in love with a nice man.'

'As soon as they realize I don't have it, they'll visit you.'

'Let them. They won't find the dossier. Not without demolishing the house.'

'I can't dump it on you.'

'Of course you can. It's the only option that makes sense. The heat will go off you and the boys, that's all I care about.' Now how's that for playing hero? But I meant every word of it.

'Yes Mum,' Fintan said.

'Yes Mum,' Felix parroted.

'Yes Mum,' I said.

Felix laughed. 'Yes Mum,' he said again, but the joke had already died.

'I'll never forgive myself for this,' Marcia said.

'And you'd never forgive yourself if the boys got hurt,' I said. I didn't elaborate, but Marcia knew. One little kidnapping is all it would take to get Marcia on her knees, dossier proffered in trembling hands.

I leaned across Felix, took Marcia's bag, extracted the dossier and put it on my knees.

We all looked at it.

It was nothing special. A plain light blue plastic document wallet, A4 size. It didn't look like a time bomb.

'How were you getting to the airport?'

'By taxi. I rang from a public phone. I don't think I was being watched. I asked the driver to come back here in about...' she looked at her watch... 'twenty minutes from now.'

'Catch it,' I urged her. 'Leave this rotten thing with me.'

'But where will you hide it?'

I winked at the boys. 'I've got a trick or two up my sleeve.' I shook my sleeve in front of them.

'There's nothing there,' Felix said.

Still, the decision was made. Fin was visibly relieved. Twenty minutes later they got into a taxi and left, Marcia with tears in her eyes. I watched while they got into the car. There was a curiously doomed quality to the scene, the boys scrambling into the back, their skinny pale legs in the wan glare of the streetlight, Marcia's last look back as she stood by the taxi, as if, even now, she might somehow change fate, the thudding of the doors in the dull, still night, the smooth departure of the taxi, the empty street...

Felix had been right. I didn't have a clue where to hide the dossier, but I had to do it immediately. I didn't know how long I had. Maybe very little time. Certainly, as soon as Marcia failed to make the rendezvous at 9.30 tomorrow morning, the cat would be out of the bag. But if Golden Fleece were following her, staying one jump ahead of her feral colleague, then the cat could well be out of the bag already. Marcia might face a little reception party at the airport before even getting on the plane.

I sat on the sofa and flicked through the dossier. Monckton nosed in for a look too. Some boring looking spreadsheets. Some photographs of two people meeting, a man and a woman, and some other photos of the same two socializing. One of the photographs unsettled me. I stared hard at the picture. I didn't know the man, but the woman… the woman was Aunty Wu.

I sat back and stared into space. Suddenly the prospect of that warm bed seemed very far off.

A second drink didn't.

45

I woke the next morning at the crack of sparrow's fart, as my father used to say. For once I'd slept well and my mind was clear. Every thought rang like a crystal flute, and had a vast, almost cathedral-like sense of inner space. Hovering like a luminous icon in that space was the face of Aunty Wu. Meilin had told me she was a family member, related to the big Boss Man, who'd argued with big Boss Man over the Odds Avenue set up, who had plans of her own, and who represented 'other factions'. Golden Fleece perhaps. And her timing was interesting. Tea and biscuits took place the day before Velvet's murder: was that a coincidence, or had someone in Golden Fleece been getting nervous? Aunty Wu was the key to all this. The link.

Aunty Wu. Not Wang. Each must represent different factions, with Blue and Sparta in the middle.

All I had to do was track her down and the case would be solved.

This sense of superior clarity lasted me to the kitchen, to Monckton's evil eye, where things started to get muddy again, as muddy as Monckton's cat box, the only place I could think of that might survive a house search; even, a professional might balk at sticking his hands into cat crap. I'd removed the papers from the folder, stuck some random papers in the folder which I shoved to the bottom of a box of my stuff, and placed the dossier, in an envelope, at the bottom of the cat-box and spread the mix back over it. Monckton had obliged in the night by leaving a nice deposit half-visible. Pathetic, I know, but that was the best I could think of after a couple of stiff drinks and a hard day.

Over an early breakfast I had a better idea. My box was full of old papers, back copies of Bellweather, hard copies of previously published articles I'd printed out for proof reading and never quite chucked away, plus wads of old bank statements and IRD bills. All I had to do, and quickly did, was distribute the contents of the dossier through the pile, page here and page there, keeping a note of where I had stored them. Still pretty pathetic, I know, but better than the cat box. It was an archival version of a cat box. One thing I couldn't do was leave the house with the dossier, not with the amount of attention I was drawing. And I could well be poised to draw a lot more. Aunty Wu knew who I was. She already knew me when she met me at tea and biscuits, so she would associate me with number 54. Now she would run into me again, in an apparently separate connection: Marcia. Aunty Wu would be as quick as me to make the link.

Good thing I never said anything about all this to Marcia or I'd have never got her into the taxi. So it was a good thing I'd lied to Marcia. There can be moral lies or immoral lies; deception, too, a part of the truth, woven into the overall fabric of things. There is a sea bird, the dotterel, that pretends to have a broken wing to lead predators from its nest. A lying bird. What was the subatomic nature of matter but layers of deception? The whole particle zoo boiled down to energy changing hands faster than hot money in a bear market. What was time but a projection of the moment?

Over a long green tea, I thought about Queenie, and the one nugget of information she'd imparted. We now had a memory stick that hadn't turned up. The fact of it, and the clandestine way

Velvet had received it, moved Velvet closer to the centre of the web of truth and deception. Yet Queenie might have chucked it away in disgust, who would trust anything important to such an unsteady agency as Queenie, unless… unless Velvet had an arrangement with Queenie. A profitable arrangement for Queenie. That made more sense than the reverse-psychology revenge Queenie claimed motivated her, and would be something Queenie would be keen to hide, zonked or not. The absence of truth and the presence of profit always went hand in hand.

I was on a second cup, and a further round of thinking, mostly about the death of Johnny Watch and why anybody would want to enrage the bros in such a grotesque way, when the telephone rang.

I looked at the clock. 10.15 and no goons had broken the door down yet.

It was Elvis.

'We're seeing a bit too much of each other,' I said.

'It appears that your daughter has just left the country with stolen property,' he said.

'Poke me in the eye with a stick,' I said.

Grimly he gave me the low down. At 9.40 he'd received a complaint from one of the partners at a prominent law firm that Marcia had failed to show for a meeting, could not be contacted, had vanished in possession of confidential documents pertaining to legal cases of national significance. A quick check revealed that Marcia flew to Australia last night. Did I know anything about this?

'I've got troubles enough of my own,' I said.

'You sure have,' he said. 'Everywhere I look, you turn up. Two murders, and now a commercial espionage case. You're branching out.'

'What do you mean?'

'The documents your daughter has stolen are commercially sensitive. The information they contain could be worth a lot of money to anyone prepared to sell. Your daughter is in serious trouble.'

'What do they contain?'

'Highly confidential material. Think threats to national security.'

'You don't know, do you?'

'I don't need to. Just tell me where your daughter is and earn yourself some goddamn brownie points. You need them!'

'Marcia is very much her own person,' I said, 'and she never talks about her work.'

'She visited you last night before going to the airport. What did she talk about?'

'Been keeping an eye on me, have you?' Pretty soon it would be bumper to bumper along Odds Avenue, guys in dark coats sitting in parked cars keeping an eye on me.

'Just answer the question, Mr Argonaut.'

'She came to say goodbye. Going to Australia on some business trip for a few days. A job interview, I think. It was a quick visit.'

'Did she leave anything with you?'

He was making me do it. Lie outright to him.

'No.'

'Did she give you an address?'

'No.'

'You're not thinking of leaving the country on some business trip are you, Mr Argonaut?'

'No. I'm staying put.'

'Good. Make sure you stay that way.'

And he hung up.

Short but not too sweet.

46

I stayed put and waited for the sky to fall. I waited twenty-four hours and the sky still didn't fall. I got a text from Marcia saying she was in Melbourne and all was well. That was a relief. But then I started wondering why the goons hadn't come to my door. They would know by now Marcia had no dossier, unless she really knew how to go to ground. It was silly to underestimate Marcia, she was a real chip off the old block; if she wanted to vanish, she would do so with typical thoroughness.

I went to work on the China article, but it was disheartening to try and figure out just how many coal-fired power plants and nuclear power plants China was building per week.

I distracted myself by going over the Melbourne ship departure schedules I'd already gone over. The Ministry's efforts to kill the story intrigued me more than the story itself. If it was nothing, why bother trying to kill it? I got hooked on the names of these rusty old container tramps. Names like *Pacific Blue* and *Pacific Paradise*. I had three Pacifics alone out of the twelve total departures over the last three days. Plus a *Flower of the Orient*, plus a provocative *Lady Jane*. Maybe I thought I might see a name like *The Argonaut*, or *The Golden Fleece* and light bulbs would go off in my brain. More likely I was just goofing off. Most of the vessels were registered in Liberia or some other suspicious place, and it was impossible to tell, at least from the data I currently had, what the ownership structure of each vessel might be. That would be a gruelling task of research.

Such a vessel wouldn't have to be loaded to the gunnels with nasty stuff the way I'd first imagined, but could be carrying some items of interest, something stashed away in a container somewhere. In which case any one, or none, of the ships might be implicated.

And so it went. Hours spent wafting around the edges of things looking for a way in. Sooner or later, however, it all came back to the one thing. Aunty Wu. I retrieved the photograph and had another look at it. The man, I guessed, was Mr Dogbane Senior. They looked pleased with themselves, as if they'd just stitched up a good deal. Mr Dogbane's eyes were crinkled up like a kindly uncle; Aunty Wu's smile was fit for a box of chocolates. However, this was no PR shot. They were looking at each other, or rather towards each other, not the camera; I doubted they'd intended to donate this moment to posterity. That meant that the photo was probably taken clandestinely, maybe with a telephoto lens, although the image looked sharp enough. Its very existence raised questions. Whoever took this photo, or had it taken, was spying, either on Dogbane or Wu or both, which meant somebody was onto them, somebody had been gathering evidence against them. Marcia's colleague couldn't have assembled all this himself – it must have been given to him, the perfect weapon to bring down Golden Fleece, handed to him on a platter. Commercial espionage, and maybe more than that.

So it went on, with not much work getting done, and a lot of staring at the cat, until another breakfast rolled around.

Tired of sitting around, I went for a drive. Mazzie seemed to know where to go, which lanes to take, which corners to turn. You've heard of racing car drivers who become one with their cars – that was me and Mazzie. Mazzie changed the gears, but those were my wheels trundling along.

We arrived, Mazzie floating to a stop right outside the front door. No parking around the corner this time. The house looked like something out of a rather sad fairy tale, gabled and peeling, with its droopy couches on the deck and even droopier datura.

I felt a bit droopy myself as I trudged up the worn steps to the door. I couldn't smell any patchouli but the rich, heady smell of datura flowers was around. The place had an empty feel, and I didn't expect anyone to answer the door, but Dr Wayne Morse did. He didn't look good.

'You,' he said.

I didn't know what to say, so said the first thing that came into my mouth.

'Velvet wanted me to come here.'

He gestured with his head for me to enter. He didn't seem so much frightened this time as defeated. He'd given up. He couldn't even be bothered telling me to piss off.

He took me through to his room. There was a derelict feel to it, even though the bed was obviously slept in. In one corner a flatscreen was growing dust. A pile of clothes that hadn't been put in the washer was growing something else in the corner. The desk was a scatter of neglected messes.

'I'm all washed up here,' he said. 'I got fired, as you call it, but I can't go home because the cops have confiscated my passport. I'll never get another job in my field, not after this. I'm finished.'

'What can you tell me?'

He shrugged. 'Velvet was into stealing code. She was a raider. She worked mostly in the darknet. She was very good.' He licked his lips as if they were especially dry. 'I got kinda drawn into it, you know, as I got to know her. There's a fascination in it. A challenge. It's a hit.'

'The thrill of committing a crime.'

'Something like that.' He stared apathetically around the room. 'I can't offer you much. You guys are always offering each other tea, like the English.'

'I think the English have taken to coffee,' I said. 'It'll probably be their downfall.'

He grinned, or tried to, pushed himself back in his chair, reached his arm behind him and pulled out a bottle. His grin went lopsided. 'But I've got some of this.' His accent had taken on a Southern drawl. It was Wild Turkey Bourbon. Dr Morse was reverting to type.

'Bit early for me,' I said.

'It's still morning, is it?' He spoke without any great interest and poured a drink in a none too clean glass he found somewhere, the same murky place he'd found the bottle. He was too busy going to pieces to take much notice of the time of day.

'Go on,' I said.

'Because of you, and your little enquiry into number 54 Odds Avenue, she hit a company called Golden Fleece.'

'I wish to God I'd never put her onto that.'

'I wish to God for lots of things.' He took a slug. 'Like, I wish I'd never come to this godforsaken piss-arse little country.'

'What happened when she hit Golden Fleece?'

'Big puzzle. It had no public profile. It looked more like a front or holding company. It cultivated obscurity. It was hardly on the radar, yet it had a highly developed IT system and some very gooey code.'

'Gooey?'

'Advanced. Sophisticated. The high end of the high end. The bleeding edge of the bleeding edge. And of course Velvet had to have some of it, didn't she? Had to get her sticky fingers in there. Couldn't leave well enough alone.'

'Could she identify any of the code?'

'Ah, here's where it gets spooky, Mr Spookman.' He was lying back lazily in his chair, his glass held on his belly. 'You sure you won't have that drink? You look like you could use one.' He swilled his around. 'Jesus, this is vile stuff.' Swilled some down.

'You were talking about the code.'

'Keeping me on track, are we? Yes. There wasn't enough of it for her to tell, but she speculated that it belonged to some kind of weapon system.'

'What kind of weapon?'

He waved his glass in the air. 'Couldn't tell. Something to do with communication systems, probably. A jamming device. I don't know. Her presence was… detected.'

'What did she do?'

'Grabbed some code and ran. It was too late by then, of course.'

'The bloodhound.'

'The fucking bloodhound. Followed her right through the darknet and smack into the university computer system. Flasheroo!'

'What was your involvement?'

'Me? Ahh, buddy 'ol buddy, I was the patsy. I distributed her code in tiny bits through the uni network so it couldn't be found. Big joke.'

'Do you think Golden Fleece took it down?'

'You know, I've got a funny *feeling* about that.' Apparently the feeling was funny enough to warrant another shot. 'Could have been taken down from anywhere in the world of course, but I think it was local.' He nodded as if I should find that of great significance. 'Think about it. Just the local broadband would do it.'

'How much did you tell the police?'

He gave me a bourbon-filled grin. 'As little as possible, buddy, you can bet your Chinese-made gumboots on that.'

'Why did Velvet go back to the university that night?'

'That's the big question. That trailer-trash woman came around that morning. Early. I dunno.'

I felt obscurely insulted on Queenie's behalf. Whatever she was, she wasn't trailer-trash. 'How early?' I remembered Elvis saying that Velvet had turned up to work that morning early but had not clocked on for an hour.

'About eight o'clock. I wouldn't've thought that women would even be alive at that hour.'

'But you don't know why she came?'

'To give her something. Fucked if I know what.'

That would be the memory stick, urgent delivery. The mystery of what was on that stick deepened, especially as Velvet kept the existence of it secret from her lover boy.

'What happened then?'

'When?' Lover boy was starting to lose track. The morning's bourbon was catching up with him.

'After Queenie came?'

'Velvet took off for work. Didn't stop to finish her coffee. Said something about beating the morning rush.'

'And you didn't know what that was all about?'

'Velvet only told me what she wanted me to know. There was plenty going on she kept from me.' He didn't try to keep the bourbon bitterness out of his voice. 'There was other stuff going on besides the weapon.'

'But you didn't know what it was?'

He drank the cup dry and yawned. 'I didn't know jack shit,' he said.

47

I'd just had my second cup of tea, and given Monckton a few extra biscuits to indulge him, when the doorbell rang. Never a dull moment, I thought. This will be the goons looking for the dossier. Finally.

I was wrong. It was Blue.

Gone was the easy-going, blonde-hair-swinging, hipster-wearing Australian Bondi-beach babe with the wide Mary Travis smile. In her place stood Miss Immaculate. A corporate executive with blonde hair almost severely styled off her face and neatly stacked on the back of her head in a chignon. She had a lilac-white blouse under a sharply cut dark-grey jacket, a matching skirt, moderately tight, reaching her knees. Stunning, as always, but this time stunningly svelte. And there wasn't a smile in sight. Those easy-going lips couldn't help but be curved, nor could her eyes stop being that stark-naked blue, but the expression was cool, almost official. And she was poised, quite elegantly, as if at a cocktail party.

'Aren't you going to invite me in?' she asked. Her voice had lost all traces of any Australian twang.

'I'm not supposed to have anything to do with you. Mr Wang's orders.'

'Things have changed.'

I waited for her to elaborate, but she didn't. I looked around for any sign of Wang's boys, the cops, Golden Fleece, the Blue Army, Uncle Tom Cobbly and all, but saw nothing out of the ordinary. Except this woman.

'I have a confession to make,' she said, when we were inside.

'They say it's good for the soul,' I said as lightly as I could.

She was holding herself steady. Calm, collected and watchful. Is she packing? I asked Jack. Not guns, Jack said.

'I'm very sorry to have caused you stress and tension, Jason. I believe you were abducted by Mr Wang. That was unfortunate.'

'I thought so. Although the ninja makes a lovely tea. Have you met him? Quiet fellow. Quicker than a cat. My cat anyway.' I stroked Monckton's head with my toe.

She didn't smile, but rather regarded me with great seriousness. Corny I know, but I felt as if she looked right into me, right to the other side of me and back again. Her lack of pretence unnerved me – maybe this was the real Blue I was seeing now.

'Jason, I was the one who put those documents in your computer.'

'Why?'

'You know the old joke. If I told you I'd have to kill you. Or, more likely, someone else would have to kill you.'

Yes, like they had to kill Velvet, I wanted to say, but held my peace.

'I wanted to implicate you.'

'Why?'

'For my own purposes.'

'Are you engaged in espionage?'

'You could see it that way.'

'How do you see it?'

'Meilin has told you that I work for an organisation in China.'

'Yes, but he didn't say its name.'

'This organisation has no name.'

'That's very deep.'

'My primary directive is to protect and guide Sparta, and I have full powers to do anything I see fit to achieve that object. Powers which I am about to exercise.' She spoke with a certain grim formality.

I waited.

'Jason, I have a favour I want to ask of you.'

'It'll cost you.'

A slight surprise registered. 'How much?'

'Tell me your favour and I'll tell you my price.'

She hesitated, and I figured that like everyone else I'd met lately, she was sorting out how much to tell me. I think she decided on the blunt approach.

'I would like you, Mr Argonaut, to accompany Sparta on a plane trip to an overseas destination.' She sounded like a travel-agent being super-efficient.

'What happened to Jason? It's Mr Argonaut now is it?'

Suddenly, like a bolt of sunlight out of a rainy day, she smiled. It was a power smile that slammed me into the back of my chair. It was Blue, and the Blue I knew.

'Fuck it,' she said, 'I was so nervous coming to ask you this.' A bit of Australian twang crept in.

'You, nervous?' I doubted it, but who knows? What I thought I was seeing was an uneasy shift between personas.

'Yes. Because while every precaution will be taken, it could be dangerous, and I don't know if I have the right to put you in a dangerous situation.'

I thought about that. To the heroes of fiction, like Jack Reacher, the promise of a dangerous situation is a red rag to a bull. Let nothing stand in the way of their pursuit of virtue! But I was no hero. I could scramble over fences to get away from pursuers and hold my own when kidnapped, but I was, or at least was trying to be, a careful old man, and I had no wish to get myself killed. And if not for Velvet then why for Sparta?

'I think you have already put me in a dangerous situation,' I said, all quiet dignity.

'Exactly. On balance, it may be more dangerous for you to stay than to go.' What a struggle just to stay at home. First Velvet had tried to scare me out, then Marcia, and now Blue.

'Go where?'

'Australia.'

'Why Australia?'

Her eyelids quivered for a moment. 'I believe you have family there, in Melbourne. You going there is perfectly natural.' For a moment I wondered if she knew about Marcia's dossier.

'You're well informed.'

'I have to be. Sparta is at stake.' She spoke with great intensity, as if she could implant her primary directive into my gullible mind. 'The situation at number 54 is becoming untenable. The place is starting to draw attention. I have to get Sparta out, quietly and fast.'

'Won't it look as obvious as all hell? Me and Sparta travelling together?' Didn't sound like much of a plan to me.

'Best I could do at the last minute. I can't buy tickets online. None of us here can make any move. You'll buy the tickets. We'll get Sparta to the airport. You'll sit in separate seats. In Melbourne you will just happen to be waiting for your suitcase at the same time as Sparta. You will walk together, as if coincidentally, to the taxi stand. A taxi will pull up and you and Sparta will be whisked away to a safe house. I will join you there in a couple of days.'

I could see the logic. It got both me and Sparta out of the way in one stroke. Made sense if some big shit was heading for the fan.

'You've got it all worked out. But it sounds implausible to me. With all the resources at your command, this organization that has no name, you could surely lift Sparta out of here without recourse to using the old geezer next door as a cover. Just drop the word in the Boss Man's ear.'

'Yes, we could lift Sparta out of here, but we are caught in the same paradox that led to the number 54 operation in the first place. The more security I provide, the bigger the operation I mount, the more obvious it becomes, the less secure it is. Getting you and Sparta out of here is about the limit of what I could do without tipping my hand. Even the Boss Man won't know about this, and he would expect that of me. There are those waiting for me to make a move. Handing Sparta into your care is the last thing they're going to think of.'

'Is somebody after Sparta?'

'At the moment they know where she is. As soon as she jumps they'll be after her all right. My guess is they'll try to provoke us into fleeing, prod us with a stick to see what we do. I want to move first.'

'Who are *they*? Golden Fleece? Aunty Wu?' She showed no surprise that I knew of Golden Fleece.

'Meilin told you there were factions at work here. I can't tell you more than that.'

'What about the old Vampire? What does he think?'

She grinned mischievously. 'This was his idea.'

His idea of a joke, I thought as I made tea. The old Vamp was a real genius. I fussed in the kitchen to give myself time to think.

'What about Sparta? What does she think?'

'She thinks it's a great idea. She likes you. She thinks you're a nice man.'

'She doesn't know me very well.'

'I realize that.'

We both laughed.

'Well,' she said, as I delivered the tea, 'what do you think?'

'I think lots of things.' For a start, the dossier. I couldn't take it with me. And if I left it, it certainly wouldn't be here when I got back. There was no such thing as a foolproof hiding place; any cubby-hole I could think of, somebody else could think of. Then there was the small matter of the police, what Elvis would make of my sudden departure.

'You haven't heard my price,' I said.

She looked at me expectantly.

'Someone must look after my cat.'

A little smile played around her lips. 'That's a high price.'

'And I want to know things.'

She kept her naked blue eyes nailed to my face.

'Like what?'

'I want to know about the old man. Where does he fit in? Meilin would tell me nothing.'

'The old man really is Sparta's grandfather. In China he has enormous… what's your New Zealand word… *mana*. Prestige, status. He's like…' It was unlike Blue to be stuck for words.

'A Godfather?'

'No, not as in Mafia, but yes, as in god father.'

'You're losing me.'

'Okay. He is revered as a something of a saint. He is a martial arts expert of legendary power.'

'*Chi.*'

'Yes. He was in on the plan to bring Sparta to New Zealand. And he insisted on coming, even though he had never left China. The Boss Man tried to talk him out of it. That's it, really.'

Really?

'Why didn't Meilin just tell me that?'

'Because it's a family matter. Meilin was just being careful.'

It didn't feel as if I'd paid been paid my price. Or I'd been severely short changed.

'Ok. Now what are these international events that Meilin alluded to?'

She was about to answer when the doorbell rang. For a moment we looked at each other like a couple of conspirators about to be outed.

48

A thirtyish man in a pin-striped suit stood before me. He had lawyer written all over him.

'My name is Harry Dogbane Jnr,' he said. 'I work with your daughter.' He was blinking against the hard sunlight like a man who had forgotten his dark glasses, and he had the pale haggard face of the terminally tired. Ah, so this was a family affair, son destroying father, for this was surely the mysterious colleague calling for his dossier.

I showed a polite interest.

'I'm sorry to bother you, but can I come in? There's a matter I need to discuss.'

'It's not a very convenient time.'

'I'm very sorry, but it's urgent.'

It didn't look like he was going to go away.

'Okay,' I said. Let the good times roll.

No sign of Blue when we got inside. I ushered Mr Dogbane Jnr to a chair, the very same that Blue must have just vacated, but he remained standing. Stiff and awkward, but stubbornly so. Before he could open his mouth I held up my hand like a cop stopping traffic. The last thing I wanted was Blue listening in to this conversation.

'Ah… Blue!' I called. From the bathroom there came the sound of running water that soon shut off, and Blue appeared. Mr Harry Dogbane looked at her once. Then twice. Then he looked at me. I smiled.

'Hi,' Blue said.

'Hi,' Harry Dogbane said weakly.

'I was just leaving,' Blue said as she tripped towards the door.

'I'm sorry we couldn't finish our conversation,' I said to her.

'That's okay. Later maybe.'

'Yes, later.'

As I showed her out I said, 'Oh, and about your niece.'

'Yes?'

'Say hello.'

Blue nodded and smiled. She understood. I'd like to think that she was grateful.

'I hope I didn't interrupt anything,' he said when I turned to him.

'You did.'

'Sorry.' Looking at him I thought of his name. Bitterroot. Looked like he'd been sucking on some.

'How can I help?' I didn't feel like offering him a cup of tea. I wasn't comfortable with him in the house at all.

'It's very urgent that I get hold of Marcia.'

I considered pretending not to know that Marcia had left town, but decided against it. A good liar only tells necessary lies. Besides, he'd probably heard from the police that Marcia visited me before going to Melbourne. Haggis would have been delighted to tell him.

'I've already spoken to the police,' I said.

'I know. But I had to come on the off-chance…'

'I don't know where she is.'

'Maybe she left some clue?'

'She said she might get a camperwagon and do a bit a sightseeing. With the boys,' It sounded like a likely story to me, so I smiled at him, as if at the peculiarities of women, but he didn't seem to notice.

'Has she been in touch? Sent a text or anything?'

'No, but I don't expect her to. She's got her own life to lead. She hates the idea of checking in with Dad all the time.' I smiled again. A you-know-how-it-is smile, but again he didn't seem to notice. Maybe he didn't know how it was.

He turned a wan face to the room as if he might magically spy what he was looking for. What was in fact very close. 'Before she left, did she leave anything with you? I'm looking for a folder with some legal papers.'

'No, I'm sorry. She never involved me in her work. I don't think she wanted me meddling.'

I tried a variation of the previous two smiles with no greater success.

He stood in the middle of the room, helpless, apparently unable to move forward or back. Like he'd reached the end of the line. The end of his tether. I didn't say anything to put him out of his misery, but I didn't feel like a great hero either, putting on my silly old man act, lying to his face; after all, he hadn't done much wrong except sit on evidence until it was too late. He'd tried to play a smart hand and had outsmarted himself. Happens every day.

When, finally, he found the power of movement, and he'd dragged himself to the door, he turned for one last desperate throw. 'You said she was getting a camperwagon, did she mention any destinations?'

'I think she said she'd go west, from Melbourne,' I said that in a hopeful voice, as if it might be some use to him.

He gave me a look, as if he were onto me, but I don't think he was. He was at a point beyond exhaustion where he didn't know what to think. He gave me his card. 'If you hear from her, please let me know.'

'I will.'

I waited for him to depart, but he didn't. Trying to sound casual in a deadly way, he said, 'You know, your daughter could lose more than just her job over this.'

'What do you mean?' I asked. The right thing to say would have been, is that a threat? But I don't always get my clichés right.

'Just think about it,' he said, and walked off with dragging steps.

I thought about it and then went back inside. Blue was sitting on the couch, Monckton purring in her lap. If cats can smile, he was smiling.

'How the hell did you get back in?'

'Through the back door.' She gave me an insouciant smile.

'But I locked the door.' I certainly had. Right after hiding the dossier.

Her smile widened.

So much bloody smiling. 'So as well as being able to speak several languages fluently you can pick locks as well. Or walk through walls.'

'I've had a wide education.'

I was going to stand on my dignity and not sit down. Then I flopped down into my chair. It wasn't even lunchtime yet and I was totally exhausted.

'I'm not staying. Jason, I want to thank you for agreeing to this, and I want to assure you that Marcia's dossier is not a problem.'

'Not a problem,' I repeated mechanically. I wasn't surprised that this astonishing young woman knew about the dossier. While I knew nothing about anybody, everybody knew everything about me.

'The people who rlly matter know where it is.'

'Golden Fleece?'

She neither confirmed nor denied. 'It suits them to leave it at your place. It's out of the way and they can pick it up any time they want.'

Of course. Silly me. It was as good as in their top drawer.

Ditching Monckton, she stood up and looked at me with gratitude. 'You're a good man,' she said softly. I couldn't quite put my finger on the emotion in her voice.

'You can't just leave it there,' I said, creaking to my feet. 'You haven't met my price. I want to know about Aunty Wu, and Golden Fleece. And I want to know why Velvet used the term 'Operation Golden Fleece' and how Velvet was involved in all this, and…'

She put up her hand to forestall me. 'I don't have all the answers, you know how it works, and some things I do know I can't tell you.'

Right. I knew how it worked. Either I was going to do this or I was going to pull my head in.

We stood looking at each other. The beautiful young woman and the silly old man.

'Then you owe me a song,' I said.

'You'll get it,' she said. Again, that same unidentified emotion underpinning her voice.

I saw her to the door. I was feeling pretty emotional myself, although I wasn't quite sure what I was feeling.

49

If I'd known the shit storm about to break, I wouldn't have tossed myself down on my bed, rejected Monckton's advances – sleeping on my bed was one of his rarest privileges, at least when I was around – and tried to think my way through this. It was a useless endeavour. As my dear old mother used to say, I couldn't think my way out of a paper bag. Everything kept getting jumbled up and swirled around. If I were to draw one of those diagrams you see movie detectives drawing to try to sort out their thoughts, with names and circles and arrows, I'd have those names, circles and arrows flying in all directions. It was enough to make me nauseous. 'Thinkin' ain't doin' me no good,' I said to Monckton, who was indifferent. It was not a problem he'd run into.

My stirred-up mind would not stay on task, and kept straying back through the decades, mostly to those five halcyon years I'd spent with Anna back in the day. And they had been halcyon years, not rose-tinged by memory, merely sepia-tinged by time. I'd been happily busy making my name as a journalist, while the birth of Marcia had been a joy to us both. We were living the life! Those five years floated free from the debris of memory and presented themselves as exemplary: that's what life can be like. Despite the pleasure those memories gave me, I seldom indulged them because that happy-ever-after tale ended in the great black hole of Anna's illness, the terrible wasting effect of dengue fever, and in that darkness brooded the dragons of despair and hopelessness.

My memories of the years since the death of Anna had a peculiar monochrome quality. After a bit of a wobble and a year that vanished into its own black hole, my career resumed – but all the colours and highlights had gone. Before she died, Anna, with all her wonderful generosity of spirit, urged me to take another wife, a woman who could love me and be a good stepmum for Marcia. Remembering her saying that, while wan and dying in her hospital bed, still gets me crying. But I never had the heart for re-marrying. That heart I'd put into bringing up Marcia. A few women had hovered but none made an impression. Eventually I adopted Monckton and settled into confirmed widower-hood.

And what had stirred all this up? *Blue*. The first woman since Anna to interest me. Fascinated would be a better word. Unobtainable, of course. But who aroused in me unfamiliar feelings, like wishing I were thirty (or so) years younger when I would have given her a run for her money. Useless feelings like that. Here I was, after all these years, a man whose heart could be bought for a song.

Blue really had me over the proverbial barrel. She knew I

wouldn't be able to resist the chance of connecting with Marcia and the boys again.

Over a late lunch my mind finally settled on figuring out some practicalities. I'd have to make some arrangements for Monckton, take him to a holiday home for cats. I couldn't be sure that Blue would be able to fulfill her promise. He'd be offended, but he'd get over it. With a rather hollow feeling I realized that with Velvet gone there was no one I felt comfortable asking to pop over and feed him. And the cops, I mustn't forget the cops. It was tempting to just skip out from under, but Elvis and Haggis would be distinctly unimpressed. A person of interest in two murder cases, and an espionage case, does a runner. Best to contact Elvis, concoct a story about my daughter needing me for a few days in Melbourne. Then there was Eddie the editor. He wouldn't go on paying me, not even Scoop his ol' reliable, for not working; you can only string Eddie along for so long. But he might be tempted. I'd tell him I was on the track of the story of the century – which, perhaps, in some weird way I was – and maybe wheedle a couple of weeks, maybe take a pay hit. I didn't spend much, didn't drink (much) or smoke, and Monckton wasn't a big eater except in his own eyes. I had a bit of money stashed away for a rainy day.

I made a list.

You do have another course of action open to you, Jack Reacher said. Grab your bankcard and jump a bus out of Dodge now. I looked around at my stuff in confusion. The world can certainly slow you down.

The doorbell rang its trivial chimes and, true to form, the next plot development arrived in all its glory. There are disadvantages to having the world come to your door, which was why Jack Reacher never stays too long behind one, except with guns drawn – you never knew who might come through.

Blue and Sparta came through mine, and fast, both dressed in loose track pants and tops and expensive trainers like a couple off to the gym. Blue's hair was pulled back in a simple ponytail. They were both in a state of hyper alertness. Not agitated or tense, but simply fully *there*, fully functional and missing nothing.

'Change of plan,' Blue said. 'No time. We have to get Sparta out *now*.'

I barely missed a heartbeat. 'Okay,' I said.

I was already doing it, grabbing my passport, my wallet, my jacket, my fucking useless mobile. Blue gave me another mobile. 'Ring the loaded number to get me. Don't use it for any other calls.' I thought about packing a bag with a few clothes, toothbrush and stuff. How about bringing your hardback copy of *War and Peace?* Jack Reacher said.

There was a boy-racer squealing of tires. A vehicle turning fast into laid-back Odds Avenue.

'Too late,' Blue said tersely to Sparta, producing another cell phone. Yet, even when we heard gunfire in the street neither of them panicked. Their movements became very economical and calm. 'Number fifty-four,' I said out loud. The impacts came like somebody knocking far too hard on the door next-door. Handguns, Jack observed. I thought of Reggie and the old Vamp.

Blue was fingering her mobile and letting off a stream of Mandarin to Sparta who was bouncing lightly back and forth on her toes as if warming up before a game. Blue's telling her to go out the back way, Jack said. You understand Chinese now, Jack? It's the same in every language, Jack said.

'A car will pick you up from Taraire St.' Blue said, shoving a roll of money into my pocket. 'Go to the airport and get the first plane to anywhere. Then do it again, get the first plane out, then go on to Melbourne. You'll travel together, no time for ruses. I'll follow in a couple of days. Use the phone when you get somewhere.'

The gunfire stopped and there was a squeal of tires again as the car did a u-turn.

Blue was already running upstairs with a not unhappy Monckton in her arms.

'Enjoy yourself,' she said over her shoulder.

Sparta had me by the hand and was dancing me to the back door. 'Don't worry Grandad,' she said, 'you're used to getting over fences now. You've got form.'

The gunfire started up again as we went through the back door. Immediately the handgun firing was joined by a deeper solid thudding. Someone in the house was firing back. 50 calibre machine-gun, Jack said. That'll make a mess of the car. It did. As we approached the fence, I looked back and saw the car through the gap between the fence and house. An old tan Holden station-wagon, silver holes opening up along the front and back doors like metal flowers. Then a great black billow of smoke went up as the Holden exploded. Sparta went over the fence in a couple of swift movements. I scrambled up behind her in my ungainly way, opening a few not so old protesting wounds. 'You're getting good at this,' Sparta said brightly.

Already, the distant wail of sirens.

We were in the back yard of what I guessed to be number 65 Taraire St. There was no one around. Muffled silence lay over the neighbourhood. We ran for Taraire St. Or at least Sparta did. On the street people were coming out of their houses to look at each other and reassure each other that the world was still there. Mostly women with children, but a few oldies too. No one paid us much attention.

An ordinary looking taxi pulled up and we got in. Easy peasy. The taxi pulled smoothly away. Piece of cake.

I kept my voice low so the driver couldn't hear. 'Do you know who they were? The guys in the car?' More like corpses in the wreck now.

Her answer knocked me over. 'The family of your old girlfriend, the one who died.'

I tried to figure the why and the how. A revenge attack? Had the bros thought that those living at number 54 were responsible for the deaths of Velvet and Johnny Watch? How had they made that connection? I tried Sparta with the question.

'They were used by Aunty Wu,' the girl said simply. She didn't have to spell it out. I could see it. After the bizarre death of Johnny Watch the feelers would have been going out all over bro-land, every Asian connection tested. They get a result. A skilled agent approaches them, pours a little poison into their ears, provides a little 'proof', wins their confidence, stirs their rage which would hardly need stirring and… Bob's your uncle. Very neat. I thought of Hiko. He might have been in that car. I never got to know him that well, but, damn it, I liked the guy.

'Did Aunty Wu want to kill you all?' I asked Sparta, who looked quite shocked at the suggestion.

'Oh no, she just wanted to flush us out. Out of number 54.'

Real killers would have busted into the house and done the job properly, I thought. I was starting to think like Jack Reacher.

'Why would Aunty Wu do that?'

'She has plans of her own.'

Which was all I'd ever learned. The same phrase.

'Who was firing the heavy machine gun?'

'That would be Reggie,' she said. 'He's got a bit of a temper.'

We travelled on in silence for a while. Sparta was still in that state of hyper-alertness that required something more than calm, but which mimicked calm. I was nowhere near calm.

'What about the old man, what would he do? Climb into his coffin?'

'Yes. While the shooting lasted. He doesn't like guns.'

'What'll he and Blue tell the cops?'

It was a silly question, and I knew the answer before she said it. By the time the cops got there the house would be empty. Maybe just a fancy coffin left behind.

'We're on our own now, Grandad,' Sparta said.

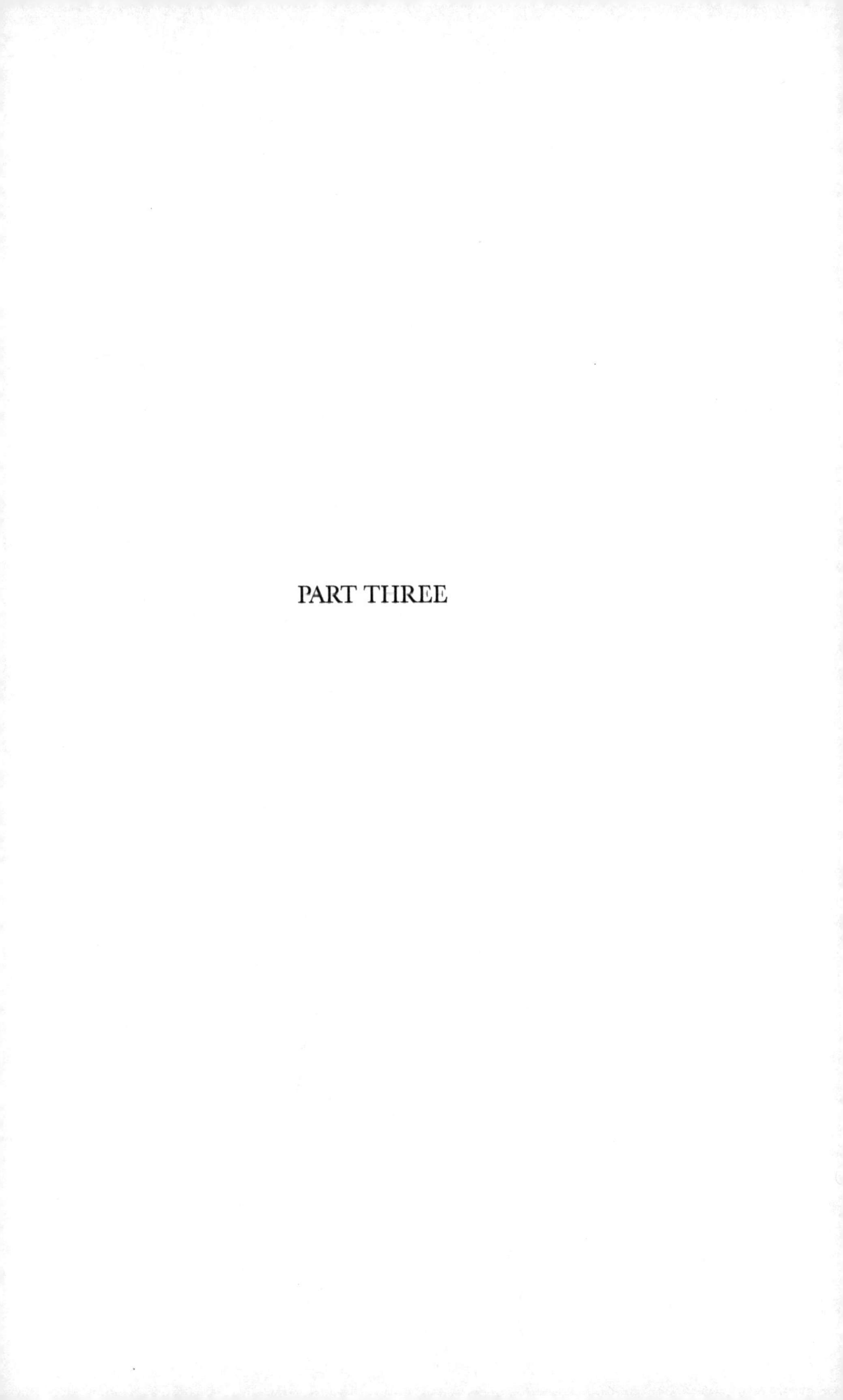

PART THREE

50

If I expected Madam Wu to make a move at the airport to prevent Sparta from leaving, I was disappointed. Which meant that Blue's gamble had paid off. Aunty Wu hadn't guessed that Blue would let herself be parted from Sparta, and if she did, the idea of hooking Sparta up with me would be the last on her list. Whatever Blue was doing now, drawing the heat away from us would be her purpose. Laying a false trail.

There was nothing alarming about the usual airport bustle, no heavies heading in our direction, no suspect guys in coats hiding behind newspapers. No one gave us so much as a second glance. It was amazing how Sparta instantly blended in, just another Asian kid; you'd have to be trying pretty hard to notice her. Old people too wear a certain anonymity. Who am I? Nobody, some old guy. We made a good pair. I was half expecting to see Elvis and Haggis, but they would have their hands full at Odds Avenue. By the time they came looking for me, I'd be gone. The first likely flight out with spare seats was to Bangkok, leaving in twenty minutes.

The first order of business was to get ourselves some plausible looking luggage. Jack Reacher's travel-with-no-more-than-the-shirt-on-your-back advice doesn't hold for airports. When it comes to airlines, you can travel too light. Sparta took some of Blue's roll and went off to buy stuff for both of us while I wandered into the bookshop to see if they were selling *War and Peace*. They weren't, and I'd already read the latest Jack Reacher novel. In the end, I settled for a *Scientific American* and a *New Scientist*. I could sit on the plane and pretend to work.

So we looked normal, with bags and everything, but we still drew the attention of a woman who was dressed like a flight attendant but might have been something else, standing behind the guy checking in the luggage and looking over the passports. Sparta, who had a handy pouch slung around her neck under her top, produced a New Zealand passport.

The woman drifted over.

'Excuse me,' she said, 'are you two travelling together?'

She was giving us what you'd have to call a hard look. Obviously our blending-in didn't work for this woman, who might have been half-Samoan, half wild card.

'Yes.'

'And you are going to Bangkok?' She held out her hand for our passports. She took her time studying them. At the same time she was covertly watching Sparta, who was watching her with earnest innocence. It wasn't hard to figure what was going on in the woman's trained, alert mind.

'How long are you staying?' She gave my passport to the guy at the computer who did what I guessed was a police check on my number.

'A few days.' Tell 'em nothing.

She was looking through our bags now. She must have seen that everything, toiletries, t-shirts and all, were just off the shelf.

'Do you work Mr Argonaut? Your passport says 'writer'.'

'I write for a living,' I said modestly. 'I'm a journalist.'

'Journalist,' she said, somehow making it rhyme with pimp, politician and paedophile.

This officious woman was pissing me off; she certainly wasn't a flight attendant, they were far more polite.

'There are a few of us left who haven't been jailed or shot or, worse, sucked into PR,' I said. She did not look reassured. Easy up trooper, Jack said. This one could turn nasty on you.

'And what's your business in Bangkok?'

'Who are you?'

Sparta stepped in to save the deteriorating situation.

'Don't yous worry about him, miss,' Sparta said with a South Auckland intonation. 'We's jus' goin' for a couple of days t' see my Chinese whanau.'

'So who's this man?' the woman asked her, gesturing to me as if I were a nearby shit-streaked statue.

'He's me uncle. He's alright. Just gets grumpy, like an old man, but he won't cause no trouble, miss, honest. The worst I seen him do is kick the cat.'

I gave the woman my best avuncular, cat-kicking grin.

The woman glanced at the man's computer. Apparently my number came up clean.

'She's lying,' I said. 'I have never kicked the cat. Monckton would leave home if I did that.'

The woman and the computer guy exchanged glances.

Then the woman grinned, and with that grin we were in.

What followed was a tedious nightmare of cramped seats, plastic food, banal magazines, shithouse movies, overpriced booze, a distinct lack of quality green-tea, and so many faked smiles you could have opened a happy shop. I'd have sold my soul to the devil for a patch of green grass, the feel of sand under my feet or a copy of *War and Peace* in my hands. No wonder Scoop chose to focus on research and work from home, and if Grandfather Detective was going to start flying all over the show, airport after airport, I would have to review my personas. Maybe Grandfather Retired.

Sparta didn't have any such problems. She moved through all that, confident and unnoticeable, as if planes and airports were her natural element. And maybe they were. What did I know about the life of this girl I was travelling with? And who was doing a good job of looking after me, steering me down the right tubes, through the correct turnstiles, and in the direction of airport officials who really wanted to see me to make their day? There was no question as to who was in charge. The only thing I was useful for was buying tickets and putting a plausible front on things. Sparta was too young to buy tickets or travel alone.

'Bangkok, a major regional force in finance and business,' I read on the plane as we were coming into land. 'The most visited city in MasterCard's Global Destination Cities Index,' and while I was there I had to make sure that I saw the historic Grand Palace and

Buddhist temples at Wat Arun and Wat Pho, grandly known as the Temple of Dawn and the Temple of the Sleeping Buddha and take time to admire the city's wonderful, mostly elevated expressway network.

We didn't do any of those things, or any of the other things suggested in the tourist guides, like visiting the nightlife scenes of Khao San Road and Patpong like all the other *farang*. Rather Sparta, with the surety of someone who knows where they are going, got us on the famous expressway and to a place out of the city a bit called Chatuchak. The suburb boasted, I read from more tourist brochures, the worlds largest weekend market, attracting visitors from all over the world, which was probably why Sparta chose it as a hide-out for a couple of days. The brochures didn't say anything about the worlds largest traffic jam. Away from the main drag, she found a run-down looking joint, run by a sweaty fat man, that still managed to qualify as three star accommodation.

We holed-up in this dive, hardly showing our faces. Sparta behaved as if Madam Wu had spies behind every garish billboard. There were plenty of grey hair and white faces around but Sparta insisted that I stay inside the little hole they called a room like a criminal on the run while she, dressed invisibly in local garb, slipped out from time to time on mysterious errands. I didn't even get to see the famous market. The best part of that was the food she brought back, food with fantastic names like *kaeng phet pet yang*, roast duck in red curry.

Our little idyll didn't last long. Soon we were back on the wonderland expressway to the airport.

'I thought we were staying longer,' I said as we watched the city flash past below, looking a bit like scenes from Blade Runner. A few years back the city suffered floods bad enough to get their prime minister talking about climate change, and repair work was still going on. It would probably go on forever.

'We were,' she said, not at her most communicative.

'So what's going on?'

'We have to keep moving.'

And we did.

Next stop, Kuala Lumpur, complete with its own futuristic twin towers called the Petronas Twin Towers.

I didn't bother with the PR guff this time. Scoop had been here before on the trail of people smugglers, most of their desperate clients being climate-change refugees. It wasn't a city I had a great affection for.

As soon as we cleared the airport Sparta had us in a taxi heading for the nearby suburb of Sepang. 'What are we doing going there?' I asked her. Nothing there but a dirty great German built race track for the Formula One Malaysian Grand Prix. As she explained it, we'd take one of the tourist hotels near the racetrack where, once again, I wouldn't be too noticeable despite it being the off-season with no races going on. There would still be few Westerners around; the famous track was a tourist attraction in itself. Sepang also had the advantage of being close to the airport but in the other direction from the central city, which we could thus avoid. We'd hole up for a couple of days.

That was the plan, and a good one, I thought, given the haste and improvised nature of this flight. We got to Sepang, booked into one of the smaller, less conspicuous hotels and I got myself ready for a couple of days of sheer boredom. I'd exhausted the joys of *Scientific American* and *New Scientist* and only had the previous weeks *Guardian*, quickly scooped up at the airport, for company.

Early on the first evening Sparta slipped out, instructing me to once more stay in the room and not show my face. I felt as if I were back under guard again. I was asleep before she returned and the first I knew was the feel of her hand on my shoulder and her voice in my ear.

'Get up, Grandad, we have to go.'

'Go where?' I sat up too fast and felt horribly disoriented. I'd been dreaming about Anna.

'Airport,' she said.

'What's the time?'

'Near midnight.'

'Christ.'

'What's all this about?' I asked, as she bundled me into a waiting taxi.

'Wu's spies are around. She knows we're in Malaysia.'

'How do you know?'

'I can smell them,' she said cryptically.

I wondered how Wu was keeping track of us. Maybe she could smell us from afar.

At the airport, we avoided the international section and took a local dawn flight to Alor Setar, which could have been a nice place to stay, having that old world charm that travel brochures love so much – romantic rice paddies where happy peasants toil for fourteen hours a day – but, as they say, there is no rest for the wicked, and we stayed only long enough for us to get a flight direct to Phnom Penh, Cambodia. Once known as the 'Pearl of Asia', Phnom Penh had once been Scoop's favourite Asian city.

I was tired. More than tired, I had that stretched feeling that only travel can bring, as if I were smeared across half the planet. Smeared too thin. According to Wiki, there were a hundred and fifty-three things to do in this tropical city and I was unlikely to do any of them. Sparta chose one of the lesser hotels near the airport. It didn't feel like Cambodia, more like some mixed-up half-way house with silent inmates that came and went like ghosts.

'We can't stay here for long,' Sparta said. 'They might expect us to come here.'

The now familiar pattern established itself. I was confined to quarters with whatever reading material I could scavenge while Sparta went out on reconnaissance. I tried to sleep, but it was too hot and the ancient colonial fan in the ceiling of our room did little more than stir the stagnant air. I lay on the bed, stared at the fan and thought about Anna and dengue fever. Sparta returned in the evening with food and nothing to report. It seemed that all was quiet on the killing fields.

I hoped to make up lost sleep that night, but after eating we were back at the airport boarding a red-eye to Delhi.

We fled the rising sun.

India. Just what I needed.

We weren't stopping. Sparta announced that we wouldn't be entering India, but catching an on-flight to Perth. Ah, Delhi airport, where even the transit lounge was chaos. Blue's magic money roll ran out in Delhi and Sparta produced a credit card that worked just as well. I noticed that she wasn't entirely comfortable about using it. All this plane hopping, sky zigzagging, had its limitations in terms of making a getaway. The quaint roll of cash helped keep our profile low, but any agency capable of wiping out a university computer network would be able to trace our flea-hopping around the Pacific with horrible ease. Surely our trail would be lit up like neon to those surveillance guys.

'You are right, Grandfather,' Sparta said when, during a tedious moment in the transit lounge sitting at a plastic table, I put it to her. 'Our strategy was a last minute improvisation. It's better to be a moving target than a stationary one. And we could always get off at the next stop and disappear somewhere.'

Yes, I thought, it's called staying one jump ahead of the posse, at least that's what my father called it, and he had lots of practice. I looked out the large windows of the airport to where India had to be. I thought of my own bed, Monckton's skeptical face, quiet little Odds Avenue, Eddie the editor chewing the end of a cellphone, and wondered if I'd ever get back in one piece. This escaping on the run could push us out on a limb rather than land us in safety. Look at what happened to those two handsome young bastards Butch Cassidy and the Sundance Kid. From raindrops falling on their heads to total wipe-out in a dusty little Mexican town.

51

The fun started at Perth, good old drought-stricken Perth. Sparta chatted away to me in a fair dinkum Ocker accent all the way through officialdom about how good it was to be back home in good old Aussie-land, charming us through, jumping from one topic of conversation to another like an agitated joey. '… and Uncle Wang and Aunty Wu will be meeting us in Melbourne, won't they Grandad? And all the cuzzies. I bet they've brought pressies for me…'

'Do you live in Australia?' The smiling customs cop said. That big smile looked like he was welcoming these weary travelers to these hospitable shores.

'Naw,' I said, 'too many Kiwis here already. Can't get away from them.'

'You keen say theet again, sport,' the cop said, giving me back my passport after a brief inspection. His attention was on Sparta. He took longer with her New Zealand passport, studying the stamps. 'You've been doing a beet of treeping about,' he commented.

He wasn't sure about us. Not sure about our hasty flitting in and out of countries, which wouldn't fit any normal tourist profile. Further, he seemed to have little time for Kiwis and less for Asians, especially Kiwi Asians with Ocker accents.

Sparta was waving her mobile at me. 'And Blue says to keep a lookout for Aunty Wu who's not quite sure what flight we're on. Good old Aunty! We don't want to miss her, you know, she doesn't know her Tuesdays from her Thursdays these days…'

'We'll find her,' I said, 'or she'll find us.'

'Is she like thees all the time?' The cop did an electronic scan of her passport.

'Tell me about it,' I said. 'She hasn't stopped all the way from Delhi. She's pretty excited about coming back and seeing the family.'

'Like a flea in a fit,' he said. 'The joys of being a grandfather, eh?' Finally I noticed that he was old enough to be one himself.

'Tell me about it,' I said, and grinned.

He didn't grin back. He gave me a look that reminded me that he was a cop and I was a suspicious character and a Kiwi to boot, probably up to no good. He studied the information leaping up on his computer screen. He evinced a mild interest in the fact that we had so little luggage, but since it wasn't a crime there wasn't much he could do.

'What's all that yabber-dabba about?' I said, after we'd cleared the last hurdle and were out the doors and into the big Western Australian sky. The air smelled of dust.

'He was going to make trouble for us, Grandad,' Sparta said. 'I made him think I lived here.'

'I thought he was quite friendly.'

'That's just a trick he plays on people.'

'To put them off their guard?'

'That's right.'

'Hot enough for you, old-mate?' A taxi driver said to me. This wasn't some jocular reference to my age, everybody was old-mate out here. And it was hot enough. There is a story told, which may be an urban myth and maybe not, about an Irishman who was not accustomed to the heat and left his dog in a car while he did some shopping. When he returned, he found that the dog had exploded. Not just died, but blew apart as if it were in a microwave.

'Change of plan, Grandad,' Sparta said. 'We buy tickets for Melbourne, but we don't fly. We go by bus.'

'They're onto us, then?'

'Yes.'

We did exactly that with due speed. For the bus trip, Sparta became Sally Ackers and I turned into Tom Maitland. We bought separate tickets and sat in separate seats and there was nothing to show that we were travelling together. Sparta gave me a different credit card to pay for my ticket. Effectively, we'd reached Perth and disappeared. That was the idea.

Blurry-eyed and stumbling, I got onto the bus, feeling like an old man with a three-day bus trip to face. Sparta was as fresh and alert as ever, as if she'd just got up after a beautiful night's sleep. Half way to nowhere I conked out and a good chunk of Aussieland passed me by, which is not hard when there is so much of the same. When I came-to the bus had stopped somewhere and Sparta was gently ushering me off. In the glare of the bus station lights I couldn't tell if it was day or night, or if I was coming or going.

'We'll get another bus here,' she said. And steered me in the direction of the ticket office.

'Why?'

'Because it's a random move, like airports only it's bus stations. They'd need a stack of people on the ground to track us.'

'Where are we?'

'Albany.'

'Oh Christ.'

'Why, do you know this place?'

'No, and I have no wish to. But let's find a place and get some quality shut-eye.'

'We can't stop moving, Grandfather,' Sparta said, very earnest. 'Booking in for a night anywhere will just expose us.'

So we sat for two miserable hours at the Albany bus station waiting for the next road to somewhere. The next magic bus. Or at least I sat for a miserable two hours; Sparta wasn't bothered. The one bright spot was that it turned out to be late afternoon and I was able to find a bookshop with a Henning Mankell, *Kurt Wallanger* novel, paid for with the last dregs of Blue's roll. As a detective hero, Wallanger was one of those angst ridden, weary men, obsessed and a workaholic with a fucked-up life. Nothing like Jack Reacher, the mystery man, scumbag waste disposal unit for honest folk, lighting up the hearts of young women as he goes; a sort of Johnny Appleseed of rough justice. And nothing like the indomitable Grandfather Detective who fearlessly sat at home and did lots of thinking and entertaining, and had a thing about not using gates when entering people's property. It was hard though to concentrate on the novel, what with the jet-lag and my own obsessive thought patterns. Wallanger was always, somehow, on the trail of the killer, whereas the famous GD was as far from finding Velvet's killer as he had been on day one. All he'd succeeded in doing was getting tangled up with the girl next door, suddenly finding himself in the wastes of Australia wondering what the hell he was doing there.

Sparta also bothered me. She was as much an enigma as Blue. Maybe it was her imperturbability. She had the knack of sitting for long periods of time perfectly self-contained. She never fidgeted or showed signs of restlessness. While flying she hadn't bothered with the crap movies or any other proffered distractions, but rather sat quietly and looked out the window at the passing parade of the sky. She had some deep place within herself where she was perfectly at ease. It seemed she was a child only when she needed to be, in front of people who expected it of her. She could be a child, but she could also be something else as well, something I'd never seen in a child and was rare enough in most adults.

'How old are you, Sparta?'

'Twelve.' She answered promptly, showing no sign of surprise at this unexpected question popping out after a long silence.

'Do you ever get bored?'

'No.'

I put it to her. 'You're a mystery to me. A mystery wrapped in an enigma.'

'That's what Winston Churchill said about China.'

'That's right. But how come you know that? And about Meccano?' That had always bothered me. 'You are certainly not your everyday twelve-year-old.'

She looked at me sympathetically. 'That's true, Grandfather. And I can see that you are bored so let me tell you a story.'

'I like stories. My mother used to read stories to me when I was kid.' There was a childlike quiver in my voice. Tiredness and jet-lag was making me maudlin. For a moment our roles were reversed and it felt as if I were the child and she the mother.

'You were lucky to have such a mother. Now listen. *There was and there was not* a kingdom, a secretive kingdom, into which a princess was born. So important was the princess that her mother, while still carrying her, was spirited away to a small satellite kingdom, which was even more secretive, to give birth. Only a very few knew that the baby girl had been born. But this was no pampered princess, Grandad. From the day she was born, she was subjected to the most rigorous training and education. She had access to the best teachers the kingdom could find in all the fields of science and art, many of whom did not know who she really was, taking her for the daughter of a rich merchant. Luckily, the princess was healthy, strong, had a ready mind and became adept in several fields at a very early age.'

'Did this little princess have friends to play with, bring home for a sleepover, to giggle and be stupid with?'

She grinned like a real twelve-year-old. 'Not quite, but every effort was made to balance training with open time, and yes, she was supplied with friends, but had little time for most them. She had no interest in playing dolls. What she liked were the survival games. They would helicopter her into some wild place, put her down with just a knife, and she would have to journey some distance over two days and two nights to a rendezvous point where the helicopter would come and pick her up.'

'What if she wasn't there?'

'The helicopter would come back in another two days.'

'How old was she when she played this little game?' Call it, abandon the child in the wild.

'They started when she was five, in easier places, but by the time she was nine she was negotiating difficult terrain.'

'Did she like it?'

'It was training. But she enjoyed every opportunity she had to get away from the satellite kingdom's palace and learned to love the wild. Sometimes she would miss a rendezvous with the helicopter just to spend two more days. She learned how to befriend the animals and birds. When she was eight the game changed and she was hunted in the wild by men who had orders to kill her. It was fun for her avoiding them. She didn't have to kill them, which wasn't so bad. They shifted her to a city, where again she would be pursued. She had to run and hide and make swift decisions.'

'Would her pursuers really have killed her?'

'If they got the chance.'

'Would her minders have let her be killed?'

'The way situations developed was not always under their control. Sometimes she had to really kill people to get away.'

'Shit.'

'Sometimes she was the hunter and had to track someone down and kill them.'

'Really kill them?'

'Sometimes. And sometimes they would track her.'

'Who were these unfortunates?'

'Murderers who volunteered. If they succeeded in killing her they would be released from prison and given special training. There were always plenty of volunteers.'

'Double shit!' I was travelling with a trained killer princess pretending to be a little girl.

'The only member of her family that visited her was her grandfather, considered to be the wisest man in the kingdom. He told her all about her history, her royal line, and of the situation in the kingdom to which she must eventually return. And one day she did return. Her grandfather came and got her and she was spirited back to the kingdom where she resumed her secretive life among many competing factions.'

'What about her mother and father?'

'They were remote figures. She lived with her grandfather. One day he introduced her to a young woman, a foreigner who'd been born amongst them, and who was almost her equal in intelligence and accomplishments, and who had a wide experience of the world beyond the kingdom. The two became friends, and the foreigner became her companion and guide. One day her grandfather told her that she would have to leave the kingdom and go into hiding in a tiny country far from the kingdom's borders, for events were taking place in the kingdom which made her situation unsafe.'

'What kind of events?'

'Politics of a baroque kind. Coming to a head. A crisis that had been building, you understand, for many hundreds of years, for the kingdom was very ancient and the factions had deep roots.'

I didn't understand, but let it pass.

'Would she ever become queen and rule the kingdom?'

'Eventually perhaps, but not in the way you might imagine. When the king of the ruling faction didn't know what to do, he would go to her grandfather for advice and instruction. So her grandfather, you might say, was the power behind the throne. The king had the appearance of power; grandfather was its substance. It is more likely that her power would be exerted that way, and that very few would ever know about it. She had met the king several times and he showed, in a subtle way - for the ways of the kingdom were infinitely subtle - due deference.

'That's why she was surprised that her grandfather was going to join her in escaping to the tiny foreign kingdom, for his place was there, behind the throne. When she explained this to him, he merely said that she should re-read the classics and try and appreciate the value of doing the unexpected. The more predictable you are, the more vulnerable you are, and she should already understand that. The green reed bends with wind whatever direction it blows from.'

'So she apologized for being a little slow on the uptake?' I asked.

'Yes, she did, for her grandfather was truly wise.'

At that psychological moment, our bus pulled up.

I said in admiration, 'You're a great story teller, Sparta. You can even arrange the bus to arrive to interrupt the story and provide a cliffhanger. Wonderful.'

'Oh, that's pretty much the story. The cliffhanger is now.'

52

On the next leg of our interminable journey we hardly spoke a word. There were too many people around for the kind of conversation we might have had, so we said nothing. It struck me that Sparta never got bored, no matter how boring the situation became. I did ask her one thing. 'What's Blue's real name? I heard Aunty call her another name but I assumed that was an adopted Chinese name. What's her real name?'

In an Australian accent she said, 'Blue. Her father named her after his father's sheepdowg.'

Someone behind me chuckled.

I had a dog and his name was Blue – isn't that how that old Ocker song goes?

Betcha five bob he's a good dog too.

Never heard Blue sing that one.

Next time I wanted to speak I leaned close to her ear. Her hair sat in a black helmet, strobed by passing lights. Her scent was light and fresh. 'In your opinion, Sparta, is Meilin my friend?' I felt like a supplicant, as if I were the insecure child and she the adult. The oracle.

She turned her face to me. In the passing shadows it was unreadable, the mere lineaments of a face like a sketch of a mask.

'Yes, Grandad. Meilin is your friend.'

And what about you, young Sparta, young fairy-tale princess, are you my friend?

About half an hour from our next destination, Sparta's mobile vibrated. She listened for some time and quit the call without saying a word. She spent the rest of the journey consulting Google Earth on her mobile.

'Change of plan,' she said. 'We'll separate in Esperance for the last leg of the journey.'

'Why?' I didn't like the sound of it.

'Blue called. The Auckland Police have put out an alert for you in Australia. You can't use your passport. It's too dangerous to travel with you.'

'So I've become a liability, is that it?'

'Yes.' She was too intent to spare my feelings. Maybe she mistook me for a grown-up and not the big baby I knew myself to be. She slipped a credit card into my hand. The bus pulled into Esperance.

'I'll catch the next bus to Melbourne. It leaves in fifteen minutes. You'll catch the next bus back to Albany, which leaves in two hours.'

I groaned.

'There you will catch the next bus to Melbourne. But you won't go all the way to Melbourne. You will get off at Kalgoorlie. Someone will meet you there and take you to the safe house. I'll already be there.'

'Will Blue be there?'

'Possibly.'

I was going to say something silly like 'will you be alright on your own,' but the words died in my throat.

'Go to a café to wait for the bus. Do the same in Albany.'

'Okay.'

She took my arm and hugged it, just like a real child might and beamed at me. 'We couldn't have done this without you, Grandad.'

It was all true. It made me feel proud. Why was I being so down on myself? I was a regular hero after all.

Then she turned and walked away. In those last glimpses of her, it seemed that she stood taller, her walk more confident, more elegant, more adult. She wants to look as old as she can since she's travelling alone, Jack Reacher said. I bought my ticket, found a café and sat feeling suitably sorry for myself with my *Henning Mankell* novel sitting in front of me, the good moment well gone, along with the vanishing figure of Sparta.

So! Elvis had run out of patience and I was a fugitive. He was probably so pissed off he would take Monckton into custody as a material witness.

I slept all the way back to Albany.

When I got off the bus I headed for the ticket office as directed.
I didn't even bother to notice what time of the day or night it was,
I just wanted to get this over with. A young woman approached
me. She had dark, almost black hair fringed in the front and was
dressed in worker overalls. She slumped along as if she had just got
off the night shift at a hellhole and was heading home. I didn't take
any notice of her until she spoke. There was no mistaking that low,
musical voice. The voice you'd just love to hear singing 'Come Fly
with Me' in a seedy nineteen-thirties nightclub.

'Buy a ticket to Perth under another name, then go out onto the
street,' she said without stopping, as if we hadn't spoken at all.

Like an automaton I kept walking. Perth! Christ!

When I bought the ticket, the bored woman at the counter
asked me what name.

'Monckton,' I said, in hindsight a dead giveaway. I wouldn't
want Monckton to get into any trouble.

I walked out onto the street. A nondescript car pulled up and
the back door swung open.

'Want a lift?' Blue said.

I slipped in beside her and we were out of there.

'Where are we heading?' I said to Blue.

'Melbourne,' she said.

53

If I thought I was going to have a cozy little chat in the back seat
with Blue I was much mistaken. Like Sparta she quickly went into
shut-down mode, that state of quietude I was all too familiar with,
and the driver never said a word after a quick hello. He looked like
a regular young Aussie guy, which I guess was the idea.

Since I was more wired than tired after my sleep on the bus, I tried to use the time to sort out my thoughts, come to grips with what was happening to me, but my thoughts were suffering from some static interference. A buzzing noise that kept coming and going. All I knew was that I was not in control. Not even when to sleep and eat or take a crap. And who was in control? Strangers. Shapeshifters. Storytellers. Powerweavers.

One way of looking at it was that I hadn't been in control for a long time, the whole ride. You could say I'd been kidnapped twice, first by Wang and then, more subtly, by Blue and Sparta – because, think of it this way, what would have happened that day if Blue and Sparta had not appeared at my door ready to whisk me away? The car would have come around the corner, gunfire would have broken out. Monckton and I would have cowered in a corner. A car would have exploded outside my house. Elvis and Haggis would have put yet another black mark against my name, but what could they have done? I was an innocent bystander. And if some heavies came looking for Blue and Sparta, I wouldn't have seen them, would I? I could have toughed it out and stayed at home, let the devil take care of his own. You could say I was panicked into fleeing the house. Manipulated at every step. And, I felt certain, would be disposed of if necessary.

After hours of solid driving we shot through Esperance, where the road takes a turn north, into the Nullabor desert. At one point I looked out the window and saw a herd of passing camels. You don't expect them in Australia but there are lots, brought over to deal with the desert conditions. Along with Afghanis to manage them. Now they run wild in the desert and are considered a pest. Hard to imagine that noble and cantankerous animal a pest. The ship of the desert and all that.

Blue saw them too and smiled at me. 'At our next stop, we… ah… switch our mode of transport for our last leg.'

I grinned weakly. 'That should finish me off.'

That was our bit of excitement for the trip. I realized that Blue's silence was not because she was trying to freeze me out or ignore me. It had nothing to do with me. Since there was nothing she had to deal with, she simply sat quietly. All I had to do to get a conversation rolling was to give her something to deal with.

'You haven't asked me how my investigation is going,' I said.

'Into your friend's death? How is it going?'

'A new twist. I'm told that Velvet stumbled on a code sequence for a weapon of some kind.'

Blue leaned forward and tapped the driver on the shoulder. He stuck a set of headphones in his ears and fiddled with his iPod.

'Who told you this?' It was hard getting used to this short-haired brunette Blue, watching me from underneath a fringe; she was more hidden than the blonde surfie girl, or at least reserved in a very Asian way. Blue was suddenly very Chinese. It was something to do with gesture and timing.

'Dr Wayne Morse, maybe you know him.' I thought of Velvet and the smell of patchouli. I could smell it now. How does patchouli smell when it turns bad? Like bitterness and rancid anger.

'Jason, are you okay?'

'Just travel sickness,' I said. 'A touch of giddiness. It's been a long time on the move.'

'You look like you were visited by a *djinn*.'

'With or without ice?'

'You know, the Muslims believe in *djinn*, supernatural creatures said to occupy a world parallel to our own, and who may appear as spirit guides, often assigned to one at birth.'

I squirmed in my seat. I wanted to get out of the car, just open the door and get out, even at full speed. I could feel Velvet all around me, dark and swirling.

Blue gave no outward sign, but I sensed that same state of heightened alertness I'd noticed in Sparta. She looked at me long enough for many camels to have gone past if there had been more camels.

'Morse was telling the truth. Velvet did find part of a code for a weapon.'

'How important is it? Important enough for her to get murdered?'

'Possibly.'

'What do you mean?'

'As I've told you, my job is to protect Sparta. I don't know everything. But this is what I understand. Chinese scientists were working on methods for disabling American drones by trying to block their transmissions. They couldn't get anywhere beaming electrons, but hit pay dirt when they started experiments with pulsed lasers. Certain frequencies can disrupt radio channels and electrical systems. They discovered a pulse that can shut down all electrical activity by interfering with the magnetic field of any engine.'

She was quiet while I absorbed that. If it were true, and not just another fairy tale, it spelled the end of modern warfare as we know and love it. Electricity as we know it and love it.

'What's the range of this thing? How big does it have to be?'

'I don't know. It can be narrowed so it goes further, or widened, which cuts down the range. When narrowed to maximum it has no trouble reaching the moon.'

So you could pick off satellites like shooting fish in a pond. Drones and rockets would fall out of the air. On the ground you could disable cities.

'Could Velvet have guessed what it was?'

'Possibly.'

'That would be enough to get her killed.'

'Yes.'

'But you don't quite believe it.'

'That's right. I don't see how she would've had enough to go on. Even though she was an expert at reading code, she could surmise. You wouldn't think she'd pose that great a threat. Not to take the risk murder involves.'

'What does Golden Fleece have to do with it?'

'They're manufacturing the weapons. The first batch.'

A suspicion entered my mind. What they call a hunch. All the best detectives get them from time to time and ignore them at their peril. Even journalists get them.

'In China?'

'No. There is no way of keeping them secret in China. It's too corrupt, and there's too much money at stake. They are made here, in Australia, at different factories that put together the components but don't know what they're for. The final assembly is done by a very small group of people.'

'Then they are shipped from Melbourne to China?'

'Will be. The first shipment is soon to leave.'

'So how come you know all of this? How are you and Sparta mixed up in this?'

She brushed her dark hair off her face. 'I've got some chocolate? Would you like some?'

'Is it Fair-Trade?'

By revealing that she knew about the weapon, Blue was demonstrating a link between her and Velvet. Blue knew what Velvet had discovered – how was that possible? And what did it mean?

I took her proffered chocolate and bit into it. It was dark and faintly bitter.

'Did you know all along what Velvet was doing?'

She caught my drift. 'No, but Aunty Wu did.'

I caught her drift. 'Golden Fleece?'

She nodded. Her tongue moved around inside her mouth, chasing a piece of chocolate. 'Aunty Wu's people picked up Velvet's hacking.'

'Are you telling me that Wu ordered Velvet's death?'

'No. I can't say that. As I've said, I can't see that Velvet would have found out enough.'

There was a big piece of the puzzle missing here, and it concerned Sparta, but I didn't know the right question to ask.

'If Velvet, why not Morse? I mean, why kill Velvet and leave Morse standing? He was in on it.'

'Morse couldn't do what Velvet did. Doesn't have the skill. Without her, and without the code she hacked, all he has is a story.'

'What about me? Now I know too – and more than Velvet knew. Why did you tell me?'

'Because, like Morse, all you have is a story. A story with not a shred of evidence.' She put her hand over mine and her warmth flowed through my skin into old bones. 'I think you are very brave, Jason. And you have never relinquished your quest to find justice for your murdered friend. Perhaps you will find it in the end.'

'Won't someone have to kill me now?'

'No one knows of this conversation but you and me and the gatepost.'

'And the *djinn*,' I said.

'Yes,' she said, without humour.

And the gatepost stays mum. But Scoop. Ah! Scoop was sitting on the hottest story in the world – and he couldn't use it. Despite Blue's misgivings, Golden Fleece came up trumps again in the suspect department. Maintenance of the greatest military secret of all time would do for a motive. In which case the murder was committed by a nameless operative just as I'd thought, and I'd never achieve any justice worth the name.

54

Nothing, but a plastic gas station plonked in the middle of nowhere. Not even a café, just a machine hoiking dirty stuff into Styrofoam cups. I walked out, and away from it, and looking back after only a few quick steps, it already looked diminished. A few more quick steps and it looked more like an alien artifact than an ordinary gas station. Garish lights and shiny surfaces of unlikely colour. It might have landed ten minutes ago. A few more steps and it was little more than a child's toy, sitting in the twilight darkness of a featureless plain. The emptiest place I've ever seen. Nothing broke the clean, abstract line of the horizon. Except for the super-real gas station there was nothing but a stony plain that fell away on all sides to the curvature of the earth.

I knew now, or thought I knew, why Velvet was killed. It wasn't my fault, I could argue. I was merely the agency. Sooner or later Velvet would have trodden on big toes. Same with Anna. Either of us could have gone with dengue fever. It wasn't my fault. Chance wears big boots, tromping over our lives. It's too easy to die. That's what guilt does, gives meaning to things, responsibility. If I was merely the agency, then I was nothing, and things just happened because they happened.

Blue wandered out of the gas station and looked idly around. She didn't see me. Casually, her back to the gas station, she drew out a pistol and began loading the cartridge. The snick of the bullets sliding home was the only sound in that opaque quiet. For a gal who didn't like guns, she seemed pretty familiar with this one.

I moved further away and the scene reduced again. The still life of gas station, car, and girl with gun appeared like a glazed miniature. This is how it would look if I were dead, I thought, taking fright. I'd reached that age when it was hard to pretend I was not going to die. Looking at Blue and at the gun I knew for certain, I could feel it, approaching, not far off… old footpad silence, the patchouli smell of graves. Ash in the air. The angel of death, that's what Blue really was, the beautiful impossible angel of death here to show me the threshold. The threshold to a place like this: a void with a gas station. That was the real meaning of her intervention in my life.

After Anna's death the spice went out of things. Life lost its taste. When Blue's voice floated through my morning window, singing of the children of the tree of life, I felt alive again. I didn't understand. I didn't see who she was. I didn't see that I couldn't escape. She found me, as she must eventually find everybody. Odysseus' crew blocked their ears to the deadly song of the sirens. I didn't have that option. Velvet's death paved the way. The closer I got to Velvet's death, the closer I got to my own. If I were ever to confront the killer, it would be my death I'd be facing. That was where this unlikely chain of events was heading.

Blue finished loading the pistol, aimed along the barrel into the air, making no move to put it away. Didn't matter out here. She placed it on the pale bonnet of the car where it gleamed with the chitinous black of an arthropod.

I understood that I'd been in the air and on the road too long, that jet-lag was bending time like a hangover can, but understanding changed nothing. Like the landscape around me, I was stripped to the barest plot lines. There was Anna, there was my life, there was Scoop off on another fool's errand of the mind. And there was the meddling GD with the missing piece of the jigsaw puzzle – *Jason knows the secret of the Golden Fleece*. And my angel of death, lounging by the car while the driver had a smoke, her piece lying on the bonnet, idly swiping at the shuffle of insects in the air.

Through all its labyrinths, the thread of my life had led me, conducted me, to this very moment, this very point in the middle of nothing, where there is nothing, and the answers to be found are all to the wrong questions.

I had the option right then, I knew, to leave it behind, to make the gas station smaller and smaller, zooming out until it disappeared. They would find me here, Blue and the Aussie driver, skin already growing pale and waxen, eyes fixed on the southern stars. I had that option, that doorway in the rose garden. The angel of death was by my side. Heedless, I'd let her in through my window. I faced the jet-lag of age, but I didn't have to bother with the end game. I could bail. I was frail enough. Threadbare enough. And, if not now, when?

When that angel knocks on the door, she doesn't go away. She keeps coming back again and again. She can take many forms, but soon you learn to recognize her. A glimpse in the street, across a room, from a window, behind a fan. This rocky nothingness plus the plastic gas station was the antechamber to her territory. I might leave, but I would be back, and I would know the place by its smell, a dry smell with the aftertaste of patchouli.

The driver had finished his ciggie. My life had lasted about as long. They were getting ready to go. Blue took her pistol from the bonnet and slipped it into her pocket and looked up, right at me. She'd known all along where I was, which was natural. That angel always knows. She never lets you out of her sight.

The other option was to stay awhile, play out the comedy for what it was worth – who knew who would be the next to die? I would come back in from the twilight, get into the car, and the engines of my life would resume. I would make smart remarks just like the great sleuths of fiction. I would play my absurdist part, live my pretence, smile and be a fool. But from this moment on I would know, I would never forget. And every time I looked at Blue I would see the angel of death looking back at me. Watching. Waiting for me.

If not now, later.

55

'Are you all right?' Blue said as I approached the car.

'I'm hallucinating,' I said. 'A big emptiness. Too big.'

'That's no hallucination.'

'I'm hallucinating me,' I said.

'That's another matter,' she said.

We hit the outskirts of Melbourne around dawn, coming in from smaller roads to the north, inching our way over towards Eltham. I buzzed down my window. The air was hot and dry and all desert. The driver was now taking directions from Blue. Last minute precautions. Make random moves. The driver won't know where he's going until he's got there. A pretty area with gates and driveways. Suddenly we go up a driveway and follow it through a wooded path of naked gum trees for quite some distance, skirting the edge of a hillside.

We pulled up at a house much larger than I expected. But I had no time to examine the house.

I was too busy looking at the three figures standing, framed in the arched doorway like a classical composition.

Marcia, flanked by Fintan and King Felix.

56

Over the next few days I had to get used to a few things, other than finding my sleeping pattern, playing horsie for Felix and getting used to living with the angel of death. Not only had the inhabitants of number 54 abducted me, but they had abducted my family as well. That was a big one.

Some 'nice men' had met Marcia at the airport when she arrived in Melbourne and explained to her that they knew all about the dossier, and while her law firm couldn't bother her, she was vulnerable to other interested parties. They had a safe house ready for her.

'And you believed them?' I said when Marcia told me this part of the story, with Fintan chipping in with observations.

'They knew in detail the contents of the dossier. They knew it was at your place. They also said that in a week or so the contents of the dossier would become irrelevant. But in the meantime they would help me go into hiding. What choice did I have?'

I knew the feeling. The invisible hand of the Plot in the free market of souls.

'Yes, Grandad. And they said you would be coming,' Fintan said.

'I'm sure,' I said.

I also had to get used to a somewhat changed Reggie. He was surly enough, but there was more. He wasn't around for most of the day, disappearing into an upstairs room in the east wing of the house, emerging hours later looking dishevelled and pre-occupied. I didn't want to spy so I asked Blue outright about Reggie's east wing room.

'That's our communications room,' she said. 'Our Reggie's a communications engineer, one of the best on his better days. He just fancies himself as a Mafia heavy. It's his upbringing, but he can use a gun when he has to, which is very handy. He can be nasty in a fight.'

'What was his upbringing?'

'In the streets of Hong Kong, where he ran with the homeless and the gangs. He became a street fighter for one of the gangs, but then his skill with electronic equipment showed. Even though he'd had no training, he put together a communications network that put his gang at the top of the ladder in terms of Hong Kong crime syndicates. Then he got noticed by… bigger fish.'

That didn't exactly tally with what Meilin had told me. He'd said the inclusion of Reggie had been a mistake, the result of a compromise between the factions, and that he was there to ensure the interest of a certain faction. Of course that might still be true – as far as it went. Thinking about Reggie got me to thinking about the house. It was a big two-storey, two-winged place with at least ten bedrooms, four bathrooms and two kitchens. In between the kitchens, on the bottom floor, there was a hall-like eating room with a sitting room attached. Generous grounds with lawns surrounded the house, with gum trees and nice guys wandering around with barely concealed guns. This was more than just a safe house. It's a headquarters, Jack Reacher said. Looks like they're keeping you close.

Headquarters was just the right word. Centre of operations. Because there was some kind of operation going on here. There was a tension in the air. A buzz. Blue was spending a lot of time with Reggie in the comms room, or upstairs in the west wing talking to the old Vamp, who was in residence but seldom showed his face. The nice guys were very alert. Everyone was preoccupied and there wasn't much conversation.

In a rare moment when I caught Blue alone I asked her directly what the hell was going on.

'The first weapons shipment leaves port soon. We are monitoring everything.'

'To make sure it all goes smoothly?'

'There are a number of things that could go wrong,' she said.

'What happens to us?'

'You go back to New Zealand. Marcia will go back to her old firm, but as head of the company. As we speak Mr Dogbane Senior is history, and his son has decided to accept an offer elsewhere. You will write your article on China. All the material has been prepared for you. Your editor will be very happy to see how busy you have been.'

57

Sparta arrived the day after I did. She was the only one who seemed unaffected by the atmosphere of the place. She changed into shorts and a top that made her look about ten years old, and joined the boys, playing with a simple, unaffected delight. She soon had Felix hanging off her neck and Fin eagerly showing her things. He'd roamed the grounds many times by now and had discovered a patch of orchids. Marcia and I tagged along as he dragged Sparta to see them. There they were with their seductive tongues hanging out in wonderfully delicate pinks. Sparta and Fintan fell on their knees to examine them while Marcia held Felix back in case he accidently on purpose kicked them or jumped on Sparta's back.

'Maybe we should pick some?' Fintan said.

'Naw, let's leave them.' Sparta said. 'They're awesome where they are.'

Fintan agreed that indeed they were, and the two of them were up and off, running through the trees having a race, with the newly released Felix stumping after them.

'What a wonderful child,' Marcia said, laughing. 'She and the boys are having so much fun.'

'She's a bit more than she seems,' I said.

'This whole place is a bit more than it seems. I take it you know more about this than you can say.'

'The mother of all confidentiality agreements, you might say.'

Marcia nodded. She didn't press me. She knew the score when it came to confidentiality. Maybe a similar thought was passing through her mind. 'But you'd tell me if our lives depended on it.'

'Yes,' I said.

'So what can you tell me about Sparta, then?'

'That she's a fairy-tale princess born to great power – and that she's a trained killer.'

'Jesus,' Marcia said. 'What's she doing here?'

'Well you may ask.'

It didn't take me very long to feel useless, and a prisoner. There was a library of excellent books and DVDs, Sky TV, the happy chatter of children, hours of talk with Marcia catching up on our lives, but nothing could disguise our incarceration, or the dual role played by the ever-present nice guys. I fretted and played chess with Marcia and watched the big blue-grinning sky.

On the third day Sparta drew me aside.

'Chun Yungzi wants to see you,' she said.

'Who?'

'Chun Yungzi. You call him the old man, or the old Vamp.' The words sounded funny coming out of her mouth.

Without speaking, I followed her up the stairs to the old man's room. It was at one end of the building with a corner view. Spacious and airy enough, and painted in light colours, but there weren't much in the way of amenities. The bed was a plank with a curved block of wood at one end for a pillow; I guess he was missing his coffin. There were a few pillows strewn on the floor. The old man was sitting on one of them. He was dressed in a colourful silk robe with the image of a double-edged sword on the front. He had a fly-whisk in one hand and beside him was a tiny tea maker powered by a candle. It was mid-morning and a dry, rich light was coming through the window making everything inside glow.

He gestured us to cushions. Sparta sat a little to one side and behind me, very still and alert.

He gave me a quick cheeky grin and lifted one eyebrow, making sure I remembered the last time we'd met. Me peering through the window at him, him peering back, me scrambling over the fence and almost losing my manhood. I had the decency to blush.

He poured me tea in a tiny cup, like kids have for dolls' houses.

'I hear you are a connoisseur,' he said. 'You must try this.' His voice was as dry and whispery as a piece of old parchment paper.

I sipped. It was exquisite, delicate but strong with a lingering spicy aftertaste.

'It might assist you to realize that, at present, at least, we are all prisoners here.' There was a curious rhythm in his speech, something old-fashioned and dusty.

'A bit like the Hotel California.'

He eye-browed me a question.

'It's a song about a hotel where everyone is a prisoner of their own device, and you can check out but you can never leave.' I didn't say anything about steely knives or the beast that couldn't be killed.

He listened attentively, as if what I was saying had some great worth.

'I like that, prisoners of their own device. English can surprise us that way, sometimes.'

'I've never been much of a poetry lover.'

'That's sad.'

'Any emotion may fade over time,' I said.

'Yet only emotion endures,' he said.

We sat for a while in the great careless generosity of sunlight and pondered imponderables, or at least I pretended to. Actually, I didn't ponder much; I was out of my depth. Despite the lightness of the room, I was starting to feel freaked, as if there were ghosts hanging around. I started to get the same feeling I'd had in the twilight zone of the gas station. All it would take is a single step.

'Who are you?' I said, all too aware of the bluntness of the question in the delicate ambience of the room, the skein of felt but not seen inner meanings into which our conversation was being woven.

'My birth name is Lu Yan,' the old man said in his powdery whisper. 'I was born in north-western China in the year 798. I became known as Lu Dongbin. Chun Yungzi is my Taoist name. Everybody calls me Grandfather.' He gave a twitch of his fly-whisk.

A blowfly had entered the room and started its mindless circling, banging against walls. The old, apparently very old man, indicated briefly to Sparta, who rose and, as the fly zoomed towards her, held her palm up. The fly zoomed back to avoid it and Sparta stepped forward. The fly pulled in a tighter circle, then bulleted for the window.

The old man smiled at me. 'She's got some *chi*, that girl.'

'I reckon,' I said. 'I could do with some myself.'

'You just don't know it for what it is.'

'Are you telling me you were born over twelve centuries ago?'

He pointed to the window. 'Your wise men tell us that the fly has only one second of memory. That is poignant. Its body lasts much longer.'

It came to me. The name, Lu Dongbin. Scoop had read something a long time ago.

'Lu Dongbin was one of the eight Chinese immortals,' I blurted.

He nodded, as if at a very clever pupil. 'Only three of us left. Lan Cai and He Xian Gu – and me.' He concentrated on his tea, filling our miniscule cups to the brim with not a drop spilled.

'He means that the immortals can die. Accidents, fires, floods, avalanches, murder.' Sparta said.

It's a cult, Jack Reacher said. A very rich cult. That would explain a lot. Centuries old. Which means they're all cuckoo. Mad people with guns and extraordinary training. Jack knew a thing or two about cults.

Sparta was standing by the window facing out. A tall breeze lifted her neat dark hair and blew it off her neck. Her face and throat were limned against the blue of the sky through the window behind. She looked serene, and beautiful with it. But there was more. Something numinous. For a split second, long enough for a fly to forget, there was the touch of Chang O in Sparta. As if the princess had been promoted. I remembered tea and biscuits, and Sparta's toast to the exiled goddess of the moon.

Maybe she looked so tall because I was sitting and she was standing, but that wouldn't do. I remembered the moment on the bus when it felt as I were the child and she the adult, wise and all-knowing, the passing lights gliding over the dark sheen of her hair.

I wasn't sure this was a cult, but I was starting to get scared in a way I hadn't up to this point except at the gas station. Cult or not, I'd hit the limits of my empirical universe and it didn't feel so great. Mysterious women and mysterious weapons I could handle; conspiracy theories, computer crashes, Chinese politics, a killer kid and a murder – I could relate to. Even the angel of death had a face. This was something else.

The old man put his hand on my arm, pulling my attention from Sparta.

'Sometimes we fail to see the desire of the mirror.'

Of the mirror? Didn't he mean *in* the mirror? How can the mirror desire? More poetry, or some cryptic Zen crossword you could begin but never complete.

'I don't know what to say,' I said. 'Speechless, that's me. Up shit creek without a phone-eme.' A pathetic effort to crack hardy, even to my own ears.

He looked as if he understood exactly what I was thinking and feeling, and that didn't help.

Sparta said, 'Grandad, you remember that story about the princess?'

'More fairy tales?' This second attempt at levity came out sounding hard and bitter. The old man grinned at me, full of good humour.

'When the princess arrived back in the kingdom she found the

268

three remaining immortals living in harmony.'

'The wine,' the old man said.

'Ah, yes, they would quarrel over the wine they drank.'

'Lan Cai has no taste.' The old man shook his head. 'And he's never changed.'

'Then the scientists of the kingdom invented a new weapon, one that could dampen the spark of life in machines, and for the first time the consensus of wisdom broke down. The princess's grandfather opposed the development of the weapon from the start. The other two supported it. The organisation, which had grown up over the centuries to protect the immortals, was itself fractured and the king's loyalty divided.'

This was something I could understand. I seized on it. To the old man, I said, 'Why did you oppose the weapon? It puts China in the box seat. Until it's replicated.'

'That box seat will quickly turn into a hot seat,' he said. 'No weapon can end wars.' There was something in the dry salvages of his voice that carried conviction. 'But people don't want the truth, whatever they may say.'

'Tell me about it. When you're tired of being an immortal, you should try being a journalist. Telling the truth can get you blacklisted for life.'

'To do that I'd have to become wise first.'

'Then you'd never make a journalist.'

'I'll live with it.'

This banter helped relieve the tension, but only a bit. Soon to be cranked up again when Sparta resumed.

'Since he was in the minority, the princess's grandfather decided to take voluntary exile to a tiny country far away, and to take the princess with him. This was a big step, since no immortal had ever left China.'

'Big mistake,' the old man said. 'The rabbit is as sure footed in the forest as she is on the plain.'

'The princess became aware that the battle between her

grandfather and the other two immortals was not only over the weapon, but also over the princess herself. The other two did not want her to go, as if they had some kind of claim over her. When she asked her grandfather about their attitude, he told her something he'd concealed from her all her life.'

'Yes?' Like the story-teller she was, she could pause at the most irritating moments. If I was supposed to be hanging on every word, then I was.

'That he was not her grandfather but her father. That she was the child of an immortal, which was a very rare event. There had only been five. Two of them were still alive. One, a man, over a hundred and twenty and herself, the princess.'

Here we go again, Jack said, once more around the fruitcake.

I took a terrible, intuitive leap. 'And Velvet found out about this?'

'The mind is a monkey,' the old man said.

'Grandad, have you heard of an organization called Anonymous?'

'Yes, like a sort of underground Wikileaks.'

'They are dedicated to publishing state and corporate secrets. Very secretive. Velvet was a member of that group. Others have stumbled on the secret of the immortals but could do nothing with it. Velvet had evidence. The organization would be exposed. The princess would be exposed.'

'I see,' I said, and I did. I saw more than I was prepared to say. I knew now who had killed Velvet, and why. The missing piece of the puzzle.

In that bright sunny room, time took a breather. The sun hung still in the sky. Nothing moved. The old man sat like a graven image, the tiny cup in his gnarled hands. Sparta stood by the window, still as a statue, face lifted to the light. A blowfly, maybe the same one, flew into the room over Sparta's head and out again in a blink, fast enough to start time flowing again.

'It is the universe that can remember only one second at a time,' the old man said.

To Sparta, I said, 'Will the princess become an immortal too?'

'No, but she will age slowly, and live for a long time.'

'And you are a real child, not twenty-five or thirty or something?'

She grinned at me. I saw the old man in her face. The same monkey impishness. 'I am a real child. I am twelve years old, but if you were to meet me in ten years I wouldn't look much over fifteen.'

Brainwashed, Jack said.

Maybe, Jack, but I'd always thought brainwashed people acted like zombies, vacant-eyed, spouting doctrine, not sharp tacks like these two.

'Okay, so you went into exile in New Zealand. What are you doing here, then? So close to the shipment. Shouldn't you be as far away as possible?'

'That I can't tell you,' the old man said.

'Can't or won't?'

'Ah, how simple yet subtle English can be. Only three words. Almost as good as Chinese.'

'And the real beauty of it is, you can answer in a single, one-syllable word.'

'Then I have to say *won't.*'

I got to my feet and got reacquainted with my legs. Didn't realize how long I'd been sitting in one place. The old man stayed sitting. By the window Sparta had returned to normal child size.

'One thing I don't understand. Now you have told me all this, and I am a journalist. Now I know what Velvet knew.'

'But you won't say anything, Grandad,' Sparta said. 'You wouldn't want all your colleagues laughing at you.'

I thought of Eddie and shuddered. Scoop has lost his marbles – the word would go around faster than a hot tweet.

'You're right. But why tell me anyway?'

It was the old man who answered. 'Sometimes it is given to the fool to learn the truth where the wise go begging,' he said.

I thought about that as I joined Sparta and looked out the window. I hadn't seen the grounds and countryside from this height, being quartered downstairs. In the distance, above the naked, skinny gum trees, some tiny black dots were circulating. They were not blowflies.

'Helicopters,' Sparta said. 'I've been watching them.'

'They've been around for a couple of days,' the old man said.

Outside the day was getting older. I stood by the girl and watched it.

58

The next morning a helicopter buzzed Headquarters.

I was sitting with Marcia in the living room, looking out the window at Sparta and the boys playing. She was teaching them a ball game. Then she stopped, lifted her head and looked at the sky. A moment later she was hurrying the boys into a clump of trees, the nice guys nicely helping her along. Then we heard it. A hard clattering, approaching fast. Some of the nice guys concealed in the trees unslung their weapons.

Marcia and I both hit the deck. By lifting my head a bit I could peek out the window. The chopper was disappearing to our left, but I could hear the engine noise change as it began to turn. Blue's voice sounded through speakers, shouting in rapid Chinese. She's telling them to hold their fire until fired on, Jack said. Don't tell me, I said, it's the same in every language.

The chopper came back. It looked as if it was heading right for the house and roared overhead. It was a muddy brown colour and had no markings.

And it was gone.

'I wonder what all that was about,' Marcia said as we got to our feet.

'It means we won't be staying here much longer,' I said.

Sparta and the boys came out from under the trees. Fintan looked very excited.

The nice guys slung their weapons.

How would I get out of here, if push came to shove? You'd take a car, Jack said. The driver has the keys. All you'd have to do is jump him, take the keys and make a run for it. Oh, and have Marcia and the boys standing by ready. If you got the driver's gun you could pop a few nice guys on your way out. Marcia driving, you doing the shooting.

Easy peasy.

That afternoon another nondescript looking car pulled up and Mr Wang stepped out. I was outside with Marcia and the kids, and he gave me a wave.

'The plot thickens,' I said to Marcia *sotto voce*.

'It's our old friend from tea and biscuits,' I said to Sparta.

'Yes,' she said. I tried to discern if she were worried but should have known better.

The door on the other side of the car opened and Aunty Wu stepped out.

'The whole gang's here,' I said.

Aunty Wu looked across at us. Her face was a painted porcelain. Like a mask; pale, with thin, high eyebrows.

I noticed that Sparta did not rush over to greet the woman, but hung close to Marcia, me and the boys.

Later Blue came out and joined us. Looking very businesslike, she handed me a mobile. 'It's time for you to ring the Auckland police. Tell them you were kidnapped and brought here. Marcia says the same. The kids can talk about helicopters and nice guys with guns. You can make up the rest.'

'They're going to be after my ass.'

'Tell them you'll be on a flight soon, with your family, but you don't know when.'

'They'll be delighted.'

I gestured to the mobile. 'Aren't they going to trace me if I use this?'

'It won't matter,' Blue said.

I wandered out of ear's reach to make the call; I wasn't expecting this to be pleasant. After some preliminary unpleasantries I got through to Haggis.

'Where are you, Mr Argonaut?'

'In Australia.'

'Taking in a spot of sun at Bondi, are we?'

I told him a story, as near to the truth as I could. Except it had been two hefty men who'd turned up at my house, rather than a woman and a girl. Even so, he didn't believe it.

'So you're telling me the Maoris, after shooting up the house next door, and getting blown up, kidnapped you.'

'Not Maoris. Asians.'

He was quiet after that. He and Elvis must have hit something, I could hear the bells ringing in his head.

'You know there's a warrant out for your arrest, don't you?'

'Then why haven't you found me? Being rescued would be nice, but arrested would do at a pinch.' I went ahead and repeated my story, with further realistic details. I didn't emphasize the plane hopping. What he didn't know wouldn't hurt him. But he already knew.

'You were abducted, held at gunpoint, yet somehow managed to swan around half of Asia in the company of a young Chinese girl. What's all that about, Mr Argonaut?'

'They had my family, Sergeant McDonald. The girl was getting away from pursuers. She was using me as a front to buy tickets.' Which was pretty much the truth, give or take.

'I'm looking forward to you explaining all that to us,' Haggis said.

'You're not going to believe me, but you might believe my daughter.' I gestured Marcia over and gave her the phone.

'Yes,' Marcia said. 'Yes, I am a lawyer… no I am not representing my father… I lost my job and came to Australia with my sons for a break and was abducted at the airport… I don't know… my father was brought in a few days later… I don't know what it's about… I

274

don't know if that has anything to do with the dossier. No, I don't know where it is. All I know is that we've been treated ok and there is no ransom demand… yes, we're told we're coming home…'

With a disgusted look she handed the phone back to me.

'We'll be waiting for you,' Haggis promised me.

I snarled down the phone, 'That's very nice. Pity you're not here now, we could sure use some help.' I screamed out the last word and cut the connection. That would give Elvis something to think about when he listened to the tape.

'How did it go?' Blue said, a twinkle in her eye, like twinkle-twinkle little star.

'*As well as can be expected,* I think is the correct phrase. *You have a lot of explaining to do,* is another that comes to mind, along with *that's a likely story* and *you don't expect us to believe…*'

Blue grinned at us. 'Don't worry, they'll believe you in the end.' She seemed to think the whole thing very funny. Me trying to explain to sceptical cops. In the right mood I might have appreciated the joke. A softness came into her face. She knelt on the grass level with Felix.

'Your grandfather calls you King Felix,' she said. 'Why is that?'

'Because I *am* King Felix.' He looked at her defiantly. 'I am King. Felix.' He spelled it out for her. 'Feel-icks.'

'I think he really is,' Sparta said.

'Well King Felix, is the king ready to go home soon, back to the castle where he lives with his mother and brother?'

'Grandad has a big box of Lego.'

'Do you like to play with it?'

'I make things,' he said reprovingly.

'What do you like to make?'

'Castle with a moat. You can put real water in the moat. But Grandad was silly.'

Blue looked surprised at the idea. 'What did he do?'

'He tried to get us to build a tower up to the sky.'

'That's very silly.'

'Yes it is.'

Felix looked up at Sparta, who was standing beside Blue, her hand lightly on Blue's shoulder. 'Princess come to Grandad's and build something too?'

Sparta was sensitive to the profundity of the compliment and bowed her head graciously, 'Princess would be happy to.'

Felix gave a regal nod, as if her promise satisfied him.

Blue sang a couple of verses of 'A Froggy Went A-courting'. She hammed it up, putting on a froggy face, making the boys laugh.

'You can come and make things too, if you want,' Felix said to Blue.

'I'd like to make a farm,' Blue said.

Felix thought that might be possible, but not likely.

'Old McDonald's Farm.' And she proceeded to sing some verses, full of quacks and neighs and moos. She looked absurd and sublime. Absurdly sublime. I envied that ability to become a child. All grandfather Argonaut had were his Lego and chocolate biscuits.

Blue got up and straightened her clothes.

'Be ready to leave within forty-eight hours,' she said.

'I'll go and pack,' I said.

'Get things sorted?' I asked.

'No,' she said.

We didn't see Wang and Aunty Wu leave, but heard their car departing into the dusty afternoon.

59

At dawn the next morning I was woken by the clatter of helicopters. Two helicopters. And behind that the sound of firearms. Marcia and the boys were not in their rooms. I raced downstairs to find them in the dining hall, staring out the windows. Reggie ran past me with a demented look on his face, heading for the comms room in the east wing. The two choppers came in low over the building and settled to the east where we couldn't see them, but we could hear the impact of heavy duty explosives hitting the east wing. The building shook. Felix started crying. I figured they were trying to take out the comms room. Now, for the keys! I knew exactly where they were, hanging up in the east kitchen where the chauffeur had left them last night.

I was halfway across the hall when the choppers lifted and came back over the west wing. They hovered in the air, doubtless getting the lay of the land. They looked like a couple of mosquitoes conversing. Below them the nice guys were shooting away. There's an attack on the perimeter, Jack said, and I think our cult friends are outgunned. Apparently negotiations yesterday came to naught.

Suddenly all the lights in the house went down. There was only rosy-fingered dawn pushing a few mellow holes into corners. Except for the small arms fire, silence reigned. The choppers! I rushed to the window. The choppers were hanging in the air, their blades turning slowly. Then they fell. Dropped out of the sky and crashed into the trees, exploding in bursts of flame. The weapon, Reggie's used it, I said. That evens up the odds a little, Jack said. I raced for the kitchen, to a back door annex where the staff hung up their coats.

I was pulling some keys from the driver's coat when, through the window, the old Vamp came into view. He was walking calmly across the lawn towards the sound of gunfire, an old man taking a stroll in the mellow morning light. But he didn't walk like an old man, his body too fluid and easy, with none of the stiffness of age. His hands hung loose and empty. He wore the same robe, which had a large embroidered sword on the back.

Look at that, said Jack in awe, he's off to battle with nothing but a silk sword.

Blue appeared beside me.

'What's he doing?' I said.

'He's going to take them out,' she said. 'The attackers, one by one.'

'But he's not armed.'

'Once he was a great swordsman, but he doesn't need one anymore. Now his *chi* is his sword. They won't have time to shoot. They won't see him coming.'

That made me shiver. One moment you are there, shooting away at your enemy. The next moment, the angel of death is by your side with ancient, skilled hands. Gentle hands.

I walked back into the hall, gripping the keys in my hand so they wouldn't jingle, Blue behind me.

'Wait a minute,' Blue said. 'Where are you going with those keys?'

60

I turned to face her. The angel of death.

So here we were, back at the gas station, back in the antechamber of hell.

'You were letting us go anyway. Now seems like the opportune moment.'

'No it isn't,' she said. 'Besides, things have changed.' Then I noticed she was armed. A heavy looking machine gun that looked like a Kalashnikov to me, but then again, I wouldn't know the difference between a Kalashnikov and a Raskolnikov.

She swung the automatic in my direction. 'I'm sorry, Jason. I can't afford to let you fall into Wang's hands a second time. Or worse, into Wu's hands.'

'Why not? I'm sure I don't know anything they don't already know.'

'It's not what you know, but how they can use you to destroy us.'

'I can't think of how they might do that.'

'That's because you can't think the way they do.'

'Okay, their evil is beyond my comprehension, but that's not the real reason you have to kill me, is it Blue?'

'That's right,' she said. 'You know what it is.'

There was the rattle of gunfire. Closer to the house this time, but, I thought, a little sparser. The old man must be going about his silent business.

'How did you know I'd figured it out?' I said. I hoped my voice would sound calm and strong, unexpectedly so, but it sounded more like the squeak of a mouse in a trap.

'By the way you looked at me after you'd spoken to Chun Yungzi.'

While the fool might discover the truth where wise men went begging, there was no guarantee he would live to tell the tale.

'And what about Marcia and the kids?'

The gun held steady, she was too much of a professional for anything else, but she bit her lower lip and I knew the answer to my question. Hold her eye, Jack said. When her expression changes, throw yourself to the left. She's aiming a little to the right and the recoil will pull the barrel to the right. Just watch her eyes.

'But they don't know anything,' I said. Of course they would soon; they would be witnesses to a murder.

'Quickly, tell me how you knew?' I guess she was wondering if there were any other leaks she had to plug, loose ends to tidy away.

'Chun Yungzi and Sparta told me.'

'How?'

'By what they avoided saying. Then I knew it had to be you.' I broke into song, a bit croaky and out of tune, but it was a song. If I were to go out, I'd go out singing. Besides, she owed me a song.

'It had to be you, it had to be you
I wandered around, and finally found
The somebody who
could make me be true
Could make me be blue...'

Blue joined me, her voice low and sweet, and we sang a bittersweet duet, me sounding more like Tom Waits than Frank Sinatra.

'or even be glad
just to be sad

just thinking of you…'

But it was an awfully short song. In fact, we were coming up to the last lines now. I gave them all I had.

'For nobody else gave me the thrill
With all your faults I love you still
It had to be you
It had to be you
It had to be youuuuuuu…'

We ended the song in a grand harmony. I was already thinking that we could do another number. How about that Nick Lowe song, 'She Used to Be a Winner (but now She's Just the Doggy's Dinner).' The last 'uuuu' was still hanging in the air as she lifted the gun. Then her expression changed just like Jack said. Her naked-blue eyes went all squinty. It was the face of a killer I saw. My very own, personal, angel of death.

Marcia screamed.

I threw myself to the left as a bullet tore a hole in my shirt on the right side and nicked the flesh in a hot, stinging wound. Even as I turned she was swinging the barrel back in my direction. She wouldn't miss the second time. See you around, partner, I said to Jack.

But she didn't get the second burst away. Sparta appeared behind her and placed her left hand on Blue's neck. She was careful, gentle, even affectionate. Blue sagged to the ground, the gun falling out of her hands and clattering across the polished wooden floor.

'Go now,' Sparta said.

And we did. In double quick time. No one tried to stop us. We didn't have to pop any scumbags. If the attackers were around they didn't show any interest. I guessed they were busy elsewhere. I thought I saw the old man one last time, standing in the trees near the gate watching us depart.

We had a clean run through to Melbourne airport.

61

It took some days, and many hours in a cozy interview room, to assure the Auckland Police that I wasn't some international criminal operative, but I couldn't have done it without the aid of Fintan and Felix. Little King Felix was particularly vivid with his descriptions of the gunfire, and the helicopter, and how the helicopters fell out of the air. Woosh! Luckily he said they'd been shot down by the nice guys.

'And were you scared?' Elvis asked him.

'Yes,' he said, because at heart he was a truthful little boy.

More details, supplied by an enthusiastic Fintan, who might have been describing some video game, and the less enthusiastic Marcia, helped fill out the picture for the sceptical cops. It wasn't until they put a call through to the Melbourne police and confirmed that a firefight had taken place north of Eltham, that they dropped the issue. That still left them with plenty. Haggis was particularly interested in my 'relationship' as he called it to Sparta, and our peregrinations around East Asia and the Pacific. The busy little bugger had traced our movements all the way from Auckland to Perth. He couldn't quite get the picture, and I didn't blame him. I kept repeating that she was on the run and only using me to buy tickets, which was true enough, but it was only when I lied and said that Sparta had told me that they were holding Marcia and the boys on the promise of my good behavior, that the suspicious Scotsman thought he understood it.

'She must be a resourceful wee lassie,' he kept saying.

'You've got no idea,' I kept answering.

I took the line that we'd been unwittingly mixed up in some Asian gang warfare, but had no idea what it was all about. Neither of them believed I was telling the truth, but since they'd arrived at much the same conclusion themselves there wasn't much they could say. They'd already decided that both Velvet and Johnny Watch's death was the result of intergang warfare. I didn't dare ask where they thought Velvet fitted in, but they told me anyway. Finally, Dr Wayne Morse had told them that Velvet was mixed up in some nefarious Asian gang. He must have been desperate to get the cops off his back. As long as they didn't have a satisfactory story they'd keep coming back to him. I gathered that he was still being held in New Zealand.

During the long hours when they just left me to sweat it out, just to see if I'd sweat any blood, I brooded to little effect over Blue and the murder of Velvet. I tried to hate Blue, cast her in the role of calculating, cold-blooded bitch-killer, but that didn't work very well. Besides, Velvet herself was not such a sympathetic figure, not given the murky depths she was swimming in, and the way she used people.

They'd let Marcia and the boys go but were still holding me when I was told that a representative of the Chinese government was here to ask me a few questions. Haggis stood by the door looking all-important as Elvis ushered Meilin into the room. Elvis moved quietly off to one side and Haggis stayed by the door. Meilin's face revealed nothing as he led me through a series of dummy questions. He asked me if I'd seen any drugs at the Melbourne Headquarters, or if Sparta were carrying drugs, and pushed that line for a while and I fed him a little. Then he asked if I'd seen any documents or Chinese artifacts. Weapons caches. I played to that one too. Said I thought there were weapons stored in the east wing but had no evidence. He asked me about Reggie, clearly happy to throw Reggie to the dogs, so I did. The cops were getting it all down on tape but Elvis was taking notes anyway. He'd be following up on Reggie. Haggis stayed by the door and glared at me. He wasn't buying it, but what could he do? This farce went on for some hours as Meilin's questioning got more detailed. I had to describe the two guys who were supposed to have kidnapped me and taken me from my house to Auckland airport where Sparta was waiting. So I described Ninja and his mate, just to make it real. His questioning became so intense that I began to sweat in amongst all the lies and half-truths and careful evasions. If he was trying to make it look good, it worked.

Eventually Meilin sat back and told the cops what they wanted to hear. The Chinese government, he said, was very concerned that New Zealand citizens had got caught up in this gangland activity. The Chinese police were investigating a large-scale drug and weapons operation centered in Melbourne, with number 54 Odds Avenue apparently used as a bolthole. They'd been aware of the activities of this group for some time, but weren't aware of the New Zealand connection. Sparta, he suggested, was the daughter of one of the bosses and was being used as a pawn in their game. With the attack on number 54, they had to get Sparta out and used Jason Argonaut to do it. All wonderfully close to the truth. Even lies have to draw their warmth from somewhere. He would do everything, he said, to keep them informed, blah blah…

When it was over he was politely ushered out.

Finally, as they had nothing to hold me on that would stand up in court, the cops let me go. Elvis had moved on from me, and was now, with Meilin's invaluable help, concentrating on the gang scene in Auckland. Silently I wished him luck. Haggis did not move on. He was too stubborn. He knew a crock of shit when he stepped in one, knew that there were too many unanswered questions, and made a point of assuring me that the case was not closed, and that one day we would meet up again. A prospect he was looking forward to.

62

I settled back into number 52 Odds Avenue without complaint. It was reassuring to see everything in its right place. I retrieved Monckton from the neighbour across the road who said that a lovely young blonde woman had asked her to look after him, that is after the awful events at number 54. 'Was she your daughter?' the neighbour asked.

Monckton seemed happy enough to be home, but it's hard to tell with cats. Certainly he was reassured by a bowl full of fresh meat. As Blue had promised, all the material needed for an article on China's energy policy was sitting in my email. And it wasn't just patsy stuff. There was some solid data there. Enough stuff for some hard hitting. Then, as I worked through the material, it slowly dawned on me that there was something else buried in here, something that the ordinary reader might not see, but a skilled intelligence analyst might. The possibility, the implied threat, of a new weapon, although never mentioned of course, merely hinted at in certain descriptions of the physics of energy and the possibilities they opened, would be evident to the trained eye. Of course, I could have ignored that material. Although Bellweather readers are avid empiricists, they can't handle too much hard science. Yet I was sure those gathered forces were confident that I would put the message in. That was my job. That was what made me useful.

I was being used, and had been all along. I spliced the material in just the way they wanted, in return for my safety and Marcia's success; the right people would get the message. As promised, the directors of Dogbane asked her to come back as company head.

The resulting article was one of Scoop's best, most sound, but not his very best, or most dramatic. At least it didn't look that way for those who couldn't read the hidden code. For those who could, they might have concluded, if they cared, that it was probably Scoop's cleverest.

Other researchers tore their hair out wondering where I'd got my information, but that was all good. Eddie was over the moon. 'You're the best, Jason old boy, the very best,' he gushed. It was nice to have someone else say it.

I surreptitiously contacted Queenie, who unexpectedly accepted an invitation to come and see me. I bought a bottle of brandy for the occasion and Queenie came supplied with spliffs. I'm not sure why I wanted to meet her because I didn't think I could learn much more from her, but somehow I liked the old scrag. I was relieved to hear that Hiko and Gary had not been in the car that did the drive-by shooting. 'Hiko didn't approve,' she said approvingly. 'Hiko's a smart boy, though he's getting fat. Those guys in the car were friends of Johnny's. Mad bastards.' She dismissed them with a wave of her hand. I remained convinced that these mad bastards had encountered Aunty Wu, who had put them up to it, but Queenie knew nothing about that.

We got on like a couple of old mates, drinking and smoking and carrying on. We talked about Velvet and I learned how to laugh again. Queenie came up with a couple of half-way coherent stories about Velvet as a kid, how she had been helping her grandfather in the garden by following along behind, pulling up everything he had just planted, and how, at the age of six, she had carefully dismantled some kid's electronic toy and then surprised everybody by putting it back together in a few moments. What she didn't tell me was how Velvet got so offside with the family, but I guessed that would come out sooner or later.

She confirmed that Velvet had paid her to bring around mail that occasionally landed in her, Queenie's, letter box. On the day of the murder and the computer crash, Queenie had gone to see her, forgetting that they were to meet at the university. Realizing her blunder, she rushed to the university where she met Velvet and handed over the memory stick. That accounted for Velvet's late check in for work that day. Queenie had no idea what was in the memory stick.

All she knew was that Velvet paid well.

'Where would I get money for the car, and the house, and the dipshit whanau?'

There it was again, the implication that Velvet, and maybe Morse, had some pecuniary interest in hacking. I'd never believed so, but a lot had changed.

'She'd give us money but she wouldn't talk to us,' Queenie said. 'Hiko knows about the money – and resented it. Not cos of the money, but her attitude. It hurt him. He loved her, you know.'

After that we got nicely incoherent and parted with promises that we'd do it again soon. And we did. I guess you can say I made a friend.

<h2 style="text-align:center">63</h2>

In the meantime the world went on its merry way to hell in the usual fashion. It felt strange making contact with all that again, as if I'd been off the planet for a while and had to make a bumpy landing in the real world of floods, famines, droughts, and the Never Ending Financial Crisis, the all too familiar hallmarks of the age. There were no dramatic announcements from China, no whispers of a new weapon being deployed. It was business as usual for the great collapse. I had my own theory as to why the weapon had not been unveiled, but there were times that, in the time-honoured traditions of reluctant heroes, for I had decided that that was really my fictional niche, I doubted the reality of what had happened to me. Blue, Sparta, the old Vamp, Aunty Wu, all characters larger than life, at least the life I knew, seemed to shift in and out of reality just like real fictional characters. Just like a gas station in the middle of nowhere.

Even the new weapon, which I'd seen at work with my own eyes, seemed to morph into mythology or urban legend. I did some research and was surprised to come up with empirical evidence for the weapon story. There was a report dated the 3rd January 2012 on wired.com on the development of non-lethal weapons. Along with those actually being developed, like the delightful "Impulse Swimmer Gun" that uses "pulsed sound waves" to cause "auditory impairment and/or nausea" among scuba divers, and a vehicle-mounted tube launcher that'll unleash "ocular and auditory impairment" combined with "thermal heating" to utterly devastate any recalcitrant occupiers, there were 'fantasy projects.'

They're also after a high-powered microwave

system that can be hooked up to a drone or a ship, and then used to trigger "electrical system malfunction" on enemy boats. Danger Room's personal favorite, though, is a system of "pulsed laser[s]" on the tip of an airplane, used to "externally control the steering forces" of a foe's aircraft, in order to "divert [it] from restricted areas.

Despite all this, the feeling of unreality remained, grew stronger even with the passing of time, until one day about two months afterwards, on another sunny morning, the doorbell rang. I was over plot developments by this stage and opened the door quite unthinkingly.

Sparta was standing there, dressed casually in a floppy jumper and skirt. Sparta, like Blue, the master of disguises.

When she came in she looked around as if expecting to see the boys.

'They're not here today,' I said, which was a lame thing to say since it was obvious.

'Of course,' she said. 'I promised them I would play Lego.'

We both knew that wasn't going to happen. I served tea the way we both liked liked it, green and fragrant.

'Did you kill Blue, that day?'

She smiled over her teacup. 'Of course not, Grandfather, I just put her out for a bit.'

'I didn't think so. Is she here, I mean with you in Auckland?'

'No. She's back in China. I'm going back later today.'

'Who are you with?'

'Aunty Wu.' She gestured to the door. 'She's waiting in the car.'

'So she got her way in the end.'

'Sort of.'

'She represents the interests of one of the other immortals, doesn't she? Either Lan Cai and He Xian Gu.'

Sparta nodded and passed one leg over the other in a very adult way. Probably in imitation of her new mentor, Aunty Wu.

'And Wang represents the interests of the other.'

Of course, I didn't really believe the story about the immortals; that was a fairy tale designed to hide the identities of the real players. Had to be. It stood to reason. Death, like causality, is a jealous God; immortality is a vain dream. The vain dream of old men. Monckton and I had had a number of conversations about it. It was absurd to imagine that the old man had lived for twelve centuries, whatever Taoist practices he might have mastered. A colourful metaphor, nothing more. A colourful blindfold for the old journo's eyes. Misdirection.

Oh, I'd done my internet searches and found out lots about the Chinese Immortals. One of the apparently surviving immortals, He Xian Gu, was a woman, her immortality due to a consistent diet of powdered mother-of-pearl and moonbeams. That should do the trick. The other, Lan Cai, was a hermaphrodite said to have wandered the streets as a beggar while singing songs about the brevity of mortal life. She/he was the patron saint of florists. Our very own old Vamp, Lu Dongbin, dressed as a scholar, roamed the earth for four hundred years slaying dragons with his double-edged sword, so he must have got lots of practice. Because he was a scholar, he was the patron saint of writers, and because of the sword he was the patron saint of barbers too. Both professions have to be sure of their cuts.

While all this was very festive and entertaining, it couldn't possibly be true. I did not, however, think that this was a powerful cult, or that they were all raving mad, although both views had their appeal; rather, I thought, that the whole story, the long afternoon and the fragrant tea drunk from dolls-house sized teacups, was all just a tall tale to knock out my reason and throw me off the scent. To fill my head with giddy thoughts while the real deal went down unseen. Further, my suspension of disbelief had been carefully built up, from Blue and Reggie's first visit to Sparta's fairy tale told on a bus to a sleepy old man to the Vamp's crowning fantasy.

In a most calculated manner, I had been set up. Monckton

agreed with me wholeheartedly; simple explanations are more elegant than the fantastic. Stick to the evidence! And that's the way I thought. Most of the time. Other times I just remembered certain moments: guns clattering to the floor at the old man's feet, his mordantly raised eyebrow at the window, his dry ancient voice whispering in the electric air of the light-filled room, his calm walk across the lawn in the gentle yellow sunlight of a Melbourne morning – and I wondered.

'That's right,' Sparta was saying, 'the organization had dissolved into three factions. After the shoot-out in Melbourne, the king of our great kingdom decided to sit on the new weapon. The ship arrived safely. The weapons are now under wraps, which is the best my father Lu Dongbin could have hoped for. The three factions all realized they'd gone too far and are now reconciled. The organization is healed. Golden Fleece is being dismantled.'

'The old man, Lu Dongbin, where is he now?'

'I can't tell you. But you know he has developed a taste for travelling. And he won't heed Lan Cai or He Xian Gu who want him to return to China.' If an immortal experienced a second childhood, how long might it last?

'He was going to sabotage the ship with the new weapon, wasn't he? That's what he wouldn't tell me, and why the helicopter attack came when it did.'

'Yes, he wanted to precipitate a crisis, which he did, but Reggie was the main motivator. He couldn't wait to use the weapon. He was going to direct it at the ship.'

'And Blue went along for the ride?'

'My father asked her to. Remember, my father is the Boss Man we have talked about. As usual she had to keep an eye on Reggie, make sure he didn't black out the whole of Melbourne or something.'

I was going to ask after Reggie's health, but thought the better of it.

We sipped tea and let the sunshine do its work lighting up the surfaces. Only the surfaces.

'How did you know it was Blue who killed Velvet?' she asked.

'Why do you want to know?'

'I'm just very curious. I'm not sure that I could have worked it out.'

'You told me. Not in so many words, but you said that Velvet had discovered not only the immortals but your existence as well. Your face was about to be plastered all over the social media, *child of an immortal*. Your face would have gone viral. That was Blue's biggest nightmare. It triggered her prime directive.'

'Exactly. Blue had to do it herself, so nobody would know except Reggie, Lu Dongbin and me…'

'And the old man had to stand aside and let her.'

'Yes. By going into exile, he put himself outside the loop.'

'Besides, he didn't want to be plastered all over the social media himself. The fourteen hundred year old man!'

'You know, Grandfather, you are not just a pretty face.'

'Hey, I'm not even a pretty face.' But I blushed with pleasure anyway. The older you get, the less it matters how absurd the compliments become.

'If Velvet had to go, why not Morse, her partner in crime?' I'd asked Blue this and she hadn't been totally upfront. The conversation in the car had been designed to keep my eyes on the weapon and lead me away from the immortals.

'Because Velvet didn't tell Morse about us, only about the weapon code. When it came to revealing the immortals, Velvet wanted to do it all by herself. Make herself famous. She wanted to own us. And she had a further reason for holding out on Morse. These secretive hacking groups like Anonymous are always being infiltrated. Police agents, Secret Service and intelligence agencies are after them. The level of paranoia is high. Morse himself, we have found out, was an American agent trying to infiltrate them.'

The bastard, I thought. All that bourbon and bullshit about being all washed-up, and the guy was a bloody operative, putting it over me when he was apparently spilling all.

'Velvet couldn't let her family, or you, or anyone else, suspect the truth. Although Queenie had a fair idea. She was working on building software that would deal to a bloodhound, a holy grail to hackers. And very dangerous work. She became covert. Then she began to discover stuff that frightened her, so she became even more secretive. When she investigated number 54 for you, she accessed, via Golden Fleece, some of the organisation's platforms and stole some codes. She and Morse might have figured out the weapon eventually. She used Queenie for snail mail. Snail mail has its advantages as it's not rigorously checked. Her group works mainly in the darknet, but math codes are sometimes sent by snail mail.'

'What was in the memory stick Queenie delivered to Velvet the morning of the murder?'

'Ah, I wondered if you'd find out about that. I might've known.'

'It can't have been the stolen codes. They were already on the university computer.'

'Velvet thought it was a post from one of her contacts in Anomymous who'd helped her assemble this anti-bloodhound software. She was desperate for some final codes she thought would protect her data on us completely. A new kind of firewall, you could say.'

I took up the thread. 'That's why she rushed into work that morning. She wanted to install the codes before work started. She and Morse had already stashed the weapons data on the university network. And she'd stashed the data on you immortals herself, unbeknown to Morse.'

'You are as quick as ever, Grandad.'

'A Chinese sage in the making.' I said as dryly as possible. 'What went wrong?'

'Blue blocked the regular post and substituted another memory stick, this one containing the virtual bomb that blew the system.'

'Pandora,' I said, remembering a conversation with Jerzy.

Always more elegant to get others to do the dirty work.

'Timed to blow at 6 pm, an hour after work, everybody'd gone home.'

'Blue thought all this up?'

'And Reggie.'

Let's not forget Reggie.

'After you left that night Velvet patched into the university system from her laptop and saw that things had gone horribly wrong. So she rushed to work to see what she could do…'

'… right into Blue's trap,' I finished.

No need to say more. The rest was history.

'Meilin told me the Chinese Government did it.'

'He's not lying. The Central Committee is a powerful faction; they politely told Blue what they expected. Blue rigged the post delivery to Queenie's house.'

'Meilin didn't tell me that.'

'It is possible that Meilin didn't know, and still doesn't.'

'With all the data wiped, why kill Velvet?'

'Velvet's very competent. She wouldn't have stopped. Maybe she could reconstruct the data. Or hidden it somewhere else.'

'How do you know this, or is that a silly question?'

'Blue and Reggie investigated Velvet. That closed room at number 54 was full of computer gear. Blue knew everything about her victim, her every movement. She knew about you, Grandad, but she didn't know how much you knew, how much Velvet might have told you. That's why she contrived to meet you, although that day she first came to use the phone she really was trying to contact Aunty Wu away from Reggie. She just used her opportunity.'

'She wanted to know how much I knew?'

'Yes, so she would know whether or not to kill you along with Velvet. She was… alarmed by your journalistic background. Remember, you'd worked with Velvet before in your article about hacking. You'd been to China. Worked with Meilin. Blue and Reggie thought she might be priming you for a big expose of the immortals. Too big to bury, that was her fear.'

'Jesus. Then she decides she can use me to get you out from under.'

'Yes.'

'Then in Melbourne she changed her mind and decided I had to die after all.'

'Yes, but that decision was not made with a clean mind.'

'What do you mean?'

'Once she knew you had her down for the killer, she saw nothing else for it but to kill you.'

That didn't answer my question but I let it go.

We sat and looked at each other. So now I knew. Now Velvet's death made sense to me, at least as much sense as there is in the world.

'Tell me why Blue put those documents on my computer. She said she wanted to implicate me.'

'Those were fakes, created to misdirect Wang.'

'You'll have to explain. I must be slowing up.'

'Wang compiled the dossier that got your daughter into trouble. He was getting ready to expose Aunty Wu and Golden Fleece. Most of all, he wanted to know what my father's plans were for the weapons' shipment. Blue guessed, rightly, that after Velvet's death Wang would visit you, go through your stuff to see if you knew anything, although she didn't anticipate your abduction. Anyway, she put the docs on your computer for Wang to find, hoping that, like you, Wang would think Velvet had put them there, that he'd take them for real, and believe that my father planned to do nothing in Melbourne but rather wait until the weapons got back to China before making his move.'

'Misdirect the master of misdirection himself. Very clever.'

'And it worked, for a while anyway. Then finally, Wang figured it out. Meilin may have played a part in that. Telling Wang might even have been the price he had to pay to get you out from Wang's clutches. We don't know, because Meilin works for the Central

Committee and we don't know how much he knows.'

'You know,' I said, because we sort of got into the habit of saying that to each other, 'if this was a proper story instead of a true one, Blue would have had to die, not end up alive and well and living in China. Morality would dictate that she pay for the murder of Velvet. Justice must be done.' In life as it is in fiction.

'Then I'm glad we're not inside such a story, with such a simple mechanical morality, because I love Blue. We are as sisters. She is very dedicated to me. True Blue, I call her. That's a real Aussie expression, you know.'

'Yeah. And Blue's a real dinkum Aussie girl too.'

We laughed.

There wasn't much to say after that.

As I walked her to the door, I said, 'You saved my life back there. Blue was going to kill me.'

'I'm not so sure of that,' she said. She looked up at me pertly, full of self-assurance. 'If Blue's intention had been clear she would not have missed.'

But I'd seen the killer look on her face. I'd seen my angel of death. That's something you don't forget. One day I will see her again. And you, Sparta? If you'd had to kill me, you wouldn't have missed, would you?

'Why did you stop her?'

Her little adult face dissolved and the twelve-year-old looked hurt at me.

'It wasn't just *you*, Grandad,' she said.

Of course. Marcia and the boys, especially the boys. Little Sparta, an only child without a family. I remembered the way she laughed as she and Fintan raced through the trees. Goddess and little girl wrapped in one.

Maybe Sparta saw the 'gee thanks' look on my face, because she put her arms around me and gave me a long hug. Monckton joined us and wrapped his tail around her leg.

Then she was up the road and out of my life.

Number 54 has been renovated. A nice old couple has moved in. I saw them out of the side window, that accursed side window. They were resuming the work that Blue had started in the garden. A retired couple pottering around. No old sweet songs.

Can't see them giving me any trouble.

ACKNOWLEDGMENTS

The title of this book is derived from a Zydeco song by Camey Doucet entitled, 'Hold My False Teeth (and I'll Show You How to Dance)'.

I am indebted to Gia-Fu Feng and Jane English for their translation of the Dao De Ching by Lao Tzu.

Also to Frances Tan for her TNW News report, 'China admits existence of a cyber-warfare team called 'The Blue Army'.' May 30, 2011.

I would also like to thank Sony Music for permission to use the song 'It Had To Be You', by Harry Connick Jnr.

Also to Kate Drummond of Wired for her article, 'Exposed: The Military's Freakiest "Non-Lethal" Weapon Ideas.'

Special thanks to AT Johnson for his reading and feedback; to Odette Singleton-Wards for her proofreading; and Māhina Marshall for the layout and project management.

Thanks to Joanna Smith and Jennifer Rackham for designing the Mike Johnson author image on the rear cover and inside cover page.

www.ingramcontent.com/pod-product-compliance
Lightning Source LLC
Chambersburg PA
CBHW020947120726
47905CB00008B/2716